ANNA

Catherine Gierlach Kennedy

This is a work of fiction and is produced from the author's imagination. People, places and things mentioned in this novel are used in a fictional manner.

ISBN-13:
978-1979593397

ISBN-10:
1979593396

Dedication

This book is dedicated to my Mom, Lucy (Leocadia) Frak Gierlach who gave me the roots to ground me and the wings to fly.

My thanks for information and encouragement to:
Both of my sisters, Diane Jackson and Marti Lutz, my daughters, Tracy Kennedy, Nancy Taravella, Marcy Knight, Coleen Crouch, and honorary daughter, Donna Petit.

To granddaughters Ashley Mezzzic, Tori Taravella, Brigid Boyet, Lucy Crouch, and Mariah Guevara.

Thanks to Sister Francine Horos and Sister Janet Schaffran.

Thanks to Nellie Swonder for her wisdom.

Thank you to the Coral Springs Writing Group, Roxanne Smolen, Betty Housey, Zelda Becht, Laurianne Macdonald, Greta Silver, Molly Tabachnikov, Janet Franks Little, Rowena Muzquiz, and Rita Cohl.

Thank you to my cheerleaders, Johanna George, Susan Donato, Sue Morgan, Barbara Hart, Kate Jones, and Dolly Conlin.

Thank you to my teachers, The Felician nuns, The Benedictine nuns, and the Sister of Mercy.

Table of Contents

ONE

April 1929

"Tata, I don't want to be a teacher. I want to become a nun and join a cloistered monastery in Kentucky." There. Anna had finally told her father.

"No, I won't allow it. I lost Mama to influenza. Now only ten years later, you are asking me to give away my daughter? No." He got up from his chair and circled the room like a fighter looking for an opponent. He took fast, huffing breaths, and was clenching and unclenching his fists.

Anna was devastated. It had been a long time since she had seen her father angry. She remembered watching his seething anger blow up after he had been sold inferior quality pork from a local farmer. Tata owned a grocery store in Petroleum City, Pennsylvania.

Last year, a customer had come in and said, "Pan Wiosnec, wieprzowina stara była." The customer reluctantly told him the pork she had bought the day before was bad. Tata had refunded her money. Then a second, third, and fourth customer complained the same day. Again, he returned money to his customers and had lavished apologies on them.

When the same seller returned to try to peddle more pork, her father had first made his children leave the store. The siblings heard Tata shout, "Don't you tell me about poor quality." They watched the quick departure of the farmer, never to be seen again.

Now, she hung her head and waited for another word from her father.

"Anna, we can discuss this later. I have nothing to say to you right now," her father said.

ಠ ಠ ಠ

Anna went to her church's convent to see Sister Laetitia, her confidant. Sister was the childhood friend of her late mother, Cecelia.

The tall slim nun wore a black habit. "How are you?" she asked. "How is your family? Your father? Your sister, Bashia? Your brother, Leon?"

Anna nodded. Her unsmiling face told her friend that all was not well.

"Did you think telling your father would be easy?"

"No," Anna answered.

"Can you understand how he feels as a parent?"

"I... I..." Anna paused. "I am not sure I will ever understand. I do not know the ways of the world. But when a person becomes an adult, as I am, shouldn't I be taken seriously? When people get married, everyone is happy. Yet my monastery choice does not please Tata."

"Yes. But can you see that you are saying goodbye to him when you enter the far away monastery?"

"But I have prayed about this for a long time. Is it selfish of me to follow my calling?" Frustrated tears pooled in Anna's eyes.

"No, but you may wait a long time for your father's reply."

ಠ ಠ ಠ

Anna spent evenings visiting her betrothed best friend, Julia. Her friend opened the hope chest.

"Julia," Anna said, "this pillowcase opening will be forty inches wide without the seam."

Julia's long dark hair swept around her shoulders as she lowered her head to inspect the fabric. "Do we attach the lace first or sew the seams together?"

"There is no place to attach it unless the seams are finished." Anna fingered the delicate snow-white piece of lace Aunt Nellie had donated for the linen. "I love this."

Julia sat at the treadle Singer sewing machine and moved her feet forward and back to propel the needle into the fabric. "Why don't you gather the lace until it measures forty-two inches?"

Anna got out the cloth measuring tape. As she measured and gathered, she said, "I don't know where I should be working while I wait for Tata's answer. My waitressing job at the Arlington Hotel is fun, but there has to be better-paying employment for me." She shook her head. "It would be best if I make as much money as I can this year since it is the last time I will help my family financially."

Julia murmured, "Um hum."

"What if I became a cook instead of a waitress?" she said. "No, there is already a good cook at the hotel. I could become a baker. No. I do not want to get up that early in the morning. I think you know what I think. I think I don't know what I want to do."

Julia finished the seams. She picked up the gathered lace, and with a wide stitch, basted it to the edge of the pillowcase. As she worked, she muttered, "Anka, your damn indecision stinks."

Anna blinked. "You haven't called me by my little girl name in a long time."

"Today you are behaving like that timid ninth grader you were in school. I can't stand it when you act so stupid." She jammed her needle into the pillowcase and put it down. Then she giggled. "Do you remember the time you almost punched Patrick McFadden? He said that I looked like a flapper when I dressed out for gym. Now you know, I loved the idea of being a flapper."

Anna smiled as she remembered that day.

Julia pulled out a length of thread and broke it with her teeth. "We're quite a pair, Anna. You are the tall slim one who can wear all those flapper clothes. I'm the short not-so-slim friend who looks silly in some of those new styles. You'll get the opportunity to follow your dream. But instead of being a flapper and suffragette, I'll get married and become a housewife. I admit I do love Adam, and he will be a good husband. But if I had my way, I'd be going to New York City."

"We had so many young-girl dreams. Now we are grown," Anna said.

"You are a good seamstress full of ideas. Maybe the convent will want to change those dour habits they wear, and you can design them. Do you think I'll go to hell for thinking that?" She put her hand over her mouth and laughed.

ಬಿ ಬಿ ಬಿ

The next Sunday after Mass, Tata sent her siblings out of the room. As they left, Anna thought about Tata's philosophy. *Tata always said that Polish people are strong. They never cry. If something is too hard, the Polish people turn it around and look at it from another angle to figure it out.*

Tata interrupted her thoughts. "Anna, I am ready to discuss your future." He sat beside her on the beige flowered davenport in the living room and looked into her eyes. His trim frame was so close she could smell his Ivory-soap-scented skin. "I love you more than you will ever know. I want you to be happy. If you have a vocation and want to go to the cloister, I will not stop you."

She smiled and hugged her father. "Tata, I love you so much."

After a long pause, he added, "But, I will still ask you to wait one year to enter. I will need that much time to accept such a loss. I know this is probably selfish, but it is my word."

Anna pulled away. That was not what she wanted to hear. *I will be like a cork bobbing along in a lake, aimlessly sliding here and there. Waiting. Ever waiting.*

"I see your Mama in so many things you do." He smiled, and his eyes sparkled with tears. "When I watch you dance with your sister, I am reminded of her love of music. She could just dance and dance. Your giggle is hers, too. And in our little garden, you pick the flowers she liked the best."

"But, Tata, a year is a long time."

"If it is a true vocation, it will still be there in a year. Do you understand?"

She nodded and lowered her head.

ಲ ಲ ಲ

In this year of 1929, things were happening in the world. To nineteen-year-old Anna, it was an era of change. President Coolidge was holding the nation together, and Rudy Vallee was crooning about it. Buck Rogers was in the comics, and Popeye was introduced. The unions were busy.

Yet her thoughts were on her future. *What will I do if Tata changes his mind and says I cannot leave?* She had a wonderful relationship with her father. Could she disobey him? She spent long moments in prayerful silence.

As she waited on the tables at the Arlington Hotel, Anna greeted her daily customers. Many were couples. One such couple, Henry and Carolyn Walker, joined her each morning. Mr. Walker would eat quickly, wish his wife a good day, and depart for work. Mrs. Walker sometimes lingered over coffee. She always dressed so classically and always wore a little lace.

One morning, Anna noted Mrs. Walker's sleeves and said, "That lace pattern on your cuffs today is very unusual."

Mrs. Walker's reply was a deep sigh. "I especially like this blouse. I had it made before I got married. This morning, I noticed this big rip." She frowned and presented her sleeve to Anna. "I think I tore it on my hatpin."

Anna studied the delicate fabric.

"I had a lady add this lace. I was told she was one of the most skilled of the handwork people in Pittsburgh."

"The stitch on your lace is intricate." Anna nodded. "If you let me take it home overnight, I could make it look like new."

Mrs. Walker looked surprised. "*You* would work on it?"

"I promise that I can fix it. Let me show you my handkerchief." She removed a cotton cloth from her pocket. It had a lace border.

"You did this yourself? It is lovely," Mrs. Walker said. "I will give you my blouse tomorrow morning, and let us see how well you can fix my accident."

The next morning, Anna was handed the blouse. When she got home, she found it was not a challenge to repair the tear in the lace. She returned it the following day.

Carolyn Walker was amazed. "Where did you learn to do this?" she asked.

"My Aunt Nellie is a fine seamstress," Anna replied, "and her hobby is lacework. She has been teaching me for years."

Anna was reluctant to accept money for the repair but finally accepted. She was already planning a purchase as she backed away from Mrs. Walker. *I saw a bolt of tiny floral print on a light blue background in the store window this morning. I will go back and buy a few yards of it. Bashia will squeal with joy when we work on a new dress for her. I have enough for the thread and a pretty button, too.*

Mr. Walker and a man about Anna's age were just entering the restaurant and were deep in discussion. In her haste to get home and tell Bashia the news, Anna had not noticed them. She and the new man stumbled, tangled, and fell onto the shining black-and-white floor.

The man assisted her to her feet, and with a bewildered look on his face, said, "Excuse me, please."

That evening, after she and Bashia discussed dress designs, Anna remembered that she had encountered a new person in town.

ౠ   ౠ   ౠ

Tuesday, Anna went to see Sister Laetitia. They prayed in the small chapel at the convent of the Assumption of the Blessed Virgin Mary. Votive and taper candles flickered before them. The scent of melting wax filled Anna's nostrils.

Later, in a tiny visiting room, they sat side by side.

Sister Laetitia covered Anna's hand with her own. "Your father is a man of action. You and I both know that he does not avoid making decisions." She paused then squeezed gently. "Sit quietly and listen to your own voice. It will serve you well."

T W O

At the Arlington Hotel the next morning, Mrs. Walker went on and on about Anna's needle skills. The most interested listener was Mrs. Elizabeth Robinson, the local dressmaker, who was breakfasting with Mrs. Walker.

After her meal, Mrs. Robinson said to Anna, "I am looking for a helper with some imagination and good hand skills with a needle. Are you interested?"

"You have to give me more details. What would I be doing? How many hours? My father will want to know."

"Tell him I need an assistant who can work with laces." Mrs. Robinson smiled, showing twin dimples on her cheeks. "Could we all sit and discuss the job at my house?"

"I will talk to my father about this tonight."

"I can expect a call soon, then?" Mrs. Robinson handed her telephone number to Anna.

Anna nodded and smiled. She felt the color rise in her face.

That night, as she served Tata his dinner, Anna wondered how to broach the subject. In her excitement, she almost burned her fingers on the hot bowl she was bringing to the table. "I have a new job offer as a seamstress. Mrs. Robinson would like to see us this week. I am going to show her a few pieces of my embroidery."

"How interesting, Anushka." He nodded and smiled. "Dobrze."

She agreed that it was a good opportunity.

Later that evening, Julia carried over a tablecloth, looking for suggestions for a design to apply to it. Anna drew a few sketches. They settled on an apple theme.

"I'm surprised Mrs. Robinson is interested in hiring me," Anna said. "I thought everyone could mend lace, put embroidery around a neckline or on a hem, and embellish a sleeve."

Julia folded the tablecloth. "You are wrong. I am always glad when you help me pick colors for my clothes and add the fancy stuff."

The following Saturday, Bashia and a neighbor watched the store while Tata drove Anna to the Robinson home. He nodded in approval when they entered Mrs. Robinson's neighborhood.

Mrs. Elizabeth Robinson welcomed them. When she saw the embroidery and lace Anna had brought, she held her hands together, as though in prayer. "I do want you to work for me. You can start as soon as possible. By the way, I like the construction of the dress you are wearing today. I am sure you saw me inspecting it. When you start, bring in another dress you've designed and made so I can see more of your style."

Anna nodded. "I need to tell you, I am interested in working here in this town for only one year."

Mrs. Robinson replied, "I think that is a fine arrangement. In one year, you will see so many benefits to this job that you will change your mind and stay."

Anna refolded her hands on her lap and just listened.

The older woman said, "I make a very comfortable living by sewing dresses for the wealthy women of Petroleum City. The sewing is done here in my home. At times, the women come here, and other times, I go to their homes for the planning and fitting of a dress. There is a steady demand for my services."

Tata looked on with interest. "Why do you need an assistant now?"

"A new dress shop, The American Woman, is opening in the downtown area and will be my competition. I need an edge. If I had an assistant to embellish, I would come out on top. I am also hearing noises from my husband regarding my being out and about alone. If I had another woman with me, Abraham would be more comfortable."

Anna wanted to accept the job offer from Mrs. Robinson immediately because it sounded exciting and the salary was much higher than at her waitressing job. Yet she only smiled.

As Tata drove Anna home, he said, "This sounds like a fine opportunity. Did you hear Mrs. Robinson say that her chauffer could drive you to her place about half of the time? I could work out the other transportation with you."

"Tata, I think I have a new job. It will help the time go faster until I leave for Kentucky."

On her last day at the Arlington, Anna saw her stumbling partner. He and Mr. Walker were having a conversation. He just stood there for a moment, listening, and then left with a lowered head.

⁝ ⁝ ⁝

Anna wondered what to wear to her new job. She finally told herself, the outfit did not matter. It only needed to be neat and clean. Aunt Nellie always said *One needs to wear clothes loose enough to show that you are a lady, and tight enough to show that you are a woman*. She laughed as she remembered. "That's the way I always dress."

Tata whistled as he drove Anna across town.

Mrs. Robinson hugged Anna when she arrived and led her to an orderly workroom. She showed Anna remnants of cloth and fringe, each of them with a name attached. "I know I am overly frugal. But I can use these scraps, perhaps. A customer would not like to recognize the fabric of *her* dress on another woman. I store it with a label because I can possibly use it on another dress for the same lady in the future."

"This is a new world to me," Anna said. "Everything is a surprise. I never thought there would be so much to consider."

Mrs. Robinson opened drawers and boxes. She unwrapped each cutting tool with the care of a new mother. After inspection, every item was placed back into its wool cover then in the proper box or drawer.

"I didn't know so many kinds of scissors existed," Anna said. *I only have the set my mother left me.*

"Oh, yes, let me show you some pictures." Mrs. Robinson pulled heavy books off a shelf and opened pages to show long scissors and short fat ones. She pointed to another pair and said, "These are to cut silk. I have ordered them."

"They must be expensive."

"You will soon see the advantage of using them, I promise." Mrs. Robinson smiled. "We need to get you some goods for your embellishments. Let's take a look through these supplier's books."

They searched through the pages and made lists to fill their needs.

At last, Mrs. Robinson put the books away. "What have you brought for me to see, Anna?"

"I brought a dress I made for my sister's birthday. It is full of pleats and soft lace, which is my sister's favorite style." She slid a light-blue, carefully folded dress out of a box and handed it to her employer.

Mrs. Robinson took the garment. "I am surprised at how lightweight it is." She looked at the stitching on the dress, then folded it over to look at the inside seams at the waist. "I like the way you bind these edges."

All afternoon, they discussed patterns, revisions, and alternate openings to dresses.

"I have a client, Mrs. Kogan, who has some weakness in her right side. We keep trying to find a better way to fasten clothes so she can put them on without getting frustrated. Perhaps you can give this problem some thought and come up with some ideas."

Anna narrowed her eyes and nodded.

The day was over quickly. When Tata arrived to take Anna home, Elizabeth remarked, "On Monday, my chauffeur and I will come to your house and pick you up. We are going to see a client. She is an early riser. Most of the ladies do not like company before eleven a.m. And," she smiled, "this is a real lady. You will like her. Some of my other customers are... I won't explain now." She shook her head, and then added, "We will see you at eight-thirty Monday morning."

Monday morning, Anna awoke early enough to eat, dress, and fix her hair.

She glanced at the clock, which was skirting past the 8:30 mark, and looked out the window, watching for the Robinson car.

It was still not there at 8:45. Anna didn't know what to think.

At 9:00, she began to worry. No one arrived, and there had been no phone call.

She thought back to the day of her interview. Had she left the family telephone number? She couldn't remember. Dark clouds swirled in her brain. Had she offended Mrs. Robinson?

Anna went out to the store to consult with Tata. He was busy with customers and people delivering foods. When he saw her, his eyes widened. "Anna, I thought you left long ago."

"Mrs. Robinson and her driver have not arrived. I don't know what to do."

"I wish I could help, but I can't just close the store."

Anna said, "Oh, no, I didn't expect you to do that." She walked out of the store. *Tata always tells me Polish people figure things out. I will be a resourceful Polish person. I must have Mrs. Robinson's telephone number. I should phone her and see what happened.* She found the number and called.

"Anna." Mrs. Robinson sighed. "I am so sorry. What a mix-up we have here today. Al, the chauffeur, wrecked the car this morning. He pulled the car out of my garage, and while going around the corner to pick me up, he hit a pole and *boom*. Even at that early hour, he had been drinking. *Again*. It seems I will be spending the next few days interviewing new drivers since I fired Al."

"Oh, Mrs. Robinson. Is the car badly damaged?" Anna was already counting her money from the bigger paycheck. Now, she would be a day short.

As if she were reading her mind, Mrs. Robinson said, "Anna, we just can't lose your skill for a whole day. I am very curious to see everything you can produce. Can I pay you for half a day today? Please take a few hours and gather a sample of everything you have sewn by hand or machine. Then have it with you when I see you tomorrow."

"Of course, I can do that."

"Can you also ask your father if he can bring you to my home for the remainder of this week since we will not have the car fixed until Saturday?"

"I will ask him right now." She put the phone earpiece down on the phone stand and went to the store. She cleared her throat. "Tata, I will need a ride to Mrs. Robinson's house for the rest of the week starting tomorrow morning. Can we manage that?"

"Anka, for you, anything."

She returned to the phone. "He can do that. I will see you tomorrow."

The next morning, she and Tata took piles and bags of things to the Robinson place for inspection.

"I was really looking forward to a big show of your sewing this morning," Mrs. Robinson remarked, "but it will have to wait until later this afternoon. Mrs. Phyllis Kidman, the lady we were going to see yesterday, will be here at any moment."

Mrs. Kidman arrived with a chauffeur. She was tiny and about thirty years old. Her eyes narrowed as she peered at Anna. "And who are you there, all dressed and ready for business?"

Mrs. Robinson said, "Meet Anna, my new assistant."

"I'm so glad she found you. She's been looking for an assistant for a long time. And I know you will love it here."

Anna smiled. "Thank you."

Mrs. Kidman proceeded to the center of the room, removed her earrings and bracelet, and began to unbutton her dress.

Anna was amazed. Mrs. Kidman showed no modesty and was soon in only her underwear. It was not the kind of underwear Anna's family wore. Mrs. Kidman seemed to be wearing shiny fabric that skimmed over her frame.

Mrs. Robinson was right behind her, carrying paper and a tape measure.

Of course. Anna tried to get her bearings. *No work can be done without accurate measurements.*

Mrs. Kidman did not appear self-conscious about her lack of clothing. "Elizabeth, my husband, Nelson, was quite taken with my new lingerie, especially the pink nightgown. We had such fun with it. All those little buttons."

Anna was embarrassed beyond belief and quietly left the room. *I am glad I went to Mass this morning. I need the courage to get through this challenge.* She kept busy by arranging the articles she had brought to show Mrs. Robinson. She heard the two women chatting. There was frequent laughter. She knew they were discussing adult, married kind of things.

What a strange, new world I have fallen into.

"Anna, I need your help."

I will be strong. Anna turned the knob of the door and prepared herself for the next assault to her modesty.

"I need three new dresses," Mrs. Kidman said. "The first, a formal for a political function next month. I am told it is a fund-raiser. Next, an all occasion frock for dinners out. The last is one of your specialty dresses." She chuckled. "The *seduce-the-husband* variety."

Anna's mouth fell open. She looked at the two women.

"Let's start with dress one," Mrs. Robinson said. "Do you have a color choice?"

"I am willing to listen to some suggestions."

"Let me show you this new crepe. I could order some of Pacquin's acid-green moiré to make a statement." Mrs. Robinson handed red, dark blue, and black fabrics to her client.

The material crinkled as they touched and crushed it. Then Anna refolded the cloth and waited for the next request.

Mrs. Robinson asked, "How would you like the all occasion dress to feel? Light or heavy? Will you be wearing it only during the summer, or do you need a heavier weave?"

Anna folded and refolded fabrics.

Finally, they discussed the last dress. Mrs. Robinson narrowed her eyes. "Just how seductive do you want to be?"

"At first, I was thinking of looking like an innocent school girl. I would be wearing scandalous undergarments. But I will keep that plan for another time. I want a dress that is so lacy and filmy that he will almost choke when he sees me."

"We want chiffon, absolutely. There is also a new silky fabric called rayon which is worth a thought. The latest colors are yellow and pink. As for personal designs, this is where my assistant comes in since she is the embellisher."

Anna gulped and whispered, "I am?"

Mrs. Robinson murmured, "I promise, it will be fun to do."

After Mrs. Kidman left, Mrs. Robinson picked up her worn tablet and tapped her pencil on the page. "I am recording any new measurements on my master list. If anyone gains or loses an inch, I better have the new figure written down."

"Oh, I never thought about your notations."

"Now comes the design part. You will see that some of the clients are wearing the new style of sleeveless or cap sleeve and scoop neck dresses for the summer. But as fall approaches, we cover the arms."

Anna assisted her in placing the patterns on the fabric for the first two dresses. They moved the papers and positioned them to waste the least amount of material.

"We always have to remember the grain of the weave," Mrs. Robinson cautioned.

After pinning and cutting the fabric, they marked the remnants.

Mrs. Robinson said, "Let's have a cup of tea. I think we have a lot to talk about. I saw you scurry out of the room when Mrs. Kidman stood there in her lingerie. I imagine, since your mother has been gone for so long, you have reservations."

"Oh, you are so right. What a naïve girl I am."

"No, the way I see it, you have been protected more than some girls. Now, what are we going to do about that? Can you handle these new things, learn from them, and work here?"

"What a big joke life is playing on me," Anna said. "Next year, I will be joining a convent. I will be praying for most of my waking hours. This year, I am being exposed to the world whether I like it or not. Can I do this for a year and enjoy the learning? I would like to try. This is all new to me. I have only seen myself in underwear. I have never heard conversations like I heard today."

"I promise, I will treat you as I would my daughter and tell you things of womanhood. However, I will not try in any way to change your future plans. Now, I hate to start with this, but we need to make a dress of seduction."

Anna took a deep breath.

Mrs. Robinson asked, "Do you know how adults make love?"

"Not really."

"Well, we will start at the beginning." In understandable language, she explained intercourse. "When a couple is happily married they enjoy each other physically not just for having babies. It is for mutual fun."

"Oh, I do not know about these kind of things," she said softly.

"Well, it happens. Women like Mrs. Kidman do many things to keep their husbands happy."

"Like dressing in fancy clothes?"

"It is not the fancy that is appealing. It is the unusual. It is the unexpected. It is the surprising. It is a dress that is easy for the husband to remove. It is a dress he can see through. It is an outfit that offers him a fantasy while it is still his wife."

"I have much to learn. I don't think it will help me in the convent, but it might be something I will want to tell my friend, Julia. She will be married soon."

"You will need to remember these things when you help make lingerie."

"What is that?"

"Undergarments and nightwear which can be very alluring."

"Goodness," she replied.

"Let's get back to work on that dress," said Mrs. Robinson.

Mrs. Robinson pulled out the gauzy fabric and began to gather it, wind it, smooth it out, and place her hand under it as if to see if she could see through it clearly. She laid out the pattern pieces for the dress. Next, she went into a small drawer, removed a bundle, and unwrapped a slim, long pair of scissors.

"This is one of the fabrics that need these shears for an extra sharp cut."

Anna listened to the distinct melody of the scissors gliding along the sewing table as the filmy yellow fabric was cut. "I think this will be hard to sew."

Mrs. Robinson smiled and nodded. "Let's make it gather around the neck, two layers with a plunge at the top, and about four layers below. We will make her panties with lots of lace."

"Should the panties be loose or tight? Do you know the size of panties Mrs. Kidman wears? And if so, how do you know?"

"I have every dimension of my clients. I measure each time for dresses. I can just glance at a client and determine whether the lingerie will fit their frame."

"I am glad you chose not to measure Mrs. Kidman for panties today," Anna whispered.

They looked at each other and laughed.

Later that afternoon, Mrs. Robinson asked Anna to draw illustrations of lace designs. "I want to look at these pictures and choose the one I would like you to add to a certain dress."

"I like that idea."

"Some of the latest styles we need to keep in mind are the acceptable fabrics of velvet, silk, brocade, satin, taffeta, and cotton. The newest length is knee-high hems and drop-waist styling."

Anna nodded. "I have seen some illustrations of lots of pleats and a stretchy knit fabric called jersey."

"As for your attire, most of these women will never notice what you are wearing unless it overshadows their outfits. We do not want that. If you occasionally have a blouse with some of your lace or embroidery, it would make good conversation and be a selling feature."

"I'm getting excited about working with you, Mrs. Robinson."

"I am just sorry that we were unable to go to see the ladies this week. I am interviewing several drivers and hope to find a suitable one soon."

⁜ ⁜ ⁜

The next afternoon, Mrs. Mary Kay Denver came to the Robinson home.

Mrs. Robinson said, "I'm introducing everyone to my new assistant, Anna, who will be helping me with all my work."

Anna smiled and said, "I am glad to meet you, Mrs. Denver."

The client never looked at Anna. "I really can't see why you are wasting my time with the measurements. You did that last month."

Mrs. Robinson said, "We want every dress that you get from us to fit you exactly."

Mrs. Denver took a deep breath when the tape measure was around her waist. "I know my size has not changed. However, I do want to tell you that the red silk outfit from last year must have shrunk during the winter. It is hard to button."

"I will be glad to let out some seams for you if you like."

"If I like? I give you enough business to hire a driver. Of course, I would like it to fit. But there better be no charge for the necessary alterations."

"I just want you to be satisfied with your clothes."

"Well, since you are willing to be accommodating, I will order a few more items." She bustled around the room, handling every fabric she could put her fingers on. "I think I would like a dress made from this thin material."

"You know, Mrs. Denver, I have another color that is more flattering to your skin tone." Mrs. Robinson removed the yellow fabric from Mrs. Denver's hands.

Anna looked closely at Mrs. Denver. Her waist did appear a little wide. Her scent was not as clean as the other clients. *I must be more tolerant. Some of the ladies I sit with at the daily early Mass smell like camphor and mothballs.*

18

Mrs. Denver appraised the drawings handed to her. "Yes, I like this one. I could use that silhouette." She tilted her head and sucked in her cheek, showing a dimple. "The gray morning dress would work, too."

Anna heard high prices discussed. *I am glad I am not responsible for that part of the business*. Mrs. Denver accepted each price. Her taste was more flamboyant than Anna had seen at the Robinson house or, indeed, at the hotel where she had served so recently. *Is it because I usually see the ladies in the mornings so their taste in dress is plain? I may know about needlework, but now I am learning the ways of the women's world.*

At the end of the day, when the two of them were alone, Mrs. Robinson said, "Next week while we are traveling in the car, I will tell you about Mrs. Denver. It is too long a story to start now."

THREE

On Friday morning, as Tata drove Anna to work, she said, "I've met five or six women this week, Tata. They are all so happy with the clothes Mrs. Robinson makes for them. We have measured and received orders for dresses, skirts, and blouses, both frilly and practical. We are busy cutting and sewing." *We also measured and sewed lacy, filmy undergarments for day and night.*

When they arrived, Anna kissed him goodbye. As her cheek brushed his, she enjoyed the sweet woods scent of his Half-and-Half pipe tobacco. She ran up Mrs. Robinson's sidewalk, eager to start the day.

"Good Morning, Anna," Mrs. Robinson said. "I think I have finally found a driver. His name is Jack. I expect him in about an hour because we will be going to see a client today. We'll try him for two weeks. Come, let's get ready for the morning." She led Anna to the fabric room. "This room is my personal haven."

Anna, more at ease with her boss now, was able to take time to look at the orderly but crowded room. The two windows on the east side were open, letting in a hint of flower scent. Morning sunlight decorated the clean, worn rug. The windowless north wall held shelves from floor to ceiling. Dark brown boxes filled each level. The packages were tucked in by size. Each container front had a handwritten label of contents. Each shelf had a master list.

"Help me pull down these cartons, Anna." She pointed to the top ledge.

Anna got up on a stepstool to remove them. Some were heavy. A few larger ones rattled when she moved them. Mrs.

Robinson opened a big box, pulled out a middle-sized one, then a smaller one, and continued until she had a tiny box.

"*Wyglądać jak Pani otwiera te mały drzweniany Ruski lalki.*"

"Anna, what did you just say?"

"Oh, it reminded me of someone opening, again and again, the nest of little painted Russian dolls."

"Yes, I too have some treasure boxes. I use them to show special things to some of my ladies," she said.

ℒ ℒ ℒ

Anna was surprised when she saw the new driver, Jack. He was about her age. He was slim, had dark wavy hair, and had a flattering cleft to his chin.

"You look familiar," she said. "Have I seen you before?"

"It's a mystery to me, too." Jack smiled at her. "We will probably figure it out since I will be driving you back and forth from your home every day."

"I will have to decide if this is appropriate for me."

"Are you worried about my driving skills?"

"No, I do not know how my father will feel about me being alone in a car with a man," she said.

"I think we need to talk to Mrs. Robinson about it."

Mrs. Robinson's solution was that Jack would never get into the back seat of the car for any reason, and Anna would never get into the front seat. "Anna, tell your father our plan, won't you?"

"I'll talk to Tata about the driving arrangement."

They loaded the car with dresses, fabrics, boxes, and bags. Everything except the tiny treasure boxes.

Anna asked, "Who are we seeing today?"

"We're going to the Krakowiak home," Mrs. Robinson said.

I see Mrs. Krakowiak in church on Sunday, sitting in the front row, wearing her white gloves all through the Mass. When she goes to communion, I notice her dresses. At least one new one each month. She always wears attractive hats. Every Easter Sunday, I can hardly wait to see her new dress and what she will have on her head.

"I am really curious about her house," Anna said. "All the people at church wonder and gossip about it. It is supposed to be dazzling."

"Oh, you will not be disappointed," Mrs. Robinson replied. "Now, you know what I tell you is confidential. This is one of the most difficult clients I have. She likes to think she is the queen of the city. The Krakowiak family is Polish. However, I have heard her say unkind things to poor Jenny, the young girl she brought over from Germany to be her maid and housekeeper. My thinking is that she likes having Jenny there because she and her husband can discuss business in Polish and no one in the house but the two of them will understand. You would be better saying as little as possible. In fact, I will not say your last name when I introduce you. We will not mention that you are Polish to her. It will be our secret unless she asks. Can you agree?"

"Of course."

Mrs. Robinson said, "As for you, Jack, stay with the car, please."

"Do you want me to just sit there for a couple of hours while you are inside?"

"No, it is too hot for that. Find a shady spot and keep close."

Anna's eyes opened wide as the car rounded the bend on the stone-bottomed private road. The Krakowiak house was on an incline as if it stood a touch above the other houses. It had black metal trim at the door. Its white paint reflected the sun, and white curtains showed at the shining windows. The lawn smelled like recently cut grass.

"Yes, that's the house." Anna nodded as if she were giving directions.

They rang the bell. A young girl wearing a starched white apron over a black dress opened the door. "Please come in. I will tell Missus she has company." She escorted them into the parlor and left them alone.

So, this is the parlor of a rich Polish house. The housekeeper must use a good pine polish. It smells woody. It is probably from all the shiny tables. Yet nobody must use this room. Every fringe on that floral couch and chair is hanging down without even one out of place.

The maid reappeared in a few minutes. "Mrs. Krakowiak said I bring you upstairs, Mrs. Robinson."

Mrs. Robinson picked up the new dresses and paperwork. She pointed to the bags and told Anna, "Gather all these fabrics samples and follow me."

In a shy voice, the girl said, "Mrs. Krakowiak does not know that two of you are coming upstairs."

"She will be pleased to meet my assistant, Anna," Mrs. Robinson said then climbed the circular staircase. Her heels tapped the stone steps.

Anna followed.

The maid knocked on what Anna assumed was the bedroom door.

"Well, why are you making so much noise, Jenny?" a voice said impatiently.

"Two dressmakers are here," Jenny announced.

"Two? Two? This is not a sideshow. What is going on here, Mrs. Robinson?"

Mrs. Robinson smiled as she and Anna entered the bedroom. "Mrs. Krakowiak, I want you to meet my assistant, Anna. I know how valuable your time is. If we both work with you, I promise, we will be out of your home in the shortest time ever, and I know you like that idea. Am I right?"

Mrs. Krakowiak breathed a deep sigh.

Yes, this is the person I remember from church, even though I usually only see her from the back. She is even taller than I imagined. Her arched eyebrows remind me of the pictures I have seen of the women called the flappers.

Mrs. Krakowiak nodded. "My Rudolph was saying just this morning how he wished I could join him for lunch. I could surprise him at the hotel. But I would need time for Jenny to do my hair and make-up. Oh, there is just so much a person can do."

"So, let us start with the dresses you ordered," Mrs. Robinson said.

Mrs. Krakowiak had been wearing a simple robe. Mrs. Robinson and Anna helped her try on the clothing. The first dress was accepted. The second was challenged.

"I picked the blue fabric, not the green," the woman said.

Mrs. Robinson countered, "Oh, remember, we decided you wanted it to match your eyes? Then you wrote your name and the color on the paper, and we attached it to this sample, just so I would not get it mixed up."

"Let me see that," she ordered.

Mrs. Robinson passed the swatch to Mrs. Krakowiak.

"Very well," she murmured.

The duel went on for each item presented. Finally, all finished items were accepted, and Mrs. Krakowiak carefully read and re-read the itemized bill. She pulled money from her brassiere and paid Mrs. Robinson.

"I will need a few more dresses. My Rudolph is such a popular man. So many functions to attend." She smoothed her hair. "He always wants me to look nice."

Mrs. Robinson showed her a few new patterns of dresses. "I suggest these summer chiffon fabrics for your evenings out since anything else would just be too hot to wear until fall. Do you like this light blue color? I will cut this fabric on the bias, so it will flatter your legs. You could go dancing in it anytime."

"Oh, Rudolph would like that."

"Let's have you pin a card with your signature on each of these pictures, then we can order the materials. Because of the new cut and the pretty way it will hang, the dress takes extra fabric."

"Extra fabric will be fine with me."

Mrs. Robinson sat, wrote numbers, and offered the bill for the cost of the newly ordered dresses. "Would you like some lace on the sleeves of the last two you picked?"

"Is there an added charge?" Mrs. Krakowiak asked.

"There will be the next time, but since this is such a new trim, I'd like you to try it. Let me know if you enjoy the way it looks. I'm sure Mr. Krakowiak will think you are even more pleasing to his eye."

That clinched the discussion. "Of course. I will be glad to show off the new lace sleeves for you."

Mrs. Robinson noted the two dresses that would have the embellishment and had Mrs. Krakowiak sign the paper.

"We must be on our way." Mrs. Robinson gathered all her belongings. "I hope you will still be able to meet your husband at the hotel today."

They left the house and soon climbed into the waiting car.

Mrs. Robinson shifted in the seat, leaned back, and let out a sigh. "Whew! I'm glad that adventure is over."

"This is the first time I have seen you ask a client to sign so many papers," said Anna.

Mrs. Robinson laughed. "She always thinks she asked for one thing but got another. I have tried to remind her, but she likes to be in control at all times. So, I have her convinced that she is the one requesting her signature on all her orders, and we both win."

Anna nodded. *I can learn some life lessons from this lady.*

"Jack," Mrs. Robinson said to her driver, "do you understand how important it is that what we say in here is in confidence?"

"My job is to drive and keep my mind and eye on the road. Right?" he said.

"That's a good policy."

"Is Mr. Krakowiak a stockbroker?" Anna asked.

"Not quite. He has people invest for him, but his fortune was made in the distillery business. And I don't mean oil."

"Oh!" Anna yelped. Had she just spent time with the wife of a bootlegger? Prohibition began in 1920. It had served many masters, making some of them very wealthy. Anna now remembered the gossip about the Krakowiak family. *Were the women who gossiped curious or jealous?*

Mrs. Robinson took out her notebook. "I always spend the

first few minutes after seeing a client with paper and pencil in hand. I write down the measurements so I can compare them. I note what we talked about so I'll remember it for the next visit. I write down what she really liked the most so I'll know more about her taste."

"So, that is your secret." Anna smiled.

"Remember when Mrs. Denver was looking at one of the fabrics, and I had to take it from her hands? She needs someone to steer her into better choices for her shape. I try to nudge her along."

"I understand."

"Anna, the more women you see in these garments, the less embarrassed you will feel."

Anna said, "Some folks seem to practice an unwritten law. They take for granted that they are receiving a service and pay little mind to the service giver. I remember Gloria, a room service worker at the Arlington Hotel, said, *I could have walked into their room, and found them naked. They would act like I was not even there.* I didn't believe her until now."

"Anna, you are the salt of the Earth."

"What does that mean?"

"It means you are unspoiled, yet you add some spice to other people's lives."

"Oh. I am adding some to my friend Julia's since I have met you. I am filling her in on all the facts of life and more. And I am making lingerie for her trousseau like she never imagined."

"I hope that's a good thing. Now, we have some fashions to create. Do you know about cloche hats, those hats without any brim, and some with a small one, and some very large edged ones? You know, we really concentrate on dresses, and yet there are some cloche hats that are worth making. Have you seen any with embroidery on the front? They are really stunning."

"Yes, I made one that is embellished with French knots. I'll bring it tomorrow."

The next morning, Anna brought a light blue cloche. The hat had white knots like a starburst on the front. She modeled it.

Mrs. Robinson tipped her head to one side and walked a few steps right then left as she examined the work. Then she nodded. "I do like this. We should make a few of these before the summer is over."

Thus, began the adventures of the threesome. The women kept busy measuring cloth, ordering new fabrics, finding buttons, and exploring new designs.

Jack arrived early each morning, opened the back door of the car for Anna with great ceremony, and drove her to Mrs. Robinson's. Anna felt like royalty being driven to and from work.

On the way home one day, she asked him, "Whenever you wait for us in the car, I see you reading. Are you keeping up with what is happening in the world?"

"I am trying to keep up with the news in the Derrick newspaper."

"What do you think is important to know?"

"Steel. Oil. And the stock market."

"I sure wish I understood more about that."

"All I really understand is that a company is not owned by just one group or one family. Most times there is a need for more money than they have, so other people buy shares of the business. It is a gamble of sorts. If the company makes money, so do the investors. If the company loses money, the investors lose."

"Can anyone buy stock?"

"I think anyone can buy it. Maybe next year, I will invest." He lowered his voice. "The main reason I want to invest is I think I found the girl I want to marry. I could make money if I could just understand steel and oil."

"That sounds like the talk at the Arlington Hotel where I worked. The men were always discussing steel, oil, and the railroad."

Jack's face went pale. "So, that's where we met. I bumped into you at the Arlington that day I was fired."

My stumbling partner. "Fired?"

"Only a few people know this. I have a cousin in Erie. His

name and mine are both Alex King. The Erie Alex has robbed a few places. Because of my name, the people I was chauffeuring didn't feel comfortable using me as a driver. I was fired. So, I decided to just start calling myself Jack. My middle name is Jacob, and I have heard people named Jacob are sometimes called Jack."

"You look honest to me. I can keep your secret. And I want to hear about your bride to be."

"Oh, the romance is just beginning."

FOUR

The next morning, when Jack picked up Anna, he was singing, "You're my little buttercup, cuddle up, cuddle up."

Anna laughed at the words. "Is that the song you sing to your girlfriend? What is her name again?"

"Clara. My lovely Clara."

When they got to their employer's house, Mrs. Robinson was bustling around the sewing room with a furrowed brow. "There's been an accident at the steel plant in town. We have a big car and will be able to help transport people. I want you two to put this oilcloth on the seats."

Anna and Jack placed the barrier on the seats.

When she returned to the house, Anna asked, "What else can I do?"

Mrs. Robinson put her fingers to her lips. "I need to just sit down for a minute and think of any other things I can take. Think. Think. Anna, can you fill some jars with water? And we'll need some clean bedsheets."

"Are the people burned, or cut, or something else?" Anna asked.

"I don't really know. I was asked to help. You two are also needed. I will still pay you as if you both were working for me today. Jack, do you know how to get to A and B Steel?"

"Oh, sure. It's in town right by the railroad tracks."

"Then let's go."

They hurried to the car.

When they pulled into the yard, Anna stared out the window. *I have always wondered what the workers did in this loud, big, sooty building.* She said, "What a lot of confusion. All those people are walking around and going nowhere." Some of the workers must have been Polish—Anna heard a few of them say the old familiar incantation, *O Moi Boże!*

Mrs. Robinson let herself out of the car. "Let's find out who is in charge here."

As the three walked into the A and B, Anna's eyes moved up the thick, concrete walls. Only slits of sunlight from the high windows slid into the room. The three-story shop felt like the kitchen at home when the oven was working at the highest temperature. The stench of sweat mixed with heat was oppressive. Deep in the bowels of the building, fires in the vast ovens belched out sparks.

Usually when walking past the steel mill, one could hear a constant loud screech of steel being smoothed, but now the silence was frightening. Beams lay helter-skelter across the floor. Under them lay accordion pleated pieces of metal. A few men wandered around. Some were spattered with blood.

Anna murmured to Jack, "It looks like they were lucky. No one is pulling at things and trying to help anyone stuck under that heap."

"Either that or they know everyone is already dead," he whispered back.

She followed her employer toward a crowd of workers. Their hands hung at their sides, and blank looks marred their faces.

Mrs. Robinson said, "See what you can do to help while I speak to these men."

Anna approached a man about Tata's age. Blood soaked his shirt sleeve. "Hello. Can you sit on this box so I can look at your arm?"

He nodded.

She eased him down to the box and poured water on his arm.

"What are you doing?" he asked in a monotone.

"I need to see how badly you're hurt."

"Oh."

The bleeding had stopped. She found one of Mrs. Robinson's sheets, tore off a square, and went back to the wounded man.

"I'm pressing a heavy bandage on your arm and tying it in place until a doctor can look at you."

She spotted Jack who was carrying more supplies and said, "Can you be sure this man has at least one glass of water? He's lost some fluid."

"Sure."

Anna hurried toward a man who was limping. His foot was covered in blood. She helped him sit on an upturned bucket. As she removed the boot, she saw a slice through the leather and a cut on his ankle. "Your heavy boot is ruined, but it saved your leg. I am going to pour some alcohol on your wound then bandage it. Is that all right?"

"Oh, sure."

She poured alcohol on the wound.

He flinched and shouted, "Hey! You should have warned me."

"My Aunt Nellie always told me to fix first and apologize second. So, I'm sorry."

As she bandaged his foot, he smiled.

She stood and almost fell over another man leaning against a wall. "Can I help you?" she asked. *What a dumb question. Of course, I can.*

She looked around and saw more people with blood on their clothes. *I detest the smell of blood. I want this to be over. I want to go home.*

She bandaged, put an arm in a makeshift sling, and soothed men by patting their hands and listening.

Jack walked a few of the injured out of the building to drive to the hospital. When he got back to Anna, he pointed to a man with a black medical bag. "Oh, look. There's a real doctor here."

"At last," she said.

"Tell me, where did you learn all that bandaging?"

"My Aunt Nellie. She's a seamstress, and that made her the local Polish self-taught nurse as well. Stitching things up, you know. She taught me about broken bones and what to do."

"She did a good job of teaching. How many men did you patch up here?"

"I have no idea."

When they next saw Mrs. Robinson, she was escorting a man to the doctor. It was Adam, the man engaged to her friend, Julia.

The doctor probed his arm. Then he picked up his medical bag and took out a bandage.

Anna hurried over.

Adam looked up and said, "Hello, Anna. I saw you helping us. We all appreciate the work you and your lady friend did."

"Are you badly hurt?" Anna asked. "Do you need to go to the hospital?"

"That won't be necessary." The doctor finished bandaging his arm and, with a nod of dismissal, walked away.

"Adam, what happened here?" Anna asked. "No one is able to tell me."

"As you know, the mill makes long steel beams. After they are constructed, little holes are put on the sides. Those holes are for attachments the customer might want to use to connect the beams. When the steel beam is finished, a big grabber called a boom is supposed to move it to a storage area. The beam slipped. I was working with the two men down there."

"The two men who died," Mrs. Robinson said.

"I was the lucky one and only hurt my arm."

"I think we are done here," Mrs. Robinson said. "Tell us how to get to your house."

Adam wobbled to the car. *He is probably in a state of shock.* He sat in front with Jack, while Anna and Mrs. Robinson sat in the back. Jack followed his directions to a rooming house.

"I will be fine now. Thank you for bringing me home." He got out of the car and walked slowly up the slight hill to the door.

"I think we have all had enough for one day," Mrs. Robinson said. "Why don't we drop you off first, Anna? Then, Jack, you can drive me home. I just need to be in a quiet, safe place to ease my mind."

Anna nodded. She wanted to climb into her bed, cover her head, and have a good cry.

When she got home, she went into the store and told Tata,

"We were at the steel mill today. Two men were killed in an accident. We helped some of the men who were hurt. Adam was one of the injured."

Tata closed his eyes and bowed his head. "What a tragedy. Such a nice young man."

That evening, she sent her sister, Bashia, over to see if Julia needed help. Julia's reply was just a thank you for what they'd done for Adam and a mention that despite no need for hospitalization, the injury was serious.

When she said her prayers that night, she said, "You know, God, I was really scared and ready to throw up today, but I didn't. All I did was work with your voice in my head. I remember the Catholic workbook saying that the best way to show God's love is to simply be present. I thank you for having my Aunt Nellie, my *Chiocha,* as such a good teacher to me. When I tell her, I know she'll say that I'm growing up."

ᛞ ᛞ ᛞ

The next morning at Mass, she prayed for the injured and the dead with a special prayer for Adam. After Mass, all the conversation was about the accident.

One of the ladies asked, "Anna, you were there, weren't you?"

"*Tak, Pani.*" Anna nodded but moved away, reluctant to add to the conversation.

Anna stopped a few doors from home to see her Aunt Nellie.

Her Chiocha said, "Anna, you did well. Go and see Adam tonight. Julia needs you."

"I will," she answered.

ᛞ ᛞ ᛞ

The next day, it was dressmaking as usual at Mrs. Robinson's. The two women worked tirelessly on the new dresses they were preparing for the clients.

Here I am working on garments for ladies while my poor friend, Julia, is dealing with her injured man. She is a strong Polish woman and will nurse him back to health, God willing.

Besides the dresses for Mrs. Denver, Mrs. Krakowiak, and Mrs. Kidman, there were new names and new measurements for other women. There had been little time for discussions on the lifestyles of the patrons.

"Anna, I am hearing raves about your designs," Mrs. Robinson said.

"I am pleased this is working well for both of us. I know we need to concentrate on the clothes, but again, I want to thank you for letting me help yesterday at the steel mill."

"You certainly were an aid to those injured men."

"Thank you. I will tell Aunt Nellie that she taught me well."

"Yes, we did our good deeds yesterday. Now, back to the clothes. What do you think we can put on this dress for Mrs. Montes?" Mrs. Robinson passed Anna a lightweight brown silk piece with loose flowing sleeves.

"Would you like a shorter stitch at the neckline?" Anna asked.

"Let me think about it. You sure are making my business grow, Anna. I'm glad I have two sewing machines. Oh, look at the time. We need to eat and be on our way to our next fitting."

Anna pulled silverware from the drawer and said, "I smell chicken."

"I noticed you like the chicken cooked the same way I do. It makes lunch easier for both of us. I hesitate to ask Jack to join us here in the house. He always says he brought his own lunch. I don't know if it is the truth or just a matter of pride for him. I'm always happy when we three are out seeing clients because all of us eat our picnic lunches together on the way home."

"I like the picnics because we are sitting outside. The fragrances of grass and flowers are like a health tonic for me."

Mrs. Robinson nodded. "I try never to eat with my clients. They seem to think I should be working on their clothes every minute we're together. If I eat with them, they think I am not busy enough or say I took forever to make the dress plan with them. As for new styles, did you notice we have not used the flapper influence in many of the dresses?"

"Yes. But it seems that your clients would like at least one of those new style dresses."

"You have to notice that most of the dresses are looser than they were ten years ago. This all started in about 1922. Women wanted a different style. It is their good fortune that the waist is only a casual hint in most of these garments. However, these clients still want the longer skirt."

The conversation went to fringe. Anna had seen the Charleston dance in the movies. She had been working with yarn, beads, thick thread, and any available item to perfect a new fringe for women's dresses. "I am sure I can make something that will wind around the lower skirt of a dress and look appropriate for the married woman."

"I know at least one woman who would like a bold look."

"Who do you mean?" Anna asked.

"Mrs. Denver is not who you think she is. Did you notice we never go to visit at her home? That is because we do not want to be seen there."

"Why?"

"Because she is a woman of the night."

"I don't know what that means."

Mrs. Robinson chuckled. "She entertains men for a living. Do you understand?"

"Not really."

"She has sex with men for money."

Anna felt her face turning red. "I should know about such things. When the ladies of the family get together, they say, *you're not married so you need to leave the room*, and I do."

"Now you will know more than anyone in your family about the women of this town. You will also know more about life than a lot of women. Many of them act like they know things, but I sometimes doubt their air of sophistication."

જી જી જી

The month of July was hotter than any July Anna remembered.

Anna gave Jack and Mrs. Robinson updates on Adam's recovery. "Adam is unable to work, and I worry about the two of them. With his not having a job, it is hard."

One morning during the drive to work, Jack said, "I am pretty excited about all the talk about the unions. It will be a strong voice for the people."

"I really am not sure I know enough about them. If Adam were in a union, would he have some money coming because of his injury?"

"I'm not sure about that. Maybe I will just get a book and read about it."

The conversation went from flappers to jazz in New Orleans to Charlie Chaplin and Jackie Coogan, the child star. It flowed from tango to tennis, from the St. Valentine's Day Massacre to the eight-mile-long tunnel through the Cascade Mountains in Seattle, Washington.

"How are you and Clara getting along?" Anna asked.

"We are having fun getting to know each other. We went to the movies last week and saw the *Wings* film that won the Oscar in May. She likes to go dancing, too. I think she would like me better if I were a good dancer."

"I'm sure she could teach you."

Anna again helped sew clothes for Mrs. Kidman, a few new clients, and the ever-present Mrs. Krakowiak.

While at the Krakowiak home, she overheard a conversation between Mrs. Krakowiak and her husband. They were talking in Polish and had no idea of Anna's knowledge of the language. They were discussing a letter Mrs. Krakowiak had received from Poland. Her end of the conversation was an emphatic, "You know, he will never be able to prove any of his ranting about the money, Rudolph."

It made no sense to Anna. *Sometimes Mrs. Krakowiak sounds mean. I will ask Tata if he knows what that money talk is about.*

Mrs. Lovell, a teacher, had a few garments made for her new

school year. "I know I could make them myself," she said in a tiny voice, "but, I just want a little something different, a new shape, or a new color, or just a change. I do think I need to take better care of *me, too.*"

Another new face was Mrs. Christine Cracker. Her husband was an oil man. She was a clever and fun-loving lady. *She always makes me smile. I hope I can do that to people, too.*

"I love the cut of the clothes and the colors. I like the whole experience of picking out the fabric, be it velvet, silk, or brocade. I like to have new looks frequently. I do not want my husband, Owen, to ever see another woman in town and say to me, *Christine, isn't that just like your dress?* Or hat? Or anything? I want to keep 'em guessing."

"It is challenging to present new looks to you. You like your hemlines a little shorter, the waists a little more defined. It is not really the style," Mrs. Robinson said.

"The style is The Cracker Style," she said. "I want a pair of ladies' pants, like Amelia Earhart wore when she was flying that plane from Newfoundland to Wales last year. It would be convenient to wear them sometimes. What kind of fabric can we use for that?"

"I will figure it out," Mrs. Robinson said.

Christine Cracker is not only funny, but also thin, tall, and pretty. With that olive skin tone, she looks exotic.

Mrs. Rachael Goral was a familiar face from the Polish church Anna attended. On their first meeting, Mrs. Goral said, "I had heard you were working for Elizabeth Robinson and doing a wonderful job."

Anna shyly answered, "Oh, you are too kind."

Mrs. Goral knew what she wanted, yet was unable to make her wishes known without sounding demanding.

After she left, Mrs. Robinson gave Anna a wry smile. "She will be a pleasure to work for."

On the drive home, Anna counted the months until she would be in the womb of the Abbey in Kentucky. *How much longer will I have to wait? I need to find a calendar and count out the weeks.*

I hope when I get there, I am as enthusiastic about it as I am about the new styles of clothes here.

Will the Mother Superior be strict? In the brochure of the convent, it says the nuns keep their heads covered with veils and wear dark woolen long dresses with ropes at the waist. I think it probably means wool in the winter. Who would wear wool in the summer? It would be so hot. What fabric does Sister Laetitia wear? Surely, it is not wool, is it? Do they wear shoes or sandals? I wish I could be a bird, fly down there now, and see their happy faces. Yes, I know they are happy.

"Anna, where did you get the tomato you gave me for my lunch?" Jack asked, interrupting her daydream.

"What? Oh, I got it from our garden. Do you have a garden, Jack?"

"I don't have a place to grow things, but I sure wish I did. If I had a place, I'd grow a lot of corn. I could eat corn every day. What do you grow?"

"*I* don't grow anything. I have tried many times. I plant things in pots in the house. I plant things outside. But everything I plant dies. I either water too much or too little."

"Didn't you tell me that at the convent they raise their own food? You better think again about what you call your vocation. If you do the farming, your fellow nuns will starve. You will be sewing them all smaller clothes because they'll be so thin."

"You know, that could be a problem."

"So, how did I get the tomato?"

"My sister, Bashia, and my father love to garden. They work on every part of it together, and it is fun to just listen to them plan."

"She has to be the girl I see looking out the window when I come to pick you up in the mornings."

"Yes, that's my little sister. We raise enough food for some of our own meals. The special spice from our soil is *koper*. That means dill. Haven't I offered you any of our dill pickles? They're so tasty, I bet we could sell them."

"Sounds great."

As she walked away from the car, she said, "I'll bring you some *koper* tomorrow. The smell is unbelievable. And I will bring you a jar of dill pickles. You do not have to be Polish to enjoy them."

FIVE

The following morning on the way to work, Anna handed Jack a leggy twig with a spicy scent and a jar. "Here are the dill weed and dill pickles I promised to bring you."

"I'll eat the pickles today for lunch. Maybe it will make me understand why you're so crazy about dill." As they rode to work, Jack asked, "Do you think there will be compensation for the two dead steel mill workers' families?"

"You make me think of things I never questioned before. This growing up is not an easy task."

They walked together through Mrs. Robinson's yard. *Even the two trees guarding the porch are the same size. Mrs. Robinson is the most orderly person I know. She teaches me so much.*

"Good morning," Mrs. Robinson said. "Today, we'll see Mrs. Craig, a new client." She handed the address and directions to Jack. "Do you know anything about the Craig family?"

"No, never heard of them." Jack looked at the directions. "I'd say this is about ten miles away. It is farther than any house we've gone to this summer."

"That's why I packed a lunch for the three of us. It will be a very late lunch, though. We might have to eat some apples as we ride."

"Or we can eat the dill pickles Anna made."

They filled the car with fabric samples and their lunches and began the journey. Outside Petroleum City, the roads were un- paved and dusty with only a few houses.

"This road looks so peaceful," Anna said.

They passed through a gate. Above the gate, there was an arch with symbols on it.

"I wonder what that funny looking C means up there." Anna looked back at the arch.

Mrs. Robinson said, "Even though we are in northwest Pennsylvania, the Craig family calls this place *The Crown C Ranch.* That explains why the *C* on the sign has a crown on the top. Ranchers brand their cattle with their unique symbol to show ownership."

"Wow. What a large piece of land," Jack blurted. "I didn't expect it out here."

Little oil machines were scattered about on the grounds of the Craig ranch. They looked like black boxes, each big enough to hide one rabbit, and sounded like loud crickets. Anna enjoyed hearing the chirp of the machines as they pulled oil out of the ground.

Jack parked the car, and the two women walked up to the house. A barking dog greeted them.

It looks like the Collie in the Saturday Evening Post.

The door opened. A lady in a dark dress and white apron greeted them. "You must be the seamstresses. Mrs. Craig is expecting you. Come in and have some cool water. Mrs. Craig will be with you in just a few moments."

The two of them sat down and drank the water offered to them. Then the lady returned. She pushed a wheelchair with a woman on it.

"I'm Adelle Craig. How do you do? Oh, from the looks on your faces, it seems I forgot to warn you. I am an invalid. At least, for the present."

"I'm Elizabeth Robinson, and this is my assistant, Anna Wiosnec. What happened to you?"

"I had an accident. I was riding my horse last year when I struck a tree. It could have been worse. If the branch had been higher, it would have hit my head, not my leg, and I'd be dead. Since then, I have been recuperating. I hope for a full recovery soon. Meanwhile, I still entertain at home and want nice things to wear. Can you help me?"

"You are offering me a challenge," Mrs. Robinson said. "I

need to know if you can stand and how much help you need to get dressed. Can a garment go over your head, or do you just turn to the side to put on clothes?"

"The injury is to my upper leg," Mrs. Craig said. "I sit up with no problem, as you can see. I have little feeling in the entire right leg. I can get up and lean against an object long enough for my helper to smooth my clothes down over my torso."

Anna watched as the two women talked. *How at ease these two are with each other. Mrs. Robinson is very direct and asks good honest questions. Mrs. Craig is not shy about her illness either. I see there is no shame in discussing such things. I will remember that. It would be good for me to know this grown-up-women kind of talk since I will probably be working at dressmaking for another year.*

"My family is happy that I am living in such a tranquil environment," Mrs. Craig said. "My life would be complete for right now if I had some new pretty clothes."

Mrs. Robinson opened her bag, took out her tape, and began her normal work of gathering measurements.

Anna walked around the room. *It looks like this family moved all little things out of the way so Mrs. Craig does not have wheelchair obstacles.* She said, "I see toys and children's books on the shelves. Do you have children here?"

"We have three, ages twelve, nine, and seven. Since we have a rather common last name, we have given the children unique middle names. Our oldest child is Anthony Nevada Craig. My husband and I liked the sound. Our older daughter is Donna Michigan Craig. We always wanted to buy a summer cottage in Michigan. Our youngest is Susan Kentucky Craig. We have considered moving to a horse farm in Kentucky."

"I admire your innovation with the names," Mrs. Robinson said. "Anna, help me show Mrs. Craig some fabrics."

They showed Mrs. Craig soft cloth in summer colors.

Mrs. Robinson drew simple drawings of skirts that wrapped instead of having seams on the sides. "Would these designs work for you?"

"Oh, you would have made the last year much easier for me had I found you sooner," Mrs. Craig said.

"Let us make the choices on color and fabric. I want to suggest some decorations to make these dresses unique," Mrs. Robinson said.

The session ended after a few hours.

"These first visits can be very long. I hope we haven't overstayed our welcome," Mrs. Robinson said. "It's been such a pleasure to get to know you."

"Likewise." Mrs. Craig smiled. "I wonder if you could help me with another problem. I'm looking for a young couple to add to my staff. They would help with the children and give some relief to our present staff. The work would be both indoors and outdoors. We, of course, have a vacant apartment they would use. I would like to have them living here at the ranch with us. Do you know of anyone?"

Mrs. Robinson looked at Anna with a knowing gleam. "We might be able to assist you with that. Right, Anna?"

"Yes," Anna blurted as realization struck. "My friend's fiancée was injured in an accident at the steel mill. He lost his job because they couldn't wait while he recovered."

"How unfortunate," Mrs. Craig said. "Yes, I heard about the steel mill accident. I would be pleased to interview them."

Mrs. Robinson asked, "Is the Craig house a place where Adam and Julia might like jobs?"

"I will stop over tonight and talk to Julia about the idea."

They said their goodbyes, packed up their fabric samples, and settled back in the car. Soon, they again passed under the *Crown C Ranch* arch.

At the crest of the next hill, Mrs. Robinson said, "Let's stop for lunch, Jack."

"Pick a spot, Mrs. Robinson."

"Right there under those enormous chestnut trees."

Jack pulled the car off the road. "There are a few dandelions here, but the lawn is short. This does look like a good hill."

"You picked my favorite kind of location," Anna said. "I bet I will be able to smell the fresh cut on the grass. I wonder if this is part of the Crown C Ranch."

"It must be. No one just cuts grass unless they own the land." Jack pulled a few wicker baskets from the trunk and put them on the ground under the trees.

Mrs. Robinson opened the baskets. "Anna, here are the tablecloth and napkins."

The tree's wide branches sheltered them from the sun. It could have also shielded a dozen more picnicking people.

Jack removed a few fallen chestnuts from the tablecloth area. "It's a good time of year to picnic under a chestnut tree. In the fall, there will be mounds of nuts here."

As Anna laid out the tablecloth and napkins, she noticed yellow and green embroidery on each piece of white linen. *Such a pretty daisy stitch.* The smell of roasted chicken made her hungry.

Mrs. Robinson unwrapped the chicken from moist cloths. "I baked this early today so we'd not go hungry."

Jack pulled a bundle from the basket and opened a loaf of cut bread. "Did you bake this today, too?"

"No, because, if I had, it would have been too hot to cut."

Anna pulled the basket closer and took out cooked green beans with slivers of bacon. A pan in the basket had cold water, remains of the ice that had melted around the chicken.

Mrs. Robinson took a jar of lemonade and some cups out of a second basket, then reached in and pulled out a cloth bag. "We have sugar cookies for dessert."

"Wait, I'll get the dill pickles." Jack walked to the car.

They sat on old towels as they ate. Fat white clouds flirted between the tree branches and then glided across the blue sky. A few blue jays scolded each other as they darted through the leaves.

Jack unsealed the jar. He bit into a pickle, and Anna heard the noisy snap of the homemade delicacy.

Anna's mouth watered when the tart garlic-dill scent passed her nose. *Am I salivating because of the garlic aroma, or did the cracking of the seal on the jar fill my head with eating memories?*

"Food always tastes better outside. I love picnics. I wonder what it must be like to eat outside every day." Anna dabbed her mouth, reluctant to put a chicken stain on the daisy embellished napkin. "Do you see all the wildflowers in the next meadow?"

"No, I wasn't looking that way," Jack said. "I was wondering about the bushes we just passed. I bet those are blueberry bushes. Wild berries appeal to me more than wildflowers."

Mrs. Robinson said, "You two sound like a travelogue. It is good to hear you rave about the wonders of northwest Pennsylvania. We really have some special things here in these mountains. I always thought of them as just hills until my husband and I took a trip, and some of the folks we met reminded me that we are a part of the Allegheny Mountain Chain."

Jack nodded and took another bite of pickle.

"What do you read to keep yourself busy while you wait for us, Jack?" Mrs. Robinson asked.

"I have a pal whose boss gets The Pittsburgh Post-Gazette, and when he is finished with it, he brings it to me. I learn about things happening in the world."

"Are you studying any specific subjects?" Mrs. Robinson asked.

"No, everything I read is general knowledge. If I read the paper from cover to cover, I learn different things. I'm not that interested in politics, but I like to read about money. Andrew Carnegie and Andrew Mellon are my favorite financial wizards. Did you know there was a monetary disaster called *The Panic of 1873?* A lot of people lost their money. It took about ten years for recovery. It almost sounds like things that are happening now."

Mrs. Robinson nodded, then turned to Anna and asked, "Have you changed your mind about next year?"

"No, I am still going. I am counting the months."

"What did you think of Mrs. Craig?"

"She has a good outlook on life. It is fortunate that she is financially able to have help at her home. Many people with in-juries end up in desperate circumstances." Anna thought of Adam. He would be unable to work for some time.

When Anna got home, she noticed Tata whistling as he moved about the kitchen. He was smoking his pipe.

"Tata, I've never seen you smoke your pipe before dinner."

"Yest dzien wielka, Córka."

"But why is this a special day, Tata?"

"I have decided to let you go and join the convent on the first of October."

"Tata." She lowered herself to the kitchen chair to catch her breath. "Are you sure? What changed your mind? You look happy about this."

His eyes twinkled. He looked at her and answered, "I prayed. I see you still wanting the convent. We will be fine here. God will provide."

"Do you think they will let me come in October? They start the new candidates on the first of September."

"Yes, I feel sure they will be happy to see you on the first of October. Many people never know what they want and just won-der and wander through life. *You know*. And I am proud of you. I will not hold you back."

SIX

That evening, Julia lamented, "Adam's arm will take months to heal. He does not have the money to pay his rent. He tries to send money home to his mother in Poland."

Anna hugged her friend. "I didn't know."

"We had saved only a little money." Tears filled her eyes. "Anna, I need your confidence. I think I am expecting a baby in the spring. There are so many things for me in this new life I have picked for myself."

"Are you sure about the baby?"

Julia lowered her eyes then nodded.

"Why, that is wonderful news."

"I always wanted to be a mother. Maybe not quite this soon, but..."

"My only regret is that I will not be here to watch you and your pregnancy and see the happy couple become a threesome. Thank you for sharing this wonderful secret." Anna hugged her friend.

They announced the banns last Sunday at the church. They said, 'This is the first announcement of the banns of marriage for Adam Bolesławiech and Julia Pewnik'. They announce them for three weeks before the wedding. This lets the congregation know of the bride and groom's intent, to be sure no one has a reason the two should not marry.

Anna asked, "How many more days do we have until you are a bride?"

"Two and a half weeks. There are so many worries. I am happy that my parents are pleased about my marrying Adam, even though his arm is injured right now."

"I have something to tell you and Adam. Where is he?"

"He is out trying to find another place to live."

"Until he gets back, we could finish the tablecloth we have been sewing," Anna said.

They sewed the last hems on the cloth.

Adam returned with no news of a place to call home.

Anna said, "Mrs. Robinson and I saw a new client this week. Her name is Mrs. Adelle Craig. She, her husband, David, and their three children live on a large estate in the country about an hour away. Her leg is injured. For the time being, she is in a wheelchair."

"How sad for her," Julia said.

"This lady is kind and thoughtful. She says they are looking for a young couple to live in and help in their home and with their land. Adam, I think it might be the answer to your living and working problem. She is so optimistic about her own healing."

For the first time that night, Julia smiled.

"Would you like to talk to her? I am sure Mrs. Robinson would not mind taking you along with us when we see her next week." Then, acting as if it were an afterthought, she said, "Now, that's my news for you. And the news about me is just as exciting. My father has given me permission to join the convent the first of October."

Julia's mouth dropped. "Oh, Anna, how wonderful."

The next morning at work, Anna said, "Mrs. Robinson, my father gave me permission to join the convent on the first of October. I would not have started this job had I known I would be leaving this soon. I am so sorry."

"I don't know what to say. You can only do what your heart tells you and your family lets you."

What should I be feeling right now? Happy? Excited? Apprehensive? I cannot quite decide.

৪৩ ৪৩ ৪৩

The next time Anna and Mrs. Robinson visited the Craig home, Adam went along. He waited outside while the seamstresses helped Mrs. Craig try on the new dresses.

"Mrs. Robinson, you have lived up to your reputation. These skirts and dresses fit wonderfully." Turning to her helper, Priscilla, Mrs. Craig said, "We will look forward to easier mornings. It will take less effort on both our parts to prepare me for each day."

"I am delighted. They do fit you well," Mrs. Robinson said. "Now, I'm sure you remember our last conversation. We brought along Adam Bolesławiech who's interested in the position you need to be filled. The young man is getting married in two weeks. He is eager and willing but can give you only his left hand for a few months. You need to hear his dilemma. He's sitting on your porch."

Mrs. Craig said, "Of course. Priscilla, will you ask him in?"

He walked in, cap in hand.

Mrs. Craig said, "Hello, Adam."

The seamstresses slipped out of the room.

A short time later, Adam opened the door and walked out smiling. He said, "I'll be back in two days with Julia to talk to Mr. and Mrs. Craig."

ဢ ဢ ဢ

The sweltering weather continued. The rumblings of the stock market were a heated topic of conversation.

"Do you have any investments in the stock market?" Anna asked her father.

"No, I don't. However, in the grocery business, the money issue is different than in a lot of other businesses. The money has to stay here in the house. When the vendors deliver their produce, I just get the cash out of my safe place. I always have it ready for them. It is the only way I know. I do read about stocks. It is not the time for me to invest."

"There is so much talk about money these days."

"Now, Anna, we need to concentrate on your going to Kentucky." He shook his head. "I can't believe you are leaving."

"Tata, there is so little they want me to bring. I will be wearing a habit, so I will not be using any of my clothes. They even supply the soap and towels. And sheets, too."

"But what can we send with you?"

"I will be thinking about that."

The next evening, Anna visited Sister Laetitia.

Sister gave Anna a hug. "I haven't seen you except in church for weeks."

"Oh, Sister, I have wonderful news."

"Is it about Julia's wedding?"

"No, Tata has agreed to let me go to the novitiate the first of October."

Sister Laetitia sat down. Her wooden rosary beads, which were attached to her rope belt, clunked against each other. "Why the change?"

"He knows I want this with all my heart."

"I see you are happy about this. After being a nun all these years, I find the happiest nuns are those who had other kinds of lives before they chose the convent. Have you ever had even one date with a boy?"

"Of course not."

"Just think about my question. I know you're busy with Julia's marriage plans these days. We need to talk again after the wedding."

ဆ ဆ ဆ

The wedding of Julia and Adam was on the last Saturday of August. The ceremony took place in the Assumption of the Blessed Virgin Mary Catholic Church. The concrete church was a cool refuge on that hot morning. Red and pink roses covered the niches around the front altar. There were flowers on the two side altars, too.

Anna and Julia stood at the back of the church.

Julia whispered, "I love the dress. I cannot thank you enough."

Anna looked approvingly at her best friend. *Julia's floor length dress looks elegant. The high neck and the lace crossing the bodice suit her. The waistline looks so tiny with the satin ribbon belt. The skirt is sophisticated with the white lace rosettes scattered around it.*

Anna said, "You look lovely. The church does, too."

"We two are quite the decorating team." Motioning with the flowers in her hand, she said, "Didn't my cousin Małgorzata do a wonderful job arranging these white roses in my bouquet? She also did Adam's corsage."

"I am glad she could be your junior bridesmaid. She was very nice when I met her at the rehearsal last night. She has some modern ideas, and I like the sassy short bob to her hair." *And she has funny stories to tell about her cousin, Robert.*

Anna looked at Julia, who despite having her face covered with a veil, had a soft glow in her eyes. *Seeing Julia looking so beautiful in her veil reminds me of my own experience. I still remember, I always will remember overhearing our neighbor, Mrs. Skrytka's, comments about me on my First Communion Day. She said that she never saw anyone as homely as I was and it was good that I was wearing a white veil. And I plan to keep my vow to never wear a white lace veil again.*

Anna walked down the aisle. She had designed her long, green satin dress with a cross draping of the bodice and absolutely no enhancements to the design, remembering Coco Chanel's adage that less is more.

The pianist, Louise, played soft music, which then built to a crescendo at a nod from the priest.

All eyes turned to Julia on her father's arm as they walked slowly down the aisle. Mr. Pewnik's eyes gleamed. At the foot of the altar, Adam seemed mesmerized as his bride drew closer.

The prayers began. The pianist played *Ave Maria* and *Serdecznza Matka*, a song about Mary, in the background. The wedding ceremony, a combination of Latin and Polish, united the couple.

What would it be like if I were getting married? Is this as close as I will ever get to a wedding? Am I making a good choice by becoming a nun?

Exiting the church, the couple hurried through a shower of rice. The reception was held at the church hall. Anna found herself with Julia's cousin, Małgorzata, as they walked next door to the hall.

The sixteen-year-old was very happy to tell Anna her life story. "My parents in Poland had too many mouths to feed. They sent me here to live with Uncle Benjamin and Aunt Janina. They are nice but old-fashioned. They call me Małgorzata, but I prefer Margaret if necessary and Margo by choice."

Anna said, "The name Margo suits you."

"I've never been to a Polish wedding. Tell me what to expect."

"Many of the people attending will bring a pot or a bowl of their favorite food, so you can expect *pierogi, kapusta, kiełbasa,* and *gołombki.* The parents of the bride supply both the majority of the food and the liquid refreshments. The local Polish band sings and plays, and we dance to *polkas, obereks,* and *mazureks*. Besides the members of the band, guests will take turns singing. Some are not quite in tune with the band, but all are met with enthusiasm from the audience."

"At least, I know how to dance, even if I don't know any of the people," said Margo. "My cousin, Robert, took the weekend off from his part-time cab driver job to bring me here. He's a good dancer. I can't wait to introduce you."

The hall was filled to capacity with about two hundred people. Polish dance music played at a brisk pace. The scent of the *kiełbasa* mixed with sauerkraut hovered around Anna's nose. The smiling faces, many pink with the heat of the room and the brisk stamping of feet, were a treat for Anna to watch.

Margo led over a tall, slim fellow about twenty-five years old. "Anna, this is Robert, and he is a spoilsport. He wants to try a polka with a really good dancer. Go, show him."

"Oh, I don't know if I should." *How can I refuse? It's my best friend's wedding.*

"So, you're that good?" he asked as he ushered her out to the floor.

They danced and danced. She could not recall ever feeling so alive. *I like his smell. My arm on his shoulder is just even with my chin, and that is nice. When we move a little apart and dance the mazurek, I see a happy twinkle in his eye when he looks at me. What is happening? This is a moment when I want time to stand still, and I want to figure all this out.*

The music was blaring yet inviting. Many times, the familiar "*Jeszcze Raz!*" was heard. The request, meaning literally, "Still, again!" was the demand to repeat a song or at least another chorus. The party went on and on, with plenty of eating, drinking, and good Polish music.

Finally, the band took a break. Anna and Robert stopped for a breather.

Robert asked, "Are you a professional dancer who has just stepped into my life to entice me?"

"No, no," she laughed.

Margo interrupted. "Anna, excuse me. They are doing some old tradition, and Julia's mother said you are needed."

Reluctantly, Anna excused herself and followed Margo. An old custom was replayed, as with every Polish wedding. The veil was removed from the bride, and a white handkerchief was placed on her head. The older women surrounded the seated bride. As they sang a song, a single violin whined out the sad ballad. It told the bride that someday she would be old, plain, and not so desirable. The older women sang the song with tears in their eyes.

When that was finished, it was back to the snappy music of an *oberek*. Robert came to Anna, touched her hand, and again they were swaying to the music.

The older women in the hall look puzzled to see me dancing. Are they my conscience?

The stars were out by the time the wedding reception was finished. Everyone was full of food, some full of liquor, and all were reluctantly deciding on how late a Mass they could attend the next day, which of course, was a Sunday.

Robert walked Anna home, her sister, Bashia, by her side.

"After church tomorrow, can I come over and see you?" he asked.

Bashia eagerly answered, "We all go to nine o'clock Mass."

"Yes, you could come and see me then," Anna said.

I will be awake all night trying to figure out what happened here. In four weeks, I will be taking the biggest step in my life. Is this a warning, a temptation, or what?

After Mass the next morning, Robert knocked on the front door.

"How nice to see you," she said. *It will not take long for me to tell you goodbye.* "Let's have coffee in the front room. I'll be back with the cups in just a minute."

By the time she returned, her father was talking with Robert. "So how are the studies at the University of Pittsburgh?"

Robert answered, "Some of those law classes keep me up late at night."

Her father stood and nodded to Anna. "We'll all be leaving for Julia's soon." He left the room.

She served the coffee.

Robert said, "Anna, sit, sit. Let me hear about you."

"Me?"

"Yes. Once in a lifetime, peoples' lives cross, then there are two choices. We can either wave to each other and pass or stop." When she didn't respond, he said, "Do you know the story of Evangeline? It starts in France. Evangeline Bellefontaine was betrothed to Gabriel Lajeunesse. They were separated by war. Both moved to America. She searched for him. One night, his boat went north on the Mississippi and passed her boat going south."

Anna said, "And they spent their whole lives—"

"Oh, no. You need to read this amazing poem by Henry Wadsworth Longfellow." He rose and offered his hand to help her stand. "I'd like to attend the *poprawienie* with you today, if I may. And may I write to you when I get back to Pittsburgh? I have never before met a girl like you. I want to hear some of your ideas and plans."

"Oh, there's not much to know about me."

"You are not giving yourself much credit. I hear you are the seamstress that designed the wedding clothes. Margo says they are almost like Chanel design and says that is admirable."

"It will soon be a part of my past. I am going to the convent in four weeks."

"That kind of talk is tantalizing to me. It will make me work a little harder to change your mind. I think you'll be worth the wait."

"It will be goodbye after today."

"I will still write to you so you can let me know when you come home."

"I won't be coming home."

"I will write in case you do come home. It does happen."

Leon walked into the room. "Hey, you two. We are going to Julia's right now. Better hurry."

Minutes later, Anna, her brother, sister, father, and Robert arrived at Julia's house.

Margo was glad to see them. She took Anna's arm. "Tell me about this *poprawienie* thing."

"The *poprawienie* is a second-day party custom. The leftover wedding food will only last for about two days, so why not have old friends come back to reminisce and have another good meal? We can see Adam and Julia, and they'll be more relaxed."

"A little drink the next day is nice, too."

"Margo. You are sixteen years old. No drinking," Anna whispered.

Anna watched her father, hoping to catch him alone. Finally, when he stepped outside, she followed. "Tata, you acted like you didn't mind Robert coming over this morning. I don't understand."

"This is the first time anyone has had enough interest to call on you. I wanted to see who you would invite to the house."

"I am still going next month."

"I won't stand in your way. Robert will be a lawyer in a few years. Did he tell you his plans?"

"No, but he will be writing me letters for a month." *I hope he forgets to write to me. It is too confusing.*

All day, everywhere she went, there was Robert. He was talking to Julia and Adam. He was with her brother playing a card game. He was sitting next to Margo eating a sandwich. And he was drinking a beer with her father.

"What are you doing near my family?" she asked him.

"Enjoying every minute. They are interesting. Your little brother, Leon, will make a good lawyer someday. He sure can argue."

"I just met you, and you are trying to turn my world around."

"I know. Moreover, after I leave, you will be hearing from me. I have learned a lot about you today. It makes me even more interested. You will like my letters. One of my best talents is persuasion."

At dusk, Margo and Robert left for Pittsburgh, and Anna went home with her family. She remembered her conversation with Julia and Adam. *They said they will be taking Monday to move to the Craig's, and they will start work on Tuesday. A few days alone for the two of them would have been nice.*

ℴ ℴ ℴ

As he drove her to work on Monday, Jack asked, "Did you see that mean blue-jay?"

"No, I missed it completely," she answered, bringing her mind back to the present.

"He was just pushing those robins away from all the food."

"All for himself?" she asked.

"It sure looked that way," he said. "So, how was the wedding?"

I can't discuss Robert with anyone just yet. "Glorious and interesting, but it was such a hot day."

He laughed, "You asked us all to pray for no rain, remember? Did you get your wish?"

She sighed and nodded. "You are right. It did not rain. I do know that by the end of the Saturday night celebration, everyone was tired. I noticed that poor Julia looked pretty pale. Sunday, just as I told you, there was the *poprawienie*, a celebration again, minus the musicians."

"Oh, that's right. I forgot about that. What a weekend you've just had."

"I could use a day of rest and calm," she admitted.

"Don't plan on it. We are going to the Krakowiak place this morning, remember?"

"I must have purposely pushed that out of my mind." She sighed. *On with life.*

At the Robinson place, they packed for their trip to see Mrs. Krakowiak. The three of them were soon off on their visit.

When they arrived at the house, the maid, Jenny, greeted them with puckered lips. "The missus is unhappy today. She forgot to tell me to open the windows early this morning. She says the house is as hot as an oven."

Mrs. Robinson asked, "What is the coolest room in the house?"

"The downstairs parlor."

They went upstairs, and soon Mrs. Krakowiak was trying on a dress. Anna tugged. Mrs. Krakowiak's bosom heaved. Yet the fabric would not slide over her body.

"I am sure I did not order this cloth." Mrs. Krakowiak scowled.

Mrs. Robinson said, "Remember last fall when you told me that the light is better down in your parlor in the summertime? I would like you to see the fabrics better. Can we move the clothes down there?"

That day, Mrs. Krakowiak had all her fittings in the cool parlor.

"I can see this cloth so much better down here," Mrs. Krakowiak said with surprise. "I should have thought of this earlier."

All decisions were made with more ease. Of course, with Mrs. Krakowiak, ease was a relative term. Even the presentation of new fabrics for the fall went smoothly. New fabrics were always of interest to Mrs. Krakowiak.

"I wonder if I will be the first in this city to wear that velvet," she said.

"You could be the first," Mrs. Robinson said, "but you would also be the hottest lady in the room. It is a very heavy fabric, best used in cold weather."

At last, they settled back into the car. After each Mrs. Krakowiak visit, Mrs. Robinson would take a deep breath and blow the air up over her face as if moving the memories of the morning out of her mind. Jack and Anna would exchange a look but never say a word.

Instead, Anna asked, "What were you reading today, Jack?"

He said, "Today's news was old news. Did you know that an agreement called the Young Plan was made in Paris in June? It will reduce the Germans' debt from $33 billion to only $27 billion. These were debts from war reparations."

"I don't even know how many zeros there are in a billion," Anna answered.

"Anna, you're a smart woman. You have to learn about money. No one will want to admit to not understanding all these terms in the modern world."

Mrs. Robinson said, "Yes. If we are making money, we need to know how best to make it work for us."

"Jack, are you reading any good books?" Anna asked.

"My buddy loaned me *The Sound and the Fury* by William Faulkner. It was a sad commentary on the times in the South. I am trying to find Ernest Hemingway's *A Farewell to Arms*. And here we are at home."

SEVEN

Two days later, Anna found a letter from Pittsburgh waiting for her. *Ugh. I do not want this letter. I do not want to read it. Why is Robert bothering to write? He had better not think I will be writing back to him.*

Reluctantly, she opened it.

August 30, 1929
Dear Anna,
What will the world lose if you join the convent?
I decided on the following ten things.

1) The laughter of Anna.

2) The dancing of Anna. Have you ever read the proverb, *the* day you were born, God danced?

3) The twinkle in Anna's eyes.

4) The curiosity in her questions to another in conversation.

5) The way Anna turns her head to listen to birds sing.

6) The gentle touch of her hand when she sees a friend.

7) The gusto with which she eats pierogi.

8) The *Ivory Soap* fragrance when she runs past you.

9) Her hair when she nods and it falls over her right eye.

10) The taste of Anna's lips.

Robert

Why did I open this? I sure am a glutton for punishment. Did I open it because I was being considerate of another's feelings or because I was curious? I wish Julia were closer so I could show it to her. How am I feeling about all of this?

"Anna, you missed the other letter you got today from Kentucky." Her brother, Leon, handed her a long white envelope. "Maybe they decided you were too homely to join their Order."

"Leon, when I'm gone, who will you torment?" She grabbed the envelope and went upstairs to her room to read it.

Abbey
Wattsville, Kentucky
August 25, 1929

Miss Anna Wiosnec
Dear Anna,

We at the convent are pleased with your request for entry. We will be expecting you on October 1.

Again, as before, we ask that you bring limited personal items. You may bring religious objects, personal hygiene items of your choice, and an address book.

We also request that you bring a compiled report of an interview with five adult women including one nun. Each needs to answer a few questions about their life choices.

The questions are:

How old were you when you decided what vocation you'd follow as an adult?

How many choices did you have?

Did anyone help you decide?

In hindsight, what else should you have known in making the decision?

How happy are you with that decision?

Remember that being a wife and mother is a vocation.

You may identify these ladies by their given name or a fictitious name. This task helps us to know you have given the vocation as nun serious thought.

Sincerely, Sister Mary Eileen

Oh, Mój Boże. Oh, good God. I have reached another obstacle. Wait a minute. I love to write. I think everyone I ask will be glad to answer my questions. I can write a good report, probably the best one Sister Mary Eileen ever read. In fact, when I ask any woman questions like that, they are usually eager to talk as long as they are alone. Maybe they will ask that I not repeat what they say, and I can let them know that all their answers will be secure in the abbey. Now, I need to pick the five women. I will ask Sister Laetitia, Julia, Mrs. Robinson, Aunt Nellie, and I will need one more.

Anna grabbed her mail. "It's only 8:30," she told Tata as she hurried out into the night. "Sister Laetitia always says I can visit until 9:00."

In a few minutes, she was sitting beside Sister. She handed her the letter. "Look at this." She waited patiently for Sister to comment.

"He seems very sincere, Anna. It is a very flattering letter."

Anna looked at Sister. She felt a blush rise on her cheeks as she realized she has given her both pieces of mail. "Oh, Sister, that was a mistake. I only planned to show you the other one. Please disregard that letter and see the wonderful one I got from the convent."

Sister read the second letter.

"I want to ask you these questions," Anna said. "Can we start now? Can I write down your answers?"

"Yes. I will answer them, but you'll have to answer mine, too."

"I will. And my first question is, why did you join the convent?"

"I decided to become a nun because my favorite aunt was Sister Genevive. She taught you in the first grade, didn't she?"

"Yes, and I loved her."

"I love her, too. I wish she would get reassigned here soon. She has a delightful sense of humor. She told me that teaching the first grade was fun and funny. She said it was fun because the children were so sweet. It was funny because sometimes when she asked an innocent question, they would reveal things. Things like who snored, who drank too much, and who didn't go to Sunday Mass. Sister said she became an expert at quickly changing subjects."

Anna smiled as she took notes.

"She spent time encouraging me to develop my art skills and my singing voice. She always said it was not a choice if there was but one option. I am not sure I understood that for many years."

"How many choices did you have, Sister?"

"Two. I could find a nice fella and get married or be a nun. I didn't see many nice boys in my neighborhood. My home life wasn't wonderful, so I chose peace for myself. I think that takes care of the next question about who helped me decide."

Anna said, "I have been told by others that you are not only happy but a little mischievous. It is said that you hold your rosary in your hands so you make no noise, then you sneak up on the other nuns and scare them."

"I only frighten the ones with a good sense of humor. Some years, that is scarce."

"How old were you when you thought about joining the convent?"

"Six. How old was I when I decided? Fourteen."

"Last question. In hindsight, what else should you have known before making the decision?"

"Fourteen is far too young to make a life decision. Many of my fellow nuns made an early choice and are unhappy. I, however, am one of the fortunate ones. Am I happy? Almost all the time. Few people can look back and say that. Now, about this other letter, who is Robert? Where and when did you meet him?"

"Sister, I'm as surprised as you. I met him at Julia's wedding.

I will at least have to be polite and write back to tell him I received the letter."

"We must continue this conversation another time. It's nine o'clock," Sister whispered and ushered her to the door.

As she walked home, Anna waved to people on their porches and said hello to those she passed.

Mrs. White, the next-door neighbor, called out as Anna got to her own porch. "Hi, Anna. You're out late tonight, I see."

"I was down at the convent talking to Sister Laetitia."

"Is everything going well for you?"

"Oh, yes, thanks." Anna smiled. *Mrs. White might be a good person to interview. I always wondered how a person with that last name could speak Polish so well. I think she would answer my questions. Maybe I'll ask her tomorrow.*

When she went inside, Tata asked, "Was Sister surprised to see you?"

"No, she doesn't mind no matter when I show up."

"Anna, I know you had a letter from Kentucky today. Are there any problems?"

"I just have to fill out a little questionnaire."

The next day in Mrs. Robinson's sewing room, Anna explained her assignment and showed Mrs. Robinson the questions.

"Sure," Mrs. Robinson said. "Let's take a break and talk about this."

"Thank you. I need to write down your answers. How old were you when you decided what vocation you'd follow as an adult?"

"I always wanted to be a housewife and have more than five children. Notice, I have none. Sometimes plans need to be revised."

Anna blinked.

"I see the next question is about my choices. My grandmother Elizabeth helped raise me. She was always making one thing or another. Her face always lit up when she saw me. I shadowed her until the day she died. We did sewing, canning, gardening, and cooking together. We had the most fun with the sewing. I wanted to be just like her. She did have seven children, though. She lived with our family. She was very short and yet very strong. I remember her chopping wood. She made the chips fly."

Anna asked, "Did anyone help you decide?"

"Yes, I came across this wonderful soldier just back from the war. His name was George Robinson. He helped me decide."

"In hindsight, what else should you have known in making the decision?"

"Probably that even though he still makes me smile every day and many nights, he had a war injury, and we were never blessed with children. Would I have still married him?" She nodded. "Yes, I would have."

"Are you happy with your decision?"

"Immensely."

On the ride home, Anna was very quiet. *Now I have two happy ladies for my report. I wonder what the other three will say. I had better remember to send a note out to Robert. I need to write it tonight.*

September 5, 1929
Dear Robert,

I was glad to hear from you because it let me know you got home safely last weekend.

Julia has moved to the Craig Ranch. I will see her next week. Say hello to Margo for me.

Your friend,
Anna

Maybe this is not a good letter. I'm just too tired to be cordial. It will have to wait until tomorrow. She crumpled the note she had written and put it in her pocket so Leon would not get it.

The next day, they delivered clothes to the Craig's. Anna was anxious to see Julia. Unfortunately, Julia was not available.

Mrs. Craig tried on the new dresses and sounded pleased with the ease of dressing in them. "Who would have thought that if one just added another panel to these dresses, they could wrap below the waist instead of at the seams?"

Mrs. Robinson knew Anna wanted to see Julia. While Mrs. Craig and Mrs. Robinson looked at fall fabrics, she asked Mrs. Craig about the possibility of Anna and Julia sharing a lunch on the lawn.

"Of course," Mrs. Craig replied.

Anna hurried to Julia's quarters only to find her friend huddled in bed. Her long-sleeved white blouse looked damp from perspiration, and her usually springy dark curls hugged her face.

"What kind of a lunch partner are you?" she asked.

"Oh, Anna, I could not eat one bite of food. Even the smell of it isn't good." She turned her head away from her friend.

Anna could smell Julia's stale breath. Remembering her mother's flu fatality, she asked, "Do you have the flu? I hope not. Can I just help you get yourself washed? When did you get sick? Have you seen a doctor? Can I get you something?"

"No, it isn't an illness. I will feel better in a few weeks."

"What? How can you be sure?"

"It's the baby," she whispered. "Now that I'm married, I can just throw up if I need to."

"Come and sit outside. At least, you won't have to smell the food."

"I'll come."

Anna sat on the floor and laced Julia's black button shoes for her. They went out to the wide lawn and sat beneath a tree.

After taking a bite of her chicken sandwich, Anna asked, "So, what work are you doing these days?"

"Oh, I dust, sweep, wash dishes, and clean. I like helping with the children, Anthony and Donna. And especially Susan. She has a sweet, freckled face and captures my heart."

"It sounds like you are happy here," Anna said.

"Can you think of a better place for me? I am with my husband, and he is working hard, despite having only one good arm. He is treated with respect. We have plenty of honest work, plenty of food, a clean room of our own. God has been good to us. I do not know what will happen when I admit that I am having a baby, but we will wait and see."

"Does Adam like it here?" she asked.

"Here he comes. We can ask him. He said he'd be cutting and clearing the bushes and chestnut trees today."

Adam walked over to them. He wore dark work pants, and a thin shirt with the sleeves rolled up. A beige straw hat was on his head and a big smile on his face.

"Hello, Adam," Anna said. "You look cheerful."

"I am," he said. "Where else but in America could a one-armed man have a job, and a new wife, and just so much happiness? I can now go and have a decent lunch and then find plenty of work to do for the rest of the day. I know my wife and I will have enough." He kissed Julia. "Ladies, I'm sorry I can't stay, but..." He shrugged and walked away.

Anna said, "Julia, what good fortune. Now, even though you are not feeling your best, I have a quiz and need some answers from you about life choices for a report for the convent."

"So, ask."

"Let me show you the questions."

Julia quickly scanned the paper. "Except for wanting to be a suffragette, my only wish was to be a wife and mother. I could not wait. When I met Adam, it was like extra sweets on the cookie of my life. I have many cousins, and all our families have at least three children. Hindsight? This throwing up all the time is ridiculous. It's temporary, so tolerable. Happy? I am, I am." Her smile faltered, and she turned her head from the scent of the pickle in Anna's lunch. "Oh, look, your Mrs. Robinson looks like she's ready to leave."

Anna looked over at the car with Jack and Mrs. Robinson nearing it. "Yes, it's time to go."

She hugged her friend and got into the car, ready for the long drive back.

At home, she faced the inevitable letter writing to Robert.

September 6, 1929
Dear Robert,
Your letter was so kind, and such a surprise. There has to be a perfect girl for you in Pittsburgh who would love to hear such sweet things from you.

I am still entering the convent in a few weeks as planned. May you have a good life.

Sincerely,

Anna

This is the kindest letter I can write. What was he thinking? I never even kissed him. He was very nice, though.

After dinner, there was time to see Sister Laetitia again. Anna met her after evening prayers.

"Hi, Anna. How did you answer Robert's letter? I have been praying that you find the right words."

"It was so awkward. I thought you would like to see my letter to him."

"I'd rather not see it. I am your friend, not your confessor. Whatever you said was what was in your heart, right?"

"The letter was only a reminder of the pleasant weekend, is all."

"Then all is well. How are the plans for the October trip? Will your whole family take you down or just your father?"

"I don't think he has decided yet. I did get two more parts of my questionnaire done."

"Did it make you think harder about the choice you are making?"

"It made me realize that all life choices are big ones and not accidental. I feel more respect for people's choices."

Sister nodded.

"I'm going to ask my Aunt Nellie the questions tonight. She always has time to talk to me. I'm surprised she still sews at night even though I don't think her eyes are very good."

"You better get on your way, then. God bless you, Anna," Sister said as she kissed her forehead.

That evening, Aunt Nellie said, "Come in and sit down. I have not had a nice visit with you in a long time. Tell me about what is happening."

"I'm leaving for the convent in three weeks. I have to ask five women questions about their life choices. Can I ask you?"

"Yes, but you may be surprised at some of the answers."

"How old were you when you decided what vocation you'd follow as an adult?"

"When I was fifteen, it became a hardship for my parents to feed all five children. My goal, I suppose you could call it a vocation, became to work at any job possible to get enough money for a voyage to America for myself. I planned to come here and work hard and send for my sister, your mother, to follow me."

"Is that what happened?"

"No. Every time I got enough money, Mama needed it for necessities for the little ones. So, I gave it to her."

"Then how did you get here?"

She said, "Czekajcie. Mam kava, mam smachne ciastko."

"That's just like you to tell me to wait because you have coffee and delicious cake." Anna smiled as Aunt Nellie hurried into the kitchen.

She returned carrying a small tray with two cups of coffee, two spoons, two forks, and plates each with a piece of angel food cake and a few strawberries on the side. She handed a plate and a cup of coffee to Anna and put her own beside her.

"I was working for a cantankerous seamstress, Pani Dorota Dziadek, whose eyes were worse than mine are now, and whose hands were beginning to cramp and shake. She thought she was some kind of a fancy lady. I overheard her saying she was moving to America. I talked to my smart Uncle Basil and asked him to help me convince her to take me along as her companion."

"That was a good idea," Anna said.

Aunt Nellie tasted her coffee. "We had heard all the stories about girls who came over that way and were indentured for many years. He and I figured one year would be plenty. We wrote an agreement with her paying my passage and me working it off in one year, and she agreed to it. We talked her into signing two duplicate papers with the agreement. That was a life plan for me. It worked. I knew she was very difficult. Anna, the trip over and the year with her in Philadelphia were terrible. At the end of the year, she tried to say she needed me for more time and was entitled to another year, but I had the paper. I also had a friend from the old country living here in Petroleum City, so I left Mrs. Dziadek and came here." She took another slow sip of her coffee.

"How many choices did you have?"

"At the time, only one." She smiled. "When I got to Petroleum City, I was one of the few with no husband and no financial obligations. I could spend some time figuring out my next step."

"Did anyone help you decide?"

"Anna, at so many points in life, one has to again decide and most decisions are made alone. Even in the convent, there will be things for you to choose or reject."

"Oh, I don't think I will have choices."

"Try to remember this conversation. Did anyone in the family ever tell you that I sometimes sense things?"

"No, I don't know what you mean."

"You tell me you are going to the convent. And I do see you there, yet I see you somewhere different with a lot of bright sun. Wherever that is, you are fulfilled there, too. We need to get back to the questions. What's the next one?"

"What should you have known about the decision in hindsight?"

"How hard it was for me to be away from my family. I was so happy when your mother came to join me. I was so sad when she died." Tears slid down Aunt Nellie's cheeks. "Being married is a bittersweet thing. Times are good, and times are bad."

"Last question is, how happy are you with that decision?"

"We make our own joy day-by-day," she concluded.

Anna hugged Aunt Nellie and walked home. *Even now, I think my choices are good.*

EIGHT

September brought thoughts of fall and new requests for dresses from the ladies. Mrs. Kidman needed a few new frocks. Mrs. Krakowiak wanted only one item. Mrs. Roebuck wanted to scan the fall fabrics. Mrs. Montes felt the need for four dresses. Anna and Mrs. Robinson were using two sewing machines to fill the orders. Anna wished for a breeze that would lift the curtains in their sewing room.

ৰু ৰু ৰু

On the way home from a dress delivery at the Craig's, Jack mentioned Julia and Adam. "It looks like the newlyweds have found a nice place for themselves. Not many couples have such good luck."

"But that accident was not good luck. He can barely move his left arm," Anna said.

"You know, he seemed to be doing his share despite his handicap. I wonder when it will be healed," Mrs. Robinson said.

"Julia did not say."

"Did you two have a good visit over lunch today?" Mrs. Robinson asked.

"It was nice," she replied. *Although, while I ate, Julia would still not eat a morsel, and her eyes brimmed with tears at the aroma of food.*

ৰু ৰু ৰু

On Saturday morning, sweat rolled down Anna's face as she

moved around the Indian Summer kitchen and exchanged the cooling flat iron for a hot one. After ironing the back of Tata's shirt, she put the heated plate on the left front.

I really like Tata's shirts to look perfect every morning when he starts the day. I have many extra metal buttons handy for him to pop into those little button holes on the left side of his shirt. Then he closes the shirt by pulling the front part of the button through the bigger buttonholes on the shirt's right side.

"Hey Anna, when will you be taking the bread out of the oven? Twelve-year-old boys can't do much weeding unless they have hot bread covered with butter." Leon rubbed his stomach.

"Sorry. I got a late start after Mass today. Now I am just praying for a little breeze. I'm using the oven temperature to heat these irons to finish Tata's shirts and aprons for next week."

"Don't bore me with details. I need bread. How soon?"

"Ten minutes. While we wait, tell me who will be teaching you in the eighth grade this year?"

"I hear it'll be Sister Mary Bartholomew."

"Isn't she the nun who considers herself kind but strict?"

"Well, my pals call her BB for Black Bart. What a—"

"Would you like anyone to talk about me like that if I were your teacher?"

"No, but when you get to your convent, you might as well be DD—deaf and dumb. You know there's no talking there."

"Right. Please go and pick me about six apples and be sure to check for wormholes. I will finish ironing the shirt. I just need to touch up the neckline then I'll pull out the bread."

As he walked out the back door, Bashia entered the kitchen.

Anna said, "Bashia, if you forget how to iron Tata's shirts, just go and ask Aunt Nellie. Please do not take them to her so she will iron them. I am sorry you had to help Tata this morning. I wanted to go over the order of ironing the parts of his shirt with you."

"You worry too much. I have ironed shirts lots of times. You do the shoulders on the inside and the collar on the inside, then the front."

"No, the collar is last."

Leon rolled six apples across the floor. "Get out the bread, please."

She opened the oven, and the yeasty scent filled the room.

Leon said, "I see cookies in there. Smells like sugar cookies to me. Why are you keeping the cookies a secret?"

"They are for Julia. This will be my last visit before I go to Kentucky. Tonight, after Tata closes the store, he is taking me to see her and Adam. Want to come?"

"No, everyone in the neighborhood is playing hide and seek tonight. Tell Julia I said hello."

ಶಿ   ಶಿ   ಶಿ

Anna and Tata sat in the parlor with Julia and Adam.

Julia said, "Oh, I love those cookies, Anna. We will both enjoy them. Mr. Wiosnec, would you like to try one of Anna's cookies?"

Anna's father replied, "No, thank you. We have more at home. Anna had to make another batch for Leon and Bashia today. He was complaining of starvation. He is just a growing boy. In fact, I think he grew two inches this summer."

Adam said to Tata, "Before it gets dark, I'd like to show you around the ranch."

"Certainly."

The two men left the room.

Now in private, Julia said, "I've been thinking about the baby. Remember the time we ran into Mr. Skolnik's store about eight times just to get out of the cold. He finally got so annoyed, he told us to *get ta hel outa.* Then remember how embarrassed he was to realize he had said bad words to two little innocent girls. If this is a girl, I hope she will be more polite than I was."

"No, you don't. What fun would that be?"

"Anna, I will need a godmother for the baby. You know you were the original choice, so I'd like to ask your sister, Bashia, to do the honors."

"She would be thrilled, I think. I will talk to her in private about that, since the baby is still a secret, right?"

"Yes, it is. Oh, I hear Adam's voice. The men have come back. Anna, I am so glad we had such a nice last visit. It is hard to say goodbye to you. I know you said I can't send you letters, but just in case they change the rules, I will keep a journal."

The girls kissed each other's cheek. Then Anna and Tata left for home.

ะ ะ ะ

Jack continued to read many books and newspapers in his multifocal studies. "I was studying the oil industry and its startup in this area," he told Anna one evening on their way home. "The first oil well was drilled in 1859, by Edwin L. Drake. He struck oil at 69 feet. Do you realize it was only a few miles from where we sit? That is why we hear all those little machines making that creak, creak, squeak, squeak noise all the time."

"I only really hear it in the mornings and at night. There are too many other noises in the middle of the day for me to notice. But I know that the machines work all the time."

"The Rock Oil Company first owned the property. Originally, the oil was used for medicinal purposes. Look how far we have come since then."

"It is pretty amazing," she admitted.

"I was also reading about the gold rush in the Rocky Mountains. Since gold was discovered in Colorado, many people have gone to seek their fortunes with the motto, *Pike's Peak or Bust.*"

"It sounds like a lot of people have lost their minds." She laughed.

ะ ะ ะ

Anna looked at the calendar and counted ten days until she would be able to move to Kentucky. She prayed long and hard for all her family to understand her need to make this life change.

A few cool breezes made the local women again want more

fall clothes. The two seamstresses and the driver were in a frenzy to fill all the orders.

ಋ   ಋ   ಋ

On Monday, September the twenty-third, Anna received a call from her father. "Julia needs you."

Oh, what can be so important? We are busy.

"I will come and get you as soon as I close the store," he said.

She was confused. "My father is on his way to get me," she said to Mrs. Robinson. "He said Julia needs me."

"He would not close the store unless it was serious," Mrs. Robinson said.

She and her father drove to the Craig farm. All he would say was, "Something happened, and I'm not sure what I heard."

When they arrived, Mrs. Craig's helper, Priscilla, ushered them into the barn.

Julia's parents stood at the entrance. Julia's father wrapped an arm around his wife's shoulder.

Her mother said to Anna, "He fell off the horse."

Anna's hands went to her mouth, and her eyes filled with tears. Her breath came in short gulps.

Inside the barn, Adam's body lay on a hay wagon atop a white cloth. Julia had a look of bewilderment and innocence. She smoothed the hair of her dead husband and whispered to him as she rearranged his rumpled and grass-stained shirt.

Anna walked over to her friend and said, "Julia, I'm here."

Julia looked at Anna as if she had no knowledge of time or place. She said, "I think Adam needs a blanket."

A young worker pulled a blanket from a stall and handed it to Julia.

She placed it on her husband.

Anna put her arm around her friend. She could feel Julia's cold and trembling body even through the brown shawl she wore.

Her mother came to Julia's side, and said, "Come, my daughter. Let us sit outside and talk."

"I can't leave my husband," Julia answered.

Julia's mother moved her reluctant daughter out of the barn. As she walked away from the body of her husband, Julia kept looking back over her shoulder.

Anna and her father joined the folks gathered by Adam's body. The ranch owner, David Craig, and his wife were there with a worker Anna had met before.

The young man, James Schultz, said, "I found him down by the crik." He cleared his throat. "We wuz workin' early this mornin' on cuttin' back brush. Suddenly, he wuzn't nowhere that I could see. I was thinkin' he went ta get a drink a water." He brushed the hair from his eyes and put his hands in his pockets.

Mr. Craig asked softly, "Then what happened, James?"

"Well, I started lookin' for him. I knew he wuz dirty, so he wouldn't go in the house. Frisky, little Miss Donna's horse, wuz missin'. I decided to do a look 'round the grounds. When I found 'em, by the crik, he wuzn't breathin'." His eyes darted up into the surrounding trees as if he were looking for his next sentence.

Mrs. Craig said, "Go on."

"The horse he wuz ridin' wuz there actin' like he been spooked. Miss Donna's horse wuz there, too. I don't know why Adam wuz by that crik, but with only one hand to hold the rein, he probly lost control and fell off the horse. I think the grass wuz wet." He looked down at the clippings clinging to Adam's shirt. "We cut grass by the crik yesterday, so it was probly covered with the morning dew." James rubbed his hand over his chin. "What wuz he doin' down by the crick when we wuz sposed to be clearin' the brush?"

Anna went outside to be near Julia. She sat on a bench under a chestnut tree. "Come and sit here by me. This sun is strong and bright. Julia, your skin was so cold in the barn. Does it feel better out here?"

Julia huddled beneath the shawl. She held a hand to her belly. A look of confusion was on her face.

Anna asked, "What can I do for you?"

"Make it be this morning again. Make him never leave my side. Anna, I am not tough. Pinch me. Wake me up from this bad dream. If I start to cry, I will never stop. Will crying hurt our baby?"

"We both know that this is not a dream. You have always been strong, and Adam has been such a good man for you. Tell me some of the good things about him, so we can both feel his spirit here with us."

"I can't even think. You think for me."

"Remember that evening when we were all three sitting on your back porch, and Adam played your favorite song on the harmonica? He made fine music, didn't he?"

"Yes, he did. I remember how he wrote to his mother in Poland every Sunday. He told her wonderful things about Petroleum City. He was counting down the months until he had saved enough money to send for her." Tears brimmed in her eyes. "What do I tell that poor lady now?"

"If your mother agrees, we can write that letter together. In all the sadness, we will tell her about the new baby you're carrying."

Tata walked up to them. "Julia, my heart goes out to you in this hour of your sorrow. Anna will be around as much as you need her in these next few days. Anna, there will be plenty for you to do at Julia's parents' place this evening. Julia, we need to say goodbye for a few hours to let you have some time with your mother and father."

ৰু ৰু ৰু

At home that evening, Anna said to Tata, "I am so glad Julia's family is here. They will be able to help her with the funeral and burial. I need to go over to the Pewnik's to be with her, but first I will call Mrs. Robinson and tell her about Adam."

After hearing the news, Mrs. Robinson said, "I want to know the funeral arrangements, please. Oh, how sad for all of them.

Julia needs her best friend now more than ever. Please phone me if you need anything. I just looked at the calendar, and it is already the end of September. I know you plan to leave in a few days. I am looking for another seamstress, but you will be hard to replace."

On the way to Julia's parents' home, Anna almost walked past the turn on Cornplanter Avenue. So many thoughts raced through her mind. *Ah, Julia, remember our innocence a year ago? We were two young, single, carefree women. Now you are a widow with a child soon to come. How strong are you, my friend? What will you do?*

When she arrived at Julia's house, the funeral wreath was already attached to the front door. A few strands of ivy and pink and red roses poked out from under the fat black ribbon.

The wreath from Mama's funeral was mostly dark fall-colored flowers since it was in December. Once the wreath is hung, everyone knows there has been a death. No one needs to knock on the door. It means all are welcome to the viewing.

When she walked into the front room, Julia's father and Mr. Fachowiecz, the funeral director, were deep in conversation.

"Unless there is a change, all church funerals are at 8 AM," Mr. Fachowiecz said. He replaced papers into the inside pocket of his heavy-looking black suit. Even across the room, she could smell the moth crystals seeping from the seams of his wool jacket.

"So, it will take place on Saturday morning?" Julia's father asked.

Mr. Fachowiecz opened a book. "Yes, Saturday at 8 AM. You probably did not realize many of the reasons. Winter is not here yet. During Indian Summer, it is cooler in the church early in the morning. It is kinder for all if the body is in a cool place. The early morning funeral gives mourners more time to get to the cemetery after the service. One could still get home and tend to the necessary things in their lives, such as a return to work for the rest of that day." He took a crumpled white handkerchief out of his pants pocket and wiped his glistening face.

What a tactless human being Mr. Fachowiecz is. Do we really need to know about the heat and all that? It is amazing to hear how some of the educated people in this community sometimes act like they are giving lectures to the masses. She paused and took a breath. *Stop. I need to be kind. This poor man has already spent hours preparing Adam for the viewing. He has had a hard day. God, forgive me.*

"I am sure the door is wide enough for the casket," the funeral director said. "The viewing will be in the front room."

Julia's father turned to some men. "The front room needs to be cleared out for the coffin. All big furniture needs to be removed, and only small chairs will be in place. We need plenty of ashtrays for the smokers."

Is this happening? Is this still the same day? How can a mind absorb all this?

Anna looked at the beautiful front room, now lacking the little reading lamps and soft pillows on the chairs. She said, "Oh, I do remember some of this from when Mr. Pasmo up the street died."

Mr. Pewnik said, "The viewing is actually a sitting. At least one person will be in the room with the coffin from the time it arrives in the house until the body goes to the church for the funeral. The hard parts are the all-night vigils. You remember when your father sat at your mother's side?"

"I will never forget. All I need to do is smell roses, and it all comes back to me." Her vision swam with new tears.

Anna walked into the kitchen. Neighbor women scurried about.

Mrs. Pewnik murmured, "It seems Mrs. Wielka is in charge."

Anna remembered Aunt Nellie saying *if either by invitation or by the inevitable final acceptance of her peers, she is put in charge, beware. She is a force the neighborhood has learned to accept.* She also said that *when Pani Wielka was appointed or accepted a task, one knew it would be accomplished swiftly, successfully, and completely. The entire workforce would be angry, dog tired, and mentally spent at the task's completion.*

The usually closed-mouthed Aunt Margaret said just a few

weeks ago, *the fable of Mrs. Wielka is well known in town. She was in a convent for a short time as a youth. The story was told that she left of her own volition. It seems the Mother Superior confidentially admitted saying to her that since the post of Mother Superior would not be available for many years, the young lady should probably move on to another vocation. Mrs. Wielka, whose first name is somehow hidden from all but the hierarchies of the local church and will never be known until the priest reads it at her funeral, then proceeded to become a teacher. Adding to her self-proclaimed résumé, she then became a person of authority in a faraway school district where she did a wonderful job. She also met and married the amazing Mr. Wielka, who had unfortunately faded out of the picture before her return to this city.*

Mrs. Wielka made the ladies empty the ice box so there would be room for the intake of funeral food. The contents were taken to a neighbor. She insisted all unnecessary furniture be carried to several close homes until after the funeral. She ordered a few men to bring in the inevitable supplies of beer and vodka. "I see we have a donation of money here for miscellaneous. I want you," she said, pointing to a young man, "to take some of this money and go out and find us a lot of ice for this food and drink."

After moving the furniture, the men were free until the arrival of the body, per declaration of Pani Wielka.

Before dark, the body arrived.

Mr. Fachowiecz said, "For the first hour, Julia and her family have a private viewing. I will stay for a few hours and be sure this all runs smoothly."

Out in the hall, Anna had a view of the room. She sat, prayed, and glanced into the living room.

During the hour, the funeral director could be seen with the family rearranging the blanket, the clothes on Adam, and repositioning the flowers. Julia walked around, examining the floral wallpaper and the position of each chair. Her mother moved her slowly to the coffin. Julia stood, looked, and swayed. She shook her head each time she was approached and offered a seat.

Lord, help us all. Give her courage. Give me powerful words to help her. I need more strength than she does to remind her of good things. I am leaving in a few days. This will be my parting gift to her. She stood to rearrange the other chairs in the hall. *I can already smell the roses, and I only see three vases. Roses and funerals.*

"Now, the rest of you can come in the room," the funeral director said as he mopped his receding hairline.

At the coffin, Anna saw that Adam was dressed in a modest dark suit. Her heart sank when she realized it was the suit he had worn so recently as a groom. A black rosary was intertwined in his scrubbed clean fingers.

The stoic men came, looked, said a prayer at the side of the coffin, and stepped aside. The women shed many tears.

Aunt Nellie had quietly joined for the first evening viewing. She sat near Anna for a few minutes and said, "As a nationality, the Polish people are silent in their lamentation. No one screams, no one falls to the floor weeping, nor is anyone, except perhaps a female spouse, expected to feel faint. Many tears are shed, but it is a quiet sorrow. By tomorrow, everyone in the parish will know that Adam died. Remember that while a member of the parish is dead but not buried, the church bell rings as usual at noon and evening. But it also tolls. That dull, low, lonesome sound cannot be duplicated. All in the parish will stop and say a prayer for the deceased."

After a long, draining evening, Anna said her good nights to the Pewnik family.

Mrs. Pewnik said, "Oh, by the way, Anna, Robert has agreed to drive Małgorzata, Uncle Benjamin, and Aunt Janina from Pittsburgh for the funeral Mass."

The next day was a steady flow of friends and relatives at Julia's home. Anna ministered to her friend with glasses of water and replacement of clean handkerchiefs as necessary.

Saturday morning, blinking the sleep from her eyes, Anna sat up and swung her legs off the bed. She looked at her bedmate sister. *Bashia needs her sleep. I will tiptoe out of here.*

The bathroom door was closed. The doorknob turned, and Leon wandered out.

Anna rushed in and brushed her teeth. Back in the bedroom, she put on clothes and tied her hair to the side. She fixed a fast breakfast for the family and went to Julia's home. *I will help her with whatever is needed. Maybe I can comb her hair and help her dress. I can help her with lipstick and a set of earrings. She will not be thinking of that. She needs to wear flat shoes so she is steady footed at the church and the walk to the cemetery.*

At Julia's, Anna found the pregnant widow lingering over a half-eaten breakfast. She guided her to her bedroom and groomed her for the day.

The funeral Mass was heartbreaking. Julia stumbled as she followed the coffin into the church. The choir sang Serdecznza Matko, a request to a tenderhearted Mary, mother of Jesus. The altar was bleak because all decorations had been removed for the funeral. The coffin was blessed repeatedly with both incense and holy water during the Requiem Mass. Bashia sneezed as the incense scent crossed her nose.

After the religious ceremony, the pallbearers removed the coffin as the choir sang, *Witaj Królovo Nieba*. This song was one a soul would sing to enter the abode of Mary, the Queen of Heaven. Women raised handkerchiefs to wipe tears from their faces.

Anna followed the hearse to the cemetery. There, Julia and her family trudged to the open gravesite. Again, prayers were said, and the coffin was blessed with holy water.

Anna watched Julia sway several times and be steadied by her father's cupped hand on her elbow. Anna heard him whisper, "Julia, you can do this. I am proud of you."

After a word or hug to the close family, everyone departed the site. Tata eased Anna away. As she glanced back, she saw Julia hug the coffin. Then she noticed Robert walking toward her.

Tata whispered, "Anna, say a kind word to your friend." Head bowed, he rushed off.

Anna stretched out both hands in greeting. "Robert."

He grasped her fingers. "I never thought I would see you again."

She closed her eyes. *Neither did I.*

"Let me walk you home."

"I can't. I am so sorry."

He said, "Think hard about the step you are taking."

"I did. I will pray for you. Goodbye." She turned and walked away.

NINE

Two days later, Anna awoke early, said her prayers, and closed her small piece of luggage. She hurried downstairs.

"Good morn, *Pani Anna,*" Leon said, calling her Lady Anna.

She saw her brother's silhouette in the kitchen as he crossed in front of the window. The sun was not up yet, but early morning light had begun to sneak into the room.

"I hear you and I see sad eyes on your face. It is only six o'clock. Why are you awake?" she asked.

"To have you fix me a breakfast for the last time. How could I resist? What are you making? French toast? My favorite?" A smile returned to his freckled face.

"No, this is just scrambled eggs with whatever I find. I am adding a little ham, chopped onion," she said as she beat eggs, added salt and pepper, splashed in a few drops of milk, and poured in the icebox leftovers.

"Again, too much information. Just cook, please. I will miss your excellent cooking. Now, I will have to break in Bashia. Take a last look at your healthy brother. Will I die of starvation? Pray for me." He laughed.

"I will pray while you cut this whole loaf of bread into slices. Some for breakfast and the rest for the trip for Tata and myself. Remember how I taught you to hold a sharp knife?"

Tata walked in, smiling. "*Córka,* my beautiful daughter, it is a fine day for a journey. The weather is crisp and clear. You know, your mama and I loved to travel, and we had wonderful plans. But, such is life. I am happy for you today. You are starting a new chapter in your existence."

"I want to go with you," Leon said.

"Son, I am sorry you cannot make this trip, but Aunt Nellie will need you here to man the store." Tata patted him on the shoulder. "Be polite, lift boxes for Aunt Nellie and Aunt Margaret, too, when they work at the store. We are so fortunate to have two such nice ladies to help while I am gone. And, Leon, when you pack groceries in a box, do make a square knot on the rope so it will not come loose when you carry it. As I have told you before, your mama was the one who taught me all the knots. She must have shown me at least twenty different kinds. She had a unique hobby."

"Yes, Tata."

Turning back to Anna, he said, "As we drive, I will remind you of the relatives we visit on the way. The trip is several days long. We will be going as fast as thirty-five miles an hour a great deal of the time. But we will be comfortable. That Mister Henry Ford sure was thinking of the working man with his car designs. It comes in four colors, you know. Of course, I still like the black best. I hear they have built a million Model A's. Can you imagine that? Your mama said to me that since I worked very hard, I should always have a nice car if we could afford it."

Bashia eased into the kitchen. Her unruly mop of curly hair was pulled to the back of her head with a wrinkled ribbon. "I was hoping you would be gone by the time I came downstairs be-cause I cannot think of how to say goodbye. When I see you in a year, you will be behind a wall, and I will not be able to touch you and hug you, so I am trying to separate myself from you now. Does that make any sense?"

"Sadly, yes it does," Anna said. "I have been so busy with Julia, we have not talked. Now, there is no time. Bashia, we two have been through so much together. Sisters sense. Sisters feel. Sisters remember. You and I," she turned her head quickly to shake the tears from her eyes, "we just know. If I hear a joke and laugh, I know you would like that joke."

Bashia continued her part of the *sister chant*. "When you are sad, I know why. When you look at the stars, especially the North

Star, I will be looking at it, too, thinking of you." She smiled. "Do you think we are twins, just born years instead of minutes apart? Anna, I will be here in Petroleum City and so proud of you." She pulled plates from the cupboard. Then she placed glasses of milk down for herself and Leon and poured coffee for Anna and Tata. As she put the sugar bowl on the table, she said, "But, Anna, I will still be pondering what Aunt Nellie said. She said she sees you in the convent but also sees you someplace sunny, dressed in light brown apparel. Is she clairvoyant, like the family insists, or just a good storyteller?"

"*Szybko.* Quickly," Tata said as he sat at the table. "I am looking for the last time at my three children together, and you all make me so proud. I know your mother is up there looking down on this momentous day." He cleared his throat and blinked tears from his eyes, opened his napkin, placed it on his lap, and said, "*Jestemy głodny.* We are hungry. Come, let us eat."

Minutes later, Anna found herself in the front seat of the family car. Tata assessed the car's contents then turned the ignition key. She looked at her neighborhood for the last time as the car moved down Warren Street. Mrs. Prosaska's summer flowers had their little heads folded down. They were now just shaggy memories of a past season of glory. Anna saw the maple tree that shaded her house, the dusty street where she and Julia had learned to ride bikes. She remembered running along holding Bashia on a bike. And then Leon. She saw the fat glistening nuts stuck in the chestnut trees, waiting to fall at the whim of an unruly autumn wind.

They passed through the center of town, across Elm Street and Seneca Street, and soon were on Route 8, headed south. He drove with his left hand gripping the wide black steering wheel, his right hand ever ready to maneuver the gearshift as they traveled up and down the Pennsylvania portion of the Allegheny Mountains.

Anna said to Tata, "I will enjoy your company. We will be alone together for the last time."

"Thank you. But now, let us have a serious talk. I see you

packed only one small suitcase."

"The booklet said that I will be given a wool habit to wear when I arrive. Extra secular clothes will go back home with the family except for my underwear and one set of clothing. I will have a storage box at the abbey where I will keep the clothes I wear the day I enter. It is the *in case I want to go home* attire. I am also putting in storage my list of telephone numbers and addresses. I cannot keep pictures, so I did not bring any. I am taking one of mama's Polish prayer books and my two rosaries."

"You picked a hard life." He slowed as they drove through Slippery Rock, Pennsylvania, then picked up speed as they continued south. "So, if you change your mind, you will call me on the telephone?"

"Tata, there is little chance of that."

"I am curious about something else. How did you resolve the issue with Robert? He seemed like a nice fellow."

"I just told him again that I was not interested in him as a boyfriend and I was still going to the convent. Why do you ask?"

"It is just a coincidence. When I was a young single man, I lived in Pittsburgh for a while. In fact, it was in the same neighborhood where Robert's parents live. You will see the area today when we stop for lunch with the Bratinski family. I worked with Edzu Bratinski when I lived down there."

"Bratinski." Anna nodded. "Then I shall remember to call his wife Mrs. Bratinska instead of Bratinski. The male of a name ending in S-K-I claims that name, while the female uses S-K-A on the end of their name."

"You are my smart daughter, *moja córka.* Then tonight, in Ohio, we will be staying with our second cousins, the Dowcipniś family. Bruno and Pearl Dowcipniś. The word dowcipniś means witty, and the whole family is quite funny." He laughed until his shoulders shook.

Anna looked at the sky, remembering that Pittsburgh was called The Smoky City. "It looks like a black shawl has been thrown over the sun. I am glad you moved up to Petroleum City where we can enjoy the blue sky."

"The city is dark during the day. Making steel is dirty work." He slowed the car, reading road signs, and said, "I am looking for the access to the Liberty Bridge. We need to cross the Monongahela River."

As they got to the bridge, Anna saw great masses of gray clouds rising from the buildings along the river. Dusty curls rose from each structure. "So, these are the dark steel mills."

"Dark in the daytime, yes. But at night, plumes of smoke and fire rise from the chimneys. Sparks of flame light up the windows. Now that I am away from it, I can look back and see beauty. This is Pittsburgh's own Aurora Borealis." He waited for the traffic light to allow him to turn toward the homes lining the hills.

"Oh, these people live right here in the smoke." A cough escaped her throat. She lifted a white lace-edged handkerchief from her purse and brought it to her lips. *This may be the last time I use a cloth with lace for myself. I will be giving it up for God.*

As though on cue, they passed a Catholic Church. They saw schoolchildren playing in the street. A Felician nun chanted a rhyme as the girls jumped rope.

"Now, if you'd become a Felician nun, I could see you once a month or at least once a season." There was a sound of regret in his voice.

"You are right."

"We've arrived." He pulled his car in front of a two-story white house. He spent several minutes maneuvering the car into a parking space then pointed the front wheels toward the house because of the steep street.

A voice called, "*Jaśu, jak dzishaj?* Johnny, how are you today?"

Anna looked up and saw a tall, thin man. His blue eyes sparkled. A dimple on his face poked in his right cheek. His wide lips separated, showing lots of teeth.

Tata opened the car door and called out, "*Edzu,* after all these years. Yes, here we are." He came around and opened the passenger door. "Let me introduce you to Anna, my oldest."

"Wonderful to meet you, Anna. Come, we have a delicious meal all ready for you two." Edzu ushered them up the three steps onto the porch. Several wooden chairs were clustered around a table which held a bouquet of yellow and rust flowers.

The door opened, and Mrs. Bratinska welcomed them into her home. *"Ah, Panienka I Pan Wiosnec, witajcie."*

"Nieh Będie pohfalony Jesus Christus." The two guests recited the blessing as they entered the host and hostess' home.

"Na *vielki viekov, Amen,"* Mrs. Bratinska said. *"Mam curcze zupa, i ciepła chleb z masłem."*

Anna's mouth watered at the idea of chicken soup and warm bread and butter. She asked, *"Crzy Pani rozumi Angelski?"* to know more of Mrs. Bratinska's understanding of English.

"Niewiele." She shook her head, admitting to only a little knowledge.

Edzu said, "My first wife, Carolćia, died in childbirth two years after we were married. Here I was with a new baby and a one-year-old. Florentyna had been in Pittsburgh for a year. She needed work and became my housekeeper and childminder. She's a good woman. At first, it was all work, then, you know, things changed." He smiled at his wife. "We married eight years ago. At the time, it was a great convenience for both of us." He moved closer and took his wife's hand. "Now, I thank God for sending me such a helpmate. I'm sorry the children are in school today. You would see how well behaved and happy they are." He looked at his wife and said, *"Florcia, yestesz ładna, sprytna i kohana."*

She shyly accepted his words of praise that she was not only beautiful and clever but also loved. *"O, Pan,"* she answered softly.

Florentyna graciously refilled bowls with soup and cups with coffee. She brought out more hot bread and soft butter. Then apple pie was served.

Afterwards, Tata and Edzu retired to the porch to reminisce. Anna and Mrs. Bratinska washed dishes.

"*Mache ładne szklanki,*" Anna said, complimenting her glassware.

Too soon, she heard Tata call, "Anna, we need to be on our way."

They all walked together to the car then said their *dzienkujes,* thanking each other for a happy visit.

"What a nice couple," Anna said as they pulled away from the curb.

She looked around at the neighborhood. Each house on the steep hill had clawed themselves into the earth. Big oak, elm, maple, and chestnut trees, all golden and brown, dropped leaves on the Pittsburgh street. High in one of the chestnut trees, Anna saw a platform.

"The falling leaves are showing us some child's secret treehouse," she said.

He looked up at the structure. "Do you remember when you had a hiding place in our maple tree?"

"Yes, I remember. I went there a lot the year mama died. And you climbed up there a few times to hold me tight."

He nodded and leaned forward as if reading road signs. "We're going directly west from here, past Steubenville where I have cousins. We cannot stop so soon, though. We will go on to Columbus." He reached into the back seat for his hat. "The sun is so bright this afternoon."

"Oh, look. We are in Ohio. It seems like more Pennsylvania. Steubenville looks like a pretty town, doesn't it?"

"Yes, it does. Help me look for Route 22."

She found the signs which led them to country roads. Hay lay in piles in the fields. Cows meandered in meadows surrounded by fences of metal or wood. Traveling south, the same trees that were shedding in Pennsylvania still had their colorful leaves attached to them. A cool wind made her pull her sweater together around her chest.

He said, "It will be dark by the time we get to Columbus."

"Tata, do you have a good gag to play on the Dowcipniś family tonight? I remember you said they always make jokes."

"No, but I did bring them the same as I brought the Bratinskis. A bag of flour, a bag of sugar, and a little chocolate."

"How thoughtful."

"And now, tell me what that crop is on the right side of the road still growing in October."

She laughed at his joke. "It's just grass. There in the far pasture are lots of sheep." *In our geography lessons, we learned this is a rugged section of Ohio because it is part of the Allegheny Plateau. Of course, coal is under the earth, so there is work in the area for the folks living around here.*

He said, "Soon we will pass Cambridge. Find Route 40 to take us to Columbus."

After Cambridge, Anna tried to think of a joke to tell their hostess. "I don't know any jokes."

"I'll think of one," he said.

"Did I tell you that Sister Felicia gave me another Polish prayer book as a farewell gift?"

"You'll have plenty of equipment for adorations, right?"

"Yes. We pray six or seven times a day. I will learn all that. I think we pray at seven AM, eleven AM, three PM, seven PM and eleven PM. Maybe it starts at three AM. Next year I can tell you all about the times of prayer. I am excited. You know, I cannot open and read any letters during my first year, but they will be waiting there for me when my year is up. Because I am entering at such an unusual time, I am not sure if they will say I am finished being a novice in October. Maybe I will be considered with a different group."

"I will still send you letters so that next year you will learn all the news. We are getting close to Zanesville. At the gasoline station, we better pull the heavier jackets out of the rear of the car. They will be needed soon. Can you feel the chill in the air?"

At the stop, he slipped into the jacket then grabbed the edge of each sleeve with his four fingers and tugged down. "I always feel that I look more presentable when I smooth out my coat."

She grinned, thinking back to cozy afternoons. She had often baked to take the chill off the kitchen at home while snow whirled around the windows. "The wind is stronger here, maybe because there are no hills to protect the land." She pointed to a sign. "It looks like we will be in Columbus in two hours."

They left the gas station and continued on Route 40. She dozed and then felt the car slow down.

"Anna, we are here," he said softly.

Anna looked out at a two-story house.

A smiling man, Mr. Bruno Dowcipniś, hurried to the car, opened Tata's door, and gave him a hearty hug. "Jaśku, we thought you'd be here in time to play a little football. Here's your hat." He plopped a leather football helmet on Tata's head. It was covered with painted pictures of bananas. "Remember, we always said you ran like a monkey?"

Laughing, they began taking the luggage from the car.

Mr. Dowcipniś said, "Meet my two sons, Marek and Łukasz."

The young men carried the suitcases. Tata and Anna followed. Anna saw the resemblance in the Dowcipniś men. The sons had their father's big shoulders and height. However, unlike Bruno's plain face, Marek had two dimples and Łukasz had a cleft in his chin. All three men had dark hair and shared hearty laughs.

In the house, Pearl Dowcipniś greeted them. Her face was flushed as she rushed into the room from the back of the house. She was a tiny lady with black hair pulled back in a bun. Ringlets snuck out all over her head. "Finally, you two are here. I'm heating our dinner. Let me show you to your rooms. We'll give you a few minutes to freshen, and my Łukasz will help me put the food on the table. You see, my daughter is married, so my son helps in the kitchen."

"Mama, don't forget, you are not supposed to tell the football players that I help you in the kitchen." Łukasz showed Anna a magazine with a male chef on a prominent page. "Did you know some of the best chefs in the big restaurants are men? I seem to have been born with a white thumb because I can cook and bake delicious food. Can you smell my turkey?"

"Wonderful smells come from your kitchen. Is that fresh bread and pumpkin pie, too?" Anna took off her jacket and folded it over her arm. "You make us feel so welcome."

Pearl Dowcipniś said, "My husband and your Tata were children together in Poland. It is our pleasure to have you here."

The dining room table was covered with a white lace tablecloth. The dark wood of the table peeked through, and under all the wonderful food smells, Anna could detect the smell of lemon oil used to polish the wood. White heavy bowls and platters crowded the center of the table filled with the turkey and side dishes.

I especially like turkey. I will eat plenty of it, and the stuffing, gravy, cranberry sauce, mashed potatoes, corn, and hot bread and butter. Who knows when I will have another chance?

At the dinner table, Bruno Dowcipniś said, "Lord, we are sorry it took Anna going to the convent for Jaśu to come and see us. But, if it is thy will, so be it. Amen." He looked at the raised eyebrows of his wife, cleared his throat, and said, "Sorry, God, I forgot to say thank you for the food and the people who cooked it. Let it nourish our bodies. We pray for a safe trip for our guests. Amen." He again looked at his wife, and a smile of relief brightened his face.

After many compliments were paid to the cooks, the only sound heard was the scraping of forks on plates.

Then Tata began a story about a solemn young lad working as a night guard in a large department store in New York City. "His name was Bruno." Tata's smile spread across his face as he continued the tale. "It seems the lad's coworker had him convinced that a front window mannequin might be alive. And, there was one beautiful lady mannequin whose head was a little loose. Bruno thought she came to life because she seemed to be nodding at him." Tata tilted his head left and right.

The dinner table trembled with the chuckles of the group.

Tata said, "Until the night a door flew open. A heavy gust of wind swooped in and knocked the head right off."

Laughter echoed from the dining room walls.

Hot coffee was served. The men moved to the porch. The heavy scent of tobacco swirled around them.

Anna excused herself and found her warm bed complete with a *piezyna.* The feather quilt made her think of home, but only for the minute it took for her to doze. In the background, she could hear the deep voices of Tata and Mr. Dowcipniś with the occasional light tinkle of a laugh from his wife.

Morning came too soon.

"We are up as early as the sun," Tata said as he kissed Anna's cheek.

She breathed in the clean soap scent from his newly shaven face.

He said, "Look. It is so early, yet the household is bustling. Łukasz is cooking, probably with his mother. Marek and Bruno will bring down our baggage."

Anna and Tata walked through the living room into the kitchen.

"No, no. Today you are company," Pearl Dowcipniś said. "We eat in the dining room again. *Hochche.*"

She ushered them to a table laden with steaming scrambled eggs, bacon, and chunks of fried potatoes. Toasted rye bread straddled a tub of butter and a cup of blueberry jam.

Soon they all had plenty to eat. Tata complimented the cook, saying the food was *smachne.* Mrs. Dowcipniś packed them a lunch. Then they had to leave.

The four Dowcipniś, Anna, and Tata stood by the car and said goodbye. Anna and Pearl exchanged special blessings, as only one leaving on a long voyage gives another. With a nod of the head and a tear in the eye, they parted. The men all patted each other's shoulders. Tata and Anna sat side-by-side in the Model T. Tata started the motor, and they were on their way.

Turning a corner, he said, "We are going west by several small routes to Cincinnati, and then we'll head south into Kentucky."

Anna saw a few white clouds slide slowly through the eastern sky as the sun pushed above the horizon. "I thought it would be warmer down here," she complained.

"Anna, you will soon be wearing brown wool and be warm all the time. Let us make a game of it and see how soon today you will be shedding your hat and gloves."

"I will watch the fields and be sure there are no loose cows, sheep, or pigs. We wouldn't want to hit them."

After an hour, she took off her gloves and looked at her father. "Tata, I will always remember this long drive and the families we saw. But most of all, I will recall the hours we spent alone together. I will miss you terribly."

"And I will miss you, Anka, more than you can imagine." He moved his hand from the gear shift and grasped her fingers.

"Tata, who will you visit on the way home?"

"I will see a cousin, Mania. We used to play together in our village in Poland. I have not seen her in many years. One does not have time to gallivant around when raising children."

Anna nodded. Soon she was taking off her hat and opening her coat. Her gloves were folded into her hat.

Her father said, "We are visiting a cemetery to pray at the grave of your mama's family. Her Aunt Gladys and Uncle Gerard are buried in Cincinnati."

Through open windows, Anna watched the landscape. The fields held mounds of hay and smelled of freshly mowed high grass. Cows silently patrolled their turf.

Once in Cincinnati, they entered the quiet cemetery.

Anna read from Tata's page of directions. "The second turn to the right, past the large statue of the Blessed Mother, then a sharp right, then park. Their graves are right next to the tall cross with the name Bell on it."

After he parked, they got out and soon found the graves.

He said, "Here they are. Gerard and Gladys Powóz. They were very nice people. I'm sorry you never met them."

Their grave was on a gentle hill. A brilliantly colored oak tree shaded the site.

"How peaceful," she said.

"Yes. Aunt Gladys and Uncle Gerard were the first people your mama stayed with when she came from Poland. They were like the pioneers that you read about in history books. They built their own house, tilled their own land, and as you can imagine, were very strong folks. They wanted your mama to stay on with them, but she was an independent woman. She did leave with good feelings all around."

After their visit, they found a nearby rest area and enjoyed a picnic lunch of turkey sandwiches packed for them by Pearl Dowcipniś.

As they ate, Anna said, "I keep remembering the questions I needed to ask as to why people do certain things. Our neighbor, Mrs. White, had some interesting insights. She is the last one I interviewed. I asked her how a lady with the last name of White knew so much Polish. She said she came from five miles away, in Franklin, and so did her husband. She is Polish, and so is he. But he changed his name from *Biały* to White because of discrimination against the Polish when he was a young man in New York. I told her I did not understand."

"And what did she tell you?"

"She told me never to judge a book by its cover. I told her I had not heard that saying. It means, she told me, that when you look at a book, to notice if the ends of the pages are plain and if the book looks worn. That is how you get an impression. Is the book stained or torn? It is either well-loved and well-read, or if the pages look new, not worth reading."

Tata said, "Interesting."

"I think you could pick up any book written in a foreign language and come to some good conclusions by opening it. If the letters are close together, then there's a lot to tell. We can't tell much by how long the words are because, as we both know, some of our simple words in Polish are fifteen letters long."

"That's an interesting theory."

"Her last thought was that every book and person you see is worth more than a glance no matter what their last name."

Tata nodded then looked at the maps again. "We'll be crossing the Ohio River going south and will be in Kentucky before you know it."

They got back into the car and drove off. For an hour, they followed map directions. They passed fields, curving right and left. They slowed because of a dirt road and found a sign carved into a large rock. The only word was *monastery*. The land now had gentle hills. All the ground looked productive, either with hay, with fences holding farm animals, or with freshly tilled soil. To the left, orchard trees faced the October sky. Most were naked of their fruit.

Tata drove even slower and said, "I'm looking at your new home, *moya córka*. My daughter, I think it is a well-kept place."

"It says in the letter that the main building is a tall castle made of stone. It sits upon a slight incline surrounded by beautiful farm country."

"I was expecting more hills. I thought highland flowers grew here."

Anna sat straight in her seat, feeling she was being inspected by unseen eyes. Both hands were on her lap. She took in her surroundings.

Tata drove through a thicket of trees, and they got their first look at the dark, stone building.

To the right side of a tower, Anna noticed a figure clad in a brown flowing habit. The person quickly moved out of sight. "Tata, I saw my first Sister."

They pulled into a parking area. Anna slipped out of the car. Tata carried her piece of luggage.

She said, "It is very quiet. Not even one oil extractor machine is squeaking at us."

"Yes, it is silent." He touched her shoulder. "Anna, are you sure? We can still leave if you like."

"No. I'm nervous but excited in a good way. It feels so solemn here. Yet it looks relaxed with all the animals nearby. Maybe I will be working with the cows or chickens, and I can whisper to them. Do you think that would be all right?"

He lifted his eyebrows. "I did not read anything in the booklet about not talking to the animals. Saint Francis always did that. Didn't he start this order?"

"I think so."

"Come. This must be the main door since it is the only one I can see."

"And now, here we are." She took a breath. "Tata, will you knock on the door for me?"

TEN

Tata tapped a few times on the door, and it swung open. A smiling nun greeted them. The Sister was dressed in a long, brown garment that seemed immersed in the scent of soap and lemon. Her head veil was the same color as the habit. A white coif framed her face. A thick ivory-colored rope encircled her waist. She smiled but spoke not a word.

Anna said, "I am Anna Wiosnec. I have an appointment today to join the convent. This is my father, John Wiosnec." *I sound like I am ten years old. Ugh.*

The nun nodded and ushered them down a long hall. A few ceiling lights were on. Muted walls were punctuated with pictures of The Sacred Heart of Jesus and a nativity scene. The Blessed Virgin portrait greeted her with outstretched arms. The sun sneaking in the windows from outside put a glow on Mary's rays of light, starting with her hands and ending on the planet Earth. Anna couldn't take time to identify any of the other artwork, although she noted that one seemed to be a drawing rather than a print.

The stone floors glistened under their shoes. She heard the echo of their three sets of feet as they moved down the hall. If not for the echo, the silence would be deafening. Anna noticed Tata glancing here and there while they walked. He held Anna's elbow as they were ushered into a room.

A nun was seated behind a desk. "Thank you, Sister Dorothy," she said. "I'm Sister Mary Eileen. You probably noticed Sister Dorothy can welcome without conversation. She does a fine job, don't you think?"

Anna looked into the eyes of the pleasant, middle-aged

woman and felt good about her new circumstance.

Sister looked at Tata and asked, "How were the directions? Was the weather good on your trip?"

He placed Anna's tiny suitcase on the floor, cleared his throat, and said, "Oh, it was a fine trip. Anna and I had hours together. We visited friends and relatives along the way."

"Please have a seat." Sister intertwined her fingers and rested her hands on her desk. "Anna, you must have plenty of questions. We will be meeting every day for a week, and you and I will talk about many things. I am here to answer any of your concerns. You arrived in the middle of the day, which is a perfect time for us. In the day's schedule, the Sisters are having Mid-Afternoon Prayers. We three can have a pleasant get-to-know-you period." She looked at Tata and said, "But once you two leave this room, you'll be going in different directions. It will be the last time you see each other. We have a comfortable suite for travelers in another building just to the west of this one. You are welcome to spend the night. One of our Sisters will bring you an evening meal. That way you can start your trip home in the morning light."

Tata said, "This is a beautiful place. At first, I was unsure, but now I am at ease with Anna being here. I wonder why this place is called a monastery and not an abbey. Then, I was wondering what you do if you become snowbound. Listen to me rattle on. I will get my bearing in a few minutes. It is not often... Actually, I have never said goodbye to my daughter before today." He cleared his throat again and ran his hand down his face. "Since you are in Kentucky, you probably don't have much snow. You seem self-sufficient. How do you handle medical emergencies?"

"One of our nuns, Sister Calista, is a fine nurse. She has always been able to help, either by what she can do or by her word that one of us needs to be hospitalized. She is suffering from arthritis but does her share as she helps with the new nuns. As for the term monastery instead of abbey, our benefactor, who chooses to remain anonymous, wishes us to go by that title. Yes, it is unusual. It makes him happy, and he is most generous. We say many prayers for him. You see how well-built our residence is and how up to date it is maintained thanks to Mister X."

"Ah," Tata said.

"Sister," Anna asked, "can you give me the prayer schedule so Tata, I mean my father, can show it to my family? They are all very interested."

Sister Eileen walked to a cabinet, took out a paper, and handed it to Tata. "The times of daily activities are listed. We have a busy day, starting at 6:00 AM and finishing at 8:00 PM. We have formal devotions five times a day. Our individual chapel time is almost continuous. You will see that many of our hours are spent in talking to Our Lord God."

Tata leaned forward in his chair. "I understand we can write letters to Anna, even though she won't be able to read them for a long time."

"Yes, they will wait for her." Sister smiled at Anna. "You will be so busy with prayers. We in the cloister want you to listen to the word of God. Cloister comes from the word *claudere* and means to shut out. We close the doors to the secular world and talk to our Creator. There will be many messages you will receive as you sit and listen to His Words."

Anna nodded.

"Today at the Evening Prayer, I will present you to Our Lord at the altar. Over the dress you are wearing today, I will cover you with the robe of our order." Sister turned to Tata. "This is a ceremony only witnessed by our Sisters. When you hear our voices rise in song, we will be clothing her as one of us."

"I understand," he said solemnly.

"If you have no more questions, I'll leave you two alone for a few minutes to say goodbye. Anna, Sister Calista will be waiting outside the door to escort you to the chapel. Mr. Wiosnec, Sister Dorothy and one of the other nuns will escort you to our guest house. It has been a pleasure meeting you."

Sister Eileen walked out into the hall and left them alone.

Tears fell from Anna's eyes as she hugged her father. "I will never forget this moment. I will carry your solemn face in my mind. The hands you have on my shoulders tell me that you are never more than one thought away from me. I love you, Tata. You know I am in the hands of God now." *I will stop crying now. It is normal for me to be shaky with all that has happened today. I want Tata to see my real happiness.*

He cleared his throat. Together, they left the room. Outside the door, Sister Dorothy and her companion sat waiting for Tata. He nodded to them, and the three of them walked away. He glanced back and met his daughter's eyes one last time.

Another nun sat on a wooden chair. She stood and gestured for Anna to follow. She whispered, "Anna, I'm Sister Calista. I am in charge of the new girls and will take you to the chapel now."

Anna looked at the nun. A wisp of gray hair pushed out from her veil. *She looks like my cousin Franja. She has a Polish nose. She has the same brown eyes, but Franja's have a sparkle to them.*

Anna and Sister Calista walked together. The nun's gait was slow and wobbly. In one of the picture's glass reflections, Anna could see that they were the same height. She could smell the wool of the nun's garment, hear the rustle of the silky cloth on her head. Light shone through stained glass. In this corridor, sun on the stone floors showed the reds and blues of the window glazing. *Joy, joy, joy. This is why I am here.*

As they walked, Sister snorted and said, "So, Anna. This is the first time Sister Eileen has ever allowed a person to enter on whatever day they pleased. Are you related to her? She must have big plans for you." She placed her bony fingers around Anna's upper arm and squeezed. Leaning her face to Anna's ear, she whispered, "Don't let Sister Eileen ever regret her decision."

"Sister, I didn't know the admission date was so important. I'm sorry for the inconvenience." *Oh, I hope I will not have to see Sister Calista too often. She could change my spirit from joy to caution.*

"Oh, it will not be a problem. I will devote an entire hour every day to your instructions."

Is she happy about that? Is she being sarcastic? I vow to do my best to make even Sister Calista proud.

As they rounded a corner, the singing of the *Ave Maria* filled the corridor. Anna wanted to burst into singing the familiar words, *gratia plena.* Since Sister was again silent, Anna's lips stayed closed.

The nun shuffled and continued to usher her down the cool hall. Pictures of saints decorated the walls. One was in color, the others were black and white prints. Again, Anna noticed a few sketches. They turned a corner and went into a small nave. Because the voices in song grew louder, she sensed they were close to the chapel. Anna heard more of the hymn, *Dominus tecum, benedicta tu in mulieribus.*

Sister Calista whispered in Anna's ear, "I have permission to speak as necessary. I will let you know when you may speak. Of course, in the church, we expect you to participate in the praying and singing. After all, singing is just prayer raised in song. Come, I will present you to Sister Eileen, and she will place the garb of our order on you. I will show you your room later this evening."

Anna was ushered into the chapel. She stood in the front just behind the communion rail. *Hallelujah. This is really happening. I am here. Glory be to God.*

Sister Eileen stepped up beside her and covered Anna's dress with the brown wool garment of the order. The weight of the wool fabric was heavy on her shoulders. A thin cross of wood on a leather cord was hung around her neck. A veil of brown thin silky fabric was placed on her head. Sister Eileen then directed her to the front pew beside several other women dressed in identical clothing.

The young Sister on her right handed her a prayer book. When the congregation sat, Anna felt the smoothness of the seat. *I bet these pews are smoothed by the bottoms of the countless nuns using them, not by a hand with sandpaper.* After the *Ave Maria,* more common prayers including the Litany of the Sacred Heart were said. She noticed that the pew kneeler was made of wood. No fabric cushioned it like the ones at home at the Assumption Church. Anna remembered Sister Laetitia telling her that the prayers all nuns said together were called common prayers. A time of private prayer happened next, Anna assumed, because all sound stopped and everyone remained on their knees. She was in the front row and could only follow the lead of the other Sisters in her pew. *Dear God, here I am. I hope you see me down here trying to follow your command.*

After a short while, a bell pealed five times, and the entire congregation rose to their feet. She followed the group and soon found herself in the dining room. Long, dark wooden tables with benches of the same color filled the room. *There are so many nuns here. One day when I am not the newest person, I will count the seats and figure out how many people are eating, but not today.* Natural light came in from four windows on her left. Overhead, exposed light bulbs shone down. Three white walls were free of adornment. A large crucifix hung on the fourth wall. Anna followed her chapel mate and sat beside her. Bowls, plates, glasses, and spoons were at each place. Sister Eileen and four other nuns sat at a front table. All heads bowed as Sister Eileen said the blessing.

Bread was passed. Anna was grateful for the warm feel of the roll in her hand. A large pot of soup was next. Following the lead of the person to her right, she filled her bowl about halfway. *Looks like I can only take half a bowl of soup. Is there a lot of stomach growling under this roof?* The smell of garlic tempted her palate. Swirls of parsley topped the soup. Meat, potatoes, carrots, celery, and beans of many shapes and colors sat in her bowl. With their napkins on their laps, the nuns ate the soup, the bread, and drank milk in silence. *If I were alone, I would wipe the bowl with this bread to get every drop.*

After dinner, a bell rang. Each nun picked up their dishes and spoons then cleaned their portion of the table. They walked to an area with two deep sinks. They placed their napkins into a bin. Each then washed and dried their dishes and returned them to their clean place on the table. This happened in total silence.

The nuns exited the room. Anna looked around, wondering about her next move, and there stood Sister Calista. Sister's gnarled right hand beckoned Anna to follow her.

In the hall, Sister propelled Anna in a new direction. The hall echoed with soft footsteps. *I know I will do a lot of praying if only for directions in this confusing building.* Anna followed Sister. Despite her hobbled walk, the nun climbed a flight of stairs, placing both feet slowly on each step as they ascended. On level two, they confronted another flight of stairs and continued the climb to the third floor. Sister breathed in deep gulps of air when they reached the top.

The two entered a small room. A tall, sparkling-clean window allowed a brilliant dose of fall sunshine to slide across the stone floor. Linens and a blanket covered a bed. A small nightstand hugged one side. On the back wall, a narrow closet held two habits just like the one she was wearing. A shelf above the garments held the valise from her suitcase and a white nightgown. Sandals and stockings sat on the floor.

A picture hung on the wall. In this portrait of The Crucifixion, Jesus on the cross wore a long loincloth. Mary dressed in blue was on one side of him, and an unknown figure was on the other side. Jesus and the two others had heads surrounded by halos. Behind the cross, a deer could be seen. Below the cross were the Latin words, *Oblatvs est qvia ipse volvit.* Anna was sure she could reason out those words with just a little thought.

"This is your room," Sister said. "It's called a cell. You will soon know where this cell is in relation to the Holy Pictures on the walls. The bathrooms are at the end of the corridor. In this closet, you will find your underwear, your hose and sandals, two more habits, and a nightgown. Tomorrow, discontinue wearing your shoes and begin to wear the sandals. Later this evening, we will be going back to the chapel for night prayers. A bell will ring, and you will have time to get downstairs. Follow the other postulants, whose rooms are all around you. In this cloister, each time the bells ring, they will do so five times for the five wounds of Jesus at His crucifixion. We do not use clocks. The bells tell us when to change activities. You may speak, Sister Anna."

Anna saw an unpainted wooden chair under the window and said, "Sister, please sit down. I have many questions."

The nun shook her head. "All you need to know for tonight is that evening prayer is the end of our day. You then return to this cell until morning. There is no conversation between any of the postulants, which is what you are now called. Tomorrow, Morning Prayer is at first bells. Daily Mass follows closely thereafter. I will find you in the dining room. I'll be with you for the Office of Reading, the next event. Try to remember all your questions, and I hope to answer them. Some tomorrow. Some in the next few days." Sister Calista turned and walked out. Anna heard her difficult breaths.

In what seemed like a blink of Anna's tired eyes, she heard the bells calling for prayer in the chapel. She rushed into the hall and gently closed her door. Her pew mate stood outside waiting for her. They smiled at each other and moved down the hall in unison. *I love this place. My new friend, here, sure looks ready to help me. I will have to name her in my head so I do not just think of her as Sister One. I'll call her Sister Red. With her fair skin tone and the freckles sprinkled across her nose, I bet she has beautiful, wavy red hair.*

They walked side by side. Overhead lights glowed. Heavy beams of dark wood crossed the high ceiling from end to end. The pictures on the wall now were a smooth blur of blacks and whites. Despite the many women moving in the same direction, there was only a soft rhythmic sound of gliding feet.

In the chapel, the organ was as silent as the attendants. A bell rang five times, and prayers began. Sister Red moved her missal to the right, showing Anna the correct page. Anna's eyes thanked her. Worship prayers started in Latin. Most prayer books had both English and Latin prayers side-by-side. Anna could easily say the *Ave Maria* without looking at the words in her missal. *This place. These words. This moment. I have waited so long for it all to happen. Of course, it is only fitting that this is the feast of the Most Holy Rosary of the Blessed Virgin Mary.*

After the evening prayer, Sister Red and Anna joined the procession of other nuns and returned to their quarters. Ceiling lights guided their paths through the halls.

In her room, she stretched out her hands and found the light cord. Soon the cell was flooded with brightness. Anna went to the window, opened the latch and let the night air into her chamber. *I want to smell the outdoors.* She smelled no flowers or tree scents. A soft breeze rearranged her veil, moving it over her face. *Who would have thought about that happening?* A new scent hit her nose and reminded her of Tata's pipe tobacco. *Could he be smoking in the house next door? Would I smell it from that far away? I did just pray for the whole family, but maybe this is a reminder and I should say another thanksgiving prayer for him.*

With no idea of the time, she decided to prepare for the night. *Do I change clothes here or in the bathroom?* Anna gathered the stiff cotton nightgown, the towel, washcloth, and bar of soap. *Smells like the soap we used to make at home and feels just as hard.* From her valise, she took out her toothbrush and toothpaste. With full hands, she walked out into the hall toward the bathrooms. Sister Red had a bed with linen folded down for the night. Another room had an open window with gentle wind noises escaping into the hall. An open book lay on a chair in a room on the right, and the light in the room to the left illuminated the picture of the Blessed Mother.

In the washroom, four young women milled around four sinks. All four looked up and smiled when Anna entered then went back to their tasks. In silence, they washed their faces and brushed their teeth. They were clad in matching nightgowns. All had short crops of hair. As expected, Sister Red's scalp showed a carrot tinged color. The other three were in the auburn family. Farther in the room stood two toilet stalls and a bathtub.

Three more nuns entered. The originals left. Anna ran a soapy washcloth over her skin, rinsed, and dried herself with the coarse towel. She walked back to her room. *When did these other Sisters get their haircuts? I will ask Sister Calista tomorrow.*

Anna knelt beside her bed for a short prayer of thanksgiving.

Then she opened her bed linens and slid into the comfort of a soft bed. She thought of Sister Calista. *She needs to give me paper and a pencil so I can write down all my questions. I have so many. Do I leave the door to my cell open or closed when I am in or out of it? Must not forget the haircut question. Do I get to know the other sisters' names? What will I do for the other parts of each day? Can I pick from a list of chores? Do we get to go outside? Will we go over the questionnaire I filled out with the five women in Petroleum City? Are there more blankets for win-ter? Do we wear the sandals only in the summer or all year round? And last but not least, do we ever tie or pin our veils back from our faces for chores and such things?*

A heavy silence settled in the dark. Then the pleasant sound of snoring from a nearby room reached her ears. *I always loved to hear Tata snore. It made me feel that all was right with the world. And it is.*

ELEVEN

*W*hy doesn't Bashia turn off that bell? I will have to get out of bed in the dark and stop that noise. Anna rolled over in bed, and yesterday's memories filled her head. Footsteps passed the door. *I do not think I need to dress to walk this hall. Where is that light cord? It is cold in this room. Did I leave the window open last night? Do I have a robe here?*

Anna found the light cord. She grabbed her toiletries and put on her sandals. *Maybe I am already late. I had better move fast.* She rushed into the hall and moved toward the bathrooms. Happy faces greeted her. Several of the nuns were already in their habits, but she breathed a sigh of relief on seeing that others were still not dressed for the day. She washed and swiftly returned to her cell. *How do I dry the washcloth and towel in my room? I will have to notice where the other sisters place their wet ones or ask Sister Calista.* She found what was probably a slip on the shelf and put it on, covered it with her habit, placed her white wimple around her face, and put her veil over it. Again, the sound of footsteps guided her into the hall and down to the chapel. *Back to the same seat, I see.*

Organ music filled the air. Everyone stood as the priest entered the sanctuary and the Mass began. The priest started with the familiar Latin words, *In Nomine Patris, et Filii, et Spiritus Sancti.* The congregation answered the familiar *Amen.* Next, songs of worship echoed through the stone room as everyone sang to their Maker. The reading for the day, the feast of St. Briget, was one honoring widows. Before she had praised, thanked, and rejoiced in being in this wonderful monastery, Anna found the Mass had ended. Behind the tide of her co-sisters, she walked to the dining room. Bright overhead lights beamed into the halls and the darkness outside.

I had better concentrate on breakfast. I am surprised I was not hungry during the night. Now I am happy to smell bacon and coffee. I hope eggs are on the menu.

She followed Sister Red. In the corner of the room, they poured coffee into their cups. Then they went back to their seats. Platters of bacon and eggs moved from nun to nun. Potatoes, toast, butter, and jelly arrived on the next two platters. *I do not think I will be hungry after this kind of a breakfast.*

Sister Calista waited beside Anna's seat when she returned with her clean dishes. The nun's palm encircled Anna's elbow as she led Anna out of the dining area. "You seem to have found a good place in this abbey. You look comfortable here. Remember, dear, we all still listen to the voice of God and do His bidding."

Anna glanced over at her companion. *What is she talking about?*

Sister Calista moved Anna into an empty classroom. "What questions do you have for me?"

"I suppose I will get comfortable with the bells instead of clocks. The hours are not that important. Could we start at the beginning? When did the other postulants enter?"

"They entered in September. Why do you ask?"

She squirmed in her wooden seat. "Will I be doing things with them, or will it be just you and me?"

"I will be with you on many occasions for the next seven days. The other girls who entered together, and there were nine of them, had a week for questions aloud in the classroom. They got to know each other before they had to be silent."

"Can I know their names? Do they keep their baptismal names, or are names given here at the convent?"

Sister Calista's tone became icy. "I don't know why you would ask such a thing. The girls will keep their own names preceded by the word Sister until they've been here a year. They then can pick a Saint's name, as long as no other nun in our abbey has already chosen that one. So, our postulants are…" She quickly turned pages in her thick tome. "Let me look them up."

Anna's eyes lit. *I will find out the names of the new sisters.*

"In alphabetic order, the names are Agnes, Angelina, Caroline, Elizabeth, Grace, Helen, Jacqueline, Rochelle, and Teresa. There you are." She placed one arthritic hand on the other and rubbed her palms and fingers again and again.

"But which is which?"

"That will remain a mystery, I believe. Perhaps if you had entered with them, you'd have the privilege of knowing."

"When did the Sisters get their hair cut so short?"

"We have an informal hair cutting for the young girls. It is so hot in the summer, it is just for convenience. When one takes final vows, there is a religious hair cutting in the church."

"So, in a month, I can get my hair cut very short?"

"If you're still here, yes, you can," Sister Calista replied.

Anna decided to ignore the insinuation and asked, "Is my cell door supposed to be closed or opened at night and during the day when I am in or out of the room?"

"There is not a rule about that."

"Do we get to pick our daily chores? Can one be outside sometimes? Who takes care of the cattle and poultry?" Her voice cracked. After hours of no conversation, Anna's mouth felt dry.

"As you saw by the morning breakfast, we are a hard-working group of people. One works inside or outside as needed. Part of our staying healthy credo is that all of us are outside for an hour a day. We can do farming, weeding, picking crops, or tending the animals, or as you call them, the cattle and poultry. After this week, you will get your assignment. Have you ever worked outside?" Sister Calista asked in a suspicious voice.

"I am better with animals than with plants, Sister."

"Can you feed them or just watch them?"

Sister Calista does not understand me, but still, I am glad to be here. "I can feed chickens and collect eggs. If one is out with the chickens, do we put a pin in our veil to hold it away from chickens flying onto our heads?"

"I suppose they do that," Sister Calista said. "This ends our question-and-answer period for today. I must be on my way. You are to go outside and familiarize yourself with the surroundings. When the bell rings, return to the chapel, then follow your group through the rest of the day."

Anna breathed a sigh of relief as she walked out of the classroom. In the hall, she tried to remember her directions to the back area of the building. She wanted to have a moment of quiet. After all, isn't that why she had come to a monastery? She found a door and walked out into a paved area with an overhang. The moss-covered walls made her think this was a perpetually shady nook. It was the size of a large living room but had only a few outside chairs. *Could I sit down and collect my thoughts? Better not. If Sister Calista sees me sitting, she will think I am not following directions. But I will remember this spot. There should be a sign on the door with the name The Sigh.*

Anna walked out into the sunshine and shaded her eyes with her hand. On her right, she saw meadows and grazing cows. Straight ahead, many trees. *Must be the apple orchard.* Looking to the left, she saw ruts of turned soil and rows of growth. *I will stay away from the farm part, or Sister will have me tending plants and that will be trouble. I cannot tell the difference between a weed and a carrot top.*

She wandered toward the cows. The fence around the animals looked straight and strong. At the edge of the meadow, nuns entered a barn. Hay flew through the air. *So that is why we eat such a hearty breakfast. One of the first pages in the booklet Sister Eileen sent me did say this monastery was self-sustaining.* The only sounds were crickets chirping and birds scolding each other as they romped through the meadow. The October sun was still beating down on the field.

Bells rang, and all work stopped. Everyone hurried to the chapel.

This time, prayer books were opened and voices chanted prayers in both Latin and English. *Hail Holy Queen* had never sounded as good as when chanted by the voices of two-hundred nuns. It made Anna's skin tingle with pleasure. She loved joining the prayers of the saints as the women responded *Ora pro nobis.*

When the prayer session was over, Anna followed Sister Red into a kitchen large enough for a dozen people to work in. Shiny pots and pans hung from overhead hooks or were cradled on shelves above worktables. A faint scent of raw chicken flowed around the room, despite some open windows. Seated in chairs around a table, two nuns cut chicken. Two others sliced carrots and potatoes. By deep sinks, several nuns scrubbed and peeled more vegetables. Nuns in aprons dashed around the stoves. Steaming pots sat on the back burners. Front burners had chicken browning. An assembly line of nuns sliced bread, added dollops of mayonnaise, placed cheese or white meat on the bread, then closed the two pieces and cut them into sandwiches.

Sister Red took Anna's hand. Together, they took a wheelbarrow out of the kitchen, across a yard, and into a cold room. Sister Red motioned, and Anna helped her move three large blocks of ice into it. Together, they rolled the barrow back into the kitchen. A husky-looking nun smiled. She attacked the ice with a pick and soon made many small pieces of ice. Anna and Sister Red placed the chunks into pitchers and then in an icebox.

Sister Red glanced around the room and kept busy. She wiped a table as it became empty, moved articles around in the cooler to make room, and kept herself out of the way yet available. Everyone who looked at Sister Red smiled. Anna could see she was irreplaceable. *And she's my friend.*

Bells rang. Anna and Sister Red went into the lunchroom and took their places. After prayers, Anna awaited the sandwiches, which were soon passed around. Ice pitchers came toward them. They were followed by decanters of cool tea with a spearmint flavor. It reminded Anna of home because she had always loved the little spearmint candies covered with hard kernels of sugar that Tata had in his store. *Tata.* She had not thought of him until now. *He had to be long gone on his trip home.* If she could talk to him, she would tell him about her first morning, the good and the bad of it. He would say that he knew she would be just fine.

After lunch, Anna followed Sister Red. They went outside by

way of The Sigh. Sister Red sat on one of the chairs and pointed to another, suggesting that Anna sit. Nothing could have delighted her more. They sat, breathed in the early autumn air, and relaxed. A few minutes later, Sister Red got up. Anna trailed. They walked towards the apple trees. In a barn, they found two baskets and a ladder. Together, they carried the ladder to a tree. While one picked and tossed, the other caught and put the apples into the baskets. Anna spotted an old wagon. She pulled it over to the apple baskets and loaded them in. They were able to bring the fruit to the kitchen easily that afternoon.

Bells rang. Prayers were said in the chapel, this time with an organ playing and much singing from the congregation. Since the previous day had been the Feast of the Holy Rosary, the beautiful songs to Mary were again sung. The strains of *Ave Maria* were heard that afternoon.

While she sang, she remembered her friend Marie at the restaurant where she had worked. Marie had heard her talking about it being the Feast of the Assumption. She wanted to know what special food made that day a feast. It was quite a while before they realized they were each using the word feast in a different way. Marie meant the word as a food occasion, and Anna denoted it as a name for a liturgical occasion.

When the prayers were finished, everyone remained. Some nuns knelt while some sat. Private prayer time had come.

God, here I am. It was a long road. I am blessed to be at this monastery. Bless my family, not just my Tata, my sister Bashia, and my brother Leon, but also all my aunts and uncles. Bless my friend Julia and the baby she will have next spring. Make Bashia be a good Godmother to the child. Bless Mrs. Robinson and her driver, Jack. Keep an eye on my friend, Robert, in Pittsburgh, and help him to find a nice wife. If I had not picked the convent, he would be a good choice, right, God? Remember all the nice people we met as we traveled here. Bless Sister Eileen who let me come into the convent at an unusual time. Bless Sister Red, whatever her name really is, since I may never know. Bless Sister Calista and help her not be in such a cranky mood. Amen.

Anna heard noises as everyone left the chapel. She felt like she had spent a spiritually moving prayer session.

Out in the hall, the wind was swirling curtains away from walls. A low growl turned out to be a distant roar of thunder. Sisters scurried about closing windows. Others rushed outdoors and dragged furniture away from the wind and rain.

After looking out the windows, Sister Red guided Anna up to their cells. *I bet we had more work outside, but it was canceled because of rain. It will be a nice break.* Sister Red pointed to her room, suggesting Anna enter. She did. Anna noticed a washcloth and towel drying on the radiator. Sister Red pointed to her mattress, raised it, and showed Anna her second veil, which she was pressing between the mattress and the bed frame. *Interesting.*

Anna went into her own room to wait for the next set of bells and realized she had been in the convent for twenty-four hours.

TWELVE

On hearing the first bells the following morning, Anna smiled. *God, here I am, ready for a magnificent day.* As she closed her window, she looked out into the approaching morning light. *I still see a few of Your stars. Thank You for Your sky with the moon and the planets. Thank you for the ebb and flow of the tide, even though I have only read about that phenomenon. Thou art indeed mighty.*

All of the postulants hurried down the hall. She washed, dressed, and followed her group to the chapel. The Saints honored that day during Mass were announced by the lector. Personal prayer books listed names of each day's saints. On October ninth, Saint John Leonardi, who lived in the 16th century, was the appointed saint. Yet, Saints Dinis, Rusticus, and Eleutherius, martyrs of the third century, were mentioned. *It is our honor to remember these soldiers of God. I will try to re-read all these prayers at another of our meditations today.*

At breakfast, French toast came out on the platters. Maple syrup and butter followed. Knives clicked against forks as the bread was cut.

Afterward, Sister Calista appeared. A strong odor of garlic settled upon the older nun's garb, skin, and breath. *I hope I can be around an open window this morning.* Sister Calista limped and shuffled more than Anna remembered. *Should I comment on this?*

Instead of taking her to yesterday's classroom, Sister Calista led her out the front door. "You need to see this door as a privilege. It is only open to a select few. I brought you outside to see the beauty of this building from the front and to give you a short tour. When you and your father entered, you knew he could only advance to the first parlor."

"Why are you telling me this?"

"Many are called. Not all are chosen."

Anna took a deep breath. "I have a question for you, Sister Calista. How did you come to this convent? Why did you pick this life?"

"No one has asked me that since the time I entered." She clicked her teeth, rubbed her right knee, and sat on a metal bench in the sun. "I grew up the youngest of ten on a farm in Indiana. We were a God-fearing Catholic family. My older brothers and sisters babied and spoiled me when I was tiny. However, when I became older, I had a neighbor who took a shine to me." She repositioned herself in her seat as if to be sure the sun warmed her knee.

Anna shaded her eyes with a raised hand. *Yes, Sister, tell me so I understand your antagonism towards me.*

"She was a nurse. She thought I could be good at it. She would have me help her with all the sick people who came to her for emergencies. I was so good at wrapping neat bandages." Her smile faded. "I figured my parents would send me to a nursing school. But there was no money for a girl's education. My parents told me that I had been the child elected to go to the convent and pray for them. I was hurt and angry. What options did I have? Actually, none. I decided to fix them. I'd go to a place where they never had to see me again. However, the funniest thing happened. I got here and loved every single thing and person. The biggest and best joke was on me." She stood and left the yard. "Let me show you more of our world."

Sister pointed out an ark on a stained-glass window and the gray stone used for the architecture. Anna smiled, seeing a pleasant side of this nun for the first time.

Sister Calista said, "I thought the sunlight would be good for both of us. This arthritis is my cross. I understand that the more I move, the less the pain. But even the garlic oil is not helping to ease the pain today. When we enter the monastery again, you will notice the Sisters are cleaning the floors and walls, polishing furniture, and washing windows."

They walked into the building and moved back into an office. Sister showed Anna to a seat.

"Let me explain some of our nonverbal communication. One's hand on one's chest means excuse me. A tug on a sleeve is to get another's attention. Each Sister is alert to the needs of her fellow Sisters. In our monastery, a life of sacrifice is a never-ending struggle for perfection. The sacrifices are bearable only if we do them with love. In order to become closer to Our Lord, you will be submitted to exercises and tests which are designed to root out your faults, curb your passions, and prepare you for acquiring grace. If you question these exercises in humility, these steps toward a closer union with our crucified Lord, you do not belong with us. The perfect nun, for the love of God, is obedient in all things unto death."

Anna nodded, trying to remember each word.

"Assignments are made monthly for tasks. Except for the postulants. They get weekly assignments to help them find their corporal talent. The postulants work with more seasoned nuns. Assignments are posted in the workroom. There is also a request box where one is free to drop a note for a preferred task. Do you understand?"

Anna nodded and followed Sister out of the office. They walked on the dry portions of the floor. The smell of lye soap wafted from still-moist surfaces. *Oh, those poor nuns scrubbing with that soap. Are they noticing their cramped knees as much as the tender skin on their hands?*

A few dark wood walls shined with reflections from windows. Parts of one wall were still dull with the wax the nuns continued to apply.

As promised, they entered the work assignment room. Sister Calista handed Anna a written list of chores divided by weeks.

Ah, my future tasks are here.

Sister Calista put her left hand behind her, reaching for the back of a chair. She took a few backward steps then slowly eased herself into the seat. Her face glistened with perspiration. "Ah, this arthritis. Let's sit and catch our breath." She lifted her right hand and pointed a bony finger. "Tomorrow, you can jot down all the jobs available and the ones not open at this time. You can make some choices. Look in that drawer. You'll find pencils and paper." She rubbed her hips. As she kneaded with her fingers, her voice rose and fell. "Make a list of jobs you might like. Keep the pencil and papers, and you can write more questions for me. After our next chore, you will follow the postulants for the remainder of the day."

"It is a beautiful autumn day. Being outside would be nice."

Abruptly, Sister Calista rose. "This next task is for me. It is a rare privilege. You need to come along because I may need assistance." She led Anna out the door of the workroom.

Anna grabbed the pencil and papers, stopped to retrieve a few sheets that fell, then caught up with the limping nun.

"The sacristan, Sister Timothy, is ill," Sister said. "I fill in for her on those rare occasions. We will be assembling the clothes the priest wears for morning Mass. Tomorrow's feast day is of Saint Francis Borgia, confessor, so his chasuble will be white."

Anna followed Sister into the chapel.

"We pray the Rosary first," Sister Calista whispered.

After the silent rosary in the chapel, they entered the sacristy at the front of the church. Sister picked up a cardboard sketch of items and placed it on a table. She dipped both hands in Holy Water, whispered a prayer, and wiped her hands on a white cloth. Then she began placing vestments for the priest in a precisely patterned pile on the table.

On the bottom was the chasuble, a robe with drapery over the arms. Next was the maniple, a long piece of cloth worn on the left arm. On these was placed the amice, a white linen cloth covering the neck and shoulders, and then the stole, worn around the neck and crossed at the breast. Over this was a thick rope called a girdle, worn around the waist. It was the emblem of purity. Then the alb, a white linen robe.

Anna watched the nun complete the laying out of articles in

the order in which the priest would put on the garments. The remaining piece, the cassock, a black ankle-length robe, was folded beside the holy objects like an afterthought.

Sister whispered, "The priest may or may not arrive wearing a cassock. The priest, of course, does not live under the same roof as the nuns."

Bells rang just as they finished the preparation. Along with the other nuns, they scurried to their seats in the chapel.

What an honor You bestowed on me today. I was so blessed to watch the preparations for tomorrow's Mass. May Sister Timothy, the sacristan, feel better soon.

Songs filled the church. Anna opened her missal and followed the words to the Latin song of praise, *Tantum Ergo Sacramentum.* Seated beside her, Sister Red's habit carried the scent of scorched leaves mixed with fresh grass cuttings. *She has probably been outside raking.* Anna smiled at Sister Red. There were pink patches of new sunburn below her green eyes.

Frequent sneezes echoed in the chapel from the leaf gatherers who had hay fever.

Concentrate. Stanza two began. *Genitori, Genitoque, lauset jubilatio.* Beside the Latin words, the English translation was printed—To the Everlasting Father and the Son who reigns on high. *God, I could sing this song to you several times a day. It is so beautiful.* But a hush descended on the chapel, and silent prayer began. *I think I am figuring out this schedule, but by hours, not bells. Lord, I am not yet into the bells. I think it starts with Mass and then varies hourly with work, prayer, and meals until the evening gatherings are finished. Then we go to our rooms to be alone for personal prayer time and sleep.*

So now is our quiet meditation time, called praise and worship. I find it hard to use the word praise. To me, that means that I, Anna, judge You, God, and give You praise. Who am I to judge? I will just worship and thank You. Anna began her own Polish prayer, *W Imię Ojca i Syna i Ducha Świętego. Amen.*

The only sounds she heard were nuns clearing their throats in the otherwise quiet chapel.

I thank You for outer space where You have put the planets in place and kept them there. I thank You for the darkness around them.

The bells rang, and Anna followed Sister Red. *It is late morning. I wonder what we will do now.* Out the door, they went. Bright morning sun blanketed Anna's face. Soft breezes tickled her cheeks. She raised her hand and shaded her view as she followed Sister Red across the grounds.

In the sparse trees, blue jays jeered at each other, and tiny brown birds that Anna thought were juncos, darted in and out of the branches. Squirrels scampered up the trunks, hiding treasures. Cows bellowed softly in the background.

Piles of orange, red, and brown leaves nestled under the trees. Sisters with wagons moved between the mounds. Anna helped them gather the leaves. They placed them in the carts then tented them with heavy canvas before moving them away.

Bells rang. *Time for lunch.*

The dining room offered no aroma to hint at the meal. After a short prayer, cheese sandwiches on dark bread were passed on platters. Bowls of sliced tomatoes covered with dill followed. Mounds of mashed sweet potatoes came around. Pitchers of foamy milk sat on the table. Applesauce, still full of juicy chunks, was served for dessert.

The chapel was the next stop. A prayer of praise, this one in English, was chanted. It was the *Magnificat. My soul doth magnify the Lord.* Quiet prayer followed. Before starting her prayer, Anna had a private chuckle. *I wonder if some of the older nuns like Sister Calista close their eyes, but instead of saying prayers, take a little nap. They probably deserve it.*

Again, she continued her silent worship. *God, I worship and thank You for our planet Earth. I see Your might in snowstorms, in fast winds, in beating rain, and in tornados, which I have only read about. The same with hurricanes, typhoons, and monsoons. Have pity on the people in the storms. Guide them to safety, if it is in Your plan.*

The bell rang. *Time for work. Will we be raking leaves again?*

I will do some stomping this time. I love to hear the leaves crackling under my shoes. I mean sandals.

However, Anna was propelled in another direction. She followed Sister Red to the work assignment room. Nuns three deep were reading a bulletin board. As the front row scattered, Anna could see the top line of the message written in large letters.

The New Mission Assignment of Our Sister Calista.

With the blessings of Sister Eileen and the Diocese, Sister Calista announces her new assignment. She and a companion will be departing within two weeks for a mission to a group of islands in the Pacific Ocean, 600 miles west of Ecuador. The islands are called the Galapagos. A doctor is working with the natives. He says that only males accept his treatments. Sister Calista, who has some nursing skills, and her companion would allow God's healing to be given to the women. Sister Calista's companion will not be announced until next week. Several of our nuns are being considered for the assignment.

Sister Red and Anna went back out to the field. Anna could see that Sister Red was in some way struck by the announcement. *I wish I could understand and talk to her about what she is feeling. What am I feeling? Why is this even important to me?*

They raked and piled. Soft breezes kept the leaves dancing away from the mounds. Canvas covers finally contained them in the wagon. Anna's joy with the leaves earlier that day was gone. Her robe felt heavy and hot. Her head felt as if it was full of leaves, and they were swirling faster and faster, making her dizzy. *What is the temperature here?* She looked up at the sun. She couldn't look away. In the center of the sun, she saw Jesus' mother, Mary. The sun glistened behind Mary, and rays flowed down from each of her hands. The image came closer to her and became life-sized. A shawl covered her head, and a gown fell from her shoulders to her toes. Sandals peeked out from under the hem. The scent of roses hung in the air.

Mary laughed. The sound bounced back and forth in Anna's head. It reminded Anna of a stream on a wooded piece of land about a half mile from her house. All the children called it *first spring*. When the water splashed on the small stones, it made a happy sound.

Mary called her. "Anna, Anna, Anna." With the water tinkling around her voice, Mary asked, "What are you doing here? This is a wonderful place for the silent ones. Your path of serving God is with a jubilant, loud voice and song. People are waiting for your help."

The light faded. It became quiet. Anna felt hands on her body moving her onto a wagon. She felt weak. She tried to open her eyes, yet her eyelids would not budge. Moments later, she heard wheels turning with an occasional squeak. A door opened, and she felt the shade of indoors. When she was able to open her eyes, she saw a new kind of room. Four beds hugged a wall. Feeble-looking women occupied each. On the other side of the room, she saw two unoccupied beds. The fresh linen smell in the room was a bouquet to the nose.

"Anna," Sister Calista said, "you are in the infirmary. You fainted."

Anna replied groggily, "I did?"

Sister offered her a glass of cloudy water. "This is just water with a little salt. It was dehydration that made you faint. This will make you better. In the infirmary, you may talk freely. The poor sick nuns here need to let me know what's wrong and how I can help them."

Anna drank the salty room temperature water. *So, I fainted. What an illusion. How did I make up Mary's voice in my delirium? I have never in my life heard anyone laugh and talk in such a gentle, sweet yet calming voice.*

Anna sat up in the wagon, and Sister Calista helped her into a bed.

"How do you feel?" Sister asked.

"Strange, confused, and weak. This will be a good place for me to rest. Thank you." Her head touched the pillow. She smelled the fresh scent of the pillowcase. Her eyes closed.

When she awoke, she felt wonderful. She sat up and looked around. Sister Calista was sound asleep in a rocking chair.

One of the ailing nuns whispered, "I need a drink of water."

Snoring noises came from Sister Calista's lips. *She is having a well-deserved nap.* Anna moved out of the bed, went to the thirsty nun, and handed her a glass of water. The older woman smiled. Anna went to the icebox and found three lemons. She sliced thin slices from one and dropped a slice into each of the water glasses. She then went around the room and fluffed the pillows of the residents.

One of the nuns held Anna's forearm and said, "You sweet child. God bless you for your care."

Behind her, Sister Calista said, "You look much better, Anna. These ladies are grateful for your help. Are you feeling well enough to go downstairs to dinner?"

"Yes, but I will need to have a very long private talk with you, Sister Calista. Can we do that tomorrow?"

"Yes, yes. Now, hurry and put on your sandals, because I'm sure the meal bell will ring soon."

Anna rushed to the dining room. Sister Red greeted her with a wide smile. Anna tried to eat an adequate portion, although her stomach was a little queasy.

Chapel time followed. The church felt cool. Flickering candles on the altar sent up thin plumes of smoke. Anna looked at a single candle while she continued to pray. She watched a thin river of wax trickle down the side of the taper. *I need to talk to Sister Eileen. Maybe I will see her after this prayer interval. My peace and quiet have been replaced by uncertainty.*

Every time Anna glimpsed Sister Eileen, the headmistress' gaze was far in the distance.

Late that night, when she should have been asleep, strange thoughts channeled through her mind. *Am I homesick? How many days have I been here? Did I think I was holy? I can almost see halos above some of the nuns' heads, both the older ones and some of the postulants. Does it come in time? It does not fall on a person like a cloak when one enters this monastery. Did all these nuns have it when they entered? They, well, most of them, look serene. How does one get to that state of mind? What made me think that I wanted to just pray all my life?*

The silence in her room was interrupted by the sound of some other restless person shuffling past her door on the way to the bathroom.

My father gave me the most valuable gift one can ever give. He turned aside his wishes and gave me the freedom to choose. Now, what? I have not been here long enough to know this life. Here I am, questioning my choice. Besides, what if I go back home now? Wouldn't everyone be ashamed of me? I could not do that to my family, especially Tata. She got up and looked out the window. The new moon flirted with her between the naked elm trees. All was quiet outside. *God, thank You for this moon tonight. Let its light put some brightness in my befuddled mind.*

Instead of getting back into bed, she knelt beside it and prayed, saying her favorite prayer, the Hail Mary. Because she was feeling vulnerable, she said it in Polish, beginning again and again with *Zdrowaś Marya, Łaskiś pełna.* Anna caught herself as her head touched the bed. *I think I can sleep now.*

With the first bells of the day, she awoke with a smile. She brushed her teeth, straightened the bed, and opened her window wide to let in the fall breeze. Her heart was light.

In the chapel, she prayed with fervor. A nun played joyful chords up and down the organ. *God, even You were plagued with doubts. Devils visited You. I will talk to Sister Eileen and Sister Calista today.*

The oatmeal was so hot it singed her tongue. *I should have used milk on it instead of the butter, as I did in Petroleum City.* The nuns ate thick slices of bread with yellow cheese. The aroma of coffee drifted around the room.

After breakfast, Sister Calista swooped over to Anna who turned, smiled, and followed.

The elder nun navigated Anna toward a new area of the abbey and opened the first door to the right. They entered a small office. A dark desk, polished to a high sheen, and two wing-back chairs, upholstered in red, furnished the room. A crucifix hung on one wall. On the other, a picture of the Sacred Heart of Jesus showed a solemn young man with long, dark hair dressed in a robe. His right hand was raised with stigmata showing on his palm. His chest had a red heart in the center, a wreath around the thickest part, and a flame above it. Anna knew that the flame represented the Holy Ghost.

Sister Calista smiled and said, "Anna, you came into my life at such an exasperating time. I'm planning a trip, as you know. My mind was filled with the voyage, and then you appeared. You made me focus on a long unfinished issue."

Where is this conversation going?

"My older sister, my parents' favorite, is named Anna Marie and most times called Anna. Now, who can forget that name? No one. Yet, what did they name me? Marlena."

"Marlena." Why *does she need to tell me this?*

"Everywhere we went, everyone knew Anna. My name was a mystery. I was always asked if it was Merlana, Marleana, or what? Even after I told them, I was always just Anna's sister. She was always happy. Like you, Anna. I was always waiting to be noticed. When I got to the convent, I decided to pick the easiest name. I wanted to be Sister Emily, but it was already taken, as were Julia, Eileen, and Margaret. I picked from the leftovers and got Calista. Do you know who Saint Calista is? No one does."

"Sister," Anna said, "I looked up Calista in the missal. I could not find it but figured it was the female version of Saint Callistus, Pope and Martyr, whose feast is next week on October fourteenth. I was planning to bring you some flowers."

"Humph." Sister's eyes sparkled as if she were blinking back tears. She eased herself out of her wingback chair, walked to the desk, and tugged hard at a stubborn drawer. When it creaked open, she removed some papers. "Review all the jobs that nuns do here. You can decide which you'd like to try for a while."

Anna walked over to examine the work list, but she barely saw it. "Sister, I need to tell you about my new thoughts since arriving here. Either you or Sister Eileen need to know about my doubts."

The older nun's head turned, and her gaze fell on Anna's face. "Oh, Anna, I've grown fond of you. I thought you were happy. I watch you praying with such devotion. You radiate joy. You have helped me think good things about my sister, Anna Marie. I wasted so much time being angry with her."

Sister Calista tried to move her chair closer to Anna's. Anna saw the struggle and, instead, dragged her own chair close to Sister Calista. They sat, and Anna leaned forward.

She said, "I'm glad you are more at peace with Anna Marie. However, I am not at peace here. I see so many holy women. I thought my calling was to quietly work and pray. Every thought and action was directed by me to be here. Only, praying all day?" Anna blushed. "Sorry. *Only* is such a wrong word to use before praying."

Sister Calista sat with her gnarled hands folded on top of the work list. She seemed to be waiting for Anna's next statement.

"Sister Calista, remember the Bible verse in the Book of John, where Mary and Martha meet Jesus at their home? Mary listens to the Word of Jesus. Martha cooks. Jesus tells Martha she would be better off listening to the Word of God than cooking and cleaning. I am the Martha. I would rather do for God, instead of just talking to him. Does it make me bad? I do not know. Does it make me wrong? Perhaps."

With a sigh, Sister Calista gathered the work list and replaced it in the stubborn, squeaky drawer. "We will make time to see Sister Eileen tomorrow. I'm pleased that you've confided in me. However, I am sad about what you've said. Sister Eileen has no doubt heard such concerns many times. I'll come with you if you'd like. With more time, your journey will be revealed. Now, I think it's almost chapel time. God Bless you, my child."

Bells chimed. As they exited the office, the hall filled with nuns. Anna hurried to the chapel. She became hyperaware of the other postulants. On one side, her pew mate had the aroma of raw onions on her hands. On the other side, Sister Red's body still radiated the warmth of the sun on her wool habit.

During quiet meditation, Anna's thoughts drifted from thanking God for all the general beauty of the Earth and centered on her home. Tata. His calloused hands. His twinkling eyes. The smell of the soap all over his face after he shaved. She could feel her heart crack a bit, and tears spilled from her eyes. Anna shook her head. *This is not a sad occasion. This is one of decision and action.*

Bells rang. It was activity time. Anna followed Sister Red to the bustling kitchen. While her friend chopped onions, Anna looked around. She saw an unattended sink with dirty pots and pans beside it. *I know this skill.* She found a piece of cloth, a plug for the sink, and soon had her hands in a pool of bubbles. Help arrived, and as she washed, another set of hands dried each piece. Religious music filled her head as she happily scrubbed. When the sink was empty, she looked for another task. She found a knife and was soon cutting lettuce into bite-size pieces. A silent chuckle hid in her mouth as she watched a nun pirouette at each salad bowl, gracing each with shakes of spices.

She smelled baked chicken as it was removed from the oven, then heard the rhythmic pound of knives as poultry was diced for the lunch salad. On a back table, hot rolls were somersaulted out of trays and into baskets.

Anna and Sister Red made one trip for ice and finished before the meal bells rang.

After lunch, Anna and Sister Red walked to the apple trees, found ladders, and picked and picked. They were not selective. Every reachable apple was removed. *The sun feels hot. I think this is Kentucky's Indian Summer. We are probably doing the last pick before the frost.* Before the hour was over, all apples were in divided bins labeled, eating, cooking, applesauce, or animals.

I remember when Julia and I fed her dog, Stashu, pieces of apple. Julia, I miss you. How are you feeling?

Bells rang. Again, it was chapel time. More songs were sung.

Joyful voices chanted in Latin to Mary. It began with *Benedicta, et venerbilis es, Virgo Maria*. Anna sang of the Virgin Mary being blessed and venerable. The singing filled her heart with joy.

The bells rang. It was the end of an extraordinary day.

Up in her bedroom, Anna composed her petition to Sister Eileen. *Help me say the right words so Sister Eileen understands. I thought for a long time that the only choices I had were to either teach or come to the silent orders. I know I want to be a nun and serve God. But I do not think I should be here. How embarrassing. I wanted this badly. I researched. I wanted to serve God. I wanted to show God's love to other people. Here, my voice is silent. How can I encourage and show love to each person I meet without talking? I want to touch people with my voice.*

THIRTEEN

Indian Summer disappeared. The morning chill woke Anna. *Did I see a blanket on the shelf in my closet? I should have pulled it out last night.*

Anna hurried through her morning routine. Then she drew the slip over her head and slid the heavy brown habit over it. A relieved sigh escaped her as she enveloped her body in the warm, prickly wool. She slipped her cold toes into her sandals.

Morning Mass and prayer time flew.

Hot oatmeal was one of her favorite food textures. She loved to bite down on the jellied kernels and feel them snap between her teeth. Yet this morning, she did not appreciate the cereal or the taste of crisp bacon. Her mind was set on her meeting with Sister Eileen.

As Anna washed her plate, Sister Calista approached and gave her the smallest nod. Anna followed her to Sister Eileen's office.

Outside the room, Sister Calista asked, "Would you like me to stay, child?"

"Yes, Sister," Anna said.

Sister Eileen sat behind a large desk of dark wood, shining and scented with the now familiar lemon oil aroma. She smiled at them as they entered the room. "Please sit down, and let's talk for a while."

The chairs in front of the desk were a buttery-brown-colored wood with dimpled spindles up each side. Anna chose one and sat with her hands on her lap. White sheer drapes flanked the open window. The drapes fluttered and curled as the fall wind intruded on their discussion.

Sister Eileen said, "Now, Anna, I want to hear about your worries. Let me start by asking questions, if I may."

"Of course," Anna said.

"How long did it take you to decide to enter a convent?"

"I'd been thinking of it since about sixth grade."

"Why did you pick our order and why did you pick a cloister?"

Anna thought for a few minutes before answering. "I wanted to be a servant of God. I like people. I did not think my calling, though, was to teach children. I searched long and hard to find you. Imagine my surprise at being here for such a short time and being disenchanted. Wait, maybe that's not the right word. I think you all are an amazing group of women. And you are all so holy."

Sister Eileen laughed. Her voice was like water falling over pebbles. "You think we are holy? Anna. God doesn't want the bland salt-and-pepper kind of people for his convent. These nuns are the spicy people. They are the cayenne pepper, the mustard, the vinegar, the onion and the garlic of the world. Think again."

"I'm honored by your allowing me to see you do God's work. I too want to do God's work. But this is not my path."

The room was quiet except for the wind ruffling the curtains and the clock ticking on the wall. It was probably the only one in the building. The rhythmic cadence of it calmed Anna.

Sister Calista wriggled in her chair.

Anna turned to her and said, "Sister, this is such a hard chair for you to sit in at this time. Are you still willing to stay?"

She nodded. "I want to be here with you."

Sister Eileen's voice rose. "What were you expecting? What is it that you imagined? What is very different? I am trying to help you to see every aspect of your problem."

"I feel like I am walking on blessed ground here. I am not that good. I am not that holy." She gulped back a sob. "I don't belong."

"You've said enough for today. I see and hear your distress. Let us continue this another time. Think about these three things. What are the best parts and the worst parts of this experience?

Next, what would be a reasonable amount of time for you to decide if you should stay? The last question will be, how many ways can you serve God?" A strong gust of wind had the curtain standing horizontally. Sister Eileen hurried to the window to pull it closed. "Maybe the Holy Ghost is trying to get in here to help us. If so, He arrived with a flourish."

All three chuckled. Anna felt as if each of them had just been blessed.

Sister Eileen said, "Because you joined at a different time than the other postulants, you haven't had a chance to get to know them. During the first year, we have a communal gathering the first Tuesday of each month. It is a prayer day and a problem-solving discussion. The postulants are able to ask questions and work out solutions. On that day, you are all in class the entire day and able to talk to each other while there. Many ideas and suggestions are debated. Next month, you'll see if that day helps. Now, off to prayer time for you." To Sister Calista, she added, "How is your packing coming along?"

"Slowly," the elder nun said.

Anna stepped into the hall and hurried toward the chapel. As in Sister Eileen's office, the hall windows were open. Some rattled with the wind. An occasional caw-caw announced the crows passing over the monastery.

The chapel had one candle lit at the altar. The peace was soothing. Her first weeks in the monastery had muddled her brain. *What is meditation supposed to be? Me talking and praising God? Or me listening to His word in my head? Are those only my thoughts?*

Instead of singing today, the congregation said The Litany of the Blessed Virgin in unison. It was a late honor to Mary, whose feast, *The Motherhood of the Blessed Virgin*, had been celebrated on October eleventh. After the Litany came blessed silence.

What had been the best part of this experience? A door to a new life was opened. A different rhythm and flow of a day unfolded for me. I was accepted graciously and immediately. What had been the worst part of the new life? Instead of only the joy and happiness of the new way of living, there was also a deep pool of dark discomfort with the act of silence. Is this normal?

The congregation began to leave the chapel. Anna moved with them.

How long is a reasonable time for me to come to a decision? I will need more help on that answer. Tata would say pomału. He cautioned me to slow down many times.

Anna followed Sister Red to the kitchen. The heat which once seemed oppressive was now a warm comfort. It was canning beans morning. Glass clattered. Pots clanged. Green beans were mounded on tables. Three nuns sat snapping beans. The discarded ends flew into an old pot on the floor. Empty, sparkling glass containers stood in rows. Anna and Sister Red helped fill the jars. Boiling water and lids were applied. *I have seen Aunt Nellie work at this, but she usually canned twenty jars. It looks like there are hundreds of jars here.* The rhythm reminded Anna of a waltz, each step and movement beautifully coordinated. As the assembly finished, bells sounded. The room emptied as the nuns moved *en masse* to the chapel.

Bouquets of red roses flanked the altar. Sitting in the front row, Anna hoped for a smell of roses, but none came. Nor could she smell the wax as it melted from the candles.

The congregation chanted a Latin verse from a Sunday Mass. The page number in their prayer book was listed on a board at the front of the chapel. *Miserere mihi, Domine, quoniam ad te clamovi tota die.* The words meant *have pity on me, O Lord, for to you I call all the day.*

Lord, how many days can I live with this uncertainty?

Lunch followed. The meal was an open-sandwich-making occasion. White bread, rye bread, or rolls could be chosen. Slices of meat and cheese were available. A tall pot with a ladle contained tomato soup. The aroma of dill pickles teased the nose.

After lunch, Anna and Sister Red joined other postulants in the fields, harvesting every ear of corn they could see.

It was a good opportunity to find flowers for Sister Calista's namesake bouquet for the next day. Anna gathered fresh pink and red blooms, not even knowing their names, yet seeing a harmony in the arrangement.

Back indoors, she found paper and labeled the bouquet, *For Sister Calista in honor of her namesake's day, Feast of Saint Callistus the First, October Fourteenth*. The postulants who read the label smiled at the note.

The rest of the day sped past, and again, at dusk, she was in her room, reviewing her needs, wishes, and dilemma.

FOURTEEN

The next morning in the chapel, Sister Eugenia, the organist, added loud cheerful chords to the melody of praise to Mary. Anna could almost see the candles trying to sway to the rhythm. The happy music echoed off the walls. Anna silently praised and honored The Almighty for the stars, the planets, the sun, the rain, the snow, even the hail.

I remember when we had hail. Aunt Nellie always said to look for a tornado. But that was usually in the spring. I remember last summer, my part in Julia's wedding. Whoops. I am off the praise prayer. Sorry, God. Back to praise and worship. I honor You for the beauty of the chrysanthemums on the altar. I honor You for the colors and volume of petals on each flower. How mighty are Your ways.

Bells rang.

At breakfast, Anna watched her coffee transform into a work of art when she poured the milk onto the edge and saw a slow swirl turn the color to the pattern of a cinnamon roll. *Will I ever get to bake those again? The smell of rolls is memorable to me.*

After breakfast, Sister Calista wandered over and together they walked to Sister Eileen's office. The three of them faced each other in the sun-streaked room.

"Good morning, Sisters," Sister Eileen said. "Let us continue on this beautiful day, the feast of Saint Callistus, Pope and Martyr, and your name day. It will be a sad day when you leave us, Sister Calista, and the day is coming so soon. The last time you were here, Anna, we were discussing the best and worst experience you've had since you arrived. Can you tell us your thoughts?"

Anna sat straighter in her chair and said, "The worst experiences were saying goodbye to my father and accepting the silence. Did I know I was a ballad tune singer and a music hummer? It did not seem important. I like the rhythm of walking, drumbeats, motors running, and the clock cadence. Can you both hear the clock's steady beat? These sounds are honey in the tea of my soul. I miss the sound of laughter. I know God sometimes asks hard things of us, but can I do this? I do not know. The best experience? Fitting into the work pattern and the prayer arrangement. Seeing us all move like the tide of the ocean to a prayer, a meal, or a chore." She looked up at Sister Eileen, and for the first time, noticed the wide gap between the headmistress' front teeth when she smiled. Anna found her warm and open. "These are my answers to the best and the worst."

Sister Calista said, "The next question was what would be a reasonable amount of time for you to decide if you should stay."

Anna shook her head. "Like other things in life, the time is never long enough or short enough. I don't know the answer."

Sister Eileen walked to Anna and placed a hand on her shoulder. "Take time to pray. It will help. Being a nun is a lifelong decision. If someone asked you to marry them, you would have to know them for longer than a few weeks, wouldn't you? How long have you known this life?"

Anna nodded. "How silly of me to give up so quickly. What was I thinking? I should probably get to know the convent life for at least six months. I will pray more intently. Thank you, Sister Eileen, for advising me. Thank you, Sister Calista, for your support. I hope when you leave for the Galapagos, your replacement will be as encouraging."

Sister Eileen said, "We still need to discuss how many ways you can serve God. Today, I want you to go to the chapel and get a chrysanthemum. Take it to your room. Tonight, touch each petal. Remember, God in His wisdom makes even each part of a flower a little different. As you touch each section, write down a way you can serve God." Sister Eileen handed Anna a sheaf of paper, a pen, and a bottle of ink. "It may take you weeks to finish this assignment. It is a good personal exercise to remind you of time. It took a while for a chrysanthemum to grow, for all the petals to form, and it will take a while for you to think of what is in your heart."

Anna hugged the papers to her chest. Outside, birds sang their farewell to warm weather. The autumn sun shone through the open windows, and cool breezes hinted of the coming winter. A peace descended over Anna as she anticipated fall and early winter at her convent. *I can see me now, scrubbing, washing, and caring for animals as the weather changes.*

Sister Eileen said, "Anna, fervent prayer is the most important part of your future here. One can change the world with prayer. And now—" She stopped to answer a knock on the door.

A tall nun huffed and puffed as she swept into the room. She wore glasses, tilted so the right lens was higher on her face than the left. A few short blonde hairs poked out of her wimple. Her habit was in place, but instead of the usual single knot of rope at her waist, she had multiple knots. A bandage surrounded her right ankle.

"Ah. Sister Gertrude. We were just finishing here." Sister Eileen smiled. "Sister Gertrude will be accompanying Sister Calista to her new post."

Sister Gertrude shook her head. "No, I can't go. My feet are swollen, I can't breathe well, and I would rather die here. Please don't make me go."

Anna gathered papers, pen, and ink as Sister Eileen ushered her out of the room.

Anna went to the chapel, took a flower from the altar near the statue of Saint Teresa, and placed it in her room. Saint Teresa had always been Anna's favorite.

The afternoon chore was scrubbing the floor of the entry hall. With soap, buckets, rags, and elbow grease, Anna and Sister Red washed, dried, and polished. They smiled as they stirred bubbles across the floor. As they scoured under the stained-glass window of Saint Teresa, the wind gusted. A branch from the field sailed into the window and shattered it. Shards of glass struck Sister

Red's unprotected right arm. Blood gushed. Sister Red cried out. Anna grabbed a clean cloth and pressed it on her partner's arm. She moved the two buckets of water to form a barricade across the debris and marched Sister Red to the infirmary. Once they were inside, Sister Calista quickly assessed and began treating the wound.

Anna returned to the broken window and cleaned up the glass. Two other postulants joined her. Anna looked for Sister Red at dinnertime and later in her room. She did not see her. Her friend must have stayed in the infirmary for the night.

In her room, Anna saw the chrysanthemum from Saint Teresa on her bed. She changed into her nightclothes. She added the blanket from the closet to the bed, picked up the flower, and stood at her window. She opened it and gazed at the starlit sky. *God, what a gift You give us with clusters of stars*. She sat on her chair. Her fingers moved to the first petal, felt the soft silky texture of the top of the petal, moved her fingers down, and felt the sturdy *base* where it was attached to the flower. *Ah. You sneaky little blossom. My nose cannot detect you, even though you are near. Am I as strong as this petal? It has no smell, and I have no voice. This petal is one of many. So am I.*

Anna climbed into bed. Instead of holding her rosary, she touched the flower between her thumb and ring finger, rolling the stem as she fell asleep.

The next morning after breakfast, Sister Calista ushered Anna back to Sister Eileen's office.

Sister Eileen smiled as they sat before her. "Anna, you were so helpful when Sister Rochelle injured her arm yesterday. I'm pleased you were able to assess her wound and hurry her to the infirmary."

So, that is Sister Red's name. What an appropriate, pretty name for my friend.

Sister Eileen said, "I have much to discuss with you. We are trying to complete the plans of Sister Calista's expedition to the Galapagos, and we find that Sister Gertrude cannot travel. Anna, instead, you are invited to the Galapagos with Sister Calista. It will give you time to think. You are offered this one-year assignment."

Anna's mouth dropped open, and her thoughts whirled. *Why did Saint Teresa drop out of the sky onto my head yesterday? Why did it happen the same day Sister Gertrude decided to change her mind about going to the Galapagos Islands with Sister Calista? Was it a sign? Is this my path? Could I help more people there? I am just a plain girl with no medical background. All I know is what Aunt Nellie taught me. But Aunt Nellie also told me she saw me in a bright and sunny place. I remember reading that the Galapagos are near the equator.*

Sister Eileen got up from her chair and adjusted the blind on the window, blocking the light from beaming directly into Sister Calista's face. "Before you decide, let's review your role as a postulant. When you arrived, you agreed as our guest to follow our rules of silence, prayer, and work. You agreed while here to wear our garb. Until you arrive on the island, you will continue to wear the habit, veil, and small cap."

Anna nodded.

"When you leave these walls, neither of you will be observing the vow of silence. We honor you by referring to you as Sister and your baptismal name. When you get to the island, you may then choose to be Miss Anna or just Anna."

FIFTEEN

A warm blush crossed Anna's face. It was as if the wind had found a home in her head and was swirling 'round and 'round. Her mind questioned, *What, what?* All the while, her lips said, "Yes, yes."

Sister Eileen said, "Anna, you look pale. Put your head down for a minute. Sister Calista and I will wait."

Anna lowered her chin to her chest. The swirl slowed. Sister Calista rose to her feet, groaned, and walked away. The next sound was water being poured. Anna sensed a glass being placed on the desk in front of her.

Sister Eileen eased Anna upright. "Anna, you need to sit back and take a sip. Raise your head, that's a girl. I'm delighted to see your skin look pink and healthy again. I think you are coming around to the Galapagos plan. Am I right?"

Sister Calista wobbled her teeth and said, "You might look at this journey and see it as a different way for you to serve God. I've seen you react to a medical emergency with quick judgment. The doctor we'll be helping, Doctor Graumann, will get two sets of medical hands. Just say yes, and we'll put together your packing list."

Anna struggled to focus her thoughts. For some reason, an image of Aunt Nellie baking cinnamon rolls came to mind. Anna used to love watching her bake. She would punch down the risen bread dough and roll it out, slather on butter and, with what looked like a casual hand, sweep sugar and cinnamon over it. Her skilled fingers rolled the dough into a log from end to end. Then her knife cut down, separating the dough into rolls, each, to Anna's eye, cut the width of the knife handle. But Aunt Nellie always, with purpose, cut some wrong fat slices, corresponding to the number of people at home while she baked. Then each person got a portion of the delicious raw dough filled with butter, sugar, and cinnamon. As this memory became clearer, Anna heard her aunt's voice. She'd said that the only decision one can always be sorry about is making no choice.

The other sage of the family, Uncle Piotr, was an avid reader. He often quoted Napoleon Hill, who wrote about overcoming fears to reach an achievement. He said that one needed to clamp down his teeth and plow forward like a buffalo in a windstorm.

"Yes," Anna said, "I want to go to the Galapagos with Sister Calista. We've grown fond of each other, I believe."

Sister Calista's seated figure seemed to grow taller by a few inches. "I'm so happy. Pack your bags. We leave in a few days. We'll be taking the train to Seattle. Next, we'll board a freighter to our new home. Doctor Graumann said it was the first livable island he saw and was near people needing medical help. They live on a neighboring island."

Anna asked, "What do I pack?"

"All your belongings," Sister Eileen said.

"This will be exciting. Where do we get the train? Do we stop at night?"

Sister Calista smiled and said, "I'll bring you the brochure. The train leaves at noon on the twenty-second of October."

Sister Eileen said, "In Seattle, you will meet the *Alexandria,* a freighter, to travel south. It is old but safe. Sister Damien's brother is the captain. He'll treat you both with dignity. We have been gathering supplies for a month. The doctor wants ointment, bandages, and oilcloth to keep articles dry. Besides medical items, he wants to again try to plant seeds, herbs, bulbs, and spices."

Sister Calista said, "The doctor describes the place as having ocean waves gently embracing the sandy beaches, and the stars so close they are barely out of reach. He writes of thatched roofs. It sounds like a beautiful place. Our diet will consist of a lot of fish."

Sister Eileen said, "Anna, we will need to let your father know. I'll help you write the letter and explain your new assignment. I will also give you any letters that have arrived for you. You may have to read them on the train. If you want to reply to them, you will have time while traveling to do that. Those can be mailed from Seattle. However, you and I will get the letter out to your father before you leave."

Anna nodded.

"By the way, usually families leave some monies in a sort of bank account here. I'll open that envelope, and you can either take it all or leave part of it here."

"If you don't mind, I will take it all with me," Anna said.

Sister Eileen pulled open a drawer of the desk and removed a set of keys. "Come. We need to get your suitcase and the mail you've accumulated."

Anna followed Sister Eileen down the hall. Sister Eileen unlocked a door. She raised her hand, searching the overhead air until she found and pulled a string. Ceiling bulbs shone on a short, wooden landing that led to a flight of steps.

As they descended, Sister Eileen said, "We are so blessed by our benefactor, Mister X. He built this entire monastery in memory of his dear mother. He had architects put electricity in each room and hallway, plumbing, thick walls to keep heat in. We never see him, but his financial advisor comes each year to plan new modern things for us. That is one reason I've been out of sorts lately. I've heard rumors of recent financial disasters. They worry me. I hope Mister X's legacy can keep up this beautiful building."

"Oh, I had forgotten about the rest of the world. We have been so isolated."

"That is exactly what a monastery does. It concentrates on God, prayers, and giving thanks."

They walked down another long hall.

"Here we are." Sister Eileen pushed open a door and pulled on the overhead light cord.

Anna saw shelves with boxes, suitcases, and cloth bags, each with a name attached to the front of the shelf. "This is the biggest closet I have ever seen."

"This is the storeroom for the belongings of our nuns. These suitcases contain the clothes each woman wore the day they arrived."

The keys in Sister Eileen's pocket jingled as she walked between the rows of shelves. She turned on another light. "Come help me." She reached toward Anna's suitcase on a high shelf.

"Let me get that." Anna lifted down the suitcase. She smelled the leather and remembered the day she and Tata picked it out. He said that it did not matter if it was used for only one day. He wanted the best he could get for her.

"Let us pull out a few more pieces of luggage," Sister Eileen said. "The doctor asked for spices. There is a whole list of things he'd like. You can carry some of it in the suitcases and put the rest in boxes. Moreover, you'll want extra habits for the trip and dark clothes if you choose to wear dresses for the next year."

"How can we take someone else's belongings?"

"These things were owned by three nuns who have recently died, God rest their souls. Instead of gathering dust, their valises will go with you. Help me find the belongings of the late Sister Agnes, Sister Francis De Sales, and Sister Hedwiga."

Anna found Sister Agnes' gray suitcase and brought it down.

Sister Eileen followed with two more. They were made of sturdy woven straw with heavy leather straps. "A matching set. These belonged to Sister Francis De Sales. She would be clapping with glee knowing her belongings were taking a trip to the tropics. They will travel well. Now, we only need Sister Hedwiga's things. Anna, you would have liked her. I always, in my mind, called her Sister Heddy. She had such a solemn face. She seemed to trudge from chore to chore. Then, when you least expected it, she would pull a good-natured prank. I could see her sizing up her next victim in advance. It would only be people who could laugh at themselves. Heddy could have run a kingdom. You know, she picked that name for Saint Hedwiga, often called Hedwig, who was a Polish Queen."

"Yes, I know the story of Saint Hedwig," Anna said. "I always thought she was a great woman."

"And Sister Hedwig could have been her double, except she developed tuberculosis. We sometimes call it consumption. Because it is contagious, she spent her last years living in almost complete isolation in one of the remote wings of the monastery. Sadly, she died at age thirty-eight."

"May the grace of the Lord be with her."

Again, Sister Eileen hurried back to distant shelves. She came out carrying a leather suitcase just a bit larger than the one Anna owned. "As you probably guessed, Sister Hedwig was also Polish. And it looks like your suitcases almost match."

Anna looked at the two cases side by side. "They could be mistaken for each other."

"I never question God's motives."

They gathered all the suitcases and returned to Sister Eileen's office, closing doors, turning off lights, and locking stairwells along the way.

"We can leave the luggage in the next room until Sister Calista gets back. This afternoon, we need to gather all the mail you've received since you arrived. Your train leaves before long." Sister Eileen shook her head as if clearing cobwebs from her brain. "Anna, I can help you with the letter to your father if you need me to."

"Thank you, but no, I'll go up to my room and think of the right words. I will need some stationery, please, for his letter and to write a few more letters while I am on the train."

Sister Eileen handed Anna a stack of white paper and envelopes. "I think you'll enjoy the train ride. I suggest you continue to wear a habit and veil until you reach the island. Otherwise, folks will be confused."

"I will, and thank you."

In her room, Anna praised God for her surroundings. *This little room is compact, cozy, and probably a haven in the winter. These brown habits keep me warm. Our bathrooms with the tubs and a shower are nice compared to many I have seen in Petroleum City. I will no doubt remember them as luxuries when I see what we have in the Galapagos. The doctor said the island was primitive. We might be using an outhouse. May the next girl appreciate this room as much as I did and give You honor. I feel Your presence.*

She moved her prayer book from her bedside table and set down the paper, pen, and ink. She repositioned her wooden chair to the nightstand, creating a desk. Before sitting, she turned on the overhead light.

She began the letter.

Dear Tata,

I have a wonderful opportunity. It involves my leaving the monastery for a year and going to the islands of the Galapagos.

She shook her head. *Not a good start. I need to start with regards to Tata.* She crossed out the opening sentence. *I wish I knew what is happening at home, but I have not read his letters.*

Needing to feel Tata's mood, she got up, turned off the light, and went down to Sister Eileen's office. She knocked on the open door. Sister Eileen waved her into the room.

"I need the packet of my letters, please," Anna said.

"Ah, here they are." Sister gave Anna her mail and handed her the suitcase she'd used when she'd arrived. "Who knew you'd be packing a bag so soon after your arrival. Besides the letters and your bag, I want you to have this Bible." She showed Anna a black leather-covered book. "You'll no doubt have many Sundays lacking a church. This was Sister Hedwig's Bible, one of the few I've seen written in Polish. She had me promise to give it to the next person who entered these gates and read the language. She'll be beside you on this journey."

Anna reverently opened the book. The inscription was, *Dziśaj, nasz familia jest błogosłavion. Nasza Elżbieta teras jest Siostra Hedwiga. Czerwiec, 1909.* She said, "Today, our family is blessed. Our Elizabeth now becomes Sister Hedwig. June 1909. Sister, thank you. I will treasure it."

With the book, her suitcase, and her letters in hand, Anna climbed the stairs. She felt enthused by her new life path. She put down the suitcase, placed the Bible on top, and scanned the envelopes. She had two letters from Tata. One from Bashia and Leon, with both their names on the return portion of the long white envelope. One from Julia in an envelope with a black line around it. *I see she is being frugal and using up her funeral stationery.* A slim envelope had the return address of the Felician Convent on Pulaski Street in Petroleum City. *This one is from Sister Laetitia.* On the dark wood floor, she found another envelope that had slipped out of the pack. It had a Pittsburgh return address. *Oh, dear. This must be from Robert.*

She put the letters in a pile, took out the first one from Tata, inserted her finger under the flap, ripped it open, and pulled out a single sheet.

October 10, 1929
Dear Anna,
My prayers and thoughts are with you and your congregation.

The ride home was fast but lonely. (I am writing as if you will read this immediately, but know I am wrong.)

You would be proud of Bashia and Leon. While I was away, they ate well and kept the house clean. I knew you would be worried about them.

Anna, I love you so very much. I am so proud of your making this choice and following it.

Love, Tata

He is in for a big surprise. She stifled the temptation to open the one from her siblings. *I need to write to Tata.*

She remembered her upbringing. All Polish adults were taught when writing letters to use the entire first paragraph for blessings and praising God.

For the second time, she began the letter.

October 20, 1929
Dear Tata,

Greetings and blessings to you from your daughter, Anna, at the monastery. I have prayed often for you and all of our family. You must be feeling the good grace flowing over you, Bashia, and Leon.

How surprised you must be to hear from me so soon.

The convent is much as I imagined and desired. What I had to learn and figured out quickly is that I am not able to praise God with silence. I feel I am a better instrument of His in word and song. (You must be remembering that I sing as well as Mitek, our cat, which is screechy.) I need to hug and talk and laugh, yet I still do not want to teach children.

I have been offered an unusual post for a year. It happened right after a stained-glass window of our family saint, Saint Teresa of the Little Flower, fell and broke at my feet. I am accompanying Sister Calista to the Galapagos Islands. We will assist a doctor in helping local residents. It will give me time to think, pray, grow, and decide.

Even though I might not be sending you mail, you will be on my mind and in my prayers.

Yours in God, Anna

I think this says it right. Sister Eileen or Sister Calista may have suggestions.

Bells rang. Anna went to the chapel.

After prayers were finished, Sister Eileen stood at the front altar. She said to the entire group, "My Sisters in God, today I have a wonderful announcement. Our Sisters, Calista and Anna, will be taking on a new challenge. We were honored to receive a request from a physician. He is working with the natives of the Galapagos Islands.

Because he is the only one there and is a man, no women are able to come to him for care. Our two volunteers will go there for a year. It will allow all people on the island to be treated. They leave in two days. After morning Mass, Father will give them a special blessing for a safe journey and a successful year of helping heal the sick."

The congregation of nuns smiled and nodded.

That evening, the cooler weather influenced the menu. Bowls of steaming stew and fresh bread arrived. Anna ate with gusto now that she'd accepted her new post. When the apple pie was served, she cut herself a generous piece, and added a thin slice of cheese, knowing in a few days, she'd be eating a new diet. *What had the doctor said? We will be eating fish and fruit.* She remembered Tata on a fishing trip to Lake Erie, showing her how to bait a hook. He demonstrated twirling the worm around the metal knob and throwing in the line. Between Tata, Bashia, and herself, they caught many walleyes. Her family had given away fish to every neighbor who wanted them.

Whoops. I will have plenty of time to remember all that. I have to get everything I own packed, plus the two other habits I have been given. How will wool dry in the salty air so close to the ocean? How muggy will this place be? I was surprised when Sister Eileen suggested I take a few dark dresses from the storage area. Perhaps she thinks it will be too warm to wear a habit in the tropics.

Up in her room, Anna folded each item and placed it in the suitcase. As she packed, she prayed. *Guide me, oh God. May my mother in Heaven and my father on Earth be proud of my decisions. Let me work doing Your good with or without the notice of other people. Let me do it for Your honor and glory. Amen.*

With her suitcase as packed as could be that evening, Anna returned to her letters. *I think I should read the one from Leon and Bashia first. I can send the reply in the same envelope as Tata's.* Upon opening the envelope, she found two sheets, each with the handwriting of a sibling.

Leon scribbled,

Dear Anna,
Bashia is slowly learning to cook. You know how slim I am already. Pray, I do not starve. I miss you. Leon

Bashia's letter was in her delicate handwriting.

Dear Anna,
I always knew you were my sister. I don't think I always remembered that you were my good friend. We are all doing well. I promise I'll do all I can to keep us safe.

Julia is fine, and I even saw her smile a few times. She is eating better. The Craig family on the farm they call a ranch are good to her.

I am wondering what I will do as an adult. What am I suited to do? What are my strong qualities?

Tata is such an interesting parent. He listens to my views on things. He thinks I do well in arguments and wonders if I might be the first lawyer in the family. He thinks I'm smart. I am sorry I never asked you for your ideas on this.

Aunt Nellie talks about you all the time. You know she is very wise. I visit her a lot. She is teaching me to sew and knit. When I learn these, I will be all set, since you taught me to embroider. While we sit, she has words of wisdom for me.

I'm sorry this letter is so long, but you know me better than anyone and know I like to, as they say, go on and on.

Love, Your getting older sister, Bashia

Anna folded the two letters, thinking of the similarities and differences of the three of them, despite having the same parents. *We are all still changing.* She looked outside and saw the moon winking between the clouds but only a few distant stars. She listened. The hall was quiet. She hurried to the bathroom. Some of the doors were open, some closed. A bed squeaked as if one of the women were rolling over. She thought of Sister Eileen's concerns for the financial future of the monastery.

As she returned to her room, she thought *I can write replies to Bashia and Leon in a few minutes in the morning. This leaves me time to tell Him how much I trust and honor Him in my night prayers.*

Exhausted, she climbed into bed. *God, tonight I thank You for the Earth. I thank You for the sky that holds the clouds, the rain, sleet, snow, mist, and fog. I thank You for the heat of the summer and the coolness of the winter.* She fell asleep.

SIXTEEN

Morning bells woke Anna. As she walked toward the chapel, she prayed. *God, thank You for this beautiful morning and for the rays of sun coming through the windows that lead me toward Your chapel. Thank You for Your wisdom, for the hard stone under my feet that wise men turned into red tile for the path to the chapel. Thank You for the minds that enabled men to cut these rose-colored stones into perfect squares.*

Outside the chapel's dark wood doorway, Anna heard solemn, minor chord music. Today, Sister Dolores was the substitute organist. *She is not playing the light music Sister Eugenia usually plays.* The somber chords made Anna think of pictures of dusty catacombs and old Roman churches with just a few short beeswax candles flickering against their altars.

Opening her missal, she searched for October twenty-first and found that the day's Mass was for Saint Hilarion, who was an abbot and head of a male monastery. The missal said he gave all his possessions to the poor and became the father of monasticism in Palestine and Syria in the third century. It was also the minor feast of Saint Ursula, who was both a virgin and a martyr in medieval times. *Now I see why Sister Dolores is playing the intense music.* Because of the serious music, the Mass felt more moving to Anna. *Tomorrow morning, I will be on my way to the train. This is my last Mass here. God bless these holy women who stay here and pray. May they continue to work and honor You with happy hearts.*

After the Mass, Sisters Calista and Anna approached the altar where the Chaplain, Father Hatfield, prayed for their safe trip and a new mission in life. They bowed their heads as he blessed them.

Next was breakfast. The scent of freshly fried bacon was in the air, while coffee aroma swirled around Anna's head. Coffee had never tasted so good. *I hope we can have hot coffee in the Galápagos', even if the weather is sultry. This coffee must be Maxwell House, like at home. I remember the cook at the Arlington Hotel telling me about Maxwell House coffee. He said it was named in honor of the Maxwell House in Nashville, Tennessee. It was rumored that Theodore Roosevelt on a visit to Andrew Jackson's home had said, after drinking the Maxwell House coffee, that it was good to the last drop.* She enjoyed a meal of bacon, eggs, fried potatoes, and toast. It was her last breakfast at the convent.

Later, in Sister Eileen's office, she said, "Sister, here is my letter to my father. I would be pleased if you would read it. Then I will go up to my room and finish my letters to my brother and sister. They can go in the same envelope."

Sister Eileen quickly read the letter. "It looks wonderful. I'll wait for your other notes before I mail this. I'm going to miss your spunkiness, Anna."

Upstairs, she began her note.

October 21, 1929
Dear Leon,

I pray for you daily. I pray for your health, your safety, and your joy at having a loving father.

Your appetite is wonderful. Remember to tell whoever cooks for you that you liked the food. It is not enough to eat a meal and walk away. Every cook spends time thinking of the eaters. The cook remembers who will not eat onion, like you, or that someone's fish choice is none and they will eat twice as many vegetables at that meal.

I am moving my life in a new direction again. I still plan to be a nun but will be working with the sick. I will be going to the Galapagos Islands for one year. It is near

South America in the Pacific Ocean. I know you will have fun both looking it up and telling all your friends that I am on an island.

I leave tomorrow. Keep me in your prayers.

Love, Your Anna

She started the next letter.

October 21, 1929

Dear Bashia,

I pray for you. It sounds like you are happy, busy, thinking, and questioning. God must be pleased and smiling on you.

Leon is happy with your cooking.

I know Tata is comforted having you near. We three are fortunate to have a parent who wants to hear his children's views.

Being a lawyer would be a worthy occupation, but requires years of hard work and study. I know you can do it. Are you interested enough? That is the question only you can answer. It would not leave much social time. I know you enjoy time with your friends. There are many decisions you will have to make. As you know, any time spent on education is never a waste.

Aunt Nellie is like a silent lighthouse beacon. She has kept us off the rocks. We do our own steering but can see her beam in our range of vision.

Thank you for telling me about Julia. Keep up the good work, Godmother-to-be.

I am leaving Kentucky tomorrow. My home for the next year will be the Galapagos Islands. I will be the companion to Sister Calista, a nun from the monastery. She has a healing hand. We will be working with a doctor and helping the people there. It will be another step in my deciding about my life choice.

All of life involves decisions. I thought joining the

cloister was my last choice. God is up there laughing at and with me as I try to figure it out.

Love, Your happy Anna.

Before the next bell rang, she'd delivered the letters to Sister Eileen.

Again, it was chapel time.

Lord, I feel pleased and excited, maybe a little anxious. Your altar today is beautiful. The fall chrysanthemums have heads of orange and yellow sitting here in vases paying You homage. I'm sure only in a monastery would we see vases of fall-colored leaves of pale yellow, vivid red, and muted brown banking the cozy altar. Of course, I always liked the three altars in the Assumption Church in Petroleum City. Lord, bless all my friends and relatives in my Pennsylvania home. Protect them from poverty and threats. Bless these holy women here. I feel you have them safely tucked under your wing of loving protection. Amen.

She looked around at her fellow postulants, all three pews of them, and mentally said goodbye.

The bell rang, calling them to lunch. Half an hour later, as she looked for Sister Calista to coordinate the next day's departure, she had no recollection of what she had eaten.

In Sister Eileen's office, Sister Calista smiled on seeing her. "Are you packed? Do you have room in the second suitcase? We have to carry more safety pins, needles, and thread. Besides, we have boxes of coffee and tea, spices, forks and spoons, a ladle, a big sharp knife—"

"I will repack," Anna told her. "I will put all my things in the larger bag, then add light things to fill it. You can put all the heavy items in the smaller bag. It will make them both easier to handle. I will bring the smaller suitcase down to the office right away."

Sister Calista chuckled. "It doesn't matter how heavy each bag is. All along, men will be very willing to lift, move, or carry our luggage. They do it both out of respect for our status in life and to prove to whoever is looking that they are strong."

"What about money? Do we have enough for our food from Ohio until Seattle?"

"We already have two paid tickets. Nuns are given free meals. You'll see."

"Sister, you look happier than I've seen you in a long time."

"I've always dreamed of a long train trip. We'll see Chicago and the mid-western states. We'll have to cross the Rocky Mountains to get to Seattle. It must be a good thing for me. I have no achy bones and am not huffing and puffing today."

Back in her room, Anna repacked her small bag and found the black purse she'd used on her trip from Pennsylvania. Opening it, she found her lace handkerchief, still with the scent of tea roses tucked deep in its folds. It brought back memories of the times she and Julia had applied drops of perfume on their wrists as they pondered their life choices.

Her wallet still held some change. She added all the monies Sister Eileen had given her. Then she took the letters that she hadn't answered yet and placed them in the purse along with the blank stationery. She looked at her train ticket again. The first paper said, one adult transportation Cincinnati to Chicago, October 23, 1929. The second paper said, one adult transportation Chicago to Seattle, October 25, 1929.

It is really happening. I am taking a train across the north-western part of the United States. Then, the two of us will be transported aboard the Alexandria from Seattle to the Galapagos. I do not feel like the quiet nun. I feel like a pioneer, taking my companion Sister Calista on an adventure. God? May I be happy and excited?

She had little sleep that night.

SEVENTEEN

Long before sunrise, she heard Sister Calista whisper in her ear, "Anna, time to wake up. Get dressed and join me in Sister Eileen's office. And bring your suitcase."

Rubbing her eyes, Anna turned on the light and tiptoed down the hall. She shivered as she washed in cold water. It would take too long for the hot water to run up through the tap. Returning to her room, she placed her suitcase on the floor and stripped the bed. Through the open window, she took a last look at the darkened grounds. A teasing breeze lifted her veil. She closed the window, turned out the light, and carried her suitcase out of the room.

In the office, Sister Eileen asked, "Do you have your tickets? Your luggage? Your reading books? Your letters?"

The two travelers nodded.

"Let's pray together that it may be a positive year." They bowed their heads while Sister Eileen said, "God, You've chosen these two servants to leave the silence of Your sacred home. They've agreed to step back into Your outside world with healing hands and hearts. May Your light shine upon them, and may Your light shine from them. Let those they serve and heal know Your love through them. And now ladies, let me add my Irish Prayer. May the road rise up to meet you. May the wind be always at your back. May the sun shine even upon your face, the rain fall softly upon your fields. And until we next meet, may God hold you in the hollow of His hand."

The three women hugged then walked to the front door. As they left their home, a cold wind blew behind them. In the early morning darkness, a car stood with its lights on.

Sister Eileen said, "Mr. Davis is here. He's been hired to drive you to Cincinnati."

He tipped his hat and put their luggage in the trunk.

Sister Calista said, "Good morning, Mr. Davis. I'm Sister Calista, and my companion is Miss Anna."

"Please call me Mike." He held the door for them.

As she climbed into the car, she said, "My bones feel the drop in temperature. I'm going to get my camphor rub from my bag as soon as we make a stop."

"We haven't started yet. I'll get your bag from the trunk." He moved Sister's bag to her feet.

Anna said, "There are two heavy blankets folded on the seat. I'll tuck you in one." She proceeded to wrap the elder nun in the clean-smelling blue blanket. "How thoughtful of you to bring blankets for us."

"My wife, Mary, told me to bring those. She said, Mike, we can't send those two souls all that way without something to keep them warm. She thinks a lot of you ladies who live in this monastery."

"Do you work with the Sisters often?" Anna asked.

He started the engine. "I've helped out at the monastery for almost fifteen years."

"You tell your Mary how much I'm appreciating this blanket," Sister Calista said.

"When our son, Thomas, was a baby, he was very sick. The whole convent prayed for him every day. After a month, he got better and better. He's ten now and strong as a bull. She wants you to keep them two blankets for the trip. When you don't need 'em, you can give 'em to someone who can use 'em."

Anna said, "Thank you."

The car started to move. Turning, Anna and Sister gave a final wave to Sister Eileen who stood in front of the monastery.

The sun peeked over the hills. The mist on the low-lying ground thinned. Anna looked at their driver as the light increased. He was a big, dark-haired man. His hands were sturdy, skin hardened with scratches both fresh and healing. A discolored bruise on the knuckles of his right hand showed as he clutched the steering wheel. He wore a heavy gray shirt and had blue cloth suspenders over his shoulders. His clean-shaven face still had a dollop of soap under his right ear.

"We both appreciate you getting up so early to come and get us," Anna said. "We're warmer thanks to Mary's blanket."

"Mary will be happy that you could use them."

"What time is it now? How long will it take us to get to Cincinnati? We have no clocks."

"It is a little after six. We'll be on the road until nine or ten. Your train leaves at noon." He leaned forward as if concentrating on the road. "The fog is still tricky when the road dips. I know there is a big elm comin' up close to the road on the right. Last week, it looked like a skeleton, bare of almost all the leaves. The elm should remind us of Halloween, don't you think?"

Sister Calista whispered, "Anna, did we bring any warm water? I need to swallow my medicine."

Anna remembered the cloth-wrapped bundle Sister Eileen had handed her as they left her office. She said that it was *for the way*. She unfolded the cloth napkin at the top and found a glass container. "We have coffee here, but you'll have to drink from the jar. Can you do that?"

"I'll do my best." Sister opened a black-leather zippered purse, pulled out two pills, and place them in her mouth. She took the coffee and drank in slow deliberate gulps, then said, "Ahh."

Anna inhaled through her nose and felt the air go up toward the top of her head. Her ears popped, bringing tears to her eyes. It had the desired effect. It was, as Sister Felicia had taught her, the secret way to yawn without opening one's mouth. *Am I sleepy or just excited?*

"Sisters," Mike said, "I know you haven't been this far from the convent lately. Look to the right. There's a little lake there, and the mist rising from it looks as pretty as chimney smoke."

Both turned to see nature's autumn show.

God, I honor Your beauty in nature.

Mike's car had the same boxy shape as her father's. The upholstery was much more worn, but it was clean. Anna remembered her father telling her how much men loved to be complimented on their automobiles. "You must be proud of your vehicle. It is beautiful. My family in Pennsylvania has a Ford, too. We always had to wipe our feet before we got into it."

"Oh, yes, we all love this car."

When he didn't elaborate, Anna assumed that he was focused on the driving.

Sister sighed. "I just want to close my eyes and let the medicine take my pain away."

Anna patted Sister Calista's arm. Her skin felt chilled even through the heavy wool blanket and her wool habit. Taking off her own blanket, Anna added another layer over her companion.

"Oh, Anna, you really shouldn't," Sister Calista said in a quiet, sleepy mumble. Her eyes closed.

Anna pulled her rosary beads from her pocket. *Even through my habit, I feel a chill on my skin. I offer this to You, to remind me of the times You were cold. In a week or so, I will be very warm as we travel south. I will want to recall my goosebumps. I want to thank You.*

Mike said, "Miss Anna, did you notice all the bales of hay?"

"There are so many, I can't even count them."

"They all belong to the Griesinger farm. He has an automobile station here, too, coming up soon. We need to stop so I can get gasoline."

"Should I wake Sister Calista?"

"No, let her sleep. It'll only be for a few minutes."

Around the next bend in the road, a white, barn-sized building came into view. A gasoline pump stood next to the road with a driveway between the pump and the building. Mike pulled the car in beside the pump.

Anna saw a storefront similar to her father's. Wide glass windows were on either side of the center door. Each window had a display. The right one had grocery items including Morton Salt,

Quaker Oats Cereal, and Ivory Soap. The left showcase had Firestone Tires and cans of Pennzoil.

Mike got out of the car and walked to the store. When he opened the door, the bell jingled.

"Where are we?" asked Sister Calista.

"We stopped for gasoline," Anna answered.

"We need to go into the store. People want to see nuns. They want to say hello. They feel like God is showering blessings on them. It adds sunshine to their day."

"All right." Anna eased Sister Calista out of the car.

Inside the building, Mike was paying the man.

As the nuns entered the store, the store owner asked, "Are these two nuns with you?"

"Yes," Mike said.

"Well, take back your money. It's our honor to fill the tank for you. I'm Joseph Griesinger. Let me call my wife. She'll want to say hello." He turned away and called, "Jane, come and see this nice surprise."

A lady walked into the store from the back room. Her dark hair was pulled back in a chignon with wisps of curls escaping toward her face. She wore a dress of white with a print of pink flowers. The front of her white apron had brown spatters here and there. When she saw them, her eyes teared. "I've been praying today for a sick friend. Now I know she'll get better. Come, come, Sisters. Coffee and cookies for you in my kitchen."

She opened the door and led the nuns back. The smell of cinnamon greeted them. Rolls cooled on the table.

"Sit down, please." She stopped abruptly and said, "Oh, I forgot all my manners. I never had Sisters in my kitchen. Would you both like to wash up while I put out coffee?" She pointed towards a tiny washroom containing a sink and a toilet.

Sister Calista hurried in and closed the door.

Anna watched the petite woman move about her kitchen. She removed five cups, saucers, and plates from the cupboard. Then she placed rolls, cookies, milk, and sugar on the table. She poured coffee into the five cups.

Sister Calista returned. Anna went to the washroom. When she came out, the other four were sitting at the table, each with sweets on their plate. They stayed only a short time. After thank-yous were said all around, the Sisters washed their sugary hands and walked back to the car.

As she settled into the seat, Sister Calista said, "That was a good stop. People here in the Midwest feel more connected to God when they are touched by a religious."

"I'm glad we stopped to visit the Griesingers. How do you feel, Sister Calista?"

"Much better, my child."

"It smells like rain," Mike said. "Best be on our way."

Anna looked up. A few dark clouds marched across the horizon, ready to block out the sun. *Rain or snow?*

They drove in silence for a while.

At last, Mike pointed. "We are coming into Cincinnati. We'll be at the station in about half an hour. It is too bad you are leaving this year. A big new train station is planned for nineteen thirty. Maybe when you return, you'll both see it."

The car slowed. Buildings old and new lined the street. Rushing people could be seen pulling up their coat collars.

A newsboy held out a newspaper and called out, "Athletics win series four to one."

Another newsboy yelled, "Wall Street fears crash."

They pulled into the train station. Men dressed in suits scurried past them. A few women bent into the wind as they walked. They were bundled in thick coats and wearing hats and gloves. A family rushed by with a man carrying luggage and a woman with a babe in arms and a toddler at her side. All hurried towards an open area full of steam and loud noise.

As Mike parked the car, Anna folded the blankets into Sister's bag. Sister Calista and Anna stepped out into the windy morning. Sister's veil fluttered. Their skirts twisted around their legs. Mist struck Anna's face, and she remembered the smell and reach of the locomotive steam.

"Come, Sisters." Mike moved them away from the car.

Anna turned to pick up her small suitcases. But two men appeared. They were dressed in suits and carrying what was no doubt their own luggage. Plus, each carried the Sisters' bags.

They approached a man dressed in blue with shiny buttons on his jacket. He gathered their luggage onto a cart and thanked the two men who had helped. Mike took the cart then escorted the nuns into the old station.

This is the first time I am in public dressed in a habit. Men tip their hats, and women put on special smiles when they see us. What respect they show. I am humbled. If they only knew. Sister Calista's the one who deserves the respect. Me? Will I ever be good enough?

In the station, they wove their way to the front. Overhead lights blazed. The windows showed gathering storm clouds. Rows of wooden seats, worn smooth from years of use, were on the right and left. Men sat and glanced at newspapers. Women hushed children. The hall echoed with muted conversations. When the announcements began, everyone stopped to listen.

Mike shepherded them to the ticket window to receive confirmation of their departure time. He turned and said, "I'm anxious to get you two settled. The wind is picking up."

Another uniformed man appeared behind their luggage cart. Pushing the cart, he followed them into the smoky canyon. The noise of hot air expelling from the engines made conversation impossible.

Four trains stood in the station, all pointing in the same direction. Each had an engine followed by a coal car and the passenger cars. At the front opening of each passenger car, a hovering man dressed in a black uniform waited with a movable box. He assisted people entering the train.

Mike hurried them past unit after unit, trying to match their tickets to the numbers showing on the side of each car. The black cars were shiny with the steam from the engines. Through the gleaming windows, green shades were uniformly lowered to the middle. Finally, Mike made the match. He handed them their tickets. When the attendant for the car saw the nuns, a big smile crossed his face. He helped them up.

Another equally gracious man ushered them to their seats. "I'm Will. I'll put all your bags near. Let me assist you with any of your needs once we get on our way. I want you both to enjoy the trip and scenery."

Mike came up into the car and smiled. "You seem to be in good hands. I'll tell Sister Eileen you got aboard."

Sister Calista said, "God bless you."

Anna, not knowing how to thank him, put out her hand to shake. "God be with you and yours."

Sister took the window seat. Anna gazed out and watched Mike Davis leave the station. Instead of the predicted rain, snow flurries decorated the hats of the people still boarding.

The older nun said, "After several weeks of the convent silence, how do you feel about all of today's noise?"

"Since coming to the monastery, I have heard the songs of birds and nuns, both with an organ and without. The noise of farm machinery was in the background, along with the animals' moos and oinks. Still, today's noises shocked my ears."

Sister Calista gave a deep laugh. "Our island in the Pacific will be a wonderful reward, won't it?"

The train blew a whistle, and outside stairs were raised.

Someone in the doorway called out, "All aboard, next stop, Chicago."

Doors slammed. A conductor in the front of the car checked names and counted each passenger.

We are on our way. Thanks be to God.

EIGHTEEN

Sister Calista wriggled in her seat as the train inched ahead. "Anna, can you put something soft behind my back?"

Anna searched for a cushion to make the nun comfortable.

The porter, Will, appeared beside her. "Sister, do you need something?"

"A pillow for my companion, please."

"Of course." He hurried away, opened a wooden door near the car entrance, and pulled out two pillows.

This busy man looks to be about fifty years old. He has dark skin, neatly combed hair, and a gentle face. His blue uniform, nicely pressed, has gold-tone buttons. He should be home sitting on a porch in a rocking chair watching the world go by.

The train slowed then picked up speed then slowed again as if it were an old lady unsteady after a long pause.

Will advanced with the dexterity of a tightrope artist. He offered the two bolsters. "This one is old, soft, and can be folded or bent. It fits into small places. This other one is new, big, and still smells like a meadow."

"Can we have both?"

"Certainly, Sister."

She smiled. "Thank you."

He nodded and moved away to serve other passengers.

Sister Calista sighed.

Anna turned. "I'll tuck the small one—"

"Oh, just hurry. My back aches. I need to take a nap."

Anna nodded. *Yes, I could use the quiet. Do take a nap.* She tucked, puffed, and adjusted the pillows. She blessed Mike for his gift of blankets as she laid one across Sister Calista's knees.

The older nun closed her eyes.

Anna relaxed into the thick upholstered seat. Almost all of the red cloth chairs were filled. Each row had two seats on the right and two more on the left. Sister Calista had claimed the one nearest the window. Flashes of sunlight crossed her face.

Anna got up to pull down the shade.

Will appeared at her side. "Sister, my job is to help you. I can adjust that."

"Oh, Will, I'm usually the doer. But we both have to follow rules, I know. Have you been doing this job for a long time?" She gushed, anxious to use her renewed permission to speak.

He positioned the shade. "Yes, Ma'am. I have been doing this job for many years."

"I see you wear a wedding ring. Your family must miss you. Do you and your wife have any children?"

"We have two sons, two daughters, and five grandchildren. My children are all decent, hard-working people, and we are proud of them."

Again, Will was called away.

The smooth cadence of the wheels relaxed her. The smell of damp wool coats filled the air. They mixed with the lemon oil on the polished wood. *Someone here works as diligently as in the convent making this dark wood on the walls gleam.* The snow disappeared as they rolled through Ohio toward Indiana. Outside, fields rested in the October sun.

She opened her purse with anticipated pleasure. Finally, *I have time to read Julia's letter.* The envelope had Julia's familiar handwriting. Holding it in her hand, she smiled as she thought of her friend. *If Julia had the extra money, she would be the first to use colored stationery. And it would be pink.* Anna opened the letter.

October 12, 1929
Dear Anna,
My greetings and blessings to you and your fellow Sisters.

Thank you for the prayers I know you send to Heaven for me.

By the time you read this (which will be October of 1930) I'll be a mother. For the sake of the baby, I'm being brave.

Forgive my blasphemy, but having both my husband and my best friend taken from me at almost the same time is one of God's dirty tricks. Can I say that? I just did.

Bashia is taking her godmother role seriously. She and I talk once a week. Unlike you and me, she speaks her mind on everything. She tells me she wants to be a lawyer.

I'm back at work at the Craig ranch. I'm comfortable here. I help with the children. I am told I'll have a job here as long as I want. After having the baby and a rest, I'll return and bring the baby with me.

There has been an interesting development. When I went to the Craig's house last week, Mr. and Mrs. Craig wanted to talk to me. They asked if my parents could be there. I was so afraid I'd done something wrong. I recall thinking I should have asked Bashia, the lawyer-to-be, to come with me.

They wanted to speak to me about the day of the accident and why Adam had left his tree cutting to ride a horse that day. Mr. and Mrs. Craig learned the answers to our questions. It seems their daughter, Donna, only nine, always had a sense of humor. She decided to have Anthony, the twelve-year-old, hide in her room. Then, she told Adam that Anthony had fallen into the creek and was hanging onto a thin branch. She begged Adam to get down there to the water and rescue him.

You know the rest. My husband died. Not almost. Really died. Probably my one and only chance of a wonderful married life. Gone. My child will never know my beloved Adam. His smile. His wisdom. His thoughtfulness.

They wanted to tell my family and me. We were heartbroken. It was a sad and needless accident. I am still crying about it. Donna and Anthony are repentant, and she has lost that sparkle of youth in her eyes. What a hard lesson for all of us. The Craigs take full responsibility for it. They have given me a gift of cash as a settlement. I am holding the money in that safe place only you and I know about. It seems everyone is nervous about money right now.

I feel the baby moving. It feels like butterflies. Pray for a healthy child for me. I'll write again in a few months.

Love, Julia

Anna had trouble getting the letter back into the envelope because of tear-filled eyes. It felt like a piece of her heart had cracked. She pulled out her white cotton handkerchief and dried her cheeks. *And we say Thy will be done. I am pleased that she hid the money. It will be safe for the baby.* She closed her eyes.

She awoke with a start. The train was slowing down.

Sister Calista was awake. "We are coming to our only stop. Didn't you hear the announcement? I need to wash my face. Where's the washroom?" She got up.

Will came and helped her down the aisle.

The train inched forward, and the station came into view. A sign with the words *Indianapolis, Indiana*, hung on the skinny roof covering the walkway.

The engine stopped with a jolt. Everyone's head bobbed. Doors opened. New voices echoed as more passengers came aboard.

Somewhere in the surrounding conversations, Anna heard, "We'll be stopping for an hour."

Sister Calista returned. Anna gazed out the window as folks boarded. A few well-dressed, laughing children almost tumbled up the aisle as they hurried to their seats. Will hurried with pillows, raised and lowered window shades, and answered questions. Impatient steam pulsed from the engine. There came the special staccato toot of the engine and a call of "All Aboard." This time, Anna was prepared for the irregular rhythm of the starting train.

As Will made his way past them, he stopped and said, "Dinner for you two is in an hour, Sisters. I'll take you to the dining car first so you can choose seats."

Sister Calista said, "Thank you, sir." Turning to the window, she said, "I love to see the midwestern countryside. As I told you, I once lived on a farm. October is such a calm time for the soil. The ground is at rest, but the workers are busy with their winter chores. They clean, oil, replace and protect their machinery and tools before the snow comes." She yawned. "What will you do, dear, for the next hour?"

"I need to write a letter to my friend, Julia. I was the maid of honor at her wedding this summer. A few weeks later, her husband died in an accident. She is now expecting a baby, and she had plenty to tell me in her letter."

Sister Calista nodded and continued to monitor the countryside. After a time, her eyelids drooped, and she nodded. Then her head bobbed up and her eyes scanned Anna's face as if to see if Anna noticed. With a smile, Anna found her pen, ink, and stationery. She addressed the envelope and placed a stamp on it. *Won't Julia be surprised to hear my news?*

October 24, 1929
Dear Julia,
I wish you God's blessings. I pray for you every day since, to me, you are part of my family.

Your letter made me homesick and sad. I am so proud of you. We are not little girls anymore. Both of us are doing new things.

Today I am on a train looking at the farmland of Indiana. The train will take my companion, Sister Calista, and me to Chicago. There, the passenger car will be attached to a different engine which is going to Seattle. Next, we will board a ship and go to an island in the Galapagos to stay for a year. We will assist Doctor Ralph Graumann, who needs females with some medical background to help him.

What a long story. Perhaps by now, Bashia has told you some of it. My vocation is questionable. I want to talk, sing, and laugh. Why did I think a silent cloister was an answer? I will have a year to figure it out. I am still planning to be a nun, but

I've had a hard time adapting.

I do not think I will get any mail in the next year, but your letters will be in Kentucky waiting for me, so do write.

Love, Anna

P.S. My traveling companion, Sister Calista, reminds me of my Aunt Caroline.

The P.S. had added spice to the note. Julia and Anna visited Aunt Caroline every month or two. She was prim, proper, and kept a spotless home. She was quick to correct any bad manners in man, woman, child, or beast. She also passed gas quite frequently, yet never admitted she was the culprit.

Will came and ushered the nuns into the dining car. Sister Calista took the seat facing forward, leaving Anna to sit in the opposite direction. Glasses of water with ice were already on the table along with white napkins with the same design as the tablecloths. Shining silverware lay in place. Pats of butter were in the center of the table.

A slim man in an immaculate white bib apron and tall white hat greeted them. "My name is Joshua. I'm the chef. Do you Sisters have a favorite dish I can fix for you?"

Sister Calista said, "I'd like white meat chicken, please."

Anna said, "Surprise me, Joshua. You must be an excellent cook to have this job. I worked as a waitress before entering the convent. I know good cooks are jewels in the crown of this business."

"Very well." He smiled and walked toward the galley compartment. As the door opened, the smell of fried onions and garlic spread through the room.

The chime of a bell echoed in the next car—one high note and one low. The porter called out, "Dinner is served."

Diners thronged into the room. The waiter asked if the nuns were willing to share their table with two ladies.

Before Sister Calista could reply, Anna said, "We'd love it."

Their table partners joined them.

The elder of the two newcomers led the conversation. "Oh,

Sisters, pray for me. My companion, Nola, and I are headed to wicked San Francisco where money and women are, shall we say, no, I can't say it." She took a breath, expanding her bosom. "I'm Mrs. Powler, a poor widow. This is Nola Judge. She wants to see the United States, so we came from Pittsburgh. We've been riding for days." The *poor* widow had brilliant stones on her fingers and around her neck. She adjusted her rings and placed her hands on the table, where the sun caught the facets of the jewels and reflected mirrors of color on the walls of the dining room. Her dress, a sapphire blue creation, was the style Anna had only seen in the preview books that Mrs. Robinson, her dressmaking former employer, had for display and ideas.

Nola nodded and gave a shy smile. But although her lips smiled, her eyes were dull. She gave a tiny throat-clearing kind of a cough and said, "How do you do?"

She looks about my age. She sounds like the cousins and friends we met in Pittsburgh, living in the smoky city. I heard so many of them do a frequent clearing of the throat before speaking.

Anna smiled at Nola, who sat across from her next to Sister Calista. Nola wore no jewelry on her clothes or her fingers. She was dressed in brown monotones. Her plain, high-necked shirt had a rounded collar. Her dark blonde hair was pulled back into a bun, but a few strands escaped, surrounding her face. The girl, for whatever reason, pulled, tugged, and twisted the hair around her cheeks every few minutes. Almost as if she were trying to hide.

Seated next to Anna, the widow fidgeted in her seat. "How can one ride backward and eat? Nola, change seats with me."

Nola dropped her napkin to the floor as she maneuvered to the new seat. With a start, Anna realized Nola was pregnant. The girl sat beside Anna, raised her napkin to her face, and coughed.

Mrs. Powler now faced forward and surveyed the occupants at nearby tables with undisguised curiosity.

Mushroom soup served with hot bread was the first course.

It was followed by Waldorf Salad. The cubed apples and walnuts reminded Anna of a dish she served while waitressing in Petroleum City.

Mrs. Powler gestured while eating, and the sunshine again sparkled off the stones in her rings.

Entrees were served. Sister Calista and Nola ate chicken breast. Anna and Mrs. Powler had the chef's choice—cubed beef, surrounded by green and yellow vegetables with quarters of new potatoes peeking out. Anna recognized rosemary and thyme spices.

Chef Joshua came to the table.

Anna said, "Only the sin of gluttony stops me from eating another serving."

He chuckled and went on to visit other diners.

Baked apples with a hint of cinnamon were a refreshing dessert. Then it was time to leave. They wished Mrs. Powler and Nola a good trip as they were led to their passenger car.

Walking back, Anna recalled that at no time had anyone asked the nuns for payment. Although, Mrs. Powler had given money to a waiter.

Will met them and escorted them back to their seats. He explained the next part of their journey. "I'm moving all passengers going to Seattle to the Pullman sleeping cars. I'll make up your berths in the sleepers. When we get to Chicago, it will be linked to another train taking you further west."

Anna smiled. "May I give you a letter to mail from Chicago?"

"Of course," he said.

NINETEEN

A s the train moved toward Chicago, they were ushered to a compartment which had two benches made up as beds and a door closing it from the hall.

Sister Calista said, "Oh, this is a cozy nook, isn't it?"

Anna nodded. Above were plenty of lights. A shelf held extra pillows and their luggage, although a few of their heavier boxes remained on the floor.

"I need to use the washroom." Sister Calista opened the door and stepped out.

Anna used the few minutes alone to wonder about Nola Judge and Mrs. Powler. *Would they ever meet again?*

When Sister Calista returned, she said, "Anna, we'll be sharing quarters for the next year. Only God has seen me naked. I'll ask you to turn your head while I change my clothes."

"As you wish," Anna said. *I wonder if God changed your diapers. Is this a preview of my life? This might be a very long year. Should I escape from this adventure in Chicago? No, I am an adult. Every quest has some risk.*

Sister shuffled around in the room. "My German family had very high standards of cleanliness and order. My surroundings are always neat and tidy."

At that, Anna took a washcloth, towel, soap, and her toothbrush and left for the washroom.

A man met her in the hall. His glistening smile brightened his dark face. "Hello, Sister. I'm Henry, and I will be your porter until Seattle. Need to brush your teeth?"

"Yes, I—"

Just then, the train shimmied.

He held her elbow as he steadied her walk. "Right this way. Easy does it." He ushered her to the washroom.

She freshened up then exited back into the hall.

Again, Henry walked with her. "Let me warn you. When we get to Chicago, it can be startling. It will be about midnight. The train will stop. This compartment will move back and forth. It will jolt. As we maneuver to disconnect some cars and make new connections, this car will get pulled from one side of the yard to the other. I'll be watching to be sure we are in the right place. When we start up again, we will be going directly west. Next stop, Omaha, Nebraska. If you don't sleep through it, peek out the window. It's fun to watch."

"Thank you, Henry. I should write about this in my journal."

When they reached her compartment, Anna knocked before opening the door as a courtesy to her traveling companion.

"Come in, Anna," Sister called.

She entered smiling. "Sister, our porter, Henry, told me about our car hitch and unhitch in the train yard in Chicago."

Sister Calista gave a heavy sigh. "I'm tired. I'll be turning out the lights."

Anna said, "I had planned to read for a while."

Sister Calista let out a long, loud breath. "I suppose." She adjusted her pillows, her face illuminated by the ceiling light. "Well, we don't have to be awake at any special time. It could be pleasant to read a while. This is an adventure, and my pain medicine is working."

Anna asked, "How are we going to store your medication when we get to the island?"

"Doctor Graumann never mentioned that. My thoughts would be to store it in a metal box. That could keep it dry. Would it work for heat, too? The three of us will figure it out when we get there, I imagine."

They each opened books. Sister Calista read a worn Bible. Anna read one on the lives of the saints. It was written in Polish, which gave her a sense of comfort and warmth. In the ensuing silence, Anna heard sobs from the next compartment.

A voice said, "Nola, that's enough. This can't be changed."

Was that Mrs. Powler's voice? It became quiet next door.

The smooth clickety-click of the tracks soon lulled Anna to sleep. She felt a bump and awoke with a start. Groggily, she reached for her bedroom nightstand. There was none. Opening her eyes, she remembered being aboard the train. *The porter. What was his name? Henry cautioned me about the rail yard frolics. If this is midnight, we must be in Chicago. Unfortunately, neither of us has a watch.* She sat up, moved to the window, and peered around the window blind.

The Chicago rail yard ballet entertained her. Glide forward. Pause. A backward thrust. A plunge ahead. Depending on direction, she was bathed in moonlight or in total darkness. The dance lasted quite a while. A mighty thrust completed the routine. A rhythmic buildup of power and speed set them in their new direction.

In the morning at breakfast, Anna heard snippets of conversation.

One woman said, "I knew about the car switching, of course. But, I was awakened from a sound sleep, and it was scary."

A man at the next table stirred his coffee and looked up at his wife. "Darling, why didn't you wake me? We might have enjoyed the moment together."

Anna said to Sister, "I didn't know what to expect next. It was thrilling."

"Did I tell you my brother worked as an engineer on a small railroad in Indiana?" Sister Calista said. "He was always trying to teach me what the various cadences in the whistles and toots meant. A certain toot means we leave in five minutes. A different signal is for here we go."

"Does he still work there?" Anna asked.

"I don't know. I don't hear much from my family," she said with a defensive tone. "They are proud of me, I'm sure, but busy with their own lives."

Their conversation was interrupted by the arrival of Nola and

Mrs. Powler. Nola's eyes were red, and her face was pale. Mrs. Powler looked robust.

"Sisters, did you see all those poor boys sitting in the passenger cars with tags around their necks? They are part of the orphan train," Mrs. Powler said as she sat across from them.

"I've read about them. Omaha and west are their destinations, I understand," Anna said.

Mrs. Powler said, "It's supposed to be a better life for them."

"At least on the train, they'll have more food than they did in New York City," Sister Calista said.

"Don't talk about food." Nola cleared her throat with a tiny cough as she held onto the side of the breakfast table. Her breakfast order was a cup of hot tea and a soda cracker. She drank a few sips of tea. The soda cracker sat untouched on her plate. She twisted her hair into a curl beside her face. Even her timid smile was missing.

"Plans for the morning?" asked Anna.

Mrs. Powler and Nola remained mum.

"I will be taking a rest. And you, Anna?" Sister Calista said.

"I have to answer one more letter."

Back in the room, Sister Calista settled into a corner and closed her eyes.

Anna unsealed the envelope from Robert. *This is strange. How did his letter even get to me? It was supposed to be only mail from Tata, Leon, Bashia, and Julia.*

October 15, 1929

Dear Anna,

By the time you read this next year, I'll be a lawyer. I've applied for positions as far away as New York State and as close as right here in Pittsburgh.

When you write back, and I know you will, you can use this address. It is my parents' home. They'll get the letter to me.

The first time I saw you on that Saturday in August, you were walking down the aisle before the bride. I can't remember how Julia looked, but YOU. You looked poised and beautiful. I thought you probably would be stuck up. Then I met you, the best polka dancer in Petroleum City. You, with that snap of life and your sense of humor. You, full of composure and joy. I plan to get to know you better.

Yes, I know you are in the convent. Be there. Pray for us.

I still have another year of hard study. I need to do this and do it well for the two of us. I am sure I can still change your mind.

I find comfort in knowing you are safe in the company of all the holy nuns.

You will hear from me again and again.

Sincerely, Robert

Anna folded the paper. *I am glad Sister Calista is napping. I must be blushing. I do not think anyone should feel this way about me, a nun. I need to answer this letter now.*

October 25, 1929

Dear Robert,

My life is taking a new course. I am going to the Galapagos Islands for a year with another nun, Sister Calista. We will be helping a doctor there give medical care.

Your path through law school has to be successful. I hear your determination. Good luck.

Sincerely, Anna Wiosnec

She sealed the envelope.

From the next compartment, she heard muffled cries, occasional moans, and Nola's familiar cough. "It hurts. I think I'm bleeding. I'm afraid."

Mrs. Powler replied, "What a time and place you picked. Nola, Nola, I don't know what my son, Dennis, saw in you. Yes, you're bleeding. We need a doctor."

"Never mind. I only need a little rest."

"What kind of a woman do you think I am? I'll ask the porter to find a doctor."

The door opened and closed. Footsteps sounded in the hall.

"Henry, where are you?" Mrs. Powler called over the clickety-clack of the train.

Anna's curiosity was piqued. *I could pretend to be looking for Henry to give him my letter for posting. No, I will sit here quietly, read my prayer book, and add Nola to the list of people I have in my prayers.*

Henry's voice said, "What do you need, Mrs. Powler?"

More footsteps. Doors opened and closed. Voices murmured. Anna could not hear the conversation. *Nosey, nosey. This is not my concern. Yet, the Bible says I am my brother's keeper.*

A groan came from Nola's room.

Henry said, "Oh, Ma'am. We need to find a doctor."

The door banged. Footsteps faded.

There was a knock on their door. Sister Calista stirred in her sleep, repositioned her pillow, and snuggled under her blanket.

Anna called, "Who's there?"

"Mrs. Stella Powler. I need a little medical help in my room."

Suddenly, Sister was fully awake. "Of course, my dear." She wiggled her shoulders and stretched her legs as she unfolded from her cozy nest. As she stood, she touched the top of her veil with each hand and pressed it smooth, running each thumb down the inside of the cloth to form sharp creases. She walked to the door, then turned to Anna. "Are you coming?"

Nothing could stop me. She tucked her letter into her prayer book and followed Sister Calista.

Mrs. Powler led the nuns into her room. Nola lay panting and sweating beneath a wrinkled bed sheet. Her long, wavy hair was moist and matted. The freckles on her face and arms were prominent against her pale skin.

Sister Calista asked, "Child, what is wrong?"

Nola looked puzzled. "It feels like something is squeezing my belly real hard. Should I be bleeding?"

Mrs. Powler said, "Nola is pregnant. The porter is looking for a doctor."

Sister Calista said, "My dear, turn on your side so I can see."

Nola started to roll to the right, looked confused, then said, "That's the wrong way." She moved to her left.

A pool of blood stained the linen and newspapers under Nola's naked buttocks. The frightened girl trembled.

I have never seen a grown woman naked before. I did want to know what was happening, but I did not want to see this. What am I doing here? I could be back in Pennsylvania helping Tata in the store. I must not act shocked. But I am. I must help her, even if it is only holding her hand.

"Let me wash." Sister Calista rolled up her sleeves and walked out of the room.

Nola grunted and twisted onto her back. She looked up at Anna. "Something slipped out. I'm scared. What is happening?"

Poor Nola. She is so afraid, she can hardly move. Anna gently unfolded the sheet. There between Nola's legs, she saw the fetus. *I have seen too much today. Blood is still coming out. Where is Sister Calista?*

Sister Calista walked in. She stood beside Anna, looked down, and whispered, "Oh, my dear. You just lost the baby. How sad for you." She picked up a glass of water and poured a trickle over the lifeless, four-inch-long baby. "I baptize you in the name of the Father, and of the Son, and of the Holy Ghost. Amen."

Nola cried, "What happened? Did I have the baby?"

Henry called out as he knocked, "Mrs. Powler, I can't find a doctor anywhere."

"The Sisters from the next compartment are helping us. Thank you, Henry."

At least one of us is helping. I have seen a broken arm and a gash on the head, but this is a shock to my senses.

Mrs. Powler looked at the nuns. "Now what?"

Sister Calista leaned and kneaded Nola's belly. She looked at Anna. "You watched me. Now, you take over."

Anna massaged Nola's belly.

Sister Calista put her hands over Anna's and forced them down. "You need pressure. Make nice little circles right under the belly button. We are trying to help her womb do its job."

Anna nodded.

Nola said, "I'm glad my baby's all right. Can I see her? I made her a cloth doll. It's in my suitcase. She'll like to look at it."

Sister Calista shook her head. "Your baby is not fine. When you felt something come out, it was the dead baby. It's called a miscarriage."

"No. I still feel something moving in there. It still might be the baby. It still is kicking."

Anna sat in front of Nola and held her hand. "Nola, look at me." With tears in her eyes, she whispered, "I am so sorry. You delivered the baby already. It was not alive. Sometimes a woman loses a baby, and it is nobody's fault."

Sister Calista moved Anna's hands back to Nola's abdomen. "Rub."

Tears rolled out of Nola's eyes, and with short gulps of breath, she muttered, "Oh," and progressed to a loud mournful "Oh, oh, oh." She looked at each woman in turn as if waiting for anyone to deny the loss. Crossing her arms, Nola continued her mournful "Oh, oh, oh" chant. Soon her nose filled.

Anna handed her a handkerchief.

Between the "Oh, oh, oh" and her own little cough, she blew her nose again and again. Then she grimaced and said, "Whoops, there's something going on again. It feels wet down there. Why did I make this happen?"

Sister Calista bustled over. "Don't worry. This is normal. This is what I was waiting for. It's called the afterbirth. It needed to come out so you can heal."

She twisted her hair. "I don't want to be here. Nobody told me about this part."

"Now, child, it is finished. We have to massage for a time and be sure you stopped bleeding," Sister Calista said.

Anna rubbed Nola's belly. "I feel a hard knot in here, about the size of a baseball."

Sister Calista nodded. "Amazing how quickly a young healthy body starts to recover. That is the uterus moving back to its normal size. It takes some rubbing for the first day to help the womb to keep healing."

Mrs. Powler looked at her wristwatch. "Now that the emergency is over, I'm ready for lunch."

Sister Calista said to Mrs. Powler, "Anna will massage for fifteen more minutes. Then you can take over. If there's no more bleeding, we'll stop rubbing, but there is a need to keep checking for the rest of the day."

"Tell me again what happened," Nola said.

"You lost the baby. When you're up to it, Henry will help us clean this room." Sister checked Anna's massage technique.

"I can't stand the smell in here." Mrs. Powler picked up her purse. "I'm going to the dining car. You two get things cleaned up. I'll pay you, of course. And, I'll expect your silence."

Anna asked, "You'll not be massaging?"

"You do it." She walked out the door.

Sister Calista asked, "Any bleeding now?"

"No," said Anna.

"I don't know what will happen to me without my baby," Nola whispered, looking at them through red-rimmed eyes. "I didn't do nothing bad. I need my baby. I ruined everything. I couldn't even take care of a tiny baby. Our baby was the plan for my future."

"You'll need to get bathed," Sister Calista said. "I'll find Henry and tell him what we need." She left.

"I need to massage for fifteen minutes." Anna continued rubbing.

"I got a watch." Nola opened the clasp on a dainty leather band. "I want you to have it."

"But I—"

"Please. I got little enough to give you for all you're doing. For all you've done."

Anna paused to look at the wristwatch. "I don't remember you wearing this yesterday."

"I was wearing this today to think of Dennis, the father of my baby." With a clenched fist, she muffled a sob. She squeezed her eyes closed and shook her head. "This will change things. It is why we came on this trip."

"It's a lovely watch," Anna said.

"It was from Dennis. There's words on the back. It says *To N from D*. When he gave it to me, he said it meant from one eNd to the other enD, or forever. But he didn't even come to see us off when the train left Pittsburgh. It *is* the end."

"What a sad story."

"I got to think about all these things. I don't know what'll happen."

"So, the trip was because of the pregnancy?"

"According to Mrs. Powler, this was an inconvenient thing that happened to her son and me. He's still in college. I met him at work. I was just a store clerk, but now I'm nothing. My family doesn't know about this baby. Now, they won't ever know. But I will always remember. It makes me want to cry and cry. I feel like my heart is breaking."

Sister Calista knocked then came into the room with Henry. They carried clean linen, water, basin, and towels.

"Come back later, Henry, please. Thank you for all your help." Sister Calista waited while he quietly closed the door. "Now, we'll make you clean and comfortable."

They washed her face, arms, and torso, and changed her clothes.

All the while, Sister Calista spoke in a quiet voice. "This is a sad event for you. I'm sure it's a day you'll never forget. A new baby is in Heaven. For that we are grateful. Why this happened, we'll never know. But remember that when one door closes, another opens. You act like you're alone in this world, but that isn't true. There must be a kind heart in Mrs. Powler. She'll take care of you. Just rest for a few days. Then decide what to do."

They moved Nola to a seat on the other side of the room and gathered the soiled linen.

Sister Calista said, "A little bleeding like a normal menstrual period will happen for a few days. But, you need to massage your belly at least once an hour until tomorrow."

180

"You'll need the watch again." Anna placed the watch on Nola's wrist.

"But I wanted—"

"I can't accept such a gift, but I will always remember your generosity."

Nola stroked the watch and sniffled.

Anna combed Nola's damp hair and found a piece of pink ribbon to wind around a few of the curls. *Sister Calista is very kind. She is a healing woman. I am glad I was here to learn and to help.*

After making Nola comfortable, they wiped and cleaned the room.

"We're ready for Henry." Sister Calista looked out the door.

Henry must have been waiting nearby because he appeared immediately. He took all the soiled articles and left.

Nola tried to get up. "I'm still shaky."

"At least, you are not as pale," Anna said.

"I'm weak but no pain." She swiped her face with the back of her hand.

"I'll get you something to eat." Sister Calista walked out the door.

A heavy silence filled the room.

Anna asked, "Would you like us to pray for your baby?"

Nola nodded.

"Does the baby have a name?"

"It's a girl," Nola blurted. "I know it must be. I want to name her Henrietta in honor of our porter who's been so kind to me."

They bowed their heads.

Anna said, "Dear God, a new little saint is in Heaven today. We believe Henrietta is beside You. Peace to the baby and peace on Earth to the mother, Nola. Our Father who—"

The door opened. Sister Calista entered carrying napkins. Henry had tea and crackers. Mrs. Powler entered the room, looked around, and nodded.

Henry left. Chimes sounded one high note and one low. Henry called, "Lunch is served."

"Go." Nola gazed out the window. "I'll be fine here. I can look out at the farms passing by. It's pretty."

"I will stay here," Anna said.

"I think Henry will deliver lunch to this room if we ask," Sister Calista said.

Mrs. Powler said, "Sister Cala... whatever. Let me treat you to lunch today. I was unable to get even a bite of food before because they said it was too early for service. Let us go now."

The nun nodded, and the two left the car.

Anna decided to massage some more. "I want to be sure, my friend, that you are much better. It feels like it has been forever since I have had a visit with someone my age. I have heard that sometimes, people who might never again see each other have long deep conversations. Do you want to do that?"

"Yes, I sure do. I haven't been able to tell anyone about this baby except the Powler family." She closed her eyes for a few seconds and shook her head. "My friends think Mrs. Powler is such a nice lady. To take me on a cross-country trip. If they only knew it's because of the baby. I'm scared of her, and what she'll do next. I can only wait and see, cross my fingers, and hope for the best." She began to sob.

Anna pulled Nola into her arms. "I'm sure you'll feel better after you get a good night's sleep."

Nola wiped her eyes. "My father always told me to stick with my own kind. He said that a goose belongs with other gooses, not with chickens. My family made me quit school. As long as I could read and sign my name, my family thought I had enough schooling." She took a big gulp of water. "As far as reading books, my mother told me that book stuff gave me crazy ideas. We needed the money for groceries and things, and what was I learning in school, anyway? They told me to go and find a job. Our neighbor worked at Macy's moving and unpacking boxes and heard about them needing one more clerk. I ran downtown as fast as I could, dressed in my Sunday blouse and skirt. I got the job because I'm good at numbers. I was so lucky to find a job right away."

"You must be pretty smart because there was only one job. Right? And you got it."

"Yeah, I am smart in arithmetic, but not with fellas."

A knock sounded on the door. Henry said, "Who in this room could eat some chicken noodle soup, still steaming hot?"

Anna opened the door.

He carried in a tray with covers of shiny metal on the plates and said, "The sandwiches are ham and cheese on fresh bread. For dessert, there is chocolate pudding and a few cookies."

Nola sat straighter. "Thank you."

They rearranged the room for dining.

Henry chuckled. "I forgot the drinks."

"Milk would work for both of us, I think," Anna said.

Henry left, whistling a happy tune.

Nola uncovered the plates. She picked up a spoon and sipped the soup. "This tastes so good." She ate a bit more. "I wanted to make a nice marriage. There's no money in my family. My brother, Frank, is only nine years old and real smart with school things. If I married somebody rich, I could help Frank to go to college, not to the steel mills. It is blazing hot, and there are lots of bad accidents."

I pray that something good comes from today's sadness. Lord, you came again and showed me the way. I can help with the sick. I can listen to people unburden a heavy heart. It feels good to help. Please keep leading me, and I will follow.

Nola smiled. "Let me tell you how I met Dennis. I was working at Macy's. I usually work on the second floor, ladies clothing. But I got moved to jewelry. I was with the necklaces and those pin things for dresses. I think they're braches."

"You mean broaches?"

"That's what I said, didn't I?"

"Yes, you did."

"Anyway, I was so happy to be in jewelry. We got paid a commission. It's easier there, too. In the ladies' department, we got to help the lady put on the clothes. Then after they try them on, the dressing area is a mess. The clerk has to clean it up, rehang every single dress, and put it back on the right rack."

Anna leaned forward and nodded.

"So, there was a big sale. Out of the blue, instead of only ladies at the necklace counter, here comes this cute guy. He was looking for a present for his mother. The rest is history. But it's bad history now. I can figure it out. I am smart."

"Yes, you are."

All conversation paused as they pounced on the cookies and pudding.

Mrs. Powler entered the room. "We'll be fine in here now. You may leave."

"Get some rest." Anna hugged Nola and left.

When she got to her own room, she picked up her completed letter, found Henry, and asked, "Could you post this for me?"

"I'll be sure to do that. We'll be in Omaha in a few hours."

Anna returned to sit quietly and reflect. *Your hand brought us here today. Now, I feel so good about my choices.*

After a time, she was aware of the train slowing down. "Omaha, Nebraska," was announced.

When the train stopped, Anna and Sister Calista watched the people coming and going outside. To their surprise, Nola, Mrs. Powler, and lots of shiny luggage and one beat up old bag passed outside their window going toward the terminal.

TWENTY

As Nola and Mrs. Powler walked toward the train station in Omaha, Sister Calista said, "I can't believe this. What could have happened? How could Henry have allowed those two to leave? I'm furious."

Anna said, "Maybe—"

"Forget the maybe. Was Nola too much trouble for him? Isn't it his job to take care of his charges? I thought he was so nice."

Anna shook her head.

"The railroad should scrutinize their help. How long has he been doing this job?"

Anna shrugged.

At dinnertime, Sister Calista and Anna had no dinner partners. They smiled graciously at other passengers. Two little boys from a nearby table played peek-a-boo with Anna behind their high-backed chairs.

Their mother came over to the table and said, "My boys are not disturbing you, are they?"

"No, it's good to see happy children," Anna said.

"It will be a fond memory for them of playing a game with nuns. My husband, sitting there at our table," she gestured toward a man in a dark suit, "is so busy with that Omaha newspaper. He is not enjoying our boys. The events of the stock market have everyone on edge. He says we will always remember October 1929, as the beginning of financial hard times."

After dinner, they passed Henry on the way back to their room.

He smiled. "Good evening."

Anna said, "Good evening, Henry."

Sister Calista kept her eyes straight ahead and proceeded to the room. It had been converted to sleep. The Omaha newspaper had been placed on their tiny table.

Anna said, "I haven't seen a newspaper since I left Petroleum City. This one is larger than *The Derrick,* which was delivered to our home every day. I love the smell of the paper. Or maybe it is the ink. It smells like moist cloth. It will be fun glancing at it after prayers."

She tried to read her prayer book, then said some Hail Mary's for Nola.

Sister Calista said, "I'm hurt. I'm disturbed. That poor girl. Is there no justice in this world?"

"Earlier today, Nola and I said prayers for her baby. She decided it was a girl and even named her Henrietta in honor of our porter because he'd been so kind to her. I think it brought her peace."

"That makes this even worse. Like Judas. He betrayed her," Sister Calista said.

"I wonder if Henry will tell us what happened."

"Whatever could he say to make it better? And he had the nerve to smile at us in the hall. I am livid. I won't get a lick of sleep tonight worrying about that girl."

"Can I go and get you a cup of tea?"

"From him? No. He might put poison in it."

"Oh, Sister Calista, he can't be that bad."

Anna watched the brilliant rosy blush of the sunset. *God, how could this disturbing thing have happened to a needy person such as Nola? She was so weary when I last saw her.* Anna opened her prayer book, feeling the need for divine intervention. Yet, when she opened it, the page was the book of Matthew, *Święty Mateusz,* Chapter 22. It began with the king who arranged a wedding for his son. *How could that fit in? Nola may have been thinking wedding, but Dennis?*

She turned back to Sister Calista with her questions. However, the older nun, still dressed in her day clothes, had her eyes closed. An occasional soft snore rippled out her mouth. *I have not heard her snore before. She must be extra tired to-night. She had a busy day.*

Anna opened the Polish Bible she had inherited from Sister Hedwig, enjoying the Polish comfort. *I wish Sister Hedwig had underlined a few words. I could feel more of her. But, we have all been taught not to damage a book. A bookmark or two would have been nice. Why don't I shake it a little, then open both the front and back cover, and see where it opens, and find Sister Hedwig's favorite passage.*

Sister Calista let out a huff, a snore, and a sigh. She repositioned herself and started a rhythmic breathing.

Outside, the setting sun cast a final glow on the train windows. *I will go brush my teeth. Maybe I'll see Henry and ask about our Pittsburgh friends.* But the hall was deserted on her trip to and from the washroom.

She opened the newspaper and read the headlines. The entire front page spoke of money, crash, stocks, fortunes, and fears. *I pray for my family's financial safety.*

She put down the newspaper then opened the tablet she planned to use as a journal and wrote. *Here I sit, serene in this little nest. We have been quartered here for two days. It feels longer because it is so snug and safe. In the daytime, I like the feel of my back resting against the padded, red fabric chair while I sit and watch the panorama of states pass before my eyes. God, Your land is magnificent.*

She gazed out the window and watched a few trees bend to the might of the moving train. *This place reminds me of the Arlington Hotel. Granted, I never saw a suite in the hotel part, just the dining room. Yet, I feel the same coziness. Lots of red on furniture and floor. Wood on the walls with a peach glow from the sun. The big difference, besides the size of rooms, is the chandeliers at the Arlington, which were frequently cleaned with ammonia. They sparkled and reflected every minutia of light.*

Anna closed her eyes for a few minutes and could sense the train's wheels sliding and bumping along. *Each night, Henry, the magician, comes in and turns our day room into a bedroom. The sheets are white and somehow smell of sun. We choose either a ceiling light or the two lights embedded in the wood walls above our bunks. The room has a high ceiling, with upholstered pieces of fabric extended over each bed on either side of the room. If Henry made one of those upper berths up for me, I would feel like I was sleeping in a treetop. The train rhythm would be rocking me like the strong wind on a sturdy branch. But, Sister Calista draws the window shade at night. I could not look out and pretend I was in a tree. Perhaps I will sleep in a treehouse on our island.*

Anna heard only the rhythmic click-clack of the wheels as they crossed more tracks.

This nest reminds me of the room of my classmate, Elizabeth, Elżbieta. We called her Betta. She lived with her grandma, babcia, near the school. She never mentioned her absent parents. She had a cheerful smile and thick blonde hair which was always in two braids with colorful ribbons at the ends and curls below the ribbons. Most of my friends shared a bed or at least a bedroom. She had her own room. It was in the attic. Other attics in the neighborhood were reached by a ladder. Hers had stairs leading up. I loved going to her place. We worked in her private room on school projects together.

Betta's bedroom was small. So was she. Big beams ran down her walls. On them, she hung pictures from magazines and her own drawings of dogs and cats. She had thin gauze cloth attached up high on the ceiling, and it flowed down around her bed. We called it a bed. It was a mattress. We classmates envied her and that private space. But I felt bad because she didn't have a teddy bear. At home, there were two bears on the bed I shared with my sister.

Actually, I only saw her during the school year. Was her room freezing cold during Christmas vacation and blasting hot all summer? Where was she now? We did not go to the same high school. Sometimes, I have learned to ask questions of these quiet people. Ask the right questions, and I hear amazing things. As for Betta and Nola, God, I put them in Your hands.

Anna closed her tablet, turned off the light, and snuggled beneath the covers.

Morning sun poked in around their window shade, but it was the feeling of the train going around a curve that woke Anna. From the corner of the blind, she saw purple mountains.

"What beauty," Anna said.

"Let me see." Sister squinted her morning eyes to half-mast and rolled up the shade. "The Rockies."

"And we move on."

Sister patted her on the shoulder. "It will certainly be a calmer day today. I prayed for inner peace before I fell asleep. And I was most tired. I'm still wearing my day clothes."

Anna smiled.

Sister chuckled. "We think we can change the world. God's joke. Even Jesus had trials."

There was a knock. Sister Calista opened the door, and there stood Henry.

"Good morning, Sisters. I didn't have time to talk to you yesterday. My apologies. I tried to stop the two ladies from leaving, but I couldn't convince them. When Mrs. Powler showed me the note on the pink stationary you had written to her, I was sure thankful. How you knew about a good doctor in Omaha, I will never know. But at your suggestion, she and Nola left the train, and Nola will see your doctor friend. I was relieved."

In the hall, another porter grabbed Henry's arm. "We're needed three cars ahead and right now."

"I will see you later." Henry hurried down the hall.

Sister Calista turned slowly. "Poor Henry. Nuns don't have colored stationery. If I tell him, he'll try to move Heaven and Earth to find Nola and never will. A person like Mrs. Powler knows how to hide her tracks. This needs to be our sin of omission. We must never tell."

A look of complete confidence passed between them.

TWENTY-ONE

There was a knock on the door that mid-morning.

Henry entered. "I have a pot of tea and some hot chocolate."

Anna smiled. "Hot chocolate. You know that is my favorite."

"Thank you for the tea," Sister said. "It will warm me. It's always cold in here."

He put down the cups. "We've just passed Cheyenne, Wyoming. Aren't the Rockies beautiful?"

"Magnificent," Anna said.

With a smile and a nod, he turned and left.

Sister poured hot water into her cup and inserted a tea bag. "I'm still not used to these things. I never saw a tea bag before this trip. Now, what should we do for the next few days?"

"This is our special time together," Anna said. "If you don't mind, I'd like to ask you questions. There is a quote from Horace we learned in school. It is *carpe diem,* seize the day. I have also heard people say seize the moment. I am seizing it."

"Very well. Ask away."

"Did you consider any other orders of nuns?"

"Oh, yes, I did. As children, we look to our parish nuns, whatever order they may be." Sister raised her eyebrows and tilted her head. "By the time one thinks seriously, we have stories and pictures of other groups and kinds of nuns."

"You mean the orders of teachers, or nurses, or contemplatives, those who spend many hours in prayer."

She removed the tea bag. "I was split in my goals. In my eyes, my family had dismissed me, and it hurt. I went to confession and talked to our pastor. He suggested forgiveness for my family. Next, he reminded me of this order of nuns. He had me visit them and discuss all my options. I would never have thought of it."

A bell chimed. "Lunch is served."

They walked carefully through the corridor. The train shimmied and curved, then moved into a pass through the mountain. At last, they reached the lunch room. A panorama showed outside the windows. Mountain shade covered the left, and the sun shone on the right. The train turned north, even though the final goal was west.

They sat at a table. Both women faced forward. The other seats at their table were unoccupied.

As if they hadn't been interrupted, Sister Calista said, "Remember Anna, we now have more modern methods to pass out information. I'm telling you about my entry time in 1908."

"You are so right. That was over twenty years ago." *Where will I be in twenty years? Will I be happy? One day, becoming a nun seems like the right path, the next, I am uncertain about it.* "Did you question your parish nuns?"

Sister's face turned toward the mountains outside the windows. "It seemed each of the eight nuns in that little house wanted to pass on some information. No one had ever asked them what they knew or had been told of other religious lives. The first nun I asked was Sister Basil. She was young, about twenty years old. She kept her head down when she walked. She told me about an order but not the one she chose."

A waiter wearing a white apron over his uniform delivered bowls of soup. The noodles in the soup varied like hair ribbons, from pencil-slim slivers to chunks as thick as Anna's Bible. Hot, shaved chicken swam in the steamy liquid.

"In that order," Sister said as she ate, "headpieces were made of white starched linen called a wimple. The neck piece, called a coif, was a pleated collar tied in the back of the neck. Under the chin, the piece went up around the face. The front top piece went flat over the forehead and was tied in back. The veil was attached to the top piece with black pins. The gown was a long cloth panel. It is best described as a fabric as wide as the person, starting at the front hem, going up with a hole in the neck, then down the back to the hemline. It is called a scapular. It's similar to the little ones we each wear under our clothing. They remind us of our commitment to God."

Anna nodded and touched the one she wore. It was two stamp-sized cloth tags attached with a string similar to a shoe-string, having a picture of Jesus on a front end and a saint's picture on a back end. It hung down about five inches on front and rear.

"The gown was held together at the waist with a rope. The rope had three knots to symbolize the three vows taken by most nuns. Poverty, chastity, and obedience."

"That sounds very complicated. I don't think I'd like to wear all that. But the dress is only a badge of distinction. The work of the order is the reason to join."

"Yes."

The waiter served toasted cheese sandwiches. Steam snuck out between the grilled slices. Sister stopped talking to eat hers.

Anna gazed out the window. "Seeing all the snow feels like a trick to my eyes. Is it a movie or actually out there? Then I hear the wind whistling and know it is real."

"Ah, yes, it is real."

"Please go on. I will pay attention while I eat." Anna bit into the sandwich and the sour dill pickle, which puckered her lips.

"Sister Frances at my parish convent told me that there were three steps to becoming a nun. The first is the postulant, second the novitiate, and the third is the professed. At the one she re-searched, the novitiate period was comprised of intense study of the order. Four family visits were allowed in that year. The postulant wore a black dress, black stockings and shoes, and a white lace cap. Prior to receiving the cap, many of the girls would cover their hair with a handkerchief. Sister Frances would have looked wonderful with that cap on her head. She had a beautiful olive complexion and curly eyelashes, so I always thought she had curly hair. When she smiled, her lips quirked to the right, giving her face an off-center sparkle."

The waiter reappeared and refreshed their tea and cocoa. Anna's tongue tingled as she sipped the hot, sweet liquid.

"Sister Frances said that in a monastery community, the head nun was called an abbess." Sister paused as if to regroup her thoughts. "This same order was described later by Sister William. Her fellow nuns called her Wills, and she loved it. She was the arithmetic whiz. She called it math. Wills said that during the postulancy, one decided if that order was a good fit. If so, the person had to write a letter to the order, asking for admission. There would be a vote among the professed regarding admission. It was a happy day when a postulant was told they could *profess*. Each girl's family bought a wedding dress including a white veil which she would wear for taking the final vows. During the ceremony, the white dress was covered with the habit, and the white veil changed to a black one."

Squares of chocolate cake with peaked white icing were served.

Sister Calista attacked her portion with vigor. "We aren't doing any physical work, yet I'm hungry at every meal."

Anna watched the rays of sun run along the mountain as the train made its curve towards the west.

Sister said, "Sister Genevive, a very quiet nun, told me that with the final vows, one received a plain gold ring. It meant the nun was now married to Christ. Sister Genevive was a retiring presence when she taught in the classroom. But that changed when she sat before the church organ on Sundays. Her music was the most vigorous the parish had ever heard."

After lunch, they returned to their room, greeting passersby.

Once settled inside, Sister Calista continued. "Sister Mercedes had lots to say. When she was in high school, she was a rebel. Many identified with her. Some of her classmates were pals. There were others who came to her quietly and alone and applauded her, saying, *I wish I had the courage to say what you did,* or *I thought no one noticed except me*. She had stories of why girls and older women wanted to enter. Too tall to find a man. Didn't ever want to be around children. Didn't want to cook for parents and siblings day after day. Constant fighting and anger under their roof. Drinking. Physical abuse. Sister Mercedes' eyes teared when she told her story." She shook her head. "That was such a big meal. I'm worn out."

"I'll read for a while and let you nap. Do you need anything?"

"No." She sighed, leaned to her side, and closed her eyes.

The speed of the train increased as if the engineer looked at the mountainous tracks ahead and accepted the challenge to climb. Gravity pushed Anna's shoulders back against the seat.

She opened her Bible randomly. It opened to *Pierszy list Sw. Pawła do Tymoteusza,* The First Epistle of Saint Paul the Apostle to Timothy. It had a heading above verse 17. It said Honor the Elders. The verse was, *Let the elders who rule well be counted worthy of double honor, especially those who labor in the word and doctrine.*

Is this about Sister Calista?

Later, Anna closed the Bible and peeked around the lowered shade. The late afternoon sun shone on mountains covered with clean snow. The wind swirled, lifting and moving the mounds of white in all directions. She touched the window and felt the snow as it dropped and slid down the glass, leaving a succession of new patterns in snow language.

The repetitive tone of the train running over tracks lulled her to sleep.

After lunch the following day, Sister Calista was eager to talk. "Sister Cecelia never confided in me. It was Sister Hubert who told me Sister Cecelia's tale. Sister Cecelia always managed to be outside doing something every Saturday morning. That's the Catholic Church's day for weddings. She watched the bride and groom with a look of genuine interest. According to Sister Hubert, her soldier who had planned to come home and marry her didn't return. Sister Hubert said she could never decide if the look on Sister Cecelia's face was one of sadness, envy, anxiety, or curiosity."

"How sad," Anna said.

"I often say a little prayer for her when I think of a wedding. I wonder how she carries her burden after these many years. A broken heart is hard to heal. But, unfortunately, almost every nun has heard of a rejected bride who entered a convent."

"Sister Calista, don't all orders have a few years from entry to profess? By then, even the Sister Cecelia's of the world should have made their peace with the stumbling blocks of life."

"Some never do. Others turn their sadness into better or bitter."

Henry tapped on their door and entered. "Sister Calista, I brought your tea. And I want to show you both the view. We are in Wyoming and will be all day. As you see, the mountains are not as tall. The highest mountains, the Rockies, are already behind us. But all their little cousins keep showing up. They are a lot easier to cross. Our next stop is Ogden, Utah, just north of Salt Lake City. From there, instead of west, we'll go north again."

Anna said, "Henry, I'm so glad I told you I was an armchair traveler. You answer questions on this landscape before I even think to ask them. You help keep my journal authentic."

"It is my pleasure." He pointed to the hills on the north side of the train. "Those are called The Badlands. Of course, as I told you earlier today, we have already crossed The Continental Divide." More to himself than to anyone, he said softly, "I wonder if that's an eagle."

"It could be. Seems like it has the right color of wings. I'm glad they do well in the cold. I imagine by mid-November there will be little travel in this area. It looks cold and damp outside."

Sister said, "Well, I feel warm and cozy with this tea, Henry. Thank you again."

"Yes, Ma'am. Oh, I must be on my way." He hurried out.

"Back to my story," Sister said. "Another nun, Sister Harold, researched the three services provided by the nuns. The nuns are either teachers of the young, nurses, or contemplatives. Sister Harold had a cousin who wanted a healing order, so joined the Sisters of Mercy." Sister Calista turned to the window, then her gaze came back to Anna. "Nuns primarily join before they are twenty years old. It is a given that they are virgins. After they enter, they receive an education. Teachers go to normal school to become teachers. The nurses go to nursing school to learn their trade. Contemplatives, like us, have classes on early church teachings and on the rites of their order. We study church doctrine, liturgy, and learn about Catholicism."

Anna said, "I thought I wanted to be Contemplative. I never expected an interest in nursing."

Sister took a sip of tea, then put her fingers to her chin to wipe a sprinkle of moisture. "My healing skills come from things I've learned from family or friends. I have no proper health education and no medical diploma. I am pleased to be passing what I know to you."

"That is quite a gift. I noticed when you talked to Nola, you used medical words. You do a lot of reading, don't you? You must never in your life have expected to deliver a baby, yet you knew what to do."

"It was one of those chapters in a medical book that I found interesting and amazing. That God in His goodness has human beings increase and multiply, and every single one, amazingly, is different from the others. That is such a powerful message from on high. I had to know everything I could about delivery. Was that a coincidence?"

"Tell me more about pregnancy, please."

For an hour, the older nun acquainted Anna with words like trimester, stages of labor, delivery, placenta, and lactation. "We may deliver some babies on the island. One basic fact is if the labor and delivery happen fast, the whole process is uncomplicated."

"My friend, Julia, is expecting a baby in the spring. Her husband died a few weeks after they were married. She probably wonders how God is giving her this gift yet took away her spouse. My younger sister will be the godmother."

"How nice that the two of them have each other. A new baby

brings so much delight and happiness to a home." Sister rolled back her shoulders and clicked her dentures.

"Did any of the nuns mention goals of a specific order?"

"No, these were simple women. I don't think anyone put their goals into words. Each talked about what they liked to do. Teach, nurse, or pray. Then they chose a group. Admittedly, some entered after the eighth grade and were innocent of even those choices. Women make choices and, once made, never change their mind. They find the good in the role."

"I am sure some must change their mind." Anna gazed out the window at the passing landscape. *Is this to be my life? Is health and healing my calling? Are my reasons for entering a cloister valid? God, I need more insight.*

"...and others grow more bitter and angry and feel trapped in their religious life."

"What? Oh, yes, we've all seen an angry religious, haven't we? Tell me more about convent life."

"Every convent has a Sister Cook. She is called that either in private or to her face. It is her duty to feed and bake. She sometimes is a music teacher or has another skill to take up her slack time. In my hometown, that convent of eight had Sister Florence. She had more time than most to read and had philosophy books in her kitchen. She called them her cookie baking books. She read while timing cookies."

"She sounds delightful."

"She told me that her order's vows were Poverty, Charity, and Obedience, but she'd heard of another order that had their nuns also promise Debility, Stability, and Conversion of morals."

"What does that mean?"

"I didn't get to ask her. Her cookies were burning, and she never finished her story. I will never forget those words, though. I always meant to figure them out."

"So, you could end up cooking for eight people or a hundred. What if you hate cooking? Could that be one of God's tricks?"

"I think the cook is either a very young girl who is still studying or a much older nun who for some reason or other is taking time off from teaching." She got up and began to walk around the little room, moving her shoulders back and forth. "I need to get out and take a walk. My bones are too cramped. Why don't you walk with me, and I'll finish our conversation?"

They stepped into the hallway.

"I'll continue my story of the nuns with Sister Luke. A lot of what she told me, she found out from the cook, Sister Florence, while they peeled potatoes and carrots. Sister Luke loved history. Her classes were full of historical facts that her students will never forget. She told me names of orders of nuns. She said the contemplatives, the praying ones, included the Poor Claire's, Redemptoristines, and the Carmelites. Many like the Felicians, Benedictines, and the Ursulines taught. The Ursulines usually taught only girls. The medical groups included the Sisters of Charity, Daughters of Saint Vincent de Paul, and Mercy."

"You have a good memory." Anna nodded as they progressed from one car to another. The wonders of Wyoming appeared outside every available window.

"In the old days, about 1901, The Holy See, the Vatican, decided it didn't want nuns teaching young children of both sexes together. For some unknown reason, The Holy See also disapproved of nuns giving direct care to young infants or lying-in women. This care was only allowed in exceptional circumstances."

"It must have changed again, or the nursing orders would be in trouble with Rome."

"Maybe tomorrow or the next day we can go on to some of the teachings of our order."

The dinner chimes rang, and the two nuns were just in time for the first servings. As a tribute to their location, the chef had labeled his choice of the day, The Salt Lake City Special—steaks smothered in onions and mushrooms. The enticing aroma was only outdone by the taste.

After dinner, Sister Calista read a bit then turned off her light. Anna read the Bible, wrote a few lines in her journal, and fell asleep.

TWENTY-TWO

In the dining car the next morning, Anna felt the train slow down.

The conductor announced, "Ogden, Utah."

The train stopped. Men and women stepped out the doors and marched into the station. Others hurried toward the train. Newcomers entered the passenger cars.

Sister said, "It looks like there will be a full train from here to the coast."

"Did you notice the heavy coats on some folks coming aboard? Others look lean and hungry and are dressed in only thin jackets. Is this part of the money scare we hear about? They keep saying recession."

"And here we are with lots of breakfast choices."

Anna nodded. *I wonder how Tata's grocery store is doing. He is such a caring man. He gives food to people, who promise to pay him back, and later, they say they forgot they owed him money. He has his credit book where he keeps records of all the money due him. He is always kind to people who have hungry children. I hope he does not lose much money on his personal charity.*

The train pulled out of the station. It headed north.

"Look at the beautiful evergreens," Sister Calista said. "This is a huge forest."

"Henry lent me a book on the things we would see. This place full of evergreens is called, wait, I have the book right here. It is the Wasatch-Cache Forest. It has fir, spruce, pine, cedar, and maple trees. It will go on for ten more miles."

The waiter approached. He was dressed in white and carried

a tray laden with food. He swung it down in front of them and uncovered each offering. "Sister, here are your pancakes with butter. You have a choice of syrups, maple or a locally made raspberry one." He sat two tiny metal pitchers in front of her. "They're hot so don't burn your fingers on them. I also brought you an extra little plate so you could taste both or share them."

"You are too kind. God bless you."

"For you, young Sister, I have oatmeal, milk, and brown sugar on the side. I hear some folks like that. Your bun is still hot from the oven." He uncovered her cinnamon roll as if show-ing off a prized item at an auction.

"Thank you," Anna said. "It smells delicious."

He motioned to the window. "Look to your left, out to the west. See all that empty space? If we were birds, we could get up high and appreciate the view. We are a few miles too far east to see our Salt Lake. It's a wonder of the world. It is so big." He laughed. "Everyone who comes to the lake wants to get into it and see if they float. There are even people there who will take your picture if you want a remembrance. I did get in and could not sink. So did all of my family. We still talk about it."

Anna asked, "Were you covered with salt like everyone tells us?"

"Yes. We looked silly and teased each other all the way home. Enjoy your breakfasts." He turned away. "It looks like we're going to have a busy day."

Anna got out the guidebook and read aloud. "The Salt Lake is 100 miles long and 50 miles wide. Can you imagine that? The book says that in the valley of the lake, the air is dry, pure, and clean. It also says gold, silver lead, and copper are mined here."

The train moved on. People entered and left the dining car. The clatter of dishes being put into a pan drew Anna's attention.

She saw Henry in an oversized white apron. "Look, Sister. It seems that our porter is cleaning off tables. I wonder why he changed jobs."

"I saw him this morning while leaving the washroom. Or, was that yesterday?" Sister said.

"No, it was today. In fact, he promised to tell me about his brother, Oscar, who lives near Salt Lake City."

The table across from the nuns became vacant. Henry carried his full basin out of sight, returned with an empty one, and began to clear the dirty dishes. He carefully removed everything from the table. With a small whisk broom, he swept minuscule breadcrumbs into a collection pan. Then, he replenished the table with fresh dishes, silverware, and glasses of water.

"You appear in the strangest places," Sister Calista said.

Henry stretched his back. "My nephew, Jonah, Oscar's boy, started here three, four runs ago. Doing good." He nodded. "Hopped off the train in Ogden to see his Daddy. Was helping his Daddy move things around in the wagon. Pulled too hard. The box wouldn't move. His hand did. Got a good cut."

"Is he all right?" Anna asked.

"Yes, Ma'am. It's a clean cut. But he needs to keep his hand quiet for a day. I'm taking his place. Jobs are real hard to find, you know. I'll do his and mine 'til he's better. He's a good boy and got to keep the job."

Henry got back to work, and Anna and Sister rose to leave the car.

On the way out, Sister said, "We may want to start your lessons about our order this morning."

"I would like that," Anna said.

As they walked to their room, the train swayed. Steam from the engine floated past the window.

Anna said, "I plan to watch the scenery while you talk. We may never again see Utah. I hear we will be in Idaho soon."

Once in their room, Sister Calista opened a fat book with handwriting along the margins. "In the contemplative orders, there are many hours of prayer. It is the reason we choose our order. These times are known as The Divine Office. As a postulant, you are eased into this life of supplication. We who are professed are part of the continuous routine of prayers. In our chapel, night and day, nuns are requesting blessings."

"How do they know when to do this during the night?"

"There are clocks in the rooms of most professed because of our night sanctuary visits. We each are honored to be included in waking during the night, going to the chapel, and praying for an hour or two. This is one of the least understood yet most spiritually rewarding deeds of our practices. It is a thing I will miss the most about leaving the monastery."

Anna said, "Before I entered the convent, we all went to bed at about ten o'clock. If I ever had my light on in my room later than that, Tata would notice. He would come in and ask me to turn it out and say I needed my sleep. I always listened to him. But, it could have been a productive time for me to be awake."

"I like the praying and being awake at night, too. Going to the chapel at nighttime was the most precious gift I gave myself each week. It was the closest I came to talking with the Almighty. It was a personal time for me to thank Him for the gifts He gave me."

"I want to hear about that, Sister."

"For me, it was a most intimate time between myself and my God. I would doze until the alarm went off. Then I'd dress and silently tiptoe down the stairs. Each night as I entered the chapel, my breath was taken away by the majestic beauty. I'd praise God for the brightness cast by the candles' glow. I'd thank Him for the smell of beeswax made by the lit tapers. I'd thank Him for the grandeur of each vase of flowers. Every color of flower, every arrangement of leaves and petal, was proof of God's vast influence. I'd marvel at the shadows all around the chapel. They were in the pews, on the pillars, all by God's intent. I'd spend minute after minute enumerating dark and light. I also praised God's giving us a brain like Edison, who helped us find light. I'd thank Him for our benefactor who provided the chapel of lights and shadows."

"Sister, were you ever sleepy in the chapel?"

She smiled. "No. The time was always too short. I'd thank God for the sweet smells. In the fall, the altar was adorned with leaves in ten shades of red, orange, and a touch of green. God is good. After my thanksgivings, I asked for blessings for my fellow nuns, the pleasant ones and the difficult ones, too. Every week, before I finished the long list of family, my replacement sneaked in beside me, tapped me on the shoulder, and pointed to the hallway, saying I could leave the chapel."

"How often did you do this?'

"We picked two times a week by choice. The list was posted for the next few days in our common room. There were times when someone was unable to go. We could fill in. By the way, we had nuns who were brilliant in music. They had special permission from our abbess to serenade at night. One would arrive with her accordion and play religious music during her hour, and the second one would play her violin. A number of years ago, we had a harmonica player. She was one of the older nuns. At first, I thought it was selfish to not let us all hear. Then I realized, the music was not for us but for God. It was tempting to go and pray almost every night, but with things to do all day, you know what it's like."

"Yes, I understand," Anna said thoughtfully. "Was this part of the seven periods of prayer you mentioned earlier? How do these hours fit in?"

"Yes and no. The prayer times I just mentioned were for individuals." She clicked her dentures, straightened her glasses, then consulted the well-worn black book. "I'll give you a fast review of the origin of our prayer pattern. The original came from the monks. And yes, it is called the Divine Office."

"It is what the priests use, isn't it?"

"Yes. Their prayers start at five a.m. and finish at eight p.m."

Anna adjusted her headpiece. "I've read about the monks and their piety."

"Remember, they too work at tasks throughout the day."

"Yet, prayer is their primary activity. What dedication they must have."

Sister Calista said, "We could go on about them, but let's focus on our order of nuns. Prayer is our calling. All work immediately ceases during our prayers unless it's an emergency. An example is when you helped Sister Rochelle after she cut her arm. In the infirmary, we are lenient about prayer time if need be." Sister stood up, rubbed her right shin, shook her head, and sat down again.

"Do you have some liniment to put on your leg?"

"Yes. I'm rationing it so it will last until we're on the *Alexandria* and have been at sea for a few days. Then we'll be in a warmer climate." She rummaged through her bag and took out a tin. Scents of camphor and wintergreen escaped when she opened the can. "It's almost gone. I'll be right back." Carrying the liniment, she made a hasty retreat to the washroom.

Anna gazed out the window at the rolling scenery. *I like the prayer life mixed with the cooking, picking apples, baking, and scrubbing floors. I understand it helps my Sisters in Christ so we all have more time to pray. The silence? No decisions on that. In a few months, I will probably know if praying or talking fit into my lifestyle.*

Sister Calista returned with the scent of camphor and a hint of wintergreen engulfing her. She picked up her book and searched for her last reading. "I lost the page."

Anna picked up Sister's bookmark from the floor. It was a prayer card with words written in a language she did not recognize. "Is this Swedish?"

"No, it's French. My origin is France, although I only know a few words of the language. My family brought this to me after my father's death. It has the date of his birth and death and his name on the card. The prayer is *The Memorare*. Our family said the prayer together if things were tough. It gives me comfort." She turned the card over and showed Anna the picture. "My brother thinks he's an artist. I didn't give him any credit for his art. Yet, he duplicated a painting inside our church and drew it on my card."

"He did a wonderful drawing. That is the same picture I had on the wall of my cell at the monastery. I never did figure out who stood beside Christ in that picture."

The older nun said, "I don't know either, but when I saw that picture in your cell, I thought it created a bond between us.

Now, back to your lessons. Even as old as I am, I learn something new each time I review these edicts."

Someone tapped on the door. Anna opened it. A young attendant dressed in a white uniform stood with a tray in hand. "I'm Jonah. Uncle Henry tol' me that we brought Sister tea each mornin', and he said Miss Anna liked hot chocolate."

The older nun said, "How nice. It will taste good today. We were looking outside and remarking on the wind and the cold."

"I was wondering what bees do in this weather," Anna said.

"Ladies, my father, he has beehives on his farm by Salt Lake City. The bees stay warm in the hives and wait it out 'til spring. Come to think on it, I never seen bees and snow at de same time. But we got lotsa bees there. My daddy say they thinkin' of callin' Utah *The Bee State*." He placed the tray on the table.

Anna said, "Jonah, I heard you hurt your hand. I do not even see a bandage. Is it all better in one day?"

"Thanks to the bees. Uncle Henry, he put honey on my cut. It sure be healin' good." He showed them the discolored line on his hand.

"That's remarkable," Sister Calista said. "I'll remember honey for cuts. You learn something new each day."

"Yes'm." He turned and left.

Sister said, "Back to work. We have lots to discuss and only two states left before our train trip is over." She turned a few pages in her book and read, "Each day, nuns follow eight sacred offices, beginning and ending with prayers in the church. The eight offices are Matins, recited at two a.m. But remember we don't all do this one. Lauds at five a.m. Prime at six a.m. Terce at nine a.m. Sext at twelve noon. Nones at three p.m. Vespers at four p.m. And Compline at six p.m. Every sect, the teaching, contemporary, or contemplative, needs to use flexibility with the hours. These are a little different than the monks' Divine Office." She repositioned herself and pulled the tea bag out of the cup.

"Are the prayers in Latin or English?"

"Some of each. Some you'll recognize like the *Tantum Ergo.* They are all lovely. Only certain nuns get up for the two a.m.

Matins. The rest of us silently say those prayers before we pray the Lauds. If we did the Matins prayer, the nuns could have accidents in the fields. There have been some. Sister John the Apostle drove the tractor over the hill and ended up topsy-turvy. She had a few bruises, including a black eye. She wore it proudly. Sister Lawrence finished milking, then carried the pails but forgot to close the gate. We had our own cow roundup. Wouldn't it have been sad if we'd lost even one animal?"

"That is a good reason for the safety of all concerned," Anna said.

"Our abbess has the authority to make the two a.m. ruling for our monastery only, and she chose to do it."

"How will we adapt this for the next year while we are away?"

"I do not know. We need to have faith that God will lead us."

The familiar chimes sounded, calling them to lunch.

Anna tilted her head and asked, "Hungry?"

They went out into the corridor. On the way to the dining car, Anna passed a young mother carrying a baby. *I smell Ivory Soap. My mother smelled that way. I still miss her. I do fine for a while, then see someone who reminds me of her or even a familiar scent, and it makes that certain crack in my heart open again.*

After being seated in the dining room and placing their orders, they watched the scenery.

Anna said, "I thought Idaho was flat. Look at those deep gullies and high peaks. This terrain is a surprise."

Jonah brought their order. "I'm glad cook placed this bowl on a dish or I'd a made a mess on your tablecloth." He placed hot tomato soup in front of each of them. "Can you feel the train curvin' when we bend around The Snake River?"

"Is that what it's called?" Sister said. "I like the way the sun glistens on the water way down below."

They ate soup, looked at the terrain outside, and watched their fellow passengers.

"We don't have enough time to get too friendly with any of

these nice people," Sister said. "Time is flying as fast as the train is traveling."

The next course was a small portion of a baked noodle and chicken dish. The steamy aroma of basil wafted through the air.

"This is still too hot to eat," Anna said. "Will you tell me about your father?"

"Not much to tell. He was hard-working and loved farming our land. We had cattle in the far fields. He liked the cattle. I hear when they first got the farm, he named each steer. But by the time I was born, he had my brothers looking after them. He liked to see things grow. He'd get out the seed catalogs in the winter, take a paper, and make a diagram of where he'd plant a certain thing and where another thing would go. He grew corn, wheat, rye, oats, potatoes, onions, peas, tomatoes, and beans. The beans were the most challenging for him."

"Why did he have trouble with beans?"

"They didn't like the climate. He tried string, kidney, and some others. Eventually, we ate a lot of corn and peas."

Anna sampled her lunch. "A farm operates every day, doesn't it?"

"My father worked hard six days a week. On the seventh day, we would feed the animals early and go to Mass. He'd do a minimum of farm work, and then we would do a family thing. Most times, it was a picnic on our grounds. We went to a few local lakes and watched ducks. We watched people sailing. We went to the dunes near Lake Michigan one time. It was a long trip for one day, but we did it. I'll never forget that. White sand from the lake covered the shore, and my father had us out running around on the dunes. He was a good man."

"Did he have a sense of humor?"

"Yes. His stories were funny ones about silly animals and such things."

Their conversation was interrupted by the announcement, *Boise, Idaho.* The train slowed and stopped.

Anna watched the new passengers. She saw a woman wearing a coat just like the one Aunt Nellie bought last year. *I miss her. She was my second mother. She taught me to sew and bake, but most of all to listen to what other people had to say. She told me that it was the highest compliment to give another, to pay attention to the person talking. We learn from being quiet, she would say.*

Anna turned back to the older nun. "And, your mother?"

Sister folded her napkin and slid back her chair. "She was a busy woman. She helped with the farming and helped at St. Joan of Arc, our parish church. I forgot to tell you. During Holy Week, the whole farming family stopped our regular lives and were at St. Joan of Arc again and again."

They left the dining car.

Anna followed the older nun through the corridor. "Did you have a procession on Holy Thursday?"

"Oh, yes, and we wore our First Communion dresses. We would get there early in the morning, parade into the church, and watch the Mass and the washing of the feet of the priest. Next, the priest would take off his vestments and put on that white long stole they call the cope. We'd sing, and he'd incense the Sacred Host in its ciborium. Then we would lead the procession around the church while he carried Our Lord in the ciborium up and down every aisle. Then they'd strip the altar of all linen to signify that it was the Last Supper and the last Mass until late Saturday morning. They would also blow out the candle in the red glass that signified the Host being at the altar."

"You must have been back in church Good Friday and Holy Saturday, too."

"Of course, we were. And each time the incense came near, I would sneeze." Sister laughed as she entered their cubicle. "What fun this has been for me, remembering all those things."

They settled inside.

"Anna, look, I think we're out of Idaho. There's no river here."

"We must be in Oregon. All I see are fields with cattle. I think we stay away from any of the big cities in this state."

"I need to take a nap. All this conversation has exhausted

me. I'm not used to talking by the hour."

Anna said, "I understand. I will write in my journal."

Sister Calista dozed, wrapped in a red blanket.

Anna took out her tablet and wrote. *The sun reflects off the trees as the train speeds through groves of evergreens. We are already in Oregon. Next stop, Seattle. I was hoping to see Walla Walla. We will be traveling too far west. I cannot say I have been to Walla Walla, but I like saying that name. Tata always talked about traveling. I am glad I brought lots of paper. I will write to him about the roads I have seen, the tracks, the train, and who knows what. I will make him think he is on this trip with me. Tata and his pipe with that Half-and-Half tobacco will always be in my memory.*

Occasionally, Anna heard Sister's gentle snore. Then the announcer woke her with the announcement, *Welcome to the state of Washington.*

Sister Calista roused and said, "Let's hurry to the dining car. They can probably tell us about arrival time in Seattle."

"Yes." Anna stood up to shake off sleep.

In the dining car, people discussed the cold weather. New arrivals were saying words like depression, market values, and stocks.

The white-clad waiter came to take their orders. He mentioned fish was the choice of the day because supplies from the northwest had been received in Boise.

"I'll try the fish," both nuns said in unison.

They looked at each other like old friends.

A short time later, dinner was served.

"I don't know what kind of fish we are having, but I am enjoying it," Anna said. "However, we may have made a mistake. When we get aboard the ship, we'll probably have only fish."

"I didn't think of that."

They ate in companionable silence then returned to their room. Evening came quickly since they ate late.

"I want to stay up for a while tonight," Anna said. "I want to see Mount St. Helens."

"Unless God gives you a huge lightning storm, I think we'll pass all of it in the dark," Sister said.

"Oh, it will have to wait until I return next year."

The train thundered through the night as they both slept. The next morning, they awoke to the announcement, "Final destination, Seattle, Washington in two hours."

TWENTY-THREE

The two women sat in their room surrounded by their boxes and luggage.

"Sister," Anna said, "I am realizing at this moment that all my worldly possessions are here beside me in these suitcases. We are wealthy in God's blessings but have only a few tokens of this world."

The train came to a stop. "End of the line. Seattle, Washington," the announcer said over the loudspeaker.

Anna heard heavy compartment doors unlatching and voices in the hallway. Through the window, she saw rain falling from an overcast sky.

Sister grumbled, "May this be our last gloomy day. I hope so. My bones are aching in protest of that wetness outside." She picked up her bag and removed her liniment. "I'll be back in a few minutes."

Anna nodded.

As Sister opened the cabin door, a damp breeze slipped in. She asked, "Do you smell the sea yet?"

"No, I only smell wet, fall leaves." Anna looked outside. *I see nothing. No ocean. Maybe some steam. No matter. It is still exciting. God lead us safely through this life-changing day.*

Loud conversation came from the hallway. Knocks and bumps came from the next cabin.

Someone said, "I'll help you with your bags, sir."

Another voice said, "Careful of that step, Miss."

Passengers dragged suitcases down the aisles.

Sister Calista returned trailing the wintergreen-camphor scent. Leaving the door open, she sat and pulled out a small tablet. "We are to go into the station. We will be met by either Richard Long, a seaman from the ship, or Captain Thomas O'Connor."

Henry approached, smiling. "What can I do for you two Sisters?"

The older nun said, "We are ready to leave this comfortable nook and move ourselves and our belongings into the station. I suppose this is goodbye. You were so helpful to me. I'll keep you in my prayers."

Henry nodded. "I have learned so much from you, Sister Calista. And Miss Anna, I hope I've lived up to your challenge of geography. I don't have any papers about Seattle, though. Sorry."

Anna said, "I found an old nineteen-twenty-seven almanac in the bookcase at the monastery. The nuns used it for weather and planting. They have a nineteen-twenty-nine version, so my superior said I could take the older one. In it, I will be able to find out things about Seattle."

"Fine. Are you ready for the next part of your journey?"

"Yes, I am. Thank you for all your help, Henry. May God be with you always."

They each carried a small bag. Henry and two assistants removed the other luggage. Once outside, they loaded it onto a large wagon and hurried through the drizzle toward the station.

"I feel that murky rain." Sister Calista held her veil down with her free hand.

Anna placed her hand on her headpiece and looked around. "All I see is haze. We're having a wet arrival." *I miss home. I want to be here. Which is it?*

As they hurried into the station, Sister said, "I'm glad to be out of the wet air."

Anna looked around a large room. "There are benches there in the middle. Let's sit while we wait. I think it will be warmer away from the doors."

Over the loudspeaker, a voice echoed, "Spokane, Washington, train 115, departing at one p.m. on track four. Bellingham,

Washington, and north, train 264 departing in fifteen minutes on track six. Portland, Oregon, and points south, train 176, now loading on track two."

I wish Tata were here to enjoy all this commotion with me.

Sister Calista said, "I wonder who will greet us, the captain or the seaman."

The two sat with their luggage positioned around them. A man in shiny overalls approached.

"That must be the seaman," Sister whispered.

The man looked at them, passed, and greeted several men a few rows behind.

Anna sighed, breathing in the scent of the sea. She blinked, and a slight man stood in front of them. He was dressed in a green suit. A thatch of red hair surrounded his freckled face.

"Where did you come from?" Anna asked.

His blue eyes twinkled. "I'm from the *Alexandria*." He removed his straw hat and bowed.

"One minute, no one was near. The next minute, there you were. As if by magic," Anna said.

"You don't say. I'm Tommy, Sister Damien's brother, happy to greet ya. When she wrote about your voyage, I was delighted to transport two nuns. But…" He put his hands on his hips. "You two are not wearing the same habit."

Sister Calista cleared her throat. "Anna and I are from the same monastery. Anna is still in training."

"So be it," he said. "It's good to have ye. Sorry about me Irish accent. Me parents came to America without yours truly. I was at sea. After some time, they talked me inta coming. But they settled in land-locked Kansas. Kin you believe it?"

Anna smiled. The slim, spry man moved from foot to foot as if preparing to turn around a few times and disappear in a cloud of dust. But, no, he stayed.

"We're both so glad to meet you, Thomas O'Connor," Sister Calista said.

"Please call me Tommy. Everyone does. I'll get you and the

baggage into the fancy car waitin' outside. That Mister X arranged a whole day of amusement, and I'm included. We'll get on board my ship, *Miss Alex*, after dark. We will be sailin' in the morning."

Anna struggled with his heavy accent. "Slow down, please."

Sister asked, "What do you mean by plans for the day?"

"We go to lunch at one of the two places Mister X suggested. He is an amazing benefactor. Wish he was in my life," Tommy said.

"Yes, he is generous and mysterious. We understand all our gifts are in memory of his mother. Most of us do not know his name," Sister said.

"Back to the restaurants," Tommy said. "The first has a seafood menu, I call it all fish, you'll be findin' at the Port of Seattle Restaurant. Or if'n you'd like meat, we be goin' to the Pacific House."

Anna asked, "How did Mister X know about this?" *How thoughtful of Mister X to take such care of us.*

"Danged if I know. Oops, sorry, Sister. I'm tryin' real hard to not say any cuss words around you two."

Tommy and two porters ushered the nuns and their luggage out to a shiny black car. The rain had stopped, and a hazy sun had come out.

A tall, slim man in a dark suit stood outside the car. He smiled and opened the trunk. "Welcome, ladies. My name is Carl. As a gift from your benefactor, I'll drive you to lunch, give you a tour of the city, offer you another light meal, then take you to your ship."

"How nice. Thank you," Sister said.

Anna asked, "Is your other career in singing, Carl? You have a wonderful baritone voice."

"No, but my wife keeps telling me I should join a choir."

The nuns sat in the back seat of the roomy car. Tommy hustled into the front with Carl.

Carl asked, "Which will it be, ladies, seafood or beef?"

Sister Calista huffed. "Our last meals on land need not be

seafood."

Carl said, "Pacific House it is. On the way, I'll point out some of our attractions. Seattle is the largest city in the Northwest."

"It is hilly," Anna said. *It reminds me of Petroleum City. It must be cold there by now. I wonder if there has been any snow in my part of Pennsylvania.*

"This city is built on seven hills," Carl said. "The water you'll see as we come up from this valley is the Puget Sound."

Sister said, "I suppose our ship is nearby?"

"Shur is. I kin hardly wait to show it to yer," Tommy said.

They came to a rise. Sunlight danced on water.

Carl said, "Way off to the west, you'll see the Olympic Mountains. Past them is the Pacific. I've been there fewer times than the fingers on my right hand. Now, turn toward the rear of the car and see the glorious Cascade Mountain Range, including Mount Rainier."

Anna smiled. "God has given us a wonderful welcome to Seattle. It takes my breath away. Water, mountains, all these fall flowers."

"The climate is mild here, and some flowers and shrubs grow year-round." Carl steered around another bend in the road.

Sister turned to gaze out the back window. "These trees still have leaves. Amazing."

Carl stopped the car. "We're at the Pacific House. Enjoy your lunch." He opened the doors.

Anna exited the car. "Smell the sea air. It is salty." *I love this day. Tata would love it, too. I will tell him about the flowers. He would probably recognize their names.* "Carl, what's the name of that yellow flower?"

"I'm not sure. But it's not a daffodil. They bloom in the spring."

Anna said, "I will draw a picture and put it in my journal. It is pretty. Oh, it could be gladiola."

Carl said, "That sounds about right. Folks, I'll be out near the car when you're ready for the city tour."

In the restaurant, aromas danced through Anna's nose. She

recognized fresh bread, onion, and garlic.

Sister said, "It smells good. I'm hungry. I can't wait to read the menu."

The two nuns and Tommy were seated.

A man dressed in white shirt and black pants handed each of them a menu. "Hello. I'm Simon. I'll be your waiter today. Our owner, Mr. Blacksmith, will be sorry to hear we had nuns as guests while he was away. He says that it is an honor to attend God's servants."

Sister said, "We thank him. We thank you. Even your name is a good omen. Today, October twenty-eighth, is the feast of Saints Simon and Jude. We will say a prayer for your Mr. Blacksmith and for you."

"Thank you." Simon opened the napkins and handed them to the women. "Let me explain the menu. We have four entrée choices. We make only a few dishes, but all are exceptional. Today, we have our Sauerbraten, which is a beef dish, a simple but tasty baked chicken, a lunch-size steak, and a turkey salad."

Tommy said, "Sauerbraten, Sister, that's a German dish, isn't it?"

"Yes," she said, "I think I'll have that."

Anna read the menu. "I will take the turkey salad."

"It'll be a rare steak for me," Tommy said.

Warm bread arrived, followed by the lunches. The older nun smiled when her dish was set before her. All bowed their head in prayer.

Then Sister said, "Just like in Indiana. Beef, onion, celery, and lots of spices. I smell vinegar, garlic, allspice, cloves..." She took a bite. "Just enough seasoning for my taste."

Anna sampled her turkey.

Tommy looked at his steak and said, "Looka that. Even onions and mushrooms. This is sure better than what I had in Ireland. We do some good cookin' on the ship, Sisters. I know you'll like being aboard."

They ate with gusto. Dessert was vanilla pudding.

At last, Tommy put down his napkin. "Let's see this city."

Outside, the car waited for them.

"Was it good?" Carl opened the car door. "I take lots of people to this place."

Tommy's eyes gleamed. "Mine hit the spot, matey."

Anna positioned herself in the seat. "The salad was tasty to me."

The older nun added, "My sauerbraten was quite tart but I enjoyed every bite."

"There's a big German population here. I bet that sauerbraten was authentic," Carl said.

As the car eased into traffic, Tommy said, "And now, we'll sit back and see the city. What's new in Seattle, Carl?"

Carl said, "Well, I can't take you to it, but you need to know the most amazing thing. This year, they completed a passageway for cars through the Cascade Mountains. They call it the Northern Tunnel. It is seven miles long."

Sister Calista said, "It sounds like we are in a big municipality. Is there any room left for farming?"

"We grow wheat, oats, and barley. We're the leaders in apple production in this state. And, the pastures have cattle and sheep."

Anna asked, "Are there dairy cows?"

"Oh, yes. But the big business is the spawning salmon. We export that fish. It is a delicacy my wife enjoys. Me? I like chicken."

Tommy turned toward the back of the car. "And don't forget about our lumber. We'll see some floating by when we leave tomorrow. There'll be more in the Puget Sound, then when we turn west, in the Strait of Juan de Fuca."

Anna said, "I love all these new names."

Tata and Mama planned to travel. In their wildest dreams, they probably never thought of the great Northwest. Her dying changed so much for everyone. It took the spark from his eyes and the laughter from his heart. For me, it muddled all my goals and made me grow up fast. It made me wonder if I ever wanted to have children then leave them motherless when they were still young.

They toured the city for several hours. Anna looked out at the sinking sun.

"This is a good way to see the town," Tommy said.

"As much as I am enjoying this tour," Sister Calista said, "I am a little dizzy. Can we stop for the day? I think I need to lay down. How soon can we be on the ship?"

"We can be there in ten minutes," Carl said. "Are you sure, you want to go aboard now? I thought you'd like another light meal."

Sister belched.

"Let's git to the Alexandria," Tommy said.

Carl turned the car into the setting sun and headed for the port.

TWENTY-FOUR

The scenery changed from houses and businesses to water.

"Port of Seattle here we come," Tommy said.

In a shaky voice, Sister said, "It can't come soon enough. I have never before been car sick." She paused and took a breath. "Carl, easy on the bumps."

"Yes, Ma'am." Carl slowed the car.

Sister sighed. Anna smelled her foul breath. She turned her head to get a gulp of fresh air. *I hope she does not throw up.*

"Sister, what can I do?" Anna asked.

"I need to lie down. Now."

"Jist around one more corner, here, and we'll be home," Tommy said.

The car turned. Two gray seagulls dove in front of the windshield then disappeared. Before them was a large gray ship. Painted in gold on its side was the name *Alexandria*.

"Looka that name on the bow. *Alexandria*," Tommy said. "I'm so proud of me home. I can't wait to welcome ye aboard."

Anna's eyes moved up the side. She scanned the portholes. *It looks so big. I can count three stories above the water.* Higher, towards the center of the ship, a two-story structure had a row of rectangular windows. *There's a statue of a lady in flowing robes attached to the front of the ship. How odd.* On the deck, men pulled and moved boxes. Their voices echoed as they yelled to one another. *Noisy. It will be interesting to see what ship workers do and say.*

Sister lowered her head onto the car seat. She gulped several times.

Anna said, "We're here, Sister."

"Let's get some fresh air. I'm cramping."

"Your legs?"

"No. My belly."

Carl stopped. He opened the back door. Air heavy with a fish odor filled the car.

It reminds me of our kitchen before dinner on a Friday night.

"I don't like the smell." Sister Calista attempted to sit up.

Anna strained to ease her partner to a sitting position.

"I'm dizzy."

"We'll get you into a bed soon," Anna said.

Tommy said, "I'm putting you two in my cabin fer your trip. Let me take you aboard."

As they walked, Anna heard a gentle thump. *That could be a boat touching a dock.* Then she heard screeching. She looked up. Large birds circled overhead, seagulls bigger than she had ever seen except in books of faraway places.

"I need a bathroom. Soon," Sister Calista said.

With Anna on the right and Tommy on the left, they escorted the sick nun up a ramp with wide slanted boards and a rope railing. *This must be the gangplank.*

On the upper deck, Anna breathed in the clean, salty air.

Tommy moved them along until they came to a heavy door. He led them into a large room. The scent of wood polish tickled Anna's nose.

Sister said, "Bathroom."

Tommy pointed to an alcove on the far side.

"Just in time." The older nun pushed her way across.

Anna closed the door.

"Welcome to my home," Tommy said. "I hope yer comfortable here, and the Sister is not sick all night."

"I am sure Sister Calista will be better by tomorrow. Do not worry." Anna gazed at the light-colored wood covering the walls. Every adornment in the room was green. "This room is so like you. Ireland lives here."

He smiled. "Yes. My treasures are all so special to me. Now, you two precious ladies are my treasures until I git you both safely to the doctor on the Galapagos Islands."

She heard noises from the bathroom. Anna went to the door and asked, "Do you need help?"

"No. I'll be here for a while," came the reply.

"Ye'll notice this room ain't on the top deck. I'm the captain, and I pick a smooth ride 'stead a bein' up high. I know it'll feel good when the seas git rough. It's warmer, too."

"Thank you," she said.

He lifted his red eyebrows. "I used ta be a gamblin' man. That's how I got me *Alexandria*, free and clear. But that's another story."

The bathroom door opened. Looking pale and with her wimple off-kilter, Sister struggled back into the room.

A bed was tucked under a slanted ceiling at the rear of the room. Anna unfolded the soft linen on the mattress and gently eased her sick friend onto it.

"Get me a pot," Sister said. "I feel awful."

Tommy ran into another corner and returned with an enamel pan. He handed it to Sister Calista. Then he turned on a light. "Easier to see with this in early evenin'."

Anna smiled and nodded her thanks to Tommy. Looking at Sister, she said, "What will help your nausea?"

"Ginger root or powder. Tea. Apples."

"I'll send one of me mateys out to find them things. And I'll unpack the car."

Thank God, this man is nice. Sister Damien has to be so proud of him. I'll have to take the time to send her a note. Anna took the white enamel pan from Sister's hands and put it on the nightstand near her head. "Tommy, before you go, tell me about your sink and bathroom for my sick friend here."

"The sink works jist like on land. Kin ye believe it? Oh, maybe the water ain't as hot. If ye need it hotter, send a message to Ladi, me mechanic. The toilet is a trap door. Ye pull the handle, and all the stuff goes away. If it smells bad, we pour bakin' sody down it."

"Having a washroom so close by is a Godsend."

Tommy nodded. "I wuz as surprised as you are when I seen that a bathroom goes with this room. It'll be nice and private fer you two. I put some towels and stuff in it. I hope ye'll enjoy yer time aboard my freighter."

Anna looked over to see if the older nun was listening, but her eyes were closed. The ship swayed. *It feels like a rocking chair*. Outside, birds demanded a fish treat.

Tommy asked, "Kin I leave this door open until I git all yer stuff in here? Then ye'll have yer privacy."

"Good idea," she said. "I want so much to see your treasures and have you tell me about them. But it will wait for another time when Sister feels better." She frowned. "We never thanked Carl properly."

"I'll take care of that," he said as he turned and left.

I hope I do not get what Sister has. I never want to get sick away from home. At home, you can curl up in your own bed. I will take care of her. I will bring her tea. No, I cannot. There is no stove in this room. What will it be like in the morning when the ship starts moving? Where do we get food? At least, I see a pitcher of water. This is going to be a memorable voyage. Dear God, I hope she gets better soon.

"Anna, help me to the bathroom."

Sister wobbled. Anna held her arm. Her skin was moist. Her wimple was askew again.

"How are you feeling?"

"Nauseous. Get me in there." Sister entered the bathroom.

Anna closed the bathroom door. She gazed out the spotted window. Reflections of the sinking sun shot through the heavens as it inched below the skyline. *These colors are astounding. Peach and yellow in the water and the sky echoes them against a blue that seems to go on forever. If I could paint those colors...*

A knock sounded on the open door. Tommy asked. "Kin we come in?"

"Oh, yes," she said.

Tommy stepped inside with two suitcases. A man followed with two more. He was middle-aged, taller than Tommy, and muscular. He wore a gray shirt with patched trousers. Dark hair peeked out of a stocking cap.

Tommy huffed and puffed as he set the cases down. "Ye got some heavy stuff in here."

Anna nodded. "Yes, we are taking a year's worth of supplies."

"This here's Brendan. He's kinda family. We grew up together in the ol' country. I trust him with me life. He took me to sea when I was a strapin' boyo."

"Pleased ta meecha, Ma'am." Brendan laughed as he set down the suitcases. "Tommy tells everyone we found each other under the rocks in Galway Bay."

Tommy's response was a high-pitched hoot.

I am happy Tommy has a trusted relative here. This could be a dangerous life on a ship. They look at each other, as Tommy said, like family.

Tommy pointed to the pile of suitcases and boxes they'd set in the corner of the room. "Kin we move these around fer ye?"

"No need to move a thing tonight, Tommy," Anna said, "but, I wonder if there is a bed here for me?"

He hit his forehead with the heel of his hand. "Jeez! Oh, excuse me. Of course. Yers is in backa the desk. It woulda been taller back there, but I had our carpenter put a bookcase cabinet up on top."

She found a low bunk behind the desk to the right. A dark wood cabinet carved with ornate swirls stood above. "It looks cozy. Thank you."

The bathroom door opened. Sister Calista shuffled out. "Tommy, do you have any tea?"

"Yes, Sister. Right now."

The two men made a hasty exit.

"How do you feel?" Anna asked.

"Weary. Nauseous. Thankful for the bed."

"How about sitting up for a while?"

"Oh, all right."

Anna took Sister's elbow and guided her to a green chair.

There was a knock and a new voice. "Tea is here."

Sister Calista whispered, "About time." Then called, "Well, come on in."

A boy entered. He was about ten years old. "Hi. My friends call me Shorty. Pani from the kitchen sent this." He put a tray with a teapot, two cups and saucers, and a tiny cup with a thimble full of milk on the round table near the windows.

"Nice to meet you, Shorty," Anna said. "Thank Pani for us."

He nodded and left the room.

"Here's your tea, Sister. Do you want milk and—"

"No, just tea." She jerked her hand to her mouth.

"Of course." Anna poured sweet smelling tea into a cup. The aroma of fresh oranges rose with the steam. She set it on the end table next to the sick nun's right hand.

"I'm left-handed, you know."

Anna tried to move the table to the other side of the nun. "This table won't budge. I wonder if the furniture is bolted down because of rough seas." *I hope there will only be calm waters.*

The nun harrumphed and managed to take a sip of the tea. "Ah, this tastes good."

Anna sat at the round table with her own tea. As she sipped, she looked around the room. Wood polished to a soft glow covered most of the walls. Three windows, two facing the front of the ship and one on the side, brought in the sunset's glow.

The ailing nun fell asleep in her chair. *Poor, grouchy thing. She can be interesting and charming when she feels good. But when she's ill, she's horrid.*

Anna found her small suitcase and took out a prayer book. *I will read for a while. I am getting hungry. I had better be a nice guest and wait patiently for dinner.*

Opening her book, she found October twenty-eight to be the feast of Saints Simon and Jude. At the top of the page, the word RED designated the color of the vestments the priest would wear that day. Red indicated that the people named for that day were martyrs. The introduction stated that in the Gospels, Simon was called the zealous one. Jude was the brother of Saint James the

Less and therefore related to Christ. Anna read the prayers of the day.

Her mind wandered. She looked at Sister, who had slipped a bit in her chair but still looked comfortable. She quietly walked to Sister's tea table and removed the empty cup. *I will have so much to record in my journal today. I will start with our leaving the train. Then the meal, the tour, the ship. No, the freighter. What a day for journaling.*

"Anna, help me to bed," Sister Calista said.

The two walked from the chair to the bed.

"Sister, I am sure we will have more visitors before the evening is over. You'll probably want to stay dressed."

"Do you think I don't know that?" she snapped. "Forgive me. When I'm sick, the wounded beast takes over, and I roar. It's a pity I'm not more Christ-like and quiet in my suffering."

Anna again sat at the table. Food aromas snuck in through the open window. *Finally.* She closed her book and heard a knock.

"It's Shorty, Ma'am. I've got dinner."

She opened the door, and he carried in a tray. One plate had mashed potatoes, meat in gravy, and green beans. The other had a banana and a bowl of applesauce.

"You came just in time," she said. "I am hungry. Do, you always help the cook?"

"No, I have lots of jobs. This boat is almost four-hundred feet long. I carry things and deliver them from one end to the other all day."

"You do? Is it hard work?"

"Sister—"

"Please call me Anna."

"Aren't you a nun?"

"Not yet. But I'm working on it."

"Anna. I was living in San Francisco. By the docks. No family. Somebody told me about this crazy Irishman, Tommy. He was looking for two boys to use as runners on this long freighter. We'd make a little money, have plenty to eat, a safe place to sleep, and learn things. They call it learning the trade."

"Interesting."

"The thought of plenty to eat caught my interest. I've been with the *Alexandria* for two years now. Since I been here, Pani's been keeping my belly full."

"Pani made me a fine meal. Thank the cook for me, please."

"I'll do that." He left.

Anna sat at the table, said a prayer, unfolded her napkin, and ate her hot meal. Outside, men yelled instructions to each other. Winches squeaked as crates were raised and lowered onto the deck. Sister Calista's snores serenaded her.

Hours later, there was a knock.

After seeing that the sleeping nun was appropriately covered, Anna said, "Come in."

Tommy entered. He wore the gray of the working dockman. "It's been a long day for all of us, right?"

"Yes."

"I'm here to warn ye. Before dawn, we'll be on our way. If you wake early, you can sit outside and watch the goings-on. Or peek out through the windows. Or you can stay asleep."

She smiled in anticipation.

"I'm bunkin' with Brendan. His room is right next door." He pointed to the wall where Sister was sleeping. "Jist pound on the wall if ye need somethin'. By tomorry afternoon, ye'll see sights never expected. And the next day, when we're out to sea, we can talk and talk. So, get all yer questions ready. Fer now, use whatever you want in the room. My house is yer house. And I'm blessed to have ye. It will be a sacred voyage."

"We are so glad to be aboard."

"Oh, we found some ginger root fer Sister's tea. How is she?"

"About the same."

"I hope Sister will be better by tomorrow. Ye met Shorty, right? He kin get a message to me tomorry if ye need anythin'." He stifled a yawn as he left the room.

"Good night." She closed the door.

I wonder if I'll be able to sleep in my new bed.

TWENTY-FIVE

Whoosh. Whoosh. Anna heard the strange noise and woke with a start. *Morning already? Is Sister calling? Does she need help to the bathroom again?* Anna listened for the clickety-*clack* of the train crossing its tracks.

Whoosh. Whoosh. The sound did not match her dream. Cobwebs filled her head. Birds squawked. *I am on the Alexandria, aboard a moving ship. Good morning, God. Life is already amazing today, and I have only opened my eyes. Mighty is Thy name. Bless us all this day.*

The rhythmic breathing and a gentle snore from the bed convinced Anna that her companion was finally comfortable. *I'll need to find some kind of a screen to put in front of her bed so she can rest with privacy.* She looked across the room as the dawn's light slid from the table and chairs to Sister's bedside stand. *We seem to be turning around.*

Footsteps passed the door. Farther away, baritone voices mixed with laughter came from the deck.

She tiptoed through the room and hurriedly washed and changed her clothes. Outside the window, men coiled a dripping wet rope. *This must be part of the process of leaving the dock. I have read about all the ropes used to tie a boat to a pier.* Several men walked along, tugging at items. They seemed to be buckling down anything that was loose. *Tommy said I could sit outside and watch the action. I will pray with the morning sun as my companion.* Opening her prayer book, she found the day's agenda. *May Saint Hilary guide me today.*

She opened the door and carried the prayer book into her new world. *I honor You for the water beneath us. It ripples, making the vessel rise and fall. It seems to be as anxious as I am to be on our way. Thank You for this water near Seattle, be it inlet or sound. Bless this crew of workers. Hail Mary—*

"Good morning, Anna. Shall I let Pani know you ladies are ready for breakfast?" Shorty asked.

"Yes. Thank you, Shorty."

Harmonica music reached her. Anna walked around a corner to better see the working ship. The ship looked longer than the road from her house to Julia's parents' home. Mist covered the front of the vessel. Behind her, pink daylight cut through the sky.

Above all the sounds and sights, she smelled coffee. Freshly brewed coffee. Coffee she would enjoy with milk and sugar. *Oh, Lord, I was interrupted. Thank You for the smell of coffee. The aroma is swirling in my nose before it reaches my lungs.*

Dishes clinked. "Anna, would you like to eat out here?" Shorty asked, showing her the breakfast tray.

"No, Sister Calista will want to eat in the room. I will take the tray in. Thank you, Shorty." She took the tray, opened the door, and carried it inside.

I need to talk to Tommy as soon as possible. What if Sister is contagious? No one else should come into our room until we are sure she is not carrying a disease. I remember when Mama got sick. At first, we thought it was a simple cold. Tata always said it was a blessing that Mama did not infect us with her influenza or we would all be dead. I remember little of her being sick, except I was never allowed to be near her in the last week she was alive. Yet I do recall her telling us, again and again, to wash our hands well with soap and water.

"Put the food on the table," Sister said as Anna entered the room. She raised her shoulders off the bed. Her gown clung to her sweaty body.

"Are you running a fever, Sister?" Anna's voice trembled. She remembered Mama's high temperature with contagious influenza.

"No. What are we eating today?"

228

"We have coffee and—"

"I won't have any of that. I need to start with tea. Maybe I'll have a slice of toast." An ugly gurgle erupted from her mouth. "I'm still sick. Where's the pan?"

Anna grabbed the pan from the bedside and placed it under Sister's chin. The nun retched and threw up foul smelling liquid.

Sister Calista gulped. "How could I still be sick? As soon as my stomach settles, I'll have tea." She handed Anna the basin. "No eating yet for me."

The dank odor in the pan put tears in Anna's eyes. "Sister, I know you will feel better tomorrow. When you are ready, I will pour your tea. I am going to find your toothbrush if you let me. You will feel better when your mouth has a fresh taste. Right? There is baking soda in the bathroom and we will use that for teeth brushing or we can find your toothpaste." Anna put down the pan and tried to open a window. It was either stuck closed or permanently shut.

"Help me," Sister said.

She helped Sister swing both legs out of the bed. "When you feel better, you will look out these windows and see how big this ship is. It is longer than all the halls at the monastery put together."

Sister groaned as she walked. "You'll find my toothbrush and a tube of Colgate toothpaste in that smallest bag. Stand beside me, will you, so I don't fall."

Hail Mary, full of grace. What could be wrong with Sister? I am sorry I did not insist that Tommy find a doctor to look at her. We will be in trouble if I catch what she has. Then, who will be our caretaker?

Once in the bathroom, Sister closed the door.

I cannot enjoy this glorious morning, Lord, for worrying about my friend. She went to Sister's bed, straightened the linen, fluffed the pillow, then tried again to open a window. Finally, she found one that opened. The breeze carried scents of grease and oil from the machinery nearby. The oil smell reminded her of home. The engine pounded louder than the noise of the seabirds. Shadows of machinery fell on the room as the ship started a swing in a different direction.

The bathroom door opened. "I feel better. I'm ready for tea and applesauce." Sister smiled and made her way to the table in front of the windows. She sat down and poured her tea. "Smell that fine brew. Oh." She moaned. "I'm sick again." She hurried back to the bathroom.

Someone knocked. Anna opened the door to see Tommy.

"How's Sister today?" he asked.

"No better. I should have insisted she see a doctor yesterday." Anna slid out the door as she spoke, barring his entry into the room.

"I wuz wonderin'. We have a choice. I kin either go straight down the coast as planned or stop in San Francisco. Pani knows a doctor there. The shippers in San Francisco wanted me to stop an' pick up cargo anyway. I tol' 'em no. But they'll probly have more cargo fer us. We kin pick it up and git the doctor to come an' see Sister."

She raised her voice over the engine noise. "What a good idea. You can make such a change?"

"I'm the captain. And me crew won't mind. They're fine folk. I'll have Pani make a special treat for their dinner."

Anna nodded. "The stop will ease my mind. I cannot let anyone into this room until I know what is happening. I am so worried it may be contagious."

"Right you are. I'll let Shorty know not to come in. He kin knock and ask questions and pass yer meals to ye."

"That's fine."

"Miss Anna, it may be dark before we git to San Francisco. Or we may not dock 'til morning. Depends on the winds an' the tides."

"Thank you, Tommy. Please tell Shorty I will need lots of soap here to clean things."

"Shure thing," he said.

Anna went back into the room. Sister Calista had returned to bed. Her eyes were closed. Anna smoothed out the blankets covering her sick friend. Then, she went to the table and ate her cold pancake breakfast. *My own fault. I should have eaten as soon as it arrived. Sister and I will not be eating together. Next meal, I will know.* She removed the silverware from the tray. *At least, I can keep Sister's silverware away from the crew and separate my utensils from hers until we know what is making her sick.*

After breakfast, she walked around the cabin and stopped at the bookcase. *I have always heard you can tell what a person is like by what they read.* On the bookshelf above her bed, she saw the titles on the book spines. Top row, strange letters. *These must be written in Irish.* Two titles sounded familiar. The first was *Candide* by Voltaire, the second was *Don Quixote De La Mancha* by Miguel de Cervantes Saavedra. On a lower shelf, she found a book called *Knots*. Pulling it down, she saw illustrations of rope tying—over, under, double, triple, and much more. *Mama loved knots. I will be sure to read this one for a while.* She returned it. The rest of the shelf was full of English primers and number books she remembered from first grade. *What respect I have for a man who tries.*

Returning to the table, she opened her prayer book.

Sister Calista sat up. "I feel better. I'll get washed and put on fresh clothes." She stood, wobbled, then threw up in the pan. "Oh, my head is spinning. I can't keep my head up." She lowered herself to the bed and closed her eyes.

Anna stood over her. *God. We honor You for our great blessings of the day. The sun and the water of the Puget Sound this morning show Your might. But, God, help me to understand what is happening to my friend, Sister Calista. Make her strong again. She needs to be her feisty old self to make this journey. She needs to put nausea behind her. Let the doctor figure it out. She is in Your hands now. I have tried all the remedies for nausea that I know. Her dizziness is scary. I need Your help.*

I thank You for Tommy. It is amazing to remember that angels come in all sizes and disguises, some even with red hair. May he be showered with Your blessings.

Anna took the basin to the bathroom and cleaned it out again. Then she sat in the green upholstered chair close to her own bed. *I pray for myself. Let me understand why I am here.* She nodded off to sleep. In her dream, her mother was asking her for water with ginger. She woke. Sister was still asleep. *Now I understand. I have been grieving these many years because I could not take care of my sick mother. Now, Sister Calista is in my care. I will treat her and give the kind of care and dignity I could not give my mother.*

There was a knock on the door. She looked at her sleeping companion then went to the door and opened it a crack.

A lady with a babushka on her head and an apron around her waist handed Anna a bundle. "Soap. From Tommy. *Jestem Pani.* Excuse me. I am Pani. The cook."

"*Dziękuje.*" Anna answered with the Polish word for thank you. When she looked up again, the woman was gone.

Is this a mirage at sea? No, the Fels-Naptha soap in my hand is real.

Anna closed the door and looked out the window. Water rushed and swirled as the boat displaced the calm sea ahead. Birds shrieked. Passing Sister's bed, she smoothed out the covers. Then, she went to the sink in the bathroom and, with soap and water, thoroughly washed the breakfast dishes.

Sister Calista sat up and looked around.

Anna said, "Sister, to my delight, our cook is a Polish lady. I met her at our door a few minutes ago. She introduced herself as Pani, the Polish word for Missus. She brought us soap."

"Oh," was Sister's weak response. "I'll drink my tea now."

"Let me pour you some hot water from the pot. The old tea is cold."

"No matter," she said listlessly.

Anna made tea and added a pinch of ginger.

Sister took it and sipped. "I'm so thirsty, but this time I'm going to take tiny mouthfuls every few minutes. It smells inviting." She sat straighter and smoothed her bonnet. "I must look a fright. My head is a little clearer. What time is it? Is this still the day we sailed? Where in the world, and I do mean that, are we?" She took a tiny sip of tea.

"I was so worried about you. To answer your questions, yes, your bonnet is sitting at a jaunty angle on your head. The time is about... I forgot. We have a clock in the room. See, Tommy has a big one mounted on the wall over your bed." The gold-colored face was about eight inches around. It had a chain and a weight attached at the bottom. "It's shortly after noon." *If I were home, the church bells would be ringing the noon Angelus.*

"Why would the poor man have a clock over his bed?"

Anna raised her eyebrows. "I hope it doesn't hit him in the head if he's asleep when the seas get rough."

Sister responded with a gentle laugh and a little sparkle in her eyes. "So, that's the tick-tick I've been hearing. In my bizarre dreams last night, I thought I was hearing drips of wax from candles in the convent chapel."

"And I was thinking it was the oil machines in the fields of Petroleum City pulling the liquid from the ground. It was so beautiful to hear that sound. The oil machines made a cadence that gave a peace and rhythm to my soul." Anna poured a little more tea into her companion's cup.

"I like the swaying of the boat. Are we at sea?"

"Not the ocean, yet. I still see land. Tommy said we would go through Puget Sound and the Straights of Juan De Fuca before we got to the Pacific."

She drank another sip.

"Sister, Tommy says we are swinging into San Francisco because we want a doctor to examine you. We want to be sure you are not contagious."

"I feel weak but better. Is the stop still necessary? I will lie down, though, for a while."

"Let me help you."

Abruptly, she stood taller and gestured to the washroom. Anna helped her across the room. After the door closed, Anna heard the familiar sound of Sister throwing up.

Soon the nun came out, eyes reddened and with a few tears

running down her cheek. She sighed, sat on the bed, tucked her feet under the covers, leaned on her elbows, and lowered her head to the pillow.

Anna closed her own eyes. *God help us.*

She heard a knock on the door. Shorty stood outside with a lunch tray. He looked like he was holding his breath.

"Just a minute." She handed him the washed breakfast dishes. She sent back the clean silverware, determined to keep only the ones already in the room in case Sister's saliva was contagious. "Thank you."

She looked at her lunch. Steam from chicken soup wafted into the air. Thick slices of bread and a large lump of butter sat on a plate. Anna poured a bit of the broth into the cup and covered it with the saucer to keep it warm. She sat, prayed over her food, put her napkin on her lap, and ate Polish *rosu.* She could almost feel the presence of her dead mother in every bite of the thick noodles, chunks of chicken, parsley, and dill floating in the flavorful broth.

As she ate, she thought about Pani. *I need to send her a note in Polish. I pray she can read.*

She wrote, *Błosłaviona Pani, Hora yest moya kolega, Siostra Calista. Yestemy isolowaćny. Wigemy doktor v San Francisco, dzisaj albo jutro. Dzienkuje. Anna. If anyone non-Polish reads this note, they will know that part of the note said I am wishing Pani a good day. The next line says the soup was delicious, especially the noodles. It tells her that Sister and I are isolated and will see a doctor today or tomorrow. Until then, we are keeping our used silverware. I thank her for her kindness and say I am anxious to meet a fellow Polish woman and visit. I hope this note can be delivered to Pani with the next meal.*

The sick nun's breathing was soft and regular. Anna took a cloth from the sink and wiped down every inch of the room. She found another cloth and wiped the floor. *I am glad Tommy cannot see me. He would wonder if his place was not clean enough. It was. This is only busy work. I think better with my hands moving.*

The music of a harmonica came in through the open window. The melody was unknown. The tempo helped her move the wet cloth left and right over the floor. Soon, the floor glistened. Chores complete, Anna pulled the *Knots* book from the shelf and read the instructions for the ten most common knots, enjoying the illustrations. While her companion slept, Anna took time to bathe and put on fresh clothes.

She sat at the table. Prayers came easily. *God, there is so much to thank You for. Bless the crew. Bless Tommy. Sister looks a little better. The water voyage is smooth. For as long as our journey takes, I will have a new friend, Pani, even if I can only send her thank you notes. Time is flying, or is it moving too slowly? Although it is autumn, this ship is taking us back to summer weather at the equator. God help us. God bless us. God protect us. Let His light shine upon us.*

"Miss Anna," Tommy called.

She opened the door.

"How's Sister today?"

"About the same." She guarded the door to obstruct the view of Sister in bed. "She took some tea, talked to me, asked questions. Then went and threw up again."

A look of concern crossed his face. "Sorry she's not better. But I came to tell ye where we are. We're not out ta sea yet. Once we git outa here, it might be a fast trip down ta San Francisco. Or, we could hit high winds and have a slow trip. We got some li'l islands ta go 'round once we're in the Pacific."

"When do you think we will be in San Francisco?"

"Late tonight or early tomorry. I'll let you know when we kin have the doctor see her."

"I know your guardian angel is right there on your shoulder, watching this ship and all of the people on it. I think of you and say a prayer when I hear your clock ticking."

"Wow." He tapped the heel of his hand against the side of his head. "Thanks for reminding me. I won that clock in a, oh, ne'r mind. Anyways, every day, ye need to pull on the chain and move the weight up ter the top to keep 'er goin'."

"I can do that. And Tommy, I love the harmonica music. Who is playing it?"

"Most half the guys here play. It shure is a fine sound ta travel in the ocean breeze. And it don't mean they're not workin'. Some men's job is just ta watch. Playin' that harmonica keeps them alert. Maybe ye'll be lucky enough ta hear a few of them playin' together. Sounds like Irish angels ta me. Well, gotta run. See ya later."

Anna closed the door. Her companion was in the bathroom. *Thank God the floor was dry.* She went to the bathroom door. "Sister, can I get you some clean clothes?"

"No, Anna, I'm coming out. I feel better. I can get clean clothes. Thank you, dear." She opened the door. Walking with a careful gait, she went to her suitcase and pulled out items.

"I'm so glad you are better, Sister."

"Maybe better. Might just be a temporary reprieve. But while I'm good, I'll put on fresh clothes. I don't want the doctor to smell bad things on me when I get examined."

"Tommy says we will be in port either late tonight or early tomorrow. That may help you decide what clothes you want to put on now. I will be sure to wash your soiled things. I got soap from the cook, Pani." Anna pointed toward the ceiling. "Look up. Tommy had a clothesline in here. I could put a sheet on the rope. You could have more privacy."

"That's a fine idea."

"Sister, can you try this chicken soup? It is lukewarm now, but the taste is heavenly. Is that blasphemous?"

"We're headed to a world where we will be making new rules. God hears, and when we say heavenly, we're making our statement into a prayer. Let me have some of the heavenly soup, dear." She left her clean clothes in a pile and moved to the table. She ate slowly then sighed. "Indeed, we bless this food and the talented hands of the one who prepared it."

Anna drew the clothesline taut and draped a sheet over the cord, creating a private area for the ailing nun. "I have so much to tell you."

"I'm listening."

"First, Tommy's clock. I am going to reset it now. I think it is like one of those Swiss or German clocks where the weight is the control. He asked me to pull up the weight to keep it moving. I hope it does not bop you in the head."

They both laughed.

Anna pulled the loose chain and the weight knob rose from the floor to the base of the clock. "This is not very practical on board a moving ship."

"What else do you need to tell me?"

"It's about Shorty. Does he get any education aboard? If he were my brother, I would want to know someone was teaching him to read and do some arithmetic. I see some simple books here he could use. I want to ask Tommy if I can set up a make-shift school while we're on board."

"What a good idea." Sister Calista took another sip. "This soup is such a gentle pleasure on my weak stomach."

"As I told you earlier, Pani came to the door. She speaks with a Polish accent. I am sending her a thank you note for lunch. I hope we can share tea with her after our visit with the doctor."

"Yes, it would be nice for all three of us."

"With the windows open, I hear harmonicas playing. I think you will enjoy the music as much as—" She smiled at the older nun who had nodded off at the table. Anna gently nudged her awake and guided her back to bed.

All afternoon, it was the same routine. Sister to the bathroom. Sister out. A few sips of liquid. Sister back to sleep.

Anna listened to harmonica music. Gradually, the sound of birds faded. The thump of the ship's motor grew louder. *We are going faster now.* Windows showed end-of-the-day shadows.

Sister sat up in bed. "I smell chicken cooking. That will taste good to me."

"Yes," Anna said. To the pace of the clock, she helped Sister move to the bathroom again.

Shorty delivered soups and two chicken dinners. A little

white lace peeked out from under the teapot. Shavings of ginger were in a tiny cup. Anna handed him the letter for Pani.

She placed the tray on the table and set out the food. They bowed their heads in prayer. Sister eagerly attacked the chicken soup. The noodles and gelled circles of chicken flavor competed with the spices swimming atop the bowls.

Sister's hand flew to her mouth. "I thought this was the perfect meal but—" She hurried to the bathroom once more.

God, let us see the doctor soon. How can we help this poor woman? Anna poured Sister's tea and added a sliver of ginger. *May this ginger do magic on my friend's queasy stomach. May Sister's guardian angel rouse the San Francisco doctor to see her and make a good diagnosis. What could she have? Not influenza because there is no fever. Not seasickness. Even when the ship was not moving, she was still sick. Dear God, help us.*

Sister came from the bathroom.

"What can be done for you?" Anna asked.

"I don't know. Perhaps the doctor will tell us. I hope we'll know something tomorrow." The smell of sickness attached itself to her companion like a cloud.

"Sit on the bed. I will bring you the small basin and let you wash your face for the night." She put hot water from the teapot into the pan, placed a washcloth and tiny cake of soap onto the tray, and carried it to her bedside. She pulled the drape for privacy. The clock ticked as if it were pacing words, *too slow, too fast, let's get finished with the task.*

Anna answered a knock on the door.

Tommy said, "I think we'll pull inta port at the break of dawn. We'll see the doctor sometime tomorry."

She took a deep breath. "Godspeed to all. And goodnight."

Night fell. The sounds of the ship motors grew softer. Harmonica music blended with the gentle splashes of the water and the rhythm of the clock.

TWENTY-SIX

It was the racket of ship motors instead of the clock that announced morning. To Anna, it felt like the shifting of a giant car gear. She looked out the window. Dark clouds marched across the sky. Salty sea air struck her coming-awake nose. She took a deep breath, closed her eyes, and reviewed the night. Sister up. Sister down. Sister throwing up. All night, Tommy's clock seemed to be saying, *Sister sick, tick, tick, tick, get the doctor, make it quick.*

Lord in Heaven let us get good news this morning. She washed and dressed for the day. Morning light snuck across the ceiling of the room. Her companion slept. Her snoring was a mesmerizing sound. The moving ship creaked and groaned. Anna pulled out her prayer book, found October thirtieth, and said her prayers. She pulled open her journal. *I am going to write only positive things.* She wrote *This morning, Sister is having a much-deserved sleep.*

The tap, pause, tap, tap, pause, tap, Anna knew, was Tommy's knocking pattern. "Good morning. How are you this fine day?" she asked as she cracked open the door.

"I hope we'll still be friends, Miss Anna. I take full responsibility fer what I gotta say. We got two more days' journey to San Francisco. I thought I knew how ta read the map. My pilot, Matt, he tol me I shuda checked with 'em. If we wuz way out in the ocean, we'd be goin' faster. But close to land like we gotta be fer the route to San Francisco, it's slow becuz the water's not real deep."

"Ah." She leaned against the doorframe. "Two more days. I'll tell Sister."

"My fault." His face was as red as the hair on his head. "Anythin' I can do to make this time easier, I'll do." He nodded and left.

Anna glanced at all the activity that she was missing. *I would like to feel the spray of the water on my face while standing on deck.* She closed the door and backed into her room. *How will I tell Sister this news?*

The bed was empty when Anna walked behind the partition. She smoothed out the bed covers and fluffed the pillow. Unpleasant smells assaulted her nose. *I am not making this bed. I'm going to air it out.* She pulled the blankets and sheets off the mattress and threw them over the furniture in the room. The pillow got several hearty punches, and then was placed near a window in the sunlight. Behind her, she heard the old familiar denture click. *I have not heard that noise in a few days. Sister must feel better. Since we got aboard, her mouth has been so dry, those dentures were stuck to her mouth. If I hear them, she has got some saliva there. Good for her.*

In stocking feet, Sister plodded toward the table. "I'm going to get dressed after I clean up a bit. Are we in the port yet?"

"No. That was Tommy at the door. There was a miscalculation. We won't be there for two more days."

She maneuvered herself into a chair. "I can wait. I will be stronger by then. But for now, let's find some breakfast."

"What a nice surprise," Anna said. "What foods would tempt you to breakfast?"

Sister said, "As a child, one of my favorite breakfasts was what we called toast in the bowl and toast on the table. Both pieces were buttered, the one in the bowl was swimming in hot milk, the other was dry." She smiled. "Maybe you had to be there to understand the appeal."

Anna grinned. "One of my fondest memories of my mother was her making me what we called French toast. It was sliced bread dipped in beaten egg and fried in butter. It was served with lots of granulated sugar on top."

"Ma'am," a voice outside called.

Anna opened the door. A boy stood there.

"My name is Charlie. Shorty is busy right now. Here's your breakfast." He gave her the tray and quickly shut the door.

"Thank you, Charlie," she said to the closed door.

She carried the tray to the table. A sliced hard-boiled egg and a thin serving of ham were on each of two plates. A piece of toast, cut into four triangles sat on both servings along with a wedge of butter, and a mound of jelly. A china pot decorated with pictures of roses hinted at hot tea. The pot was on a stiff white doily. There were two cups. A tiny vessel again held ginger shavings, but this time it also held a blot of honey. Both ladies sat, prayed, and began breakfast.

"This is what I think is being served for breakfast in Europe," the nun said.

"If it is good enough for them, it is fine for me."

"I will take it slow. First, I'll fix our tea." She poured water and brewed their drinks.

The tea aroma was fresh and inviting.

Anna burned her tongue with her first taste. She said, "You had so many interruptions to your sleep. I am surprised you are so cheerful this morning."

"I won't let a little sour stomach do me in," Sister told her. "Where I come from, we don't talk about illness."

Anna nodded.

Sister said, "We can work on some lesson plans for the boy."

"It seems there are two of them, Shorty and Charlie. Since we do not know if they can read at all, let us decide where to start."

They pulled out the primer, and an hour later, had arranged a reading program and some simple arithmetic for the two youngsters.

"How do you feel?" Anna asked.

"I'm worn out from all this planning. I think I'll rest."

Anna grabbed the linen she'd scattered about the room, re-covered the divan, and topped it with the aired pillow. Sister crawled into her nest.

Anna found a numbers book and continued working on a study plan for the boys. *It makes me think of my baby brother.* She chuckled. *I remember his reaction to being called the baby. He would say that he was grown. After all, he was twelve years old. His brown hair used to tumble over his eyes. Whenever Tata came near, Leon would sweep the hair to the side. Tata thought long hair across the eyes was too modern for his son.*

Sister took some deep breaths and repositioned her pillow. Sunshine glided into the room.

Anna smiled, thinking of Leon. *When we two were alone, he would say, Anna, I know enough to run Tata's store. I'd put a table or booth in here. People could come, buy a cup of coffee, and visit. Her reply had been sarcastic. Leon, what an idea. No one stops to drink coffee until after supper. Do you want Tata to work after five o'clock in the evening? His answer had been a firm, no.*

A slight breeze fluttered her arithmetic papers. She covered them with the inkwell. "What a foolish move. If the ink spills..." She replaced the bottle with a treasure box from Tommy's bookshelf. *Surprisingly heavy. This must be where he hides his gold.*

Sister coughed a few times. It sounded like the preamble to the gulps that hurried her to the washroom. Before Anna could reach the bed, Sister was up and scuffling along. Anna silently walked her companion to the bathroom door. Sister was sick again. She soon came out, and with lowered head, moved unsteadily back to her bed.

Anna took Tommy's treasure box off the papers. She searched the book for more addition problems that included *carry the one to the next column*. Her thoughts returned to Leon. It seemed her baby brother had a new idea every week. Once he suggested placing a basket of fruit on a stand in front of the door to attract customers. Her rebuttal was that if the fruit were outside, Tata would have to hire someone to sit there.

I remember the intense look Tata would give Leon when he shared his plans. Tata never laughed at the ideas. He listened with the same courtesy as when he served his customers who bought groceries in the store.

Harmonica music rose over the soft swish of the waves. Anna found and wrote down the double-digit addition work. She made three copies—one for the instructor and one for each of the two students.

She turned toward a noise. Sister exited the bed, gait unsteady, color pale, making gulping noises. Anna dropped the pen, scattering a few ink droplets on the lesson plan. She moved to the nun, placed an arm under a shaky elbow, and helped her walk across the room. The too familiar swallowing noise came from Sister's throat.

Anna heard the clock's rhythmic pace. *Sister's sick from head to toe, here we go, take it slow.* And so, the monotonous day continued through lunch, dinner, and the night.

The next morning, on opening her prayer book, Anna remembered it was October thirty-first, only one day away from the Feast of All Saints. *I will miss all the novenas and prayers said in the churches. Yet, it seems I am praying more here in this room.*

With Sister asleep, Anna had time to wonder about Tommy's heavy treasure box. *It could hold money. It could have irreplaceable family pictures. Possibly it held letters from a love and maybe a lock of her hair.*

He must have left her behind in Ireland. She probably was a fair-skinned girl, with curly hair, red as fire, and with a lilt to her voice. Did she sing to him? Is dating different in Ireland? I hear they are all Catholic there. Every date must be chaperoned and proper. But, Tommy's such a mercurial guy. He would be able to find a secret spot for a few kisses.

This is a part of life I passed by. I thought I heard God calling me. Yet, in church, the priest said few of us in the New Testament hear the voice of God. Her heart twisted a bit. *When I am at peace, is it His voice I hear? Lord, in the quiet times, show me Your direction for my life.*

By midafternoon, Sister seemed stronger. She laid out her

clothes for the doctor's visit the next day.

Anna said, "Tomorrow is the Feast of All Saints. Maybe we can pray together."

"We should pray with the crew. Remember, even now God asks us to spread His word and love." She opened her hands toward Anna, fingers splayed. It looked like she was a statue of the Virgin Mary with blessings flowing out from her palms.

"Sister, you always have something new to teach me."

"You need to arrange a time for me to tell a Bible story to the crew. I have an amazing story of the Good Shepherd that I'll share with them."

"I will speak to Tommy about it."

As the sun went down, harmonicas serenaded the sea and the two ladies.

TWENTY-SEVEN

Anna was awakened before daybreak by the *Alexandria's* motors belching then picking up speed. She knelt and said her morning prayers as they continued the smooth journey over the water.

I feel the ship speeding us to San Francisco and the doctor. Sister was only up twice last night. I pray she will feel better today. I offer You, God, all my actions of this day.

Anna looked at her sleeping companion. Sister's skin glistened. *Was she perspiring? Was she running a fever?*

She opened the window wider so the nun would be comfortable. The sea breeze blew, and Anna tasted the salt on her lips.

God, I thank You for the wonderful crew of the Alexandria. Bless them on this journey. She opened her prayer book. It was November first.

Sister took a deep breath. In a weak voice, she said, "Anna, is this the doctor day?"

"Yes," Anna said.

"I'll get up and get ready." As she tottered across the room, she hummed Ave Maria.

"I like the tune," Anna said.

"I dreamed our organist was practicing the Bach Gounod version of this hymn." Sister got her clean clothes and went to the washroom, still humming.

Anna answered a knock on the door.

Shorty stood outside with their breakfast tray. "Tommy sez we'll be stopping soon." He backed away from the doorway.

"Thank you, Shorty," she said.

The two nuns sat at the table and prayed over their meal.

Anna ate warm eggs and toast. Sister Calista took a few bites of dry toast and an occasional mouthful of tea.

The ship slowed and stopped. Horns blew. Birds squawked. Voices filtered into the room, muffled by the wind and the waves hitting the resting ship.

"Over here."

"Tie that line tighter."

"Hurry back."

Through the window, Anna watched winches lift crates onto the ship. They landed on deck with a loud thud.

Sister opened her prayer book. The nun gulped and swallowed hard. Yet, she continued reading.

An hour later, there was a knock. "May I come in?" said a deep, unfamiliar voice.

He sounds like Uncle Stanley who used to visit us after church each Sunday.

Anna opened the door to a tall, slim man dressed in black. His hair was curly and disheveled. A mustache ending with an elegant curl decorated each cheek.

"I am Doctorr. Doctorr Biały. Muy cousin, the lady cook, sent me to examine the Sisterr Calista." He spoke in the familiar Polish sing-song with much tongue rolling. He stepped into the room.

Sister described her gastric problems. "I want to know exactly how sick I am and what to expect."

Doctor Biały nodded. After asking her permission, he used his stethoscope to listen to her chest and back. He palpated her abdomen. He pinched the flesh of her forearms and pressed her ankles. Then he pulled down her lower eyelids and looked into her eyes. When he examined her mouth, he flinched as if at Sister's rank breath.

"Sisterr Calista, you arre not contagious. But you have a bad problem. You arre suffering from ptomaine poisoning, often called food poisoning. You no doubt ate some bad food."

"In Seattle," Anna blurted, thinking of the Sauerbraten.

"And now?" Sister asked.

"Yourr body is trying to heal. You arre verry strong woman.

246

But your body is too drry. The only way to heal is to take in much more fluid." He bundled up his stethoscope and laid it on the table beside him. "I know you want only the trruth, so I will be blunt. Looking at yourr condition," his voice elevated, "I would say most people so dehydrated as you will die from this. Unforrtunately, therre is no medicine to cure ptomaine. My rrecomendation is that you leave the ship. I would like to take you home to stay with my family."

"I can't do that. I have a mission to complete. I must stay aboard."

He held out his hands as if in supplication. "Nonetheless, I offerr you my home and family. They arre good Catholics. They would offerr you drrinks and brroth frrequently."

She looked away. "Thank you, but no. I've come this far."

He sighed. "Trry tea with honey, waterr with gingerr, thin soup. Then prrogress to toast if it will stay down."

Sister said, "Thank you, Doctor. I appreciate your honesty. I will pray for you."

He wiped his equipment with cotton balls drenched with alcohol. Anna recognized the smell from the monastery infirmary. Then he repacked his bag, snapped it shut, and walked out the door.

Anna followed. "Doctor, what more can I do?"

"You arre taking good care of herr. Let herr eat whateverr she wants. If she doesn't improve in the next few days," again his voice elevated, "she neverr will. I think she knows that. It must be a most imporrtant jourrney forr the two of you." He gave her a fatherly pat on the back and ambled away.

Anna watched Dr. Biały disembark. Men untied ropes. Others pulled them in. The ship's motors grew louder as the *Alexandria* turned away from San Francisco. She looked up at the city as the ship maneuvered its exit, but a mantle of fog blanketed her view. The haze was so thick she couldn't see the front of the vessel. Condensation felt wet on her skin. Like tears.

Sister will get better or not. What kind of advice is that? Maybe when we get to the Galapagos, the doctor there will have more remedies. I am so afraid. God, give me strength.

After a lunch of chicken soup, Sister napped.

Tommy came to visit. His green eyes darted around his room. "Ye look settled in here. I like the curtain ye put up fer Sister. Is she sleepin'?"

"Yes. Tommy, it is important that we get to the islands quickly. How soon will we be arriving?"

"*Miss Alex* goes twelve to fourteen knots an hour. A knot is a little short of a mile. We have 400 miles ta go. With the wind and current, it could be three days or seven days, dependin' on the weather. I need ta ask Matt, the pilot. I'll git back to ye on that."

"I understand. You are all doing such a fine job. I want to thank Pani when she is free, too."

He nodded. "I'll tell Pani you said thank you."

"Let me walk you to the door," Anna said. Outside, she told him everything that the doctor said. "I am sure you'll keep it confidential."

"Yes, yes." His face turned grim. "A death at sea is the worst thing that can happen. It follers the ship. It's the first thing mates remember when they say a ship's name. We'll be a hurry'n. Ya kin believe it."

Back in the room, Anna helped Sister wobble to a chair. The sun shone on her pale face as she took a few swallows of tea. A few minutes later, she gulped and threw up in the bathroom. When she returned to her bed, she turned to face the wall.

Sister's breath is foul. How can I face her dying on the ship? Maybe she will die in her sleep. I need to listen to her breathing during the night. I volunteered for this journey. With God's help, I will see this through.

Anna opened her journal and recounted the doctor, his diagnosis, and the lift of the quarantine. It was all the good news she had for the day. To keep busy, she found her sewing kit and sewed French knots on two of Tommy's throw pillows. *This will be a nice Thank You Gift to our host.*

There was a soft knock on the door. "*Prosze?*" That was a way of saying hello in Polish. It meant *please*, as in *excuse me, am I bothering you?* or *is this a good time to visit?*

Anna opened the door. A smiling woman of about forty stood there. She wore a long, floral-print dress covered with an apron as white as new snow. Her chestnut hair had strands of silver. It was clustered into a bun at the nape of her neck. She held out a loaf of bread with wisps of steam surrounding it.

Anna saw her own Polish roots in the woman. "Pani. It is good to see you again."

They hugged like long-lost relatives.

Anna drew her inside and ushered her to a chair. "*Dziękuje,*" she said, thanking her for the gift of bread. Speaking in Polish, Anna told Pani about Sister's illness.

On hearing the diagnosis, Pani brought her hand to her mouth then offered to help in any way possible. "*Móy Boże. Jeszcze coś, Panienka?*"

Sister stirred.

Anna went to the nun. "We have a guest. Our gracious cook and baker."

Sister got out of bed and came to the table. "I am delighted to meet a woman who works so well on a ship. Can I ask you how you became—" She stopped. "No, how a lady from Poland came to be aboard?"

"*Nie rozumje,*" Pani said to Anna.

"Sister, I will have to translate." Anna passed along the question and got Pani's answer. "Pani says she and her young son, Władysław, came to America hoping to stay with family. But it did not happen. They struggled for years. Włady, called Ladi by his friends, dreamed of a life at sea. After he became an adult, they moved to San Francisco. Along came Tommy. He was looking for a cook and a machinist. Tommy did not know about the stories of bad luck with having a woman aboard. By the time he heard of it, he and his crew were already enchanted with Pani's cooking."

Sister said, "Tell her how pleased we are to meet her, and that we are enjoying the food."

Anna did. Pani nodded and smiled.

Sister said, "You remember, Anna, that I wanted to meet some of the crew and tell them a Bible story. We are women of God and need to teach when possible."

"Yes, but you have been so weak."

"With this diagnosis, I could get weaker. I'd like to speak to the crew tonight, if possible. Can Pani take you to ask Tommy?"

Anna and Pani left the room to find Tommy. He answered her request with a big smile. After dinner, as the sun was setting on the Pacific, the men gathered on the deck to listen to Sister.

"I want to tell you about The Good Shepherd," Sister said. "This is the 23rd Psalm and is the one most of us have heard. It is Jesus telling us he is the good shepherd. In the Psalm, which is only a few paragraphs, it says, *thy rod and thy staff give me courage.* The parable means the good shepherd is watchful for the poor sheep that are caught in the briars. He pulls them out with his staff because it is a big wooden hook. The rod he carries is a heavy piece of wood shaped like a baseball bat. The shepherd individually whittles the part where he places his hand for a good fit. Then he spends hours perfecting his aim by tossing it at specific stationary targets. The man develops a very accurate throw. Whenever a wolf circles the sheep, he flings his rod at the predator and scares it away.

"Another phrase is, *He maketh me lie down in green pastures.* Sheep are very squirmy beings. They prefer to stand because of wolves. Only when a shepherd presses his hand on the sheep's back will the animal feel secure enough to lie down. The shepherd calms his flock.

"The last phrase is, *You anoint my head with oil.* Sheep, unfortunately, have runny noses. As each day progresses, the mucus attracts bugs. This annoys the sheep so much, they bang their heads against anything handy to stop the discomfort. The shepherd carries a sack of oil and liniment. Each night, he pours some oil on the head of each of his flock. It runs into their noses, kills the bugs, and comforts the sheep.

"If ever any of you men feel alone, think of the Good Shepherd and know peace," she said in a quavering voice.

She got up from her chair and walked back into their room. Anna helped her to the bathroom where she threw up again.

"I think I'll turn in early. It's been a long and eventful day." Sister walked at a snail's pace to her bed.

"Sister, your lesson on Psalm 23 was such a gift to the crew. I heard a few members of the group clearing their throats because they would not want to shed a tear in front of the others."

"Thank you, dear. I heard that story at a mission one evening, and it made Our Lord so touchable."

"It did. I do not know if I have anything that beautiful in my head to share."

"Pray for it." She turned to the wall and repositioned the pillow under her head.

In the quiet of the room, Anna heard Tommy's clock. It seemed to say, *Sister's trying, time is flying.*

"I am going out on deck, Sister. I want to see the moon."

Rhythmic breathing came from the sleeping nun.

Anna went out and gently closed the door. A new view opened to her. Far to the front, which she knew was called either the bow or the stern, lights twinkled. They looked so far away, it made the ship seem miles long. Above her, moving to the east, a few clouds swept the sky. A half-moon peeked out. Its glow sparkled on the ocean's surface. The ever-present harmonica music beckoned mermaids to the ship.

She found the chair Sister had used and sat down. *These men sound cheerful in their work. I need to copy them and be happy in my mission to help the doctor and learn from Sister. I want her to get better. Lord, please listen to my prayer.*

Nearby, Pani and a male voice approached speaking Polish.

Pani said, "*Syn, ile dnia idzymy do Galapagos? Shiostra bardzo hora.*"

His reply was, "*Mama, nie znam. Moze trzy, sztery dnia.*"

A muscular man with short, brown hair came around the corner with Pani. Seeing Anna, they said, "*Dobry wiechór.*"

Her answer for the greeting of a good evening was a comment on the moon. "*Dzishaj księźyc wielki.*"

"*Chiekajce. Władzu, tu jest Panienka Anna.*" Pani introduced Anna to the man. "*Moi syn, Władek.*"

Anna felt hard callouses when she shook his hand. *So, this is Władysław, Pani's son.*

Władek said in stilted English, "Nice to meet you, Anna. Mother told me so much about you. I feel we are friends already." Władek then kissed his mother and wished her a good night. "*Dobra noc.*" He left.

Anna said in Polish, "I heard your conversation about the travel time to the island."

"Yes. His guess was three to four days."

Anna said, "I want to sit and visit with you. But, I need to be near Sister Calista. Could you join me inside?"

"I would like that."

Anna turned on a light in the room. She peeked at Sister and was relieved to see her asleep.

The two women sat on the soft, green chairs.

"It's so nice to hear someone speak Polish again," Anna said. "I would love to hear about growing up in Poland."

"Life was hard in the old country." Pani shook her head and examined her hands. "When I look, I still expect to see dirt caked on my fingers and under my nails. I grew up with siblings, including a twin sister. My baptismal name is Mary, so I am known as Mania. My twin's name was Frances, and we called her Frania. She married and had her son, Władysław, a year later. Sad to say, when he was three, Frania caught a bad cold. She died before the spring flowers burst out of the ground. Losing my twin was like misplacing my right arm."

"How sad for you and your family."

Pani said, "You know how men are. One year after Frania died, her husband found a new wife. She did not like Włady."

"So, you became his mother?"

"In many families, there are numerous children, and some are raised by sisters or cousins."

Anna said, "Yes, we had several families in our church with eight or more children. One girl in my class, Dorothy, was being raised by her Aunt Rose, and her brother, Bernard, lived with his grandmother."

"Older boys who helped with the farming were in demand. But Władziu… He was such a tiny boy. My married sisters did not want him." She clutched her chest. "It was breaking my heart. I had wanted him from the time Frania died. I took him and said he was mine forever. No one dared to remove him from me."

"It looks like you never regretted that decision."

"He's been my son since. When he was fourteen, I'd had enough of the village. I had worked hard and saved some money. We booked passage to America."

"That's a lovely story."

Pani stood. "I must return. I hope we can talk again."

Anna said, "I hope so, too."

They hugged goodbye.

Behind her, Sister cleared her throat. "Anna."

Anna hurried behind the curtain.

Sister trembled. "I feel so weak. I can barely stand. Can you help me to the bathroom?"

"Of course." She guided the unsteady nun to the washroom. *The skin on her arms feels loose.*

Anna waited at the door for Sister to exit.

Sister said, "I dreamed I heard harps. The sounds were sweet and soothing."

"It might be the rhythm of the water." She helped the nun back to bed. Her gait had slowed to a waddle.

"I heard you say you were going out. Remember, Anna, you cannot be on the deck unless accompanied by another female. The men will not be respectful."

"Yes, Sister." *Will I ever learn the correct behavior of a nun?*

After Sister had fallen back to sleep, Anna looked out the window at the stars. *I am not even sure the North Star is visible this far south. But I am thinking of you, Bashia. Do you feel me?*

She washed and changed into her nightdress. Then she knelt at her bedside. *I am full of sorrow at not making good decisions.* After her prayers, she climbed into bed still holding her rosary.

TWENTY-EIGHT

Anna washed and dressed for the day. In her prayer book, she noted that the saint of the fourth day of November was Saint Charles Borromeo. He was a young Bishop when he started a group called the Confraternity of Christian Doctrine. It became an early worldwide method of teaching the young the ways of the church. *He will bless my plan to teach Shorty and Charlie.*

She heard a *Tommy* knock.

"Miss Anna," Tommy called.

She glanced at Sister and saw the nun asleep. She pulled the curtain as far as possible for privacy before saying, "Come in."

He entered. Happiness sparkled in his green eyes. "I have good news. We been movin' at fourteen knots an hour 'cuz we knew how much ye wanted to git to the island. We'll see the Galapagos on the horizon tonight and git you there tomorry."

"This is wonderful news. I cannot wait for Sister to wake up so I can tell her."

With a bow, he was gone. *What a funny little man. I did feel the motors moving most of the time in the last few days. I suppose they want us off as soon as possible. I will say a quick prayer of thanks to Saint Charles Borromeo. He must have speeded our arrival.*

"*Przepraszam?*" Pani knocked, saying the Polish excuse me.

Anna answered the door wishing her a good day. "*Dzień dobry, Pani.*"

She asked about the nun's health. "*Siosta lepiej?*"

"*No, jeszcze bardzo hora.*" Anna felt bad as she told Pani

there was no improvement. She added the good news of an arrival date. "*Jutro, będziemy v Galapagos.*"

Pani nodded and handed the breakfast tray to Anna.

Under the white cloth, Anna saw toast, soft boiled eggs, and applesauce. There was hot tea for Sister and steaming coffee for her.

"The coffee smells especially good this morning," Anna said. "Dziękuje."

Pani smiled and left.

Anna ate her breakfast. *God help me make this last day on the ship a good day for Sister.*

Sister awoke. She sat at the table and began yet another story of Christmas past. "When I was a little girl, I only wanted a baby doll for Christmas. I had seen one in the Sears and Roebuck catalog. The doll I liked had blue eyes that opened and closed." She gave a wistful smile. "On Christmas morning, I got a doll. She had brown eyes painted on her face. The eyes did not open and close. I tried to act happy but was smiling with tears in my eyes. My parents could not afford better, and I knew it. But, I had wished so hard."

Anna said, "Tommy came, and the news is good. We could be on the island tomorrow."

"Glory be to God." Sister folded her hands as if in prayer. "I hope to live to see it."

Anna frowned. "Of course, you will."

"Please take me to the bathroom," Sister said. She came out holding her belly. "I have such cramps."

"Perhaps Pani has something to soothe you."

Sister tapped her forefinger against her head. "I have paregoric in our medicine bag. It will cure the cramps. Let me look." With unsteady steps, she started across the room. Her face paled. "Help me. I'm dizzy."

Anna rushed over. She held Sister around the waist and moved her back into a chair. From the shelf, she got down the satchel, opened it, and placed it in front of the nun.

Sister looked up. Dark bags showed under her eyes. "You

should always carry paregoric. I think we packed enough for at least a year." She measured the medicine into a glass and added sugar and a splash of water. "This better stay down," she whispered. Then she tossed it in her mouth. She gagged. Her eyes watered. She placed a hand on her throat and swallowed hard. "Please, walk me to the bed."

Anna settled the nun on the bed. *What if she dies on board? Do I have the courage for this? I will pray for peace in my heart.*

As Sister slept, Anna paced anxiously.

Someone knocked with the tempo of Tommy's hand. "Hi, Sister and Miss Anna. Kin I come in?"

"Shhh. Sister's sleeping again."

"Is she back thure in the bed?"

"Yes." She stepped out of the room, keeping the door ajar. "Tommy, I feel so bad. Our journey is almost over, and I never got a chance to tour your ship."

"Ah, yes, she's a beaut."

"How long is the ship?"

"*Miss Alex* is a three-hunert ninety-seven-foot carrier. Her bottom is shaped like a quarter moon, high at the bow and stern, but the difference is, the middle has like this high house. It holds some motors and stuff, and this cabin, as you kin see. *Miss Alex* moves cargo all aroun' the Pacific, especially in the Americas. She's been mine fer 'bout six years, give er take a bit."

"Have you had any problems with the crew in the six years?" she asked.

"No big 'uns. Every couple of years we git a bad egg aboard. He'll last one trip, and we git rid of 'em." His eyes twinkled, and he added, "Nah, I don't mean we throw 'em overboard. We jist fire 'em. The regular guys'r glad ta have a job, a place ta sleep, and good meals. They stick 'round."

From the room behind them, Sister called weakly, "Anna?"

"I have to go," Anna told Tommy.

He nodded. "I jist stopped ta say I'll be sendin' Shorty 'round ta help with yer things."

"Thank you." She went inside and closed the door.

Sister stirred fitfully. Anna wiped her brow with a damp cloth.

"Anna, if I die before we reach the Galapagos, here's what you do. You close my eyes. Fold my hands on my chest. Look in the medicine bag. There's a bottle of Holy Water. Sprinkle it on my body. Pray a Bible verse. Then you make that crew throw me into the sea."

"Sister, I cannot believe you are telling me this. Will the Catholic Church bless such a thing?"

"God is much more understanding than we think in times of challenges. Your dedication will get me up to see my Lord."

"You are very brave."

"Facts are facts. I am getting weaker by the hour. I may not be able to get out of bed again. If I make it to the island, I don't think I'll last long after we arrive."

"Maybe we should stay here, ask Doctor Graumann to—"

"Won't work. No ship wants a death on board. We're better off on the island."

"Maybe you will be better soon."

Sister raised her eyebrows. "Perhaps the doctor will have a miracle cure."

"We will both pray for that today and see what happens."

"Is there any tea left?"

Anna helped Sister raise the lukewarm cup to her lips. She took a sip then lowered her head to rest.

Anna quietly removed the cup from the bedside. She rushed to the bathroom, turned on the water, and wept. *I am so afraid. I am so alone. I feel so useless. Help me, God. Give me some of Your strength.*

After several minutes, she dried her eyes and straightened her shoulders. T*omorrow, when we arrive at our island, birds, sunshine, and trees will surround me. Leaves will sway in a gentle wind. But for today, there is so much to do.*

She pulled out her notepaper, pen, and supply of ink. *I need to write thank-you-and-God-Bless notes to everyone who has helped us. Can I send letters to Pani after my year on the island? Can she read? That reminds me. I must give my lesson plans to*

Tommy and ask about the person on board who can teach the two boys.

Sister made a loud, gurgled sound. Anna's heart beat faster. She ran over to check on her, but she seemed to be sleeping comfortably again.

My top priority is to have Sister ready to get off the ship as soon as we dock. I had better be sure all our bags are packed. And I will pull out the holy water just in case. Her eyes felt heavy with tears. She ran into the bathroom and splashed handfuls of cold water on her face.

A gentle knock made her look up. "Anna, it's Shorty. I'm supposed to help you move boxes and stuff."

"Come in. We need all of these containers moved closer to the door. And I need to look into the middle-sized black one marked with the word *medicine*."

"Ma'am, I don't read big words." He hung his head. "I don't even read a whole lot of little words. Every now and again, I want an answer to something. The answer is a gift. I know this ship has books. But I can't read the covers and know which one has my answers." He stood taller and added, "I do know how to write my name, though."

She smiled. "That is such a good start."

The two of them tugged, moved, opened and closed, and re-arranged suitcases and packages. Anna pulled out the holy water from the medicine bag. She laid out clean clothes for herself and Sister for their departure.

Tommy knocked. "I came ta see if anythin' else needs ta be done. Is Sister feelin' any better?"

Anna shook her head. "I worry about her more than you can imagine. I will be relieved when we finish the trip tomorrow and she will have a doctor's attention."

Tommy nodded. "I'm sorry ta say it will be a relief for the crew when she's safe on the island, too. Until then, don't ye ferget, Brendan and I are jist one knock away. 'Member, I tol' ya we two were bunked next door?"

"That gives me comfort. After you leave us off tomorrow, you will be on your way to where? South America?"

"Yes Ma'am, Sister, I mean Miss Anna."

"On another subject, I wanted to give the gift of knowledge to your runners. I made some lesson plans for the boys. Who of your crew will be able to teach them reading and arithmetic? These skills are so important. And, I found your book on knots. The pages are well illustrated. These two boys could use it to learn the ten most common knots. I think anyone they meet would be impressed if they could identify the square, the over-hand, and the barrel tie. You men know all these, I'm sure, but the two boys would feel awfully good about themselves if they knew the names and how to make them."

"I'm glad you thought of that. Men sometimes fergit and no one teaches that stuff to the young'uns. This is a good time fer me to git Sebastian up 'ere." He smiled at Shorty. "Go ask Sebastian to come 'n see us if he kin, so Miss Anna will know she didn't go through all this trouble fer' nuthin'."

"I bet I can find him in a few minutes." Shorty hurried away.

Anna sighed and looked at their belongings on the floor. Then she brightened. "I am curious about your treasure box."

His eyes twinkled as if he were a leprechaun. He hurried across the room, picked up the case, and placed it in her hands. "Guess."

"Jewels? A lock of hair from an Irish lassie? A treasure map?"

"Nah. Open it."

She did. It held a clump of black dirt with tufts of dead grass.

"It's Irish loam from the Galway Bay." He put the box to his face and breathed in the musty scent. "It's part of me mother-land and a reminder of me childhood with all the good and hard times saved in a box fer me."

"You are a sentimental fellow."

"I am."

A sharp knock and Shorty's voice interrupted. "Here we are."

Anna pulled open the door. "Come in."

A middle-aged man with thinning hair and glasses stepped in behind the boy.

Tommy put his arm around the man's shoulder. "Sebastian, meet Miss Anna."

Anna expected the soft hands of a schoolteacher but shook the hard-calloused ones of a laborer.

"Good to meet you." He smiled.

She showed him her lessons.

He adjusted his glasses as he examined the papers. "These are excellent. You would make a good teacher."

Anna never thought of herself as a teacher. Although she had enjoyed drawing up the reading and arithmetic study plans.

He shuffled the papers. "My big sister always said I'd make a good teacher, but I had to quit school and go to work at an early age. Now, I'm just a deckhand. When I write and tell her I'm teaching two boys what she taught me, she will be pleased. I thank you for this opportunity. Maybe next year when you are leaving the islands, we will be the ship that takes you home, and these boys will read you some stories."

"We better git back ta work so these ladies kin arrive on schedule tomorry mornin'. Anythin' else ye need?"

"No," she answered. "Thank you."

Later that evening, Pani arrived with a dinner tray. Anna invited her inside. She gave Pani a note of thanks and was delighted that Pani was able to read it.

"I would like to write to you, my new friend, and let you know of my island adventures," Anna said.

"Oh, my. The only letters I have ever received were from the old country. When a ship comes to your island, you can give them the letter. Send it to the name of the ship, *Alexandria*, in Seattle. That is our home port. Then, I will get it. Be sure to tell me everything." Pani smiled, hugged Anna, and left.

Anna sat down with her dinner. Even Pani's wonderful cooking tasted like grass. She peered behind the curtain to watch Sister breathe. *Do I see any movement? No.* Anna moved closer. *Oh, yes, she is breathing. Please, God. Let her keep breathing for at least one more day.*

Anna swiped a cake of soap through the basin, giving the water a fresh scent, and wiped the nun's brow with a cool, damp cloth. *God, I can only do this with Your help. Why am I afraid? Sister is not anxious, but she is old and may be ready to die. I hope the island is beautiful since we have traveled so far. Will I have a room of my own? How do people stay cool? What am I thinking? I should be concerned about Sister.*

She left the sleeping nun. *This is my last night aboard. I will say a blessing on this room.* She picked up the bottle of holy water and walked to the windows. *May the light of the stars, moon, and sun come in through these spaces and warm the room. Make holy those within.* She sprinkled holy water near the windows. She walked to the table. *May all who eat here be nourished by the food You give us. May all here find purpose in their work and wisdom in their choices.* She continued to touch, pray, and sprinkle around Tommy's room.

Finally, she sat in a chair and closed her eyes. *Bless Sister Calista, and bless me, as we leave the Alexandria. May we find a kind and smart doctor to help Sister heal and to partner with us as we work with the needy. Keep me strong so I can help her. Know my fear and be with me. Amen.*

She realized the engines were quiet for the first time in several days. *We must be here.* She looked out the window but saw only water. She opened the door just as Tommy came around the corner.

"Miss Anna, we're finally here. Kin ya believe it? We made it. How's Sister?"

"I regret to say she will not be able to walk off the ship."

He gave her a brotherly pat on the back. "I'm sorry ta hear that. It's been a rough journey fer ya. I know it's a trip I'll never ferget."

"Tommy, you have been so kind to us. Sister Calista and I appreciate all your compassion and thoughtfulness. I have a note here for you to send to the monastery when you get to a port that takes mail. It will explain to the convent nuns about Sister's illness and all your good care."

"I'll be sure to see it off." Tommy took the letter. "Ye'll probly have a boat come by ta drop stuff 'bout once a month er every other month. We might even swing by again. Ya plan ta be here fer a year, right?"

"That is the plan. It will depend on how well we do."

"I un'erstand." He stifled a yawn. "Sorry. We sea folk are part of the early ta rise group, ya know."

"Yes," she said.

"Goodnight, Anna."

"Goodnight, Tommy."

He walked away.

She closed the door. Sister coughed. Anna checked on her. Sister's dull eyes were wide open. She seemed to be staring ahead. Anna touched the nun's arm, horrified at how loose the skin was.

"Sister? Are you all right? Sister?"

Panic welled in Anna's stomach. Then breath rattled in Sister's throat. Her eyes slowly closed, and she resumed her gentle snore. Anna bit back a sob. She took the moist cloth and sponged off Sister's face and hands again. Then she walked to her own bed, knelt, and said a Hail Mary before sliding onto the mattress.

TWENTY-NINE

It seemed only ten minutes later, yet Tommy's clock said it was five o'clock in the morning. The silence of the sea surrounded her. Anna rushed behind the curtain. Sister took a long breath. Anna took one, too. *She never woke up last night. I think I know what that means. We had better move along quickly.*

There came a knock on the door. *"Dzień dobry, Panienka,"* Pani called to Anna.

A young girl? I feel like a gnarly boned old lady today. But she answered, *"Dzień dobry."*

Pani entered with a light breakfast of bread and cheese. "Do you want some help from me this morning to get Sister ready for the departure?"

Anna nodded. "More than you will ever know."

Together, they washed Sister Calista and changed her into fresh clothing. As they worked, they said a few Polish prayers. They placed a clean, dry sheet under the nun. All the while, Sister continued her slow, laborious breathing.

"I will sit with her while you eat and get dressed," Pani said.

Anna ate. She had just finished dressing when Tommy knocked. Two men followed him inside carrying a long canvas sling supported by a wood pole running down each side. Anna remembered seeing a stretcher used when she'd helped with the factory accident so long ago.

"Are we ready?" Tommy asked.

"Yes," Anna said.

The three men lifted Sister onto the sling. Sister took another deep breath.

Pani kissed Anna. "Bȯg z ciebie."

I hope God will be with me. Anna followed the stretcher out the door. The men lowered Sister into a small boat. *She looks so tiny*. Anna joined them. She looked around to see her new home. *My island must be on the other side of the ship. All I see is a ragged piece of land filled with palm trees.*

The men rowed the boat.

Tommy said, "After you two ladies leave us, we'll go back and git all your belongings and bring 'em over."

They reached land in only a few minutes. Anna gaped. There were no buildings. Only a pile of logs. A man stood on the shore, waving at them.

"Doctor Graumann," Tommy called out.

"Yes, I've been expecting a ship. I was watching for two nuns." His voice had a pleasant southern drawl like the ones she had heard while she was a waitress. His hair was light brown and curly. He had a mustache. His frame was slim yet muscular, and his stride was long as he joined them. "I was not expecting a patient. Who have we here?"

Anna shielded her eyes from the blinding sun. "This is Sister Calista."

Sister took a long breath.

"Bring her up to the logs, and we'll make a cozy place for her," the doctor said. "We had a terrible storm two days ago. All my structures were destroyed."

The men carried Sister on the stretcher and lowered her onto a deck of timber. Then they got in their boat and rowed away.

The doctor took Sister's pulse and looked into her eyes. "What happened to her?"

"We saw a doctor in San Francisco," Anna told him. "He said it might be food poisoning. She has been getting weaker and weaker. I tried my best to take care of her." She held her breath, waiting for Sister to breathe again. It did not happen for what seemed like forever. Then the nun took another breath. "We could not have her die aboard the ship."

"Miss, I understand. Ship's crews feel it's bad luck." He

shook his head. "I'll try my best to pull her through this. I am not making any promises, though."

"It's in God's hands, then."

"Are you a nun, too?"

"Postulant. I am her companion. My name is Anna."

"You're pretty young to have this flung on you. Will you return to the ship or stay here? I'm sure it will be a hard choice."

"I need to stay with Sister Calista."

"Miss Anna, that ship will be sailing within the hour. These men can't wait. What if she dies today or tomorrow?"

"I have to stay."

Tommy and the crew returned. They carried the nuns' belongings and laid them at Anna's feet.

"Miss Anna," Tommy said, "The crew and I wish you and Sister Calista health and luck."

"God bless you, Tommy."

He nodded and left. When their little boat reached the *Alexandria*, the ship gave a great belch of smoke and glided toward the horizon.

Anna looked down at Sister. She waited a long while but did not see the nun take a breath.

Doctor Graumann took out his stethoscope. He put the plugs in his ears and listened to Sister's chest. He looked at Anna and shook his head. Then he covered Sister's face with the sheet.

THIRTY

Anna stared at Doctor Graumann. "I can't believe this is happening. It is like a bad dream."

She walked away from the body and the doctor. She needed to get out of the sun, needed to stop and think. *After all of this voyage, my hopes and prayers have failed. Sister Calista is dead.*

The doctor took her arm and led her to the pile of logs. He brushed leaves and sand from one and helped her to sit. "Miss, you know this is real. If it's a dream, we are in it together."

She heard the softness of his voice but couldn't make sense of his words. "What did you say?"

"Miss, you are in a cloud. You need to come on back to Earth. We have plenty to do." He disappeared and returned with a cup. "Here, drink some water. Miss Anna, you've had a big shock. Look at me. Focus." He placed the cup in her hand then moved her hand to her lips.

Water dribbled over her chin. "Oh."

He took the cup away. "Miss Anna, tell me all about Sister Calista. Tell me everything you remember. I want to know."

"We met in the monastery." She glanced around the shaded area where they sat. "Can I lie down, just for a bit?"

"Come." He led her deeper into the thick stand of palms toward a hammock. "Let me help you get into this thing." He seated her, lifted her legs to one side, and placed her into the cool nest. "My Mammy used to relax this way. You rest now. Nod off. I'll be back." He walked to the beach.

The surf glided in and out. Her head filled with the scent of flowers. Above, palm fronds swayed in a soft breeze.

Whistling awoke her. Was she still dreaming? She lifted her head. The doctor had carried her belongings from the beach. He nestled them beneath a rickety sort of tent—a ceiling but no walls. He whistled as he worked.

He looked over at her and wiped his brow. "Ah, you're awake. How do you feel?"

"Better."

"My whistling doesn't disturb you?" He pulled up a tree stump and sat on it.

"No, I like music."

"Good. I made some lunch. Ready to get out of the hammock?"

"Yes." *What an embarrassing situation.* "I don't know how."

"Let me help." He held the ropes and talked her through slipping out. "I'll bring the food up here. Then we can make a plan." He walked away.

Anna stumbled then sat on the tree stump. There were two more nearby. When he returned, he carried a basket of fruit with berries peeking from one side.

"I think I'm hungry," she murmured.

"So am I." He set the basket on one of the stumps then sat on the third. He peeled a banana and handed it to her.

She turned it over and over in her hands. "I had so many pictures in my head of my arrival day, but none quite like this. Thank you for being so kind… Doctor?"

He nodded. "Just call me Doctor for now. And I'll call you Miss Anna. I was brought up in Virginia. Petersburg, Virginia. We call every lady Miss."

"That will be fine." She looked at the doctor's face. *How are the two of us going to live here together?*

"Well, Miss Anna, I have to put all my energy into today's task. We need to be finished with Sister's body by the end of the day. There are wild boars here and…" His voice trailed off.

"And what?"

"I'll spare you the details. Tell me about how you two were

picked for this journey. Tell me more about Sister." His words rolled out of his mouth like slow-melting brown sugar.

"She was raised on a farm. At the convent, Sister worked in the infirmary." She paused and listened to the palm fronds rubbing each other. "We are a praying order. But when your letter came, the nuns were determined to find two medical people and send them to help you. They realized that you thought our order was a nursing one. They knew it could take a year to send a letter, tell you to try another place, and keep you waiting when you needed help now."

"So, neither of you are nurses?"

"No, but Sister Calista knew about herbs and other things to stop pain and cure maladies."

"And you?"

"I... I helped accident victims in a mill in my hometown."

"As my Mammy used to say, Miss Anna, *ya got guts*."

"Either that or no brains."

"You sure you're not from ol' Virginny?"

She blushed and shook her head. "Pensylvania."

He got up. "Ready for some work? I was raised by my grandparents, Mammy and Pappy. Pappy always asked if I was ready for work then said, *Son, you'n me's gonna do it whether we want ta or not*."

"I thought you were from Chicago. And from your name, I thought you were German."

"I went to school in Chicago. Sometimes, I lose my Southern accent. Then I think of Petersburg and fishin' on the Rappahannock, and my drawl is back. My Daddy was German but he was long gone while I was still growing up. My family saw to it I had a proper education. Well, better get to it." He headed toward Sister.

Anna gasped and jumped up. "I need to find the medical bag with the holy water inside. And my prayer book, too. Sister told me if she died, to bless her and dump her off the ship."

"She was a wise woman."

"Why do you say that?"

268

"Because I will be taking her out to sea today to drop her body into deep water."

Her fingers covered her lips, and her eyes opened wider.

He said, "The natives who come to see me are from the east. I call them the East Ones. Recently, they brought a very sick, old man here. He died. The natives insisted on a sea burial. The volcanic terrain here is too hard to dig deep. I went with them to learn how they do things on these islands. I think they have been here for a few centuries. I honor their ways."

They walked to the rickety lean-to. He moved a few boxes to help her search for the medical bag.

"I found it." She picked out the holy water and prayer book then followed him to the beach.

The nun was covered with a tarp.

"Can we unwrap her?" Anna asked.

"Sure." He removed the tarp and sheet from her face.

Anna prayed over her companion. Tears slid down her cheeks as she sprinkled the body with holy water. "Goodbye, dear friend." Her hand traced Sister's face for the last time.

"I need to take her out soon," he said. "Incidentally, do you want to come along?"

In my mind, I have already rehearsed this several times. I can bite my lip and show some courage. "Yes, I do."

"All right, let's get going. The sun is blazing hot. We'll be gone for hours. I need to get some drinking water." He walked back up the slope.

Sister Calista, what did we get into here?

When he came back, his pockets bulged. Each hand held a Mason jar. On his head, he wore two pith helmets. He put down the water jugs. "You need to wear one of these. It will save you from the heat of the sun." He placed a hat on her head.

"I appreciate your thoughtfulness."

"Come along."

With water jugs in hand, they walked past Sister's remains and continued to the shore. A wave came up and wet her shoes and the bottom of her skirt.

A canoe and a raft rested on the water's edge. The raft had four logs tied to each other with one loose log resting on top. He placed another short tree branch on the floating logs. He pulled out a rope, made a slip knot, pulled a folding knife out of his belt, measured, then cut the rope. The rope was placed between the logs then was knotted to the slip knot. The top branch was removed.

"I'm making a raft for Sister's last voyage," he said. "Incidentally, don't you have a shorter skirt and older shoes?"

"No, I do not."

"Then they'll be ruined."

"I am sorry I did not plan ahead. Yes, my clothes are already wet." *I feel so dumb. I'm wearing my woolen habit. Sister Eileen told me to wear the habit until I reached the island. I should have put on one of the dresses she gave me from storage.*

He tied the raft to the canoe. "It's time to bring Sister down."

They went back to Sister's body. The doctor wrapped her securely in the tarp. Then he picked her up and carried her. Perspiration rolled down his face.

At his instructions, Anna pulled the raft to the shore.

"Hold it right there." He placed Sister on the raft. "We need stones to help her sink. I got five, think we could use about five or six more, the same size."

He motioned toward stones the size of cabbage heads. She searched the beach, found more, and added them to the ones in the canoe.

"Get in. We need to be away." He held the canoe for her.

Water squeezed between her toes as she put one wet foot and then the other into the boat. "Do we sit on the floor?"

"You can use the brown pad, Miss."

It smelled like fall leaves when she sat on the cushion.

With the oar in his hand, he stepped in, sat down, reached into a pocket, and took out a compass. "I had this with me when I went with the East Ones. It's a bit of a long way, so you best get comfortable."

"I will."

There was no breeze. Except for an infrequent ripple, the ocean was flat. The only sound was a rhythmic slapping as the paddle sliced into the water on either side. The boat slipped forward, cutting through the sea like a knife.

"Is the ocean usually so calm?"

"No, it's like a fickle woman. Some days calm, some days moody, and other days stormy."

"I'm glad for the hat. Thank you. Even out here on the ocean, it is hot. Did you ever see pictures of women in the tropics carrying sun umbrellas?"

"I can't remember seeing that. But it is mighty hot." He looked at his compass and pulled the boat to the right. "There. This is the way the East Ones came. Miss Anna, it was an odd trip. They seemed so sure of the way. It was straight west of my settlement. Then a gradual turn north after we lost sight of the land. Like now."

She looked back. *Only water there.*

"An elder man guided the rowers. I could hear him call, *no, no*, when the others wanted to turn. It seems like *no* is a universal term. He kept looking in the water at the reefs but wouldn't go over them. As if he were scared. I think they're beautiful. But they could be fragile. I'm gladly going around them. Finally, the old one agreed to let the rowers turn because there were no more reefs in the water." He consulted the compass again. "We're almost there."

She said, "It is hard to say goodbye to Sister."

"Were you two always close?"

"No." She laughed. "When I met her, she was so angry—at me. I had joined the cloister in October. All the other postulants joined in September. Sister Calista was in charge of admissions. I was an inconvenience."

"Why in October?"

"I wrote a letter to the head of the order at that Abbey, Sister Eileen. In it, I explained that since I finally had the blessings of my father, I needed to go as soon as possible, or he might change his mind."

He chuckled. "So how did you and Sister Calista become friends?"

"We slowly warmed up to each other. She had some breathing problems. She would climb the three sets of stairs to our sleeping quarters and think she was surprising us. She sounded like an old furnace firing up." Anna shook her head, surprised to feel her eyes wet with tears. *I will not cry out here on this boat.* "But you, Doctor. What brought you here?"

"I was married for only two years. A fast-moving car killed my wife, Amy, and baby boy, Ralf. In Chicago. Two blocks from my hospital. Two blocks the other way from my office. I passed that corner every day. That is what I called hell. Everyone reads and hears about the Galapagos Islands. They talk about the beauty and the inaccessibility. It seemed like the right place for me. So, here I am. I came to cure my deep melancholy. And that's the story of how I got here straight from Virginny by way of Chicago."

"I am so sorry."

"Not as sorry as me." He consulted the compass. "We're here."

He pulled the trailing raft alongside. All the stones were placed on the body. Then it was rewrapped and tied.

Grief threatened to overcome her. *I can watch this.*

"Say goodbye to Sister Calista, Miss Anna."

She touched the tarp. "Sister, the Good Shepherd is waiting for you. Goodbye."

The ropes holding the logs together were cut. The wood spread apart, and the body sank into the water.

The ocean became as quiet as a sigh.

Anna was surprised. "She was such a big personality. I cannot believe she left with only a ripple." She reached into her pocket, pulled out her rosary, and prayed for Sister Calista. She heard a splash to her right, turned, and saw a fish jump. It was so close, ocean spray struck her face. The heat of the sun pressed upon her.

"Time for water." He handed her a jar and drank from the

other. "We go home, now, Miss Anna. I imagine you have many stories about you and Sister Calista, and I want to hear them all. But I need to change the subject to the East Ones. I am so sorry to put you in this position today. I wanted to have time to talk to you about this when you were rested. But, here's the fact. You are white, young, and lovely. They are an inquisitive people. They will know a ship stopped by, and they'll all want to see the new person on the island. Unless you show great interest in me, you will be courted. You may even be taken against your will if they think you are not my mate."

Her hands flew to her mouth. A lump the size of one of the stones used at the burial tried to slide down her throat.

"I am so sorry, Miss Anna. I did not expect a young nun."

Anna twisted the rosary in her hands. She could not look up. In too short a time, he pulled the canoe to the beach.

THIRTY-ONE

Back on shore, Anna said, "The heat has dried my clothes. Praise God for the power of the sun."

The doctor looked past her down the shoreline and motioned to another canoe. "We're not alone."

"Are we in danger?"

"We have visitors. They are the East Ones. I see the one they call Sno. To myself, I call him Sir Sno the Snoopy One."

"I'm frightened."

"Miss Anna, don't say a word of greeting to him and don't let go of my hand." He picked up the water jars and led her to the clearing.

Sno stood statue still. He had mahogany-colored, glistening skin and long dark hair. He was dressed in a loincloth and wore a leaf arrangement tied with a vine around his left thigh. He looked to be about twenty-five years old.

"Don't look frightened, Miss Anna." The doctor had not let go of her hand. "Incidentally, I know he didn't come alone."

I feel silly holding his hand. I don't know him. She tried to let go, but he held tight. *What did I get myself into?*

At Sno's side, the doctor released her. He knelt, poured clean water on his hands from the water jar, and removed the vine wrap. He added water to the leaves and removed them slowly. "It looks like you've got a deep, nasty wound. I bet you were up to no good. Fishing? Chasing women? Climbing trees?"

Sno pulled a knife out of his waistband. He made little circles in the air with the blade.

The doctor leaned back. "I think you want me to suture it up, Sir Sno."

Sno answered in what Anna assumed was Spanish. It sounded like he agreed.

The doctor smiled at Anna and took her hand again. They walked to a lean-to harboring his supplies. He got out a black bag then removed a needle and a long, yellow thread from a pouch. A second visitor appeared from the trees. He gazed at Anna. Both East Ones nodded.

"Ah, Sir Sno, it seems you brought Frah with you. Miss Anna, meet Frah. I call him the frightened one. He is always looking around, and whatever he sees alarms him. But he looks at you with envy."

She gulped. "I hope I can be a good actress today, Doctor."

"Call me Ralph. My name is really Rolf, but we don't need a pronunciation problem today. These folks don't know what we are talking about, but they will remember your name. I knew Sno was not alone. There are always two or more of them. Don't act frightened. You can either look at the wound or look away, but stay by my side."

"I would not dream of leaving. I do not know where to go, anyway." She gave him a tremulous smile.

He motioned to Sno to sit down, but Sno stood with his arms crossed. *At least, the knife is back in its sheath.*

"Stay close." Ralph reminded her as he knelt beside Sno.

I would rather not look. I do not want to see the injury. I do not want to be here. God help me. She glanced to her right. The terrain was flat for a distance then rose in a gentle slope. A wooden structure was tucked into the bushes. It still looked intact. The ground around it was covered with greens. Palm trees shaded most of the area. To the left, the sun was going down over the ocean. In front of her, the doctor continued to sew the wound. *Is he that gentle, or is Sno simply unwilling to show pain?*

When Ralph finished, Frah handed him fresh leaves as a wound cover. The doctor tied the bandage with the same vine.

Sno gurgled a response then walked away.

"I'm surprised," Ralph said. "Usually, they bring a gift."

The two visitors went to their boat. Frah returned, carrying a basket dripping with water.

"Here come the fish. They will be a welcome dinner. Stand close to me and nod to the men, Miss Anna."

She did. *Are all nuns required to become actresses? I do not think so.*

Frah opened the basket and proudly showed them a half-dozen fish, all with a fresh, salty smell. They were surrounded by seaweed.

"We will eat well tonight," Ralph said.

Standing side-by-side, they watched the East Ones leave.

"I'll build a fire. The first thing we'll make is tea for you. What a day this has been." He walked around, whistling and picking up pieces of wood.

Anna wanted to help, but she didn't know what to look for. She picked up a single piece of driftwood. He accepted it with a smile. In a pit area, he started a fire. He set a pot full of water on a hook suspended over the dancing flame. Then he and Anna moved the three tree stumps near the fire.

"Come," he said. "I'll show you around my camp. I keep food supplies in what's left of this lean-to. It was solid before the storm." He took out a tin of tea and shook it beside his ear. "Incidentally, I found a cave. It is back where the hill starts and is well hidden. The East Ones have never discovered it. I keep most of my supplies there and sleep in it most nights."

They walked back to the fire and sat on the stumps. Ralph spooned tea leaves into two cups then poured in hot water. He handed a cup to Anna. Then he put round fruit in the boiling pot and returned it to the fire.

"These are guavas from our tree right there," he said. "I think you will like them."

"I am so hungry, I will like most anything. It seems like lunch was yesterday, doesn't it?"

"I am sorry for such a wild start to your adventure here."

"One of my main concerns is about the East Ones coming back at night."

"Don't worry about that. They have never visited after sundown. It must be because of the reefs."

"That is a relief."

He sprinkled herbs from a shaker on the fish, rolled them in banana leaves, and put them directly on the coals. The sparks from the fire reminded Anna of Pennsylvania lightning bugs.

Her belly growled. "I do not know what you put on the fish, but it smells wonderful."

"I've become quite the chef of fish."

Minutes later, he pulled the fish out of the fire, and they ate. The unwrapped banana leaves worked as bowls.

"I hope you and I will get along here, Miss Anna," he said. "I need to tell you, I am quite sarcastic and have a nasty temper. You will see it, as time goes on, but I didn't have the heart to be mean to you today."

"So, tomorrow is another day. By the way, shall I call you Doctor or Ralph when we are alone?"

"It better be Ralph. We will need to play out this spouse role so we won't forget whenever they are here."

She nodded. *I need to be on my toes every minute. This is an uncomfortable game we seem to be playing.*

"Do you think you can sleep in a hammock tonight?"

He motioned, and she realized there were three hammocks.

"As you can see," he said, "I thought there would be two nuns, not one."

So did I. "I could probably sleep standing up. I am quite tired." *And weary. I want to cry. I need to be alone.*

"You may have noticed the one building left standing. It resembles a small shed. Four walls. Thatched roof. I have some storage items in there. I will check first to be sure there are no iguanas to scare you. Then, you can go in and change into your sleeping clothes."

"Those iguanas. How big are they?"

"They can be longer than a yardstick. They look like little dragons, but they won't harm you. The iguanas on this island are brownish-red, but some of the other lizards are green." He moved the hot coals around in the fire. "After you come out, I'll show you a few of the constellations in the sky. Miss Anna, there is no place in the world where you will see a more beautiful night. You will even see twinkling stars from your hammock."

He walked her to her suitcase. By the light of the fire, she pulled out a change of clothes. He checked the walled area, pronounced it lizard free, and led her in.

"We have pounds of tea," he said. "I'll make another cup for us while you change."

She came out wearing a nightgown that covered all of her down to the ankles. The gown smelled of the soap she'd received from Pani. *I miss her.*

"Your tea is ready." He served it on the tree stump.

Together, they watched the stars.

THIRTY-TWO

The morning sun teased Anna awake. A bird in the tree above her practiced his four-note song again and again. The other two hammocks were empty. *How do I get out of this sling? Should I call for help? No. I should figure it out myself.* She swung out a foot, lifted her head and shoulders, swung the other foot out, and dumped herself on the ground, landing face down in the sand. *I'm glad no one was here to see that.*

Brushing her hands on her nightgown, she walked deeper into the woods to relieve herself. *And I was afraid we might be using an outhouse.* She went back to the clearing and the lean-to with her belongings. All the suitcases had been lashed to the support poles. She untied her suitcase and pulled out a dark dress. *No more habits for me. I need to do laundry today. Do I wash the clothes in the ocean?* Looking around for the doctor, she walked to the shed and put on her clean dress.

When she returned to the lean-to, Anna said her morning prayers. *Lord, You have made this beautiful island. I thank You for the noise of the tide, for the smell of the salty air, for the sight of the morning sun.* The fresh scent of blooming flowers filled the air. She heard the doctor whistling.

"Ah, you're awake," he said. "Did you sleep well?"

"Surprisingly well, thank you."

"I've made tea for you. Don't get used to being waited upon, Miss Anna, but for today, so be it."

She followed him to the cooking pit. Two cups, a bowl of fruit, and a plate of fish sat on the wooden stump.

"This looks tasty. Thank you, Doctor."

He shook his head. "Ma'am, it's got to be Ralph at all times. For your safety, we cannot forget. I know they speak another language, but they will hear us as we address each other."

"This makes me very uncomfortable."

"That's a good honest answer, Miss Anna. Sit down and have some breakfast. I have something to tell you."

She filled her plate then took a cloth that looked like a napkin. She didn't see any silverware. She sat down, picked up a slice of mango, and took a bite.

He said, "When you arrived yesterday, it felt like a bucket of ice water had been thrown over my head. I did not want you."

The fruit slipped down her throat. She sputtered. "What? You sent a letter."

"I sent that letter six months ago, back when I thought we had friendly neighbors. Three months later, I sent another letter retracting my request."

The balmy breeze changed into a harsh wind.

"My second letter must not have reached the motherhouse in time. Here comes this innocent girl—and you are just a girl in many ways—into my protection. What to do? Should I send you and your dying friend back to the ship?"

"Oh, my," was all she could say.

"Those sailors who dropped you off." He pointed to the shore as if each member of the *Alexandria* crew were standing there. "Every one of them was as polite as possible but were almost running backward down the beach, anxious to get away from the dying nun."

"And I insisted on staying."

"You insisted. I agreed."

"Are you furious with me?"

"No. It was my decision to make. For better or worse, we're here together. Until another boat comes, we need to make a plan. It might be a thirty-day plan or a ninety-day plan." He rubbed his hand over his chin and lightly stroked the stubble of a light-blonde beard. "Incidentally, I was still whistling this morning."

"And why is that important?" She looked at him, eyes squinting in the sun.

"It means we will figure this out, Miss Anna. I do my best thinking when I whistle. I whistle when I'm alone, too. I don't want anyone to jump out at me and think they scare me. It's a defense tactic." He got up from the stump. "We've rested long enough. There's lots of work to do. We can talk and walk at the same time."

"Where are we going?" She scurried to walk at his pace.

"Today, we need to make a decent shelter. I'll cut down trees for logs. You can help remove the tops. We'll construct a roof with the palm fronds."

They walked to his supply lean-to. He put on a straw hat. Opening a chest, he drew out two hatchets and some cloth.

He hoisted the drab, brown fabric onto his shoulder. "This is canvas. I'll use it to haul the trunks back out here to our living area." He handed a hatchet to her. "Do you know how to use this?"

"My father runs a grocery store. He taught me how to use a cleaver. They look similar to this. Lethal and sharp. He told me many times about needing to be alert when I held it. He told me to respect the tool and to be careful."

"Smart man." He looked at her dress. "Don't you have any shorter skirts or short-sleeved shirts? It's mighty hot here."

"No, I will be fine."

"I don't know how to fix your clothing problem."

They walked into the trees.

Dropping his voice, he said, "We need to be together at all times. The tribe might be watching when we're not."

She gulped. "I'll have to follow you around, then."

He put his ear to a tree trunk and tapped, shook his head, and did the same to the next. "We need to put up trunks as posts and weave the fronds into a ceiling. The East Ones did it the last time. I bet we can figure it out."

"Why can't we use the logs from your old structures?"

"Some were damaged in the storm. Others simply floated

away." He tapped again. "I find the best trees have a certain sound when struck. I can't quite say how it resonates."

Anna tugged her dress away from the prickly brambles. She glared at the doctor's back. He was dressed in a short-sleeved shirt and long pants. *Why is he worried about my clothes? He is all covered.*

Finally, he stepped back from a tree and chopped it with his hatchet. The tree came down. Looking pleased with himself, he placed the hatchet in his belt. He rolled the tree trunk onto the canvas and dragged it to the clearing.

They removed the fronds from the tree. The stems were serrated and harsh. Then they went back into the trees and cut down another. By the third trip, the sun was beating down.

As they pulled apart the branches, Ralph asked, "Didn't you think about the climate when you packed to come to the equator? You're going to turn into a prune and die of dehydration."

"The garb for a nun is long and dark. When I agreed to this adventure, I was given old clothes from the closet. These were the dresses the nuns wore the day they entered the convent."

He laughed. "Well, if this weather keeps up, you could feel like you're in hell soon. When I researched this place, it said the temperature from June to November was an average of twenty-two degrees Celsius or seventy-two degrees Fahrenheit. From December to May, it has an average of seventy-seven degrees Fahrenheit. It feels a lot warmer to me."

"And to me."

He stood. "Let's stop for lunch. I caught fish this morning."

They walked to the cooking pit. Anna sank gratefully onto a stump.

As he started the fire, he said, "Later this afternoon, when it's too hot to drag trees, I'll show you the twelve drums of clean rainwater I keep for personal use."

"Can I use that for washing clothes?"

"Of course. I even have a washboard." He cooked the fish and handed her one. "Now, tell me some nun stories. You lived in a convent?"

"They called it a monastery. Usually, nuns call their places cloisters. Yet this one was called a monastery. I believe it had something to do with the benefactor's wishes. It is in a beautiful part of Kentucky. The grass is so healthy it looks blue. There is someone praying in the chapel at every hour of the day and night." She stopped to take a bite of fish. "I was told that one nun prayed by the music of an accordion she must have brought from her home. Another played the most unbelievable violin compositions, also at night. Perhaps they played on special occasions during the day as well. I was not there long enough to see the happenings on certain Holy Days."

"And why did you pick that place?"

"I loved the idea of prayer and isolation. When I got there, it was just as the brochure stated. Yet, the quiet that I thought would be serene was," she shook her head, "unsettling. I thought silence was a relative thing, not a one-hundred-percent state. Sister Calista said—" Her eyes flew open at a sharp pang in her chest.

Ralph leaned as if to touch her hand. "I know you have not mourned for her. It could take days and days for an aching heart to show sorrow. Everyone grieves in his or her own time and way. If you need a few hours alone now and then, be sure to tell me. I will understand."

"That's the kindest thing I could hear today. Sometimes my heart is so heavy. In the Polish culture, we rarely show tears or sorrow. We save it for alone times. I have heard of cultures where people at funerals cry aloud. But I have never seen anyone do that."

"We'll have to arrange some alone time for you then," he said. "Incidentally, I began moving some of your belongings to the cave. They will be safer there. I took a couple of boxes and two bags."

She lowered her head. "The bags belonged to Sister. The black one was her medical bag. The other one held personal items."

"They belong to you now."

"I suppose." She looked away just as a canoe landed on their beach. "Oh!"

He got to his feet. "I think we're in for Act Two."

She stood beside him. Sno and Frah came on shore. One carried a shovel, the other a heavy ax.

Ralph placed his arm around her shoulders. "Anna, you can do this."

She forced a smile as the two East Ones approached. Sno pointed to the ocean. Six more canoes appeared.

"What is going on?" Ralph murmured.

Sno pressed Ralph gently but firmly into a sitting position and pointed again to the boats. The canoes slipped on shore with the surf. Eight men walked up carrying shovels and rope.

Four women followed. They had dark, curly hair long enough to cover them to their waists. They wore skirts of leaves and grass. Only that. None of the women wore a top. Two carried baskets of fruit. With a smile, they placed the fruit gifts in the eating area. The third woman was heavy with pregnancy. Her grass skirt hung low to allow room for her ample belly. The fourth was a girl about fourteen years old. She kept near the pregnant lady as if she were an attendant. The pregnant woman stepped close to Anna. She reached for Anna's pinned up hair. Then she touched and tugged her layered dress.

Ralph smiled at the group. "Ah. These ladies are sure jealous of all your skirts and things."

Sno came over. He bowed to Ralph, nodded to Anna, and pantomimed cutting down trees. Sno twined two of his fingers against each other, twisted them, and gave a leering smile.

"No need." Ralph gestured. "I can provide our living quarters." He tried to stand, but Sno guided him back to his seat. He said, "This seems to be our wedding gift. I wonder what strings are attached."

"Maybe none."

"You are naïve. Have you ever heard the saying that no good deed goes unpunished?"

"No, but that is a confusing phrase."

"The more one thinks about it, the more confusing it gets."

Two of the men dug deep holes. The others dragged tree trunks from the woods. The women who had brought the fruit baskets removed the tops of the fallen trees. Soon a structure was marked off by sturdy vertical logs.

Ralph said, "This might be a good opportunity for you to have some girl talk with this pregnant lady. What is her name? Does she have any living children? Who is her spouse?"

"I will do my best." She looked at her two guests, pointed to herself, and said, "Anna." Pointing to the pregnant lady, she opened her hand as if asking.

The woman shook her head. Sno walked over and put a protective hand on the pregnant lady's shoulder.

Anna pointed to him and said, "Sno." She touched her own chest and said, "Anna."

The pregnant woman pointed to Sno, repeated his name, then pointed to herself and said, "Flor."

Anna nodded and looked at the younger girl. She repeated her own name and Flor's then asked with an open hand.

"Naranja," the young girl said.

Anna said to Ralph, "I could use a drink of water, and I am sure you could, too."

"Let's imitate drinking from a glass." He gestured. "Agua."

The young girl nodded and left.

Anna spelled to Ralph, "I think S N O is F L O R's guy. Agree?"

"I think so."

"I will try to ask about previous babies. Why is that important?"

"I think she may have a problem with the pregnancy. She needs an exam. I could never do it because I'm a male. But, you could."

"What? Are you serious? And I would do this where?"

She looked at the site and saw a wall-less structure. The roof was being woven. The leaf ends of the palm fronds showed, but the stems were hidden. Not a streak of sun reached the floor.

"Solid shade," she said.

"Amazing, isn't it?"

"Do you think we can get close and watch?"

"Business first, Anna. Ask her about her babies."

"All right. But I feel like the construction is going up by magic, and I would love to observe."

Naranja returned with four coconut-shell cups and a pitcher carved from a gourd. She poured a fruity liquid into the cups.

Anna sipped. "Oh, this is so tasty." She emphasized her words to show pleasure.

Naranja smiled and nodded.

"Back to the history, please, Anna."

Anna rocked an imaginary baby in her arms. She pointed to herself and shook her head. Then she pointed to Flor and her belly. Flor mimicked Anna's baby in arms. With a sad expression, she shook her head. Without any thought to propriety or custom, Anna reached over and hugged the woman. Flor stiffened as if in surprise but then relaxed.

"Ralph, I think you are right. She seems to be telling me she has tried for a baby or two."

"That's our puzzle. Does she have trouble carrying a baby, or trouble delivering one?"

"Can we stop now and watch the house go up?"

"Let's you and I get up and walk over."

They stood. Naranja helped Flor to her feet then led her toward one of the hammocks.

Anna took her other arm. "Our guest looks strong but feels unsteady." She helped get Flor into the sling.

Naranja brought over one of the tree stumps and placed it and Flor's drink near the hammock. Then she joined Anna and Ralph. The three of them walked to the building area.

"This is large," she said.

Ralph stood beside her. "I figure it's twelve feet by twelve feet. The roof is looking very solid. It will be good except when the wind blows hard because it lacks walls."

The East Ones continued working around them. Some were

barefoot, some in soft, form-fitting shoes. Their conversations varied from abrupt words to long drawn out sentences.

"This is amazing," Anna said. "All this made of trees."

"Trees and twine. Incidentally, I read that Norwegian settlers inhabit one of these islands. One of our friends has an ax. It must have come by way of Norway."

Naranja turned to two workers coming out of the clearing. "Padre," she said of the first. Then with a crimson sheen on her face, she motioned to the other man. "Regalo."

"He must be her beau," Anna said.

"Well, look there," Ralph said.

The two other ladies approached with Flor between them. Naranja took Anna's arm.

"I think they want you to join them. I wouldn't be surprised if you're expected to examine Flor inside our new home."

"Oh, my," she said. "What will I do?"

"You'll look at her and nod, touch her belly, feel the baby move, and smile. I want to know the location of the baby in her. It will help me know when she will deliver." He handed her a coil of twine. "Measure her. Take the string, put an end on her belly button, and measure upward until you get to a flat part of her belly. Put a knot there on the string. Next, touch the other end of the string on her belly button and measure down until you get to a flat part. Put two knots there on the string. It will help me to know how far along she is. Can you do that?"

"You sound as if you expected this to happen."

"I suspected. Why else would they bring her here?"

"Why did you not tell me earlier?"

"So you wouldn't act nervous around all these men."

"You best be watchful every minute." She followed the ladies into the new hut.

As her young attendant made a screen of branches, Flor took off her skirt. Anna gulped. *I am an adult. I am here to help.* She felt the moving baby and smiled. She measured. She nodded. Naranja dressed Flor. They stepped back into the sun where the group of solemn men stood waiting. Flor nodded to Sno.

Anna handed the knotted twine to the doctor. "I'm happy that's over."

"You did fine. From your knots, I suspect she's at seven months gestation."

"And that means?"

"She is seven months pregnant. That's good and bad. How much longer can she travel? Will she deliver here? Or when she starts labor, will we have to go to her home?" He placed his arm around her shoulder.

Without a word, the East Ones picked up their tools and headed toward the shore. Their canoes skimmed over the smooth ocean as they paddled away. The ebb of the sea made a soft lapping noise as it pulled back the tide. Birds sang in the trees. Mockingbirds repeated their calls. Pearls of perspiration rolled down Anna's forehead, around her ears and the back of her neck. Her many layers of clothing absorbed the moisture.

"You were going to show me where I can wash my clothes."

"This way. I have pans for holding water. Incidentally, I've also got bars of Fels Naphtha soap." He guided her out of the sun and past their new roofed hut. Deep in the trees, he showed her the drums of rainwater and the cleaning equipment. "There is a freshwater pond in the jungle. When the rainy season is over, I can get more water for drinking or laundry there."

"Do you have a clothesline?" she asked.

"No, I use rocks and bushes. Lay the garments on them."

She scrubbed the salt from the hem of her habit. The clean scent of the soap reminded her of the convent. His whistling in the background was a soothing sound.

She said, "Ralph, how do you know all these tunes?"

"Some are from my college days, others from my coworker's radio. There are children's songs, spirituals from church, and ragtime. Don't forget, dear, I lived in Chicago."

"Dear? No need for charades now."

"Well, it seems I feel better when I am around another person. I missed companionship. Does it make you uncomfortable if I call you dear?"

"No, but I've never had one person who cared only for me ever before in my life. I do not know how I feel about that."

"Let me know when you figure it out." His amusement mixed with his southern drawl.

She completed her laundry. Her drying clothes formed bouquets on the bushes. When she looked for Ralph, she found him dressed in pants cut above his knees and a sleeveless shirt.

"Time to go fishing for our dinner." He showed her a bulky fishing net. "Can you find a task in the clearing? I'll want to see you safe each time I look at the shore."

"Yes. I will get my prayer book."

"I find this a good time of day to fish. Let's see what I catch." He walked to the water, took off his shoes, and disappeared into the sea.

Anna sat on a stump with her prayer book.

Alone. Prayer time. God, this whole adventure is more remarkable every minute. I am in Your hands. Thank You for the gift of a roof over our heads. The roof will cover us from the beating sun and the driving rain. Bless our house. Thank You for the gift of labor from the East Ones, whatever their intent. Bless the workers. Each time she looked at the ocean, she saw either Ralph's head or waves. She pulled out her rosary and immersed her mind in prayer. Fifteen minutes of silence later, she felt serenity fall on her like a cloak of love.

She fanned herself with a palm frond. *It is brutally hot in the sun. What will I do to keep cool? Ralph said the temperature was only in the mid-seventies. It must be the humidity that makes it so uncomfortable. My dress is already splashed with sea salt. Will my clothes fall apart? Should I shorten a few of the skirts to mid-calf? They might last longer if I did not wet them every time I walked to the beach. The surf sneaks up like a naughty little brother.*

Whistling interrupted her thoughts.

"Hello, dear."

"Hello," she said. *He has a dimple in his cheek. I wonder if his little boy had that same dimple.*

"I've caught two days' worth of fish. We'll be eating our supper before the sun goes down."

"I'd like to help."

"Good. In our supply lean-to, you'll see some metal boxes with lids. Inside is fruit that I've dried. Can you pull some out for our dinner?"

"Can we save it for another day? The two ladies brought lots of mangos."

"I forgot that. It's been one hell—" He stopped with a silly look on his face.

She laughed. "Yes, it has been one unusual kind of a day."

"Indeed."

"What else do we have to eat around here?"

"Ah. You said *we* as if I was winning you over. So, do you like my South Seas paradise?"

"It is much more entertaining than the abbey." *Why did I say that?*

"As for food, I understand the pirates that invaded used to eat the giant tortoises you see roaming around. They weigh over four hundred pounds." He shook his head. "History says there were whalers here, too. They also butchered the tortoises for food. But for me alone, why in the world would I kill one and waste so much meat?"

"I'd like to see a tortoise."

"No doubt, you will. Anyway, if you get tired of fresh fish, I have canned tuna fish as a substitute. And I have rice. The rice takes too long to cook for us to eat tonight, however. I have more spices than you can imagine. In addition, I have garlic. There are many crabs, too. Did you ever eat garlic crabs, Anna?"

"No, are they good?"

"I'm as sure they're good as you're sure God is in Heaven. We Virginians love our garlic crabs. Mmm."

"Are you teasing me?"

"No. I'm trying to decide if you're only a praying person or a working one, too."

"I'm used to labor from working at my father's store with my family. In the convent, we did some farm work. I never got to milk a cow, but did pick apples, clean animal stalls, and at the kitchen, helped with a little cooking and quite a bit of cleaning. Look at my hands." She lifted her palms towards him, pointing to her callouses and scars.

"Ah." He nodded.

They feasted on fish and fruit. Purple clouds encroached on the setting sun. After they doused the fire, they walked to the roofed hut. The scent of freshly cut wood lent a clean smell to the room.

"They put palm leaves on the floor," he said. "It will work until the first heavy rain. No matter what the direction the rain falls, there's always run-off from the wooded area. I wonder what this roof will do in a big wind."

"You sound worried. Is it because of the last storm?"

"I researched the weather before I came. Simply put, from June to November I could expect cloudy, windy weather with frequent drizzles." He laughed. "Last week's drizzle needs redefining."

"At least it will be daytime shade." She examined the high-arched ceiling. "It's the roof that amazes me. Each frond is laced into the one on the next row like threads in a plaid skirt."

"Should we move our hammocks inside?"

"If we do, we won't be going to sleep looking at the stars or following the clouds like we did last night when the moon was so bright."

He smiled and shook his head. "By the way, did your clothes dry?"

"I'll have to check. And Ralph, I am thinking of cutting a few dress sleeves to the elbow."

"I think it's a good start."

"Start?"

"Maybe the East Ones will bring you some of their shoes. Yours will soon be waterlogged, and they'll fall apart."

"Oh." She looked down. Ralph's feet were covered in leather. "Did you make yours?"

"No. I got them as a gift. I have an extra pair. Let's see if we can make them fit."

They walked to the supply lean-to. In the growing dark, he rummaged in a metal box and pulled out the flat, leather foot coverings.

"Why don't you take off your shoes and try these on? They have a strip of leather that goes over the top. See if you can tighten it enough."

She sat on a stump, unlaced row after row of laces, and removed her shoes. *I wish I'd brought my sandals from the convent. Saint Francis always wears them in the pictures I've seen, and so does Jesus.*

She put on the East Ones' shoes. Her feet did not fill them. She tugged the straps and tightened them with knots.

Ralph smiled. "Not bad."

The wind picked up. Anna felt sprinkles of rain. "My laundry."

She ran toward the water drums with Ralph beside her. They gathered her clean garments. By the time they sprinted back to their roofed hut, the rain was pouring down. The wind shifted, and water assaulted them from all four sides.

Over the racket, Ralph shouted, "Regarding this new hut, I smiled too soon. This place looks fine in the sunshine, but in the wind and rain, it's awful. We need to make our way to the cave."

Ugh. That cave again. It sounds so foreboding. "Can't we just run to the shed?"

"Sadly, the roof was damaged in the last storm. It won't be much drier."

She bit her lip and looked out through the sheeting rain. Another gust drenched her. With a sigh, she dropped her neatly folded laundry into a puddle.

He laughed a hearty hoot. "You are a trooper, Anna. We'll make it through this adventure, I believe."

"We do not have a second choice, do we?"

"No. Here's my plan. Remember when you arrived on the island? Even though my camp was wrecked, I was not injured. It was because I spent the night in my cave. That is where we will go now. It is dry. There are provisions. There is a chimney of sorts. I can burn some wood in the fireplace."

"And if the East Ones come?"

"They may be curious, but they are also cautious. They never travel at night. None have ever arrived on a windy day. It is still night, and there is the wind."

"I have been dreading the cave since you spoke of it."

"I could tell by your expression. You will have to trust me."

"I do need to be dry. I feel like a saturated sponge."

"Hold my hand."

"Ready."

He took her hand, and as the rain slapped their faces, they walked into the jungle. The blackness of night surrounded them. She couldn't see more than six feet in any direction. She stumbled over the rough terrain, splashing mud to her knees. Bushes grasped her skirt.

Dear God, help me. What part of the Bible can I think of now? I cannot even remember the date or the day of the week. I know it is always a good time to say the Rosary. She prayed for every person she had met on her journey, starting with those in Pennsylvania. The walk was long. She was enumerating in prayer the people on board the ship when Ralph stopped.

"Lower your head, dear. We have a short ceiling."

The rain on her head ended. She prayed the first line of the Memorare. *My soul doth magnify the Lord.*

"Here we are."

His voice was to her right, yet she dared not move. She didn't know if the cave was large or small. She waited, breathing hard, in total darkness. Then came a sound like the striking of a match. Ralph's silhouette showed in front of the glow of a fire.

"You will feel better when you can see your way around this place," he said.

The fireplace was a pit. The walls were dry earth. Wooden shelves lined the walls. In the center of the room was a small table and more of the tree-stump chairs. One side of the room held a cot. The other side held two more. Each had straw poking out from the underside and striped ticking on top. A folded white sheet lay at the foot.

"Three beds," she murmured.

Ralph nodded. "The motherhouse said there would be two of you. Incidentally, the belongings I carried up are right over there."

"Oh, yes."

"Make yourself at home. You are safe here. I feel like an old dog that has been on watch night and day for over forty-eight hours. I need about twelve hours of sound sleep. Don't wake me until it stops raining. You're free to look around. The smoke from this fire goes out a complicated flue, so it will not attract attention. You can add more sticks to the fire if it gets low."

She heard a familiar noise. Ralph was snoring. *Oh, my. He fell asleep immediately, just like Tata at home. That is such a comforting sound.*

She found Sister's bag. *I know everything in here because as she got weaker, I was the only one who touched these things.* She pulled out Mike's worn blanket. *At least I will be dry.* Anna moved out of the light, stripped off her sodden dress, and wrapped herself in the wool blanket. It felt warm and comforting.

She sat near the fire. *God bless Sister Calista. May her hard journey to You move her past purgatory and straight to Heaven. Bless Doctor Graumann. I know I am safe with him, but he scares me with all his cautions. He is like a fairytale troll who came up from under a bridge and is annoyed to see someone walking in his territory. Bless me and help me. I am in Your hands.*

The sounds of Ralph's snores mixed with the noise of the wind and falling rain. Her eyelids fluttered. She curled up on the cot. Despite being in a cave, the scent the bedding was of dry flowers and autumn leaves. *Bless this house, oh Lord, we pray. Make it safe by night and day.* She fell asleep.

THIRTY-THREE

Anna sensed it was morning before opening her eyes. The sound of rain slid in through the cave opening. Whistling came from the left.

"Good morning," she said.

"Ah, you're awake. I have water on for tea. By the deluxe fireside seats, in one metal box you'll find dried fruit and in the other beef jerky. The jerky is from one of the ships that passed by. They collect fresh water and a giant tortoise or two, and drop me off this and that." He walked closer to her. His clean-shaven face still smelled of soap.

She said, "This and that?"

"They ask, and we trade. I get tools, a sharp blade or two. Twine is nice, but it is not a good idea. It is damp here, thus cotton cord has a short life. Leather strips are better. I've given them a few shirts and some coffee. Do you like coffee?"

"Yes. In Petroleum City it was a start-the-morning thing or a ladies' get-together-and-sew-or-mend event."

"Unfortunately, we can't use it here in the cave. It leaves a residual smell. A fire smell is easy to explain because that happens sometimes, especially if one of the little volcanoes on one of the near islands erupts."

She closed her eyes and shook her head. "Volcanoes?"

"There are some on the islands only a few hours away. Incidentally, none have exploded on this island since I've been here."

They moved to sit before the fire. A branch cracked and sizzled as the middle of the wood went up in flame.

He handed her a cup of tea. "Anna, about the East Ones. I don't trust them at all. It is a gut feeling. They come. I don't

295

know when or how many. I don't know why. They always smile. However, one of them usually wanders into the jungle. They might find our cave. I cover my tracks well, I think, and I always walk a slightly different path. So far, they've not discovered this place."

"How do you know they haven't been in here?"

"Because of my secret set of threads. If anyone walks through them, they mess up the pattern. My Pappy showed me the trick. When I was about six, I was always afraid the Yankees would come back into Petersburg when we weren't vigilant and capture us again. So, I have plenty of thread practice. Bet you didn't even notice them at the cave entrance, now, did you?"

"No. But now I will be sure to look for them. What would the East Ones want to take?"

"Beats me. But that's why I only eat dried food in here. With your fresh eyes, what do you think they might be up to? Any ideas?"

"I will pray and think hard about it. Tell me about the volcanoes."

"I'd rather we get to know more about each other. Have you always wanted to be a nun?"

"No. Not when I was a child." The flames warmed her face. She was still wrapped in the blue blanket. Her hair fell loose and disheveled.

"Incidentally, you don't look like any nun I've ever seen."

She sipped her tea. "You seem to be secure in your life choices. As for me, I am waiting for something, yet I cannot even think what it is."

"Anna, rarely do we hear a voice from above saying you should be this or that. It is kind of a see-what-fits thing. Does being a nun fit?"

She took a deep breath. "I needed a different life. Every time I saw my classmate and neighbor, Rose, with her mother, I was jealous. They did everything together. They looked like they had a special secret between them. When the flu epidemic happened, Rose's mother was sick. My mother took care of her. Rose's mother got better. My mother caught the flu and died. How unfair. I did not want to stay and have my heart broken again and again every time I looked at her."

He handed her a piece of beef jerky and took one for himself. "I never knew my mother. But, I always had Mammy and Pappy and didn't know I was missing anything."

"You missed a great deal."

"So, why didn't you join the nuns at your church?"

"Something there was not right for me. I searched for a perfect match. I always liked the quiet. And I wanted to do something different than the rest of my peers. A convent where there was no talking sounded perfect." She shook her head. "But it was not a perfect fit."

He laughed. "You wanted perfect? Really?"

"Yes, I did."

"So, you're not a nun. Are you a half a nun?"

"I was there in the convent. I was studying to be a nun."

"Well, kid, I can't help you study. I'm not a practicing Catholic."

"I know," she said emphatically. "Before we leave this tell-all session, let me ask. What are your aspirations?"

"First, I want to stay alive. And I want to keep you alive and safe, too. You're getting under my skin in a good way, Anna, or should I say, my dear? We make a good team."

She picked up another piece of dried beef jerky out of the tin. "This is salty."

"It's garlicky, too. I knew you'd love it."

She chewed. "Did you always want to be a doctor?"

"Yes. No lightning bolts from above, though. I liked every part of the classes in medical school."

"Then you got married?"

"Well, no. Whenever my friends and I would go out for a few beers, we'd meet lots of girls. We always said we were studying to be doctors. It attracted the ladies. Ooh, la, la." He laughed.

"You had time to go out and study, too?"

"Yes, we managed both. When we were carousing, it was Chicago beware."

"I've read about such things."

He put up a hand. "You don't know the half of it. Incidentally, my wife knew a bit about my wild past when she married me. She said my life had been spicy."

"And then?"

"There came a magical Christmas when I was courting her. Next was a poignant wedding. The next Christmas, we were waiting for our baby. We had only two short years of marriage. Then the accident happened." He got up and strode to the fireside. He added more wood. Sparks flew from the blaze. "I died, too. I know how your father felt."

"How did you get better?"

"I didn't. For three months, I was deep in hell, excuse the language. My buddy, Carlos, another doctor, finally sat me down and told me to leave town." He reached into the fruit can, pulled out a few pieces of dried mangoes, and popped them into his mouth.

"So, you came here."

"I did. Carlos helped me plan. He had some Spanish culture in him, so he tried to tutor me on the language before I came. I didn't learn much. However, I have a Spanish-English dictionary. Carlos knew some seaman up on Lake Michigan, and that seaman had a buddy who worked on a ship that supplied and delivered things to South America. So, here I am. I planned to spend five years." He walked to the cave opening. "The rain is stopping. We'll have to leave soon."

"Do we put out the fire?"

"Yes, but it's the last thing because it is our light. Go ahead and get dressed. I have a screen there on the left. You could change behind it."

"Thank you." She went to the rear of the cavern and dressed. Her clothes felt damp and cold.

As she stepped back around the screen, he came into the cave with an armload of fresh branches. He stacked them beside the fireplace. She rinsed the cups in a barrel of water and put them back on the shelf. Then she smoothed the cover on the bed of straw and leaves and folded the blanket neatly on top.

Lastly, he poured water on the fire. "Come, Anna dear, let's greet the new day." He clasped her hand.

They walked out of the cave. Songs of birds greeted them. The air smelled of fresh, moist earth. The misty morning allowed a bit of sun to peek through the palms.

"Let me show you how I set the thread trap." With nimble fingers, he wove a web at the cave entrance.

Anna paid close attention.

Hand-in-hand, they walked through the jungle. The damp foliage wet her skirt, but Anna was in too good a mood to care.

"This dawn fog pleases me," she said. "We had mornings like this in Pennsylvania."

"I remember those mornings in Petersburg. Happened in the fall. I'd scrunch leaves I didn't quite see all the way to school."

"In Petroleum City, when it was foggy, I liked to walk in the woods. If I walked quietly, I would see rabbits. Or even a deer. Once, I nearly stumbled on a brown fox." She laughed. "He and I were both surprised when I almost tripped over the poor thing."

"Here you'll see tortoises. They definitely will not run away. They know no fear. They command respect because they are so big."

"You mentioned them before. I am anxious to see for myself."

"The islands are named for them. Carlos told me the Spanish name for these animals is Galapagos."

Ralph guided her around a stand of trees. They walked toward the sound of the surf.

"There is so much beauty here," he said. "The scents are better than any store counter of perfumes. One day soon, I want to take you up to the cliffs on the north part of the island, and you can see many tortoises. Another time, we'll go south where you can see the rocks covered with seals. When we go there, we will hear the bark long before we see the animals."

They reached the beach. The sandy portion was as wide as

four backyards in Petroleum City. Past it on both sides were rocky areas.

"I already love the music of the ocean," she said. "It sounds like a rhythm of life. I feel at home with the sand and sea. It gives me a sense of peace."

He laughed. "That will be short lived. Look at this mess."

The tree-stump chairs sank lopsidedly in the sand. Boxes from the supply tent and Anna's suitcase were scattered around.

"I thought I'd lashed all your suitcases against a post in the lean-to."

"I am sorry. I untied one to pull out my dress yesterday."

"But, dear—"

"It only contains small items of clothing. They may be wet, but I don't think I had any breakable items in it."

Ralph carried her case under the roof of the new structure. "So much for our floor of palm fronds. The rivulets of rain washed most of them away."

She motioned upward. "The roof still looks solid."

"It's almost lunchtime, and I'm already hungry after our trek through the jungle. Think I'll start a fire." He walked out to the firepit.

Anna placed her suitcase on a stump chair. It dripped water. She lifted the clasp and examined the contents. Her undergarments were soaked. *I can wash these.* She then removed two books. She opened each. Her mood darkened. *These hold the prayers given to me by Sister Eileen. How will I say the devotions of the day? Can these pages be dried?* She carried them to Ralph.

He stood by the newly lit fire. "Anna, how about we make a schedule. One day I cook, one day you do. I've already started the rice and—" He stopped. "What's wrong?"

"Look at my books." Her head hung.

He took one. "Oh, I see. We'll have to prop them up in the sun, and as they dry, put small stones between the pages. There's hope."

"They are prayer books. This one is called a Daily Missal. It has lists of devotionals."

"What does that mean?"

"Every day in church, we follow the calendar and say prayers about a specific saint."

"And you are following this?"

"As best I can."

"And the Rosary?"

"I say it daily."

"So, you are a nun."

"Lots of people read devotionals. Young and old. Men and women. Single and married. They pray for a half hour to an hour a day."

"For what?"

"For you, for me, for my family, for your family. I could go on and on."

He laid chunks of fish wrapped in seaweed on a grate over the fire. The smell of brewing tea and roasting fish mixed with the briny wind from the sea. He rolled more fish in seaweed, placed them on the grill, then turned the already heated food onto the other side. It sizzled, and her stomach growled.

"Don't worry about the books. We'll fix them." He handed her a cup of tea.

"Thank you." She sat on a stump.

He showed her a large white bag. "Here's our rice. Tomorrow morning when you get up, please measure one cup of rice and place it in the pot, add two cups of water, heat it to a boil, then put it aside for twenty minutes or so."

She laughed. "Do I time it by the sun or the tides? I have no watch."

"Pardon me. You can use mine." He rolled the top of the bag closed and placed it into a metal container. "You are like the swans I saw on Lake Michigan. On the surface, they look serene, yet under the water, they are paddling as fast as one can blink his eyes."

Behind him, a dark shape moved over the sand. It looked like a boulder slowly getting larger.

She gulped and whispered, "Look behind you."

He spun around. "Ah, one of our tortoises. Does it scare you?"

"You said big, but I never thought... They don't bite, do they?"

"Never have. Incidentally, they usually travel with three or more."

They got to their feet and watched the tortoise's slow advance. Ralph pointed out a second one following. He put a hand on her shoulder and guided Anna forward. "Go ahead. Touch it."

"It feels warm and dry. Like the biggest shell I have ever imagined." She raised her gaze and shielded her eyes from the sun. "How mighty is God."

"Why do you say that?"

"He made these beautiful creatures." She watched the pair walk south.

"Yes."

Ralph went back to the tree-stump table, placed the fish on plates, and added rice cooked with canned peas. They ate in comfortable silence.

After a while, he asked, "How are you at fishing with a net?"

"I will not know until I try."

"I'd like to teach you to fish."

"I can't swim."

"Then swimming lessons come first."

"The clothes might be a problem."

"Right. You need to think about that. And, while you're out here in the sun, please keep a pith helmet on your head. When the East Ones come back, see if they'll make you a straw hat and some shoes."

"I'll think about how to ask Flor for them."

After lunch, they rinsed their dishes, then set about to tidy the area. Ralph returned the boxes to the lean-to. Anna located her laundry from the previous day full of sand and seaweed at the water's edge. *I'm lucky I didn't lose anything.* She carried everything to the hut.

Ralph hammered a nail into a post and hung a helmet on it. "We need to call the lean-to just that," he said. "This roof on sticks, we'll call—"

"How about the East Ones' Gift?"

"Good idea."

He hammered in another nail for the second helmet. Then he found small stones. He propped open her soggy books on a tree-stump chair near the firepit and placed the stones in between the pages to keep them from sticking together.

"No canoes on the horizon," she said. "It looks like we have a quiet day. What have you planned?"

"This is going to be a picnic day. Let's pack a snack and go see the seals. I do have an ulterior motive. This is the first day the two of us have had to talk without interruption. We need some alone time." He took a cloth bag and placed a few pieces of fruit, some jerky, and two jars of cool tea in it. Then he slung the pack across his back and secured the parcel to his shoulders with a belt.

Anna went to the East Ones' Gift and pulled the two pith helmets off their nail hangers. She handed one to him. The other, she placed on her head.

After they doused their cooking fire, they left the camp, heading south.

THIRTY-FOUR

As they entered the wooded area, Anna said, "How did we end up alone together? You and I have a situation neither of us expected."

"That's true." He led the way, looked at the trees, and then glanced at his compass. "Now, Anna, I am going to explain how we two got here. If you've heard me tell you this before, just raise your right hand, and I won't say it again."

"Why am I raising my right hand?"

"When I was in college, I was with the same group of guys almost all the time. We got tired of hearing the same tale repeatedly. So, if we already heard it twice, we'd just raise our right hand, and the story would stop."

"I see."

"Back to my saga. When I lost my wife, it was the loss of my one true love. And I lost our son. It was like being pounded by bricks. I left Chicago." He stopped, swallowed, and took a few deep breaths. "I got here by boat. For the first six months, I was content to play Robinson Crusoe. That Daniel Defoe had some good ideas. In fact, there is a copy of his book in the cave."

Leaves rustled under their feet. Mockingbirds repeated their songs.

Anna walked in and out of the shade. "And then?"

"I started getting visitors about once a month. On their part, I was only a curiosity at first. Then one of the East Ones fell and broke his leg while here. I pantomimed fixing it. We made a splint. I won't go into all of that. Anyway, they began to visit every two weeks, then every week."

"Only the men?"

"No, they kept offering me one of their women. I was *not* interested. But I noticed, incidentally, I only treated the men. I did see two women who were obviously pregnant. Then they were not pregnant. I did not see any babies. I asked as best I could about them. But I realized I needed a female helper." He glanced at the compass and forged ahead.

The sun peeked through the trees. Palm fronds slapped Anna's head, nearly knocking off her hat. She detoured around a beehive.

"So, you wrote to request help?" she said. "Why our place?"

"I didn't bring an address book with me. But one of my college roommates had a relative at your convent. I helped him write so many letters to his cousin, I could never forget the address. So, I took a chance."

"But our convent was for praying, not for nursing. Did you know that?"

"I didn't really consider it. I figured there would be some good women who wanted to come and help. I sent the letter. By the next time a ship came by, I regretted sending it. That Frah is a sneaky kind of guy. He's always disappearing after they get here. What is he looking for? So, I sent a second letter, canceling my request for help. Obviously, it was too late because in that same posting I received a reply. Two nuns would be departing soon to give me a hand."

She didn't know what to say.

He sat on a log, handed her a jar of tea, and drank from the other. The drink was tart and refreshing.

"I need to whistle for a while. I have never seen anyone on this part of the island, but don't want to startle a soul."

He whistled a melody she had not heard before. It sounded like a march.

"Is that the Battle Hymn of the Republic?" she asked.

"Madam, no. I beg your pardon. This is *Dixie*, the Confederate Hymn."

"Harrumph," she said in a fake southern accent, "I forgot you were a rebel."

He laughed.

Soon she heard the roar of the surf and the barking of seals. They climbed an elevation and looked down from the top of the hill. About fifty feet away, hundreds of seals sunned themselves on the rocks and frolicked in the surf. Some were brown, some gray.

"Look at those eyes," she said. "They are dark and so big. I do not see their ears. The fat cheeks make them resemble puppy faces. But they are bigger than any dog I've ever seen. I wish we could climb down closer so I could see their whiskers."

"I don't think it would be prudent to be near them. Besides, it's hard to believe anything that beautiful could smell so bad."

She took a breath and coughed. "There is an awful fish odor. Did you notice there are lots of baby seals?"

"Yes. The fur seals here in the Galapagos give birth in early October."

He opened the pack he'd had on his back and withdrew a folded cloth. They laid out the cloth on a large level spot, then sat to share their fruit.

"I want to look at each one of the seals," she said. "They look so playful and relaxed."

"I understand they usually go to sea and feed as the sun goes down. These animals are beautiful. And plentiful, too. Was it worth the hike?"

"Oh, yes. Thank you for this day."

"Can I continue with the story?"

"There's more?"

"Unfortunately, yes. You are at risk here. Those men are watching you. That's why we need to act married in their eyes."

"I am honestly not safe here? This makes me frightened. It also makes me furious. What do you think could happen?"

"If the men of the tribe decide to take you, a white woman, you will be impregnated soon after your abduction. I imagine there will be some dissension and discussion as to who would get the honor. You know how men can be."

"What are you talking about?" she said shrilly. "I don't know a single man who would act that way. I am safe with you, and you're a man. You are like a dependable friend or a cousin from my hometown."

He rolled his eyes and looked away. "I don't think you are in danger as long as Flor is pregnant because they probably want you to help with her baby's delivery. Here's my plan. I am going to teach you some midwifery skills."

"I am not sure if it is the seals barking or my mind squeaking, trying to fit these ideas into my head."

"Can you do it?"

"Yes, I can. You will have to tell me all about delivering a baby. Except tell me a little every day so I will remember and not be nervous when the big day comes. I will touch her gently each time I see her, as a mother would touch a daughter. I will let her feel my kindness. If she's in her seventh month of pregnancy, she should deliver about Christmastime." She looked out past the seals and saw a deep blue sea with gentle ripples moving across it. "All this uncertainty on an island that looks incredibly peaceful."

"Yes, and we need to have a good plan, Anna. I don't even know what day it is."

"It is between November the fifth and the tenth, the feast of Saint Andrew Avellino, or maybe November eleventh, the feast of Saint Martin of Tours. I have lost track with everything that's happened."

"I think you can be excused, my dear. We will figure it all out." He gathered their belongings and placed each item into the bag. "We do not leave one scrap behind. Not even the mango pits. This is an ecologically clean place."

"What does that mean?"

He cleared his throat. "We could be the first people ever to step on this rocky promontory. It makes us obliged to keep it pristine."

"May it stay this way for these beautiful seals."

He put out his hand and pulled her to her feet. They walked back into the jungle.

He said, "I want to take you out in the boat to my fishing spot and let you watch. The fish out there are colorful. Almost to the point of bewitching. If I ever don't come back, it's probably because I followed the beckoning of a mermaid."

"You better not, Ralph."

"I'll try to remember. Besides, I need to tell you so much more to keep you safe. There is usually a ship around here every month or—"

She raised her hand.

He laughed. "Back to pregnancy. Did you know that when the baby is inside the mother, it is kind of floating around but turns itself head down before delivery?"

"I had no idea. So, I will know what to look for first."

"The usual full growth of a baby is in the seven-pound range. Have you seen a newborn baby before? Do you have an idea of the size?"

"Yes, I have seen a few new babies," she said. "Not many, because women don't take them out of the house for about a month until they are baptized."

"Of course. Anyway, when Flor delivers, if the baby comes back of the head first, which is the most frequent, called the cephalic presentation, it goes most easily. But there could be a more difficult presentation. It could be facial, which is called brow. Or, it—"

"Enough of the delivery talk for the day, Doctor." She laughed nervously. "Can we change the subject? Tell me how you found the cave."

"I was here for a few months and was getting bombarded with rain and wind. It seemed every time I dried things out, a new storm hit. Being drenched gets old." He checked the compass and pointed a little more to the west.

She walked and listened to his southern enunciations.

"One day, I was out hiking in the jungle and doing an inspection of the area. I sat to rest near a high hill. I was idly watching the antics of an iguana when suddenly it disappeared from my line of vision. Out of curiosity, I looked for the varmint and found it in a cave. It was my great secret. Every few days, I began to put certain things in there. Enough was left out so the East Ones did not think I had another place."

"How do you decide what goes in?"

"A little of everything. I have acquired oilskin from passing ships so it is wrapped around my books and a few of my suitcases so they do not get moldy. Those stay in the cave. Extra food is there in barrels, and there are wood boxes to hold my tools. Incidentally, I found a sideways hole at the top that works as a vent when I make a fire."

She trudged over the uneven terrain, trying to keep up with his steps. "I have another question," she said. "How do you get or send mail?"

"That is a strange process. Each time a ship comes, they will take mail. They either deliver it to the target country or at least put it in a destination station. The next ship that goes that way picks it up and moves it along. It could take a few weeks or a few months to be delivered."

"So, it is an honesty thing. The letter may never get home."

"Oh, ye of little faith."

"Now you are quoting Matthew 8:26 in the Bible," she said.

"I'm making a joke. It does seem like my letters got through, though."

"Yes, they did."

"If you have some letters to write, Anna, do it, and the next time a ship stops, we will send them on their way. However, *you* will only get aboard a ship if it appears harmless. Although you need to leave as soon as possible, it is paramount that your journey home is safe. In any case, your letters can be on their way."

"I do have a few to write."

They arrived at the camp. He got his fishing net.

"Why don't you put on one of my short-sleeved shirts and share my boat while I get dinner. You can look at the fish."

"I'll take you up on the trip but not the shirt. And remember, Ralph, I do not know how to swim."

"You've traveled around a quarter of this planet without

knowing how to swim? We need to talk about swimming lessons soon. How will they work? With all these clothes, you might sink."

They refilled the jugs with water. Anna got into the canoe, and he rowed toward the channel between the reefs. The little splashes from his oars that hit her clothes were refreshing. Above, puffy white clouds slowly paraded before the sun.

I need to rest my mind from all this new information, if only for the time at sea. It is all so scary. My motto has always been God, family, and fellow man. Yet, my survival comes before the care of a fellow man like the East Ones. I must remember that. For now, I will enjoy this mighty ocean You have put before me today, dear God.

She gazed over the edge of the boat. Down in the water, yellow, striped, and silver fish swam past.

"Look at these gorgeous fish," she said. "I especially like the multicolored ones. They move incredibly fast."

He nodded, yet Anna sensed he seemed more interested in the fish than conversation.

Ralph threw a net out in a circular twist. It hit the water and sank, except for the lone cord he held in his hand. "The net is caught on something. Hold this rope, and hold it tight. It's your dinner." He smiled at her and jumped into the sea.

Warm water sprayed her. Anna narrowed her eyes against the sun's reflection on the blue, still water. Beneath the surface, fish darted away. Several jumped. Ralph returned and rolled his wet self into the canoe, pulling the net with him.

She giggled. "That's an amazing maneuver."

"I haven't quite figured out the graceful entry yet. Now, with you watching, I think I better practice." He threw the net again, then jumped back in the water and repeated his rolling reentry.

They both sat and had a hearty laugh. Water dripped from his face. Then he hoisted the net and dropped it and the contents into a bucket.

Two large fish flapped and splashed. Her clothes became damp with the pleasant feel and smell of seawater.

He lifted the oars and turned the boat toward land. "My reward for the way home is the tide pushing me toward the shore."

The canoe soon slid onto the sandy beach. Along the tree line, low ferns waved at them. They secured the boat then moved toward the cooking area. Ralph carried the newly caught fish.

Anna placed wood chips in the firepit over the half-burned driftwood. He handed her matches, and she lit the fire. While he filleted and seasoned the fish, she placed the pot of leftover rice and peas from lunch over the flames then filled an empty pot with water for tea.

He said, "We seem to have some rhythm here."

Together, they fixed the meal.

As they ate, he said, "I have managed to take some honey out of a nearby hive. It should add a new taste to your palate."

"Besides a doctor, you are a bee man?"

"Anna, I have talents even I have yet to discover."

The sun fell into the sea.

She stretched out her arms. "For the first time since my arrival, I am tired from a busy day."

He stoked the fire. Sparks flew and wood crackled. "I hope I haven't upset you with my talk about the East Ones."

"Yes, the news you gave me is a wild revelation, but I always prefer to open the door and see the monster than to imagine it. Can we start the swimming lessons tomorrow? If need be, I can at least try to swim back to land if I am abducted. By the way, do you have any weapons in the cave?"

"I have some heavy pieces of wood that could be used as clubs, but two against a tribe makes no sense. There has to be another way." The firelight bounced off Ralph's face. He looked like a kind, family friend. His voice was soothing. "My dear, it's going to rain. Let's go to the cave and get a good night's sleep. Tomorrow, we can put fresh boughs in our cots and have sweet smelling mattresses. But for tonight, I think we are both exhausted."

Hand-in-hand, they walked back to the woods and the cave.

THIRTY-FIVE

Anna opened her eyes.

"Did you hear the rain last night?" Ralph asked from across the cave.

"No, I slept soundly. Has the rain stopped?"

"Yes, finally. We'll be postponing stuffing our mattresses with fresh grass and palm fronds. Maybe this afternoon, if all is dry and no East Ones appear, we can pick new stuffing for our bedding."

"New bedding will smell sweet."

After setting up the threads, they exited the cave.

As they walked, Anna looked overhead at the white clouds. "The skies here are breathtaking."

"It's good to hear you feel that way. I can't see enough of them myself."

At the camp, she cooked rice. *I wonder if I can find a spice in our stock to add a touch of tang.* She placed the pot with water on the fire for tea.

"Not tea today, Anna. We'll have coffee." He appeared with a coffee pot and grounds ready for the heat.

Soon, she heard the popping sound of water moving up the stem of the percolator. "The smell is delightful." She glided around the eating area. "I feel good this morning. It is November thirteenth, I think. The feast of Saint Didacus, a Spanish Franciscan lay brother. I've asked him to watch over me today as I take my first swimming lesson."

He smirked. "You're going swimming in that?"

Anna tugged at her long-sleeved top then fluffed her skirt, which she had cut to mid-calf. "Here is my thinking, Ralph. I cannot change my style of dress quickly. But I have only one layer of clothes on, and I can learn, I know. So, let me give it a try."

"As soon as we eat, we will. You are a stubborn one. Instead of your hair all over, do you think you could braid it?"

"Right after breakfast."

They ate. She sighed with her first sip of coffee, although it was a bit bitter. Afterwards, she braided her hair. They walked to the surf.

"We will start with you learning to float," he said.

He demonstrated. She listened, swallowed a few gallons of water, sputtered a few times, and learned.

She said, "I'll never swim like Gertrude Ederle, but I am staying on top of the water."

"Who's that?"

"She swam the English Channel a few years ago."

"Ah." He nodded and took her arm. "That's enough practice for today. You've done a fine job despite all your clothes."

"It's been a delightful morning, and I thank you."

They walked back to shore.

"Do you have a plan for the rest of the morning?" he asked.

"Yes, I want to write some letters as you suggested. My supplies are in the cave. Do you mind if I go there alone?"

"I mind. Besides, it's warm. The sun is bright. The palms are dry. We can gather the fronds for the mattresses." He took a last look at the sea. "Change of plans. Here come the East Ones. The boat looks different, but—"

"I will run into the shed and put on dry clothes and more of them." She hurried away.

By the time Anna returned, wearing her usual several layers of tops and skirts, the East Ones were on the beach. Ralph accepted a basket of fruit from Sno and Frah. The other two boatmen carried a log sliced in half lengthwise, exposing a flat surface.

Anna walked close to Ralph, and he put his arm around her shoulders. She looked up at him. *I will pretend I am Julia looking at her new husband, Adam. Maybe I could have been an actress like Clara Bow.* After a while, she turned her attention to the two men carrying the wood. They walked past her and up to the East Ones' Gift then placed the log flat-side-up in the center of the shelter.

"What is happening?" she asked.

"It seems we're receiving flooring for the East Ones' Gift. Somehow, they have hardwood. They are cutting it in half at their place, tying it back together, and floating the pieces across the water to our island. And they are doing it two logs at a time. It will be a solid floor."

But Anna shook her head. "Ralph, they are placing it three feet off the ground."

"I see that," he said. "It will allow the water to run under the structure. They must have figured that out a long time ago."

"It will still be wet when it rains. No walls."

"I think the walls are yet to come. They're doing this piece-meal as a ploy to have them return again and again. Incidentally, that was some good acting. I thought you were Mary Pickford."

"Thank you. Now, Ramón Navarro, when is lunch? I am getting mighty hungry after all that floating."

He held out the East Ones' fruit basket. "See if you can find something to eat. Hopefully, they won't stay long."

She picked out a red, apple-looking fruit and bit. Pain shot from a lower tooth all through her jaw, face, and head. "Oh." She pressed two fingers into her jawbone. Tears welled in her eyes.

"What happened?"

"I think I broke a tooth." She separated the teeth inside her closed mouth and rubbed the aching spot with her tongue. "This is so painful."

"Do you want me to look at it now? I'm afraid all four of our guests will want to take a look, too."

"I will wait." She lowered her hand. Eyes still wet, she pasted a smile on her face. *I can endure anything for an hour or two. I will offer it up for the poor souls in purgatory.*

The rest of the day passed in a blur. The men hammered logs

into the posts holding the roof, making a sort of brace. The noise was louder than any Anna had heard since her arrival. It seemed they pounded hundreds of spikes into the support beams.

Every time Ralph offered to help, he was rejected. He whistled as he watched. "I wonder where they got so many nails?"

"Probably from pirates. Maybe from outer space. I do not care. I want them to leave. My entire right cheek is throbbing. My right eye feels numb."

"Why didn't you tell me it was so bad? I'll get some aspirin for you. Come." They walked around the East Ones' Gift, to the supply lean-to. He pulled out a tin box, opened it, and rummaged through the contents. "Ah. Aspirin. Here's a jar of water. Swallow two of them. Then place the third on the sore tooth. Sometimes on the tooth helps."

She did. They walked back to their eating area.

His arm was around her waist. "Mary Pickford, put some love in your eyes."

She looked into his face and saw caring and concern. The tablet sat on her tooth. "Aspirin tastes horrible."

"Shall I look in your mouth now?"

"Absolutely not. I have waited this long. They have to run out of nails soon."

They did. The smell of freshly cut wood perfumed the air. Sno invited the two of them to inspect the work.

They smiled and nodded. The four East Ones left.

"Please explain what I am looking at, Ralph. They put boards on the floor then took them out and nailed them to the what?"

He cleared his throat and smiled at her. "Here's how it goes. Incidentally, this structure with all these nails will be standing here for the next fifty years, I believe. The side braces will hold a floor." He walked around the perimeter. "This opening will be our entrance." He pointed to three planks leading up. "The steps look pretty weak right now. I don't think they're finished."

She nodded.

"You look mighty tired, dear. Finally, I get to see the tooth."

"Oh, and it hurts. Let me show you." She opened her mouth.

He stood closer than he had ever been. Gently, he held his fingers to her lips and peered into her mouth. "Move your tongue, Anna. Let me get a good look."

She did. Her mouth was open wide. It felt like he should be able to see down into her lungs.

"I see. It's that right lower premolar. I'm not going to touch it. Looks very jagged." He took his hand away from her face.

"What will we do?"

"Unfortunately, the tooth has to be pulled. The sun is going down. The light is not good. I can't work on it today. For now, you'll take aspirin and use cotton saturated in alcohol—"

"I cannot take alcohol into my—"

"You're not swallowing it. Just letting it sit there on the tooth. It's a medicine I'm prescribing as a doctor, you hear?"

"The pain is awful. I suppose I could try."

"Yes. But for now, dinner. See you soon." He walked out to the water carrying the fishing net.

She started the fire, began to cook the rice, and washed a few pieces of soft fruit. *I should have squeezed these pieces of fruit and bit into a soft one. Not the jawbreaker I tried to eat at lunchtime.* Her tongue kept rolling around the sharp tooth. *I need to stop that before I hurt my tongue.* She turned to the ocean, and there was Ralph with a heavy net.

"The fish were there waiting for me." He grinned. "I'm glad. I'm hungry."

"So am I."

He filleted the fish and cooked them. Dinner was quickly served.

"I feel like I have been fasting for days." She took her first bite. It was on the wrong side of her mouth. It brought tears to her eyes.

"Slow down. We have all evening here."

"Yes. Tomorrow, the pain will probably be gone," she said.

But it did not stop. For the next three days, each time he asked to pull the tooth, she refused. "I cannot bear the thought. No.

No. No. It will stop hurting. No pliers. No pulling." Aspirin became her companion every four hours.

Every day, the East Ones came. They put the trunks flat-side-up on the braces, making the floor wider and wider. While they built, she sat in the shady place near the hammocks. She took only sips of liquid, carefully letting it touch only the left side of her mouth. She tried to write to Tata and the family, but the pain was distracting. She prayed for relief. *O, Matka Boska, skończyć ból.*

On the fourth day, the East Ones came and pounded again.

Ralph asked, "Anna, how's the mouth today?"

"Bad. Do we have a large supply of aspirin?"

"Glad you asked. It's getting low." He handed her a cup of tea and a sliver of fruit.

"The tea smells good. But I cannot eat. I cannot bear anything but warm tea or water."

"I've noticed. If you were home in Pennsylvania and couldn't get to a dentist, whose opinion would you trust?"

"My father's, of course."

"Now, you just pretend I'm your father. And hear the truth. Anna, you've had four days of this."

She nodded.

"What will happen next? Do you reckon the pain will go away? On its own? It will not. Because by now, with an open cracked tooth, it's infected. Germs are having a good time."

"I… I suppose."

He put a calming hand on top of hers. "Let's finish this problem today so tomorrow you can complete your letters. Here's the plan. By the time the East Ones arrive tomorrow, and arrive they will, you'll only have a hole where you had a cracked tooth."

"But it will hurt."

"Yes. At lunchtime, we'll mash you up a mango and add some liquor to it. And you make it go down. The tooth pulling will not hurt as much. You do a second one in the middle of the afternoon."

"I am not sure."

"You haven't been opening your prayer book, Anna. Each morning, you used to announce whose Saint's day it is. Not the last few days. And I know you like moving those rosary beads in your fingers. Where have they been?"

She nodded and whispered, "I have not been praying, have I?"

"No, I don't think you have. Incidentally, let me remind you. A bad tooth unattended can cause jaw complications and facial problems in your near future."

"Really?"

"The minute these East Ones disappear over the horizon, I will pull your tooth."

"And, it will hurt."

"Yes. This is one of those things you'll offer up for the souls in purgatory. I've heard you say that again and again."

The East Ones nailed.

Anna forced herself to swallow a mashed, awful-tasting bourbon mango for lunch. At midafternoon, she ate the second fruit with bourbon and tears in her eyes because of the difficulty getting it down.

A few hours later, the East Ones left.

She staggered toward Ralph. "It's now or never, buddy."

He nodded and guided her weaving gait to the hammock. With his help, she climbed into the sling.

"Sorry I don't have a sturdy chair," he said. "It would make the job easier."

"What job?"

"Pulling your tooth. Remember?"

"Is that the plan?"

"Yes, before the sun goes down."

"Is this a party?" She burped.

"Yes, a dental party. You have to do two things for this party. First, hold this ball of rags and don't let go. Squeeze it hard whenever you want. Second, open your mouth and leave it open." He came close. "Your halitosis takes my breath away."

"Wha?" She tried to answer, but his fingers were in her mouth. She could not close her lips. She gripped the rag ball. Her head spun.

ജ   ജ   ജ

When Anna woke up, she was still in the hammock. The sun was just a smudge above the sea. Her tongue went to the sore tooth, but there was only a hole. It felt as big as the Grand Canyon. She felt again. The tooth was gone.

A whistling figure drew near. "Congratulations. Let me show you your premolar. It was hard getting it out because you wouldn't stop talking. But, here it is." He handed her a piece of cloth containing her ragged tooth.

"Oh." She looked at her tormentor. It was black on the chipped edge. "Amazing. I will forever be grateful to you."

"I made a late dinner. See if you can eat a bite or two. I know you've not had much sustenance the last few days." He helped her out of the hammock and guided her to the fireside.

She ate a few bites, but her head still spun. "My mouth feels better, but I am nauseated."

"Probably too much bourbon. You'll sleep it off and feel better tomorrow."

She listened to the snapping branches in the fire and the soft pulling sound of the water moving from the shore. The night sky glistened with stars. *God, Mighty is Thy name.*

THIRTY-SIX

The next morning, she awoke in the hammock to the song of birds under a clear sky. *Dear Lord, thank You for this day. Thank You for my painless sleep. Each leaf waving in these palm trees honors You.* She hurried out of the sling, washed her face, changed her clothes in the shed, then walked to the firepit. The flames in the center greeted her. A pot of water bubbled. The bag of rice and a faded life vest sat propped by a tree-stump seat.

Behind her, Ralph whistled his Confederate melody.

She turned toward the sound. "Good morning."

"You slept well, I hope?"

"Yes, and free of pain. Thank you, good friend." She turned to the fire. "I'll start the rice?"

"Fine." He carried the fishing net.

"Off-shore fishing, I see." She added rice to the pot.

"Right. After breakfast, I hope to get in a short swimming lesson before the East Ones' visitation. They may finish the hut today." He hurried to the shore, got into the boat, and paddled out to sea.

Anna stirred the rice and replaced the cover on the pot. She found her prayer book. She opened it to the twentieth of November. The Feast of Saint Felix. She prayed that he would help her with her swimming lesson.

Ralph returned with fish in a bucket. Water slid from his wet head to his shoulders. He plopped down on a log chair and quickly fileted the fish. "Is the rice ready?"

"Yes."

"Use my knife to cut the fruit into pieces. And keep water

near. You don't want even one grain of rice in that cranny from the pulled tooth."

Anna's stomach stopped rumbling after a few bites.

As they ate, she asked, "What is the next step with the swimming?"

"Kicking your feet."

"Does that help?"

"Yes. Makes you go faster."

"All right. And I decided I am not wearing stockings for swimming."

"Astounding. Why?"

"I only have two pairs left without holes."

"Good idea."

Anna finished eating. In the shed, she put on her bathing clothes then walked into the clearing.

Grabbing the life jacket, Ralph moved near her. "I saw an old man improvise with one of these at a lake in Virginia. He used it as a waist innertube. I thought he was crazy, yet the fellow was obviously teaching a pal to swim. The vest was tied on his friend's belly. Until the student could swim well, that funny circle kept the non-swimmer above the water." He secured it around her waist.

She had no idea where the conversation was going but nodded. "This feels strange."

"I know you think this is silly, but it works. Concentrate on your feet and kick as hard as you can. Watch how swiftly you travel in the water."

With bare feet, she walked to the beach. The tiny grains slipped between her toes. Her steps were timid. "The water is cool this morning."

He smiled at her. "You'll get used to it quickly."

"In I go." The flow of the tide smacked her knees, then her thighs. She soon stood in waist-high water.

Ralph stood beside her. "Lie on your belly and raise your head. I'll swim to your left. You'll be pleased."

Anna put her chest into the sea then elevated her head.

"Now move one arm front to back and continue to alternate left and right. Then kick like the devil is chasing you."

Her body slid across the water. Salt clung to her lips. A few brown fish the size of her finger darted around her, urging her forward. She turned to the left. He was lagging behind. "Ralph, come on, keep up." An unexpected wave splashed. She took a big swallow, blinked a few times, and coughed.

Ralph tapped her shoulder and pointed to the shore.

"We're done already? I was having a good time."

They headed for the shore. The water became waist high. The wet jacket pulled her down. She staggered instead of walked.

Ralph said, "There's no graceful way to exit the ocean."

"Is this a sea rule?"

"Yes." He took the jacket from her. "I expect the East Ones soon."

"I'll go and change. The water was delightful. The tiny fish were enchanting." A smile crossed her face as her gaze met his, then she rushed to the shed to put on dry clothes.

As she returned to the firepit, the East Ones approached in their canoes. Anna, completely clothed, including hose and shoes, with braided hair still moist from the sea, stood close to Ralph. Men carried logs past her.

The last boat held women. Flor grandly and slowly moved toward them.

Anna saw a look of distress on Flor. She hurried to greet her. "What is wrong?" she asked in a soft, comforting voice feeling sure Flor would understand the question from her tone.

Flor took Anna's hands, placed them on her pregnant belly, and said sadly, "Bebe."

I do remember this one word. It means baby.

"Is something not right?" Ralph asked.

Anna took the length of unknotted twine he handed her. "I will find out. I will take her to the shed."

Even the birds stopped singing as they walked to the structure. Anna and all four women went inside.

Ralph followed as closely as possible. "I'll be outside at a discreet distance. Talk as loudly as you can so I can hear what you say. Remember, there is still a lot of pounding going on."

Once inside, Flor removed her grass skirt. With her head lowered sorrowfully, she pulled a bloody cloth from between her legs and handed it to Anna.

"Ralph, Flor has been bleeding. I am holding a wad of cloth with dried blood."

"Oh, no," he called back. "How much blood? Does it cover a foot of the cloth or—"

"No. It's only an inch or two."

"All right, can you get close enough to look for new blood?"

Anna pantomimed then examined. "No bleeding now."

"Get the twine and make the knots. And feel her belly. Is there movement? Is she in pain?"

Gently, Anna measured as before. She placed the twine around her own neck for safekeeping and stayed so close she could hear every breath Flor took. Anna touched Flor's stomach. All was still. Then she felt a belly full of butterflies. Next, something in the belly poked Anna's hand.

"The baby is dancing." She nodded, and with hands still in place, looked up and smiled. A slow smile brightened Flor's face like a ray of sunshine after a storm. Again, the baby made Flor's belly tremble. "It feels like a strong baby."

"Assure her this happens sometimes. I think it was a fluke."

Anna smiled. Again, she touched Flor's belly, mesmerized by the baby sensations. *God, bless this woman, my new friend, Flor. Let her baby be born in good time with good health. I feel so privileged to have touched the moving baby.*

They exited the structure. As they walked back to the eating area, all the women smiled. The pounding of the floor at East Ones' Gift ceased. The only sound was the splash of the surf.

I have never felt a baby moving in a mother-to-be. This could be the way Julia's baby is doing about now. How can I live my life and never feel a baby inside me? What is going on in my head? Where are these thoughts coming from?

"Anna," Ralph said, "you look lost in a conundrum."

"I will tell you after I figure it out."

Flor pulled a straw hat and a pair of leather slippers out of a basket. She handed them to Anna.

"What gifts I have received today." Anna bowed her head as she thanked Flor.

When the boats were out of sight, Ralph said, "We haven't looked at the cave for several days. This would be a good time to be sure it's still secure. Incidentally, I haven't seen Frah lately. I wonder what he's up to."

"He is probably checking out another island."

As they walked through the jungle, they gathered handfuls of greens from surrounding bushes.

One bush caught Anna's eye. "Oh, look. Flowers." She picked some of the blossoms and carried them, too.

At the cave, Ralph examined the security threads. "All is well here today."

They went inside. Anna put the flowers in a teacup filled with water. Then they re-stuffed the mattresses with new leaves.

Ralph examined the twine Anna had used to measure Flor that morning. "You were so deep in thought today. Care to share?"

"I am even more confused. I was happy with my decision to dedicate myself to God. But today, I felt that baby move again. Do I want to give up being a mother? I believed I did. Now my head is spinning. Flor has made me think again."

"It never hurts to think new ideas. By the way, the baby is fine and growing as expected. I think she'll deliver around Christmastime."

"That makes me happy for her. But for me, I am befuddled about my religious decisions."

"Anna, in all of life there is never just black and white. Sometimes our lives move so fast we don't look at the other colors. But they are there."

"I try to think and think. I am looking for answers from my heart."

"I've told you about being happily married to Amy, and about my son, Ralf. Incidentally, he was named after my German great-grandfather who had the good fortune to come to America. But I digress. I want to talk about the ups and downs of my marriage."

She sat on one of the newly stuffed beds, breathing in the fresh, green scent.

"Amy was my true friend. She could be enchanting and exciting. She could be quiet and gentle. Or she could show me an ugly temper." He rubbed the back of his neck.

Anna whispered, "You must miss her so."

"I miss her every single day. Yes, she was my chosen one. But our life was far from perfect. Once, she surprised me at my new office. I introduced her to my nurse, a grandmotherly Mrs. Bruce. I showed her the new equipment I was so proud to own. When she left to go home, I felt puzzled. It seemed like she was not waltzing to my ragtime beat. I came home to a holy terror." He smiled, and his eyes glistened.

"What was the problem?"

He stood, gathered the discarded leaf bedding, and placed it in the box next to the firepit. "It seems I had embarrassed her in front of Mrs. Bruce by not commenting on her new dress. She had secretly saved money for the fabric and spent many hours sewing it. This long, flowing blue outfit hid her pregnancy. I had not made one comment about it. The whole evening was a mighty cold one. I will never forget it."

"So, you learned all about her."

"I should have spent more time with her because, in hindsight, our time together was short. But I was busy starting a practice. Some days, she was bone tired taking care of the baby."

"Why are you telling me this?"

"You never get one-hundred percent. Every marriage, every job, every event requires concessions. Do you want to be a nun? The silence is hard?"

She got up and walked to the flowers on the table. *Why am I unable to make good decisions?*

"We should get back," he said.

He picked up a bag of rice and jerky. She carried a bag with ink, pen, stationery, and envelopes. They replaced the threads, then stepped out of the cave. Sun sifted through the surrounding trees like confectioners' sugar over warm cake.

Ralph narrowed his eyes. "I'm looking for signs of intruders."

"It's good that you're cautious."

They walked through the jungle of trees and shrubbery. Anna wished to see a blackberry bush. She was becoming very tired of eating fish and rice.

Suddenly, out of a bright blue sky, it began to rain.

"A sunshower." Anna laughed and danced in the refreshing spray.

He smiled. "Do you enjoy dancing?"

"I did."

"There are no dancing nuns."

The moment was over as quickly as it had begun. They walked the rest of the way in silence.

At last, they reached the East Ones' Gift. He dropped the food items on the three-foot-high surface. Mounds of ropes, thick and thin, were piled on the floor.

He shook his head. "Something isn't finished. Looks like they'll be back tomorrow."

"I don't imagine Flor will make the trip two days in a row. Speaking of Flor, I need to try on the hat and slippers she gave me." Both items sat on the lumber floor. She unbraided her hair and put on the hat. "It fits like it was made for me. Oh, it was." She laughed, then untied and wiggled out of her shoes. She put on the new ones and gave a soft, "Ahh."

They walked to the eating area. While he started the fire, she picked through the fruit basket, found the softest fruit, and washed them for dinner.

"So, Ralph, about your story. You are telling me to think more realistically about my future goals."

"Yes. Think of where you will be most happy. Not all the time, but half the time. Many people settle for that. Next, try to think of a place where you can be happy three-quarters of the time."

She placed water and rice in a pot and on the flame. Then she diced mangoes, guava, and bananas into a fruit salad. He sprinkled spice on a fish, folded it in a banana leaf, and added it to the fire.

"Incidentally, I see you brought back writing supplies."

"Yes, I have not finished my letters. I would like them to be ready in case a ship comes by."

"I think you're right. It's about time for another ship to take away a few tortoises." He nodded. "But it could be months, dear, until you receive any mail."

"I am not even sure if the monastery will forward letters to me. If I were still there, the notes would all be saved and given to me on the anniversary of my entry day."

"When your supervisor—"

"Sister Eileen."

"Gets your message about Sister Calista, what will happen?"

"Only God knows."

He stirred the pot. "So, tomorrow, you write. But first, you'll have another swimming lesson. You are a good pupil. In fact, it's hard to believe you never swam before."

"Thank you. Little fish do it so why not me?"

"Incidentally, I'd like to look in your mouth and see how the toothless area looks."

"Sure."

He walked to the water supply, poured some over his hands, then approached. He touched her cheek. She opened her mouth.

"Looks mighty healthy. Maybe the ocean water worked as an astringent."

"Again, I am so grateful you helped me in my time of need."

As they ate their meal, they watched the sun sink into a flaming orange puddle. The hush of evening fell like a damp quilt over their camp.

Anna said, "I miss the sounds of crickets. It is so quiet, I can hear you breathing." Looking up at the sky, she added, "And I think I can hear those stars blinking."

His laugh echoed in the quiet night.

"I do have lots to think about. I am going to slip into my hammock and pray myself to sleep. Good night." She walked to her hammock and climbed in. *God, today we honored Saint Felix. Help me to exist as a God-fearing person here on the Galapagos.* She fell asleep as a breeze pushed her swaying bed gently to and fro.

THIRTY-SEVEN

The sun woke her to a new day. Beads of warm, moist air clung to her hair, skin, and clothes. *Good morning, God. Today is the Feast of the Presentation of the Blessed Virgin Mary. It will be wonderful today to think of three-year-old Mary being taken to be blessed at the temple. I can only imagine the pleasure her parents, Anne and Joachim, felt in offering her to the house of God.*

She followed Ralph's whistling to the firepit where he was already brewing coffee. Today's song was *When Johnny Comes Marching Home.*

He walked toward her through the morning haze. "You may be aware, Madam, that this song was a Civil War tune and was popular both above and below the Mason Dixon Line."

"I did not know it was used by both the blue and the gray."

"That's your fact for the day."

"I keep planning to wake up first one morning, but it has not happened yet." She pulled out plates. In the fruit basket, she noticed berries. "What a treat." She rubbed her tongue over her mouth and felt the empty socket. *I hope seeds do not fall into the tooth pocket. Thank You, God, for healing. I feel no pain.*

"The fish were biting right on shore today." He held up a string with about a dozen small fish attached.

"They look like yesterday's swimming companions. I must re-member in my letter to my family to tell them about the abun-dance of sea life. The colors and shapes are wonderful. The yel-low and black ones are my favorites."

"Some days in that clear water, all I see are those little yellow fish. But today, I saw a long, gray shark. So, I caught lots of little fish on the shoreline. You know, we have three main currents passing through these waters. The different catch of the day depends on those streams. I'll look out for sharks again tomorrow. They are a very smart fish. They sense things so much faster than we humans do. Tomorrow the winds may come from a different direction."

She lifted the lid on the pot of rice and stirred the grains. "Will you be teaching me to fish soon?"

"I reckon. When you finish the swimming lessons, my dear."

She nodded and poured coffee into two cups. "This mist we see each morning is magical to me. One minute, I feel I am surrounded by a cloud. Then it disappears like a vision from the Almighty."

"Nothing mysterious about it. Just a local phenomenon. It happens because we are so near the equator. Incidentally, I expected warmer temperatures, too. I thought it would be a hundred degrees here, but no, it's in the seventies and eighties."

"Surprisingly, the water temperature is cool." She handed him his breakfast.

After a few bites, he looked out at the sea. "The water looks gentle for you today."

"Yes, it does look flat."

"This will be your first day of swimming parallel to the beach. You'll be practicing your hand movement, coordinating it with the feet kicking. Wear the vest one more day. Are you anxious?"

"Excited." She watched the slow, smooth, ebb and flow as the waves skimmed the sand.

"Good. Let's do it soon. The East Ones seem to be arriving earlier every day."

They finished eating then cleared dishes and food from the area. While Ralph extinguished the flame, Anna walked to the shed and changed into her swimming attire. She returned carrying the life jacket. She tied it around her waist and entered the ocean.

She walked as quickly as possible into the deeper water. *Blessed Mother, I thought this was warm water. Oh, Pacific, you are chilly today. I will offer it up for the souls in Purgatory. I find your temperature less distracting than the little nibble of fish. Yipes. When the tide hits my thighs, it makes my eyes water. I will get used to it, same as yesterday. It is up to my waist now. Keep walking. Courage. Saint Anne, Mother of Mary, make me brave.* She placed her body flat on the surface and swam.

Beside her, Ralph said, "Put your right arm into the water, face to the left, then your left arm in and face to the right."

She slid ahead. *Jesus, Mary, and Joseph, it works.* She smiled. With her mouth open, seawater ran in. She coughed.

"Were you laughing, Anna?"

She nodded, reluctant to say a word and invite another wave attack. *I will tell Tata I can swim, and tell Julia, too. I wonder if they know anyone who can swim.*

Ralph pointed in a circle, wanting her to turn and repeat. She nodded, swam, turned, and swam back.

"Good. Wonderful arm action."

She felt a rhythm come to her effort. *Right arm, head left, left arm, head right. This feels nice.* A bigger wave rolled toward her. Despite it crashing over her head, she managed to stay on course.

"Let's try back and forth a few more times."

She did and was pleased.

"Put your toes down. Can you feel the bottom?"

She nodded as her feet touched the ocean sand. Strings of seaweed clung between her toes.

"Do you think you can take the belt off your waist and try on your own?"

She nodded again, but more hesitantly. She removed the belt and handed it to him. She put her feet on the bottom. With one step, she felt the smooth sand. With another, she felt sharp shells. *I had better lift my feet.* Anna stretched out over the waves. She replayed his mantra in her head. *Kick like the devil is chasing you.* She moved through the water. *This feels too slow. I better kick harder.* She punched the water with her feet. Her speed increased.

He touched her shoulder. "We need to end our lesson for to-day. I think we'll have visitors soon."

They turned toward the shore.

She laughed as the water receded to her waist and then her knees. "If I could keep my mouth closed, I would move faster and swallow less."

"You will be a seasoned swimmer soon. I'm glad you chose bare feet. There are, however, stones and rocks along here, so step lightly. I don't want you to slip and fall."

They walked to the beach.

"Thank you again for these lessons. I cannot wait to tell my family and my friend, Julia. She is expecting her baby about the same time as Flor."

"So, this is the reason you feel so protective of our pregnant native."

She nodded. "I will go and change."

She walked away. Sudden uncertainty brought tears to her eyes. *Flor. Julia. And it is the Feast of the Presentation of Mary as a three-year-old at the temple. What is my message here?*

She changed her clothes and exited the shed with her writing supplies. As expected, two canoes approached the beach. Frah and Sno with two more men sat in one canoe. Four men sat in the other.

Anna stood next to Ralph. His arm went around her shoulder.

The East Ones seemed eager to get to work. They wrapped heavy rope several feet above the hut's floor on three sides. Others climbed to the roof to hang woven mats. The mats unwound from ceiling to floor, creating grass walls which could be raised and lowered.

Ralph watched the construction. "I am amazed at the inge-nuity of these folks. Look at the walls that are appearing."

"That should stop the rain."

"Yes," he said, almost to himself, his gaze on the hut.

Anna gathered her skirts and sat near Ralph on a stump chair. With her writing supplies on her lap, she began a letter.

Dear Tata, Bashia, and Leon,

Zyche chi Wesoły Świąt Bożego Narodzenia i Szczęśliwego Novego Roku. I am wishing you a Blessed Christmas and successful New Year even though I do not know when you will receive this letter.

During my sea voyage, the storms reminded Sister and me of the might of the Lord. The quiet of a calm sea with the night sky having an amazing shine to it also recalled the presence of The Almighty.

When we arrived on the island, I saw many new things from the sand under my feet to the palm trees overhead to the quiet night sky too full of stars for one to count.

The kind doctor who requested our help on the island is helpful and sympathetic. He has treated natives of the other islands with knowledge and tenderness. He pulled an infected tooth from my mouth and has taught me to swim. Can you imagine me swimming in the Pacific Ocean? Yes, I am swimming and getting better every day. Doctor Graumann plans to teach me to fish soon.

The natives I mentioned live a few hours away. They speak a language I do not understand. But we use our hands and our heads to communicate. One of the ladies is expecting a baby soon. I am helping her stay in good health before she delivers.

I pray for you daily and think of you often. Now that I have written you one letter, I will add more about my life here and put it into the same envelope until a ship comes by to pick up our mail.

Love, Anna

The letter was put into an addressed envelope, but not sealed.

The note to Julia was not as easy to begin. *What do I say? Do I ask her, so many miles away, if she has ever been uncertain? How does it feel to be carrying a baby, the baby of her dead husband? Who listens to her dreams? I do not know the answers. How can I write? How can I not?* She tossed down the pen, walked to the eating area, picked berries from the basket, and washed them.

"Anna, is something wrong?" Ralph asked.

"I cannot find the words to send to Julia. She is pregnant, as I told you. Before I left Petroleum City, her husband died when he fell off a horse."

"Tell me more."

Her eyes burned with tears of frustration she didn't want to shed. "All afternoon I have been wearing this straw hat that Flor brought me. I have been teary eyed and thought it was because the hat did not stop the bright sun from assaulting my face. I am wrong. I am annoyed. This letter is to my friend. We have always been so close. In a way, I think I am writing it to myself."

"So, do that. If you think alike, she'll understand it, too."

With a huff of breath, she sat on the stump chair and picked up the pen again.

Dear Julia,

May the angels of the Lord look down and smile on you and your baby.

I miss you more than you can imagine. I wish I were there looking into your eyes. I am living on a beautiful, primitive island. The other resident is a doctor named Ralph. He is awfully nice and like a big brother to me. We have natives from another island visit us. We call them the East Ones.

One of them, a lady named Flor, is expecting a baby around Christmastime. Today is around November 21. I think you are going to have your baby in January. Are you healthy? Can you feel the baby moving? Is my sister, Bashia, seeing you every now and then?

My big problem is that I felt Flor's baby kicking, and I am adding it to my other confusions. Do I want to be a cloistered nun? Or any nun? Fortunately, there is plenty of time to pray here. I say the Rosary as I watch the palm trees sway.

Can you believe, I now know how to swim in the ocean with little fish nipping at my bare toes? (Do not tell even my sister about the bare toes.)

I miss you terribly and miss my family. I am praying and waiting for a sign from God to show me my way.

My heart is full of love and blessings for you.

Love, Anna

Again, she addressed the envelope, inserted the letter, but did not seal it. She placed both envelopes in the box Ralph had designated for outgoing mail.

When she looked toward the sea, a big, orange sun flirted with the ocean waves. The East Ones' voices resounded along the shoreline as they cast off on their voyage home. *When their voices hit the water, they take on a different tone, as if echoing through a long hallway. This is a part of the island phenomenon I will never forget.*

Ralph said, "You look more relaxed."

"I am. I did as you suggested, and the letter writing went so quickly. When I looked up, our guests were leaving."

"I'm glad you put your thoughts on paper for Julia." He got up from his seat, brushed sand from his short pants, and moved toward the new dwelling. "Now, let's see the finished hut."

He helped her climb the three steps into the East Ones' gift. She tripped on the top step.

He caught her before she fell to the floor. "Careful, dear, we don't want any broken bones," he said softly.

Heat rushed to her cheeks. "How embarrassing to be so clumsy." His face was closer than it had been when he examined the infected tooth. "I hope my breath is not offensive."

"You're fine, dear." He cradled her elbow as he guided her away from a corner post.

"The rope smells like drying grass." She held a piece of it. "I expected soft, but it feels rough."

"Same as your skin. The longer you stay, the rougher your skin will become."

"I am not sure I want to get tough."

"Hmm. I'm listening." He walked around the elevated room, lowering and raising each grass shade, and nodding as they went up and down smoothly. He began to whistle. The melody reminded her of a hymn she had heard coming from a church in downtown Petroleum City.

When the music stopped, she said, "Thank you for the lovely hymn. We need to eat. I am hungry. Are you?"

Together they cooked, ate, and watched a pink sunset fill the sky. The surrounding clouds blushed with soft color as they slid across the setting sun. Dusk followed so quickly, Anna could not read her prayer book when she opened it. She picked up her rosary to finish the day with the praises of Hail Mary.

THIRTY-EIGHT

Soft rhythmic breathing came from the other hammock when Anna awoke the next day. *Finally, I am the first one awake. I will start the coffee, measure water, and rice...* Anna hurried to her suitcase in the shed and dressed. While putting on her dark smock, prayers filled her mind. *God, thank You for the beauty of the day. Thank You for the soft wind. I felt it nudge my hammock this morning as a gentle wake up. Thou art mighty, and Holy is Thy name.*

Small pieces of wood and leaves were in the center of the pit at the cooking area. She put a match to the tinder and ignited the mound. Then she placed water and rice in the pot and got it cooking.

Behind her, Ralph cleared his throat. "Madam, I'm glad to have slept in a bit. But now, we have only rice for breakfast."

"I thought you could use a little rest from early morning fishing today. I am planning to open a container of tuna."

"That's a mighty fine idea."

"How long have you had these tins?"

"They arrived the same time I did. I've used a few. Incidentally, the taste is pretty good, as I recall." He took the can and pried it open.

The scent of tuna jumped to her nose and brought a lump of nostalgia to her throat. "This is the only fish served at my Pennsylvania home. We usually ate it for dinner with *placki*."

"And those are?" Ralph filled his plate with tuna and rice.

"Grated potatoes, an egg, flour, and salt to taste, all fried in Crisco. It's best eaten when it is still so hot it burns your fingers and your tongue."

"Sounds delightful. I'm sorry we have no potatoes."

"You have never tasted *placki*?"

"I think I have. The Germans call it by a different name. They serve it with applesauce and sometimes with sour cream."

They cleaned up their breakfast dishes and walked to the shoreline. Both of them threw seaweed back into the water.

She said, "Every day, the waves are different. Some days, I see weeds way up on the shore. Flung there by the tide. Those days, I smell salt and strong fish. Other days, the water is so motionless even the sand is unruffled. The breeze of fresh air is wonderful. I cannot believe we are right here in the Pacific."

"It is a part of paradise most days, isn't it? You seem relaxed, dear. You have not even announced the Saint of the day yet."

"Saint Cecelia," she said. *It is good to relax. I can read my prayer book and concentrate on the Saint of the day, Cecelia. I do not even know what the day of the week is, but—*

"Wait." He frowned at the sea. "Do you see that fleck on the horizon?"

"Where?"

He pointed.

She squinted and saw a small, dark shape sitting far offshore. "I see something. Is it a ship?"

"It's almost hovering there. Is it trying to find a way in past the reef?"

"If the ship stops, we can send our letters." Her heart stirred when she thought of Pennsylvania, her family, and Julia.

"Now remember. They could be pirates. Our story is I'm your spouse, the doctor. You are my wife, my assistant, and nurse."

"Yes. I will act like Helen, my neighbor. She and Henry are a couple from our church. They have been married for two years. They act cozy around each other."

He nodded absentmindedly. "If they question all your dark clothes, we'll say—"

"Could we say it is my religion and change the conversation?"

He smiled. His eyes reflected the morning sun. "Good idea. You amaze me, my Anna."

He got the pith helmets, placed one on his head, and handed her the other.

"Now we look like a couple," she said.

The bobbing vessel remained far offshore.

"The longer it does not move, the more threatening it becomes," he said. "Why are they not seeking land? Or maybe they can't see us, so they think this is a deserted island and of no use to them."

Or they see Ralph and me and are making an ambush plan.

"Are you nervous?" he asked.

"Yes. But, I am sure you can handle any problem."

"Thanks for the vote of confidence."

They walked back to the firepit. The vessel on the horizon seemed to be tied to its spot on the sea.

"I feel tense not knowing anything about that ship," she said as she sat on a stump chair.

Ralph went to his supply lean-to and brought out a pair of binoculars. He gazed through them. "Oh, for Christ's sake. Excuse me, Anna. I'm looking at a *small* vessel. It's almost too tiny to be worthy of getting around the ocean." He lowered the glasses. They hung around his neck on a leather strap. He rubbed his chin as if sizing up his shaved face and took a long slow breath. He squinted. "I wonder."

"What?" she asked.

He tilted the pith helmet to a jaunty angle and put the binoculars to his eyes again. "I can see better with this little bit of shade." He nodded. "I think we'll have visitors. And my guess is because the vessel is so small, they are non-threatening and only curious." He handed the glasses to her.

She took off her helmet and tried to look through the binoculars. "How do you see through these?"

"Put the two eyepieces to your eyes, then turn that dial up on top." He placed them on her face and guided her fingers to the center.

She turned the knob. Two small rowboats came into focus. She saw people aboard heading toward the shore. She continued to watch, as intrigued by the binocular's magnifying ability as she was with the guests.

"Anna, do put on your helmet, the sun is so bright."

"All right." She dropped the glasses around her neck, placed the hat on her head, and again peered at the panorama of water and boat through the viewer.

Five men came ashore. They walked up to Ralph and Anna.

"*Bueños Dias, señor y señora*," the first man said. He was of medium height and had a happy face.

Ralph smiled, shook hands, and said, "We are Americans. Does anyone in the party speak English?"

"Oh, yes." He nodded. "I am Jean Claude Pont, a French photographer and explorer. This is my party." He pointed to a middle-aged man. "My assistant, also French, is Boudreaux."

"How do you do?" Boudreaux tipped his hat to Anna. He was rotund with an unruly mop of curly, gray hair.

"My guides," Jean Claude continued, "are these three wonderful local men. Carlos, Diego, and Luis."

The three men smiled and nodded.

Jean Claude patted a large black box he snuggled to his chest. "Here, I carry my prized camera."

Ralph said, "Let me introduce myself. I am Doctor Ralph Graumann, a physician. And this is my wife and assistant, Anna."

"How beautiful. You two. Lovely. I would like to photograph the island and take pictures of such a handsome couple. May I?"

Ralph looked at Anna. She nodded. To Jean Claude, he said, "Of course. How long will you be here?"

"A few days, a few days," he said. "I... May we sit?" He motioned to the three guides, who brought a small cask from a rowboat. "I bring nice French wine for you as a housewarming gift. Yes?"

"That's very considerate," Ralph said. Turning to Anna, he said, "Let's take these three strong men to bring more chairs out for the group."

Anna took that to mean she should stay by his side, so she did. Ralph beckoned to Carlos and his cohorts. They found two tree trunk stumps near the supply lean-to and two more by the East Ones' Gift and carried all four to those already by the firepit. Ralph brought out a wooden box that contained glass tumblers.

Jean Claude said, "Good, good. We would *love* to sit and watch your ocean with you, have a drink of wine, pass the time, and tell you our plans for photography here."

He poured the wine. Anna shook her head at the offer.

Jean Claude lifted his glass in a salute to Anna and Ralph. "I love your reef, I love your reef. And so many colorful, fast-moving fish. We also encountered many sharks. You must be aware of those."

Ralph nodded.

"Sadly, no camera on Earth can peek into the water and photograph them. But on land, another story," Jean Claude said.

"How long have you been taking pictures of these islands?" Anna asked.

He leaned back as if catching his breath. "These Galapagos. I have been here now for over one year. I keep finding new islands. I keep finding new animals. I keep finding new birds. Beautiful. How can I stop? When will I stop? Only God knows, or when I run out of film." He lowered his head and said as if in confidence, "But, I brought much, much film."

"Interesting," said Ralph.

"But for you two, another gift. Give me the name and address of family in the United States, and I will send them some pictures of you here in the Galapagos."

Anna said, "Oh, how thoughtful. My father would love to see the island." She found paper, wrote down her father's name and address, and handed it to Jean Claude.

"And you, Doctor?"

"No, Anna's pictures will be enough. Thank you."

The group finished the glasses of wine. With smiling nods, the three guides headed toward the rowboats. As Jean Claude prattled on, Anna watched the men. Carlos and Diego strolled away looking benign. Luis' gait, though, reminded her of someone from home. Luis' legs seemed to glide as if he were ice skating, leaning on each skate. His arms hung nonchalantly with hands on his hips. His head turned side-to-side in a rhythmic movement as if his eyes took in every inch around him.

Suddenly, she recognized the memory. It was of Ginusz, a neighbor. Ginusz had been in and out of jail for robbery. Another thought passed through Anna's head. Ginusz's face was replaced with the face of Frah. A chill rolled down her spine.

"My dear, we need to say goodbye to our guests." Ralph pulled her to her feet. "We'll see you all tomorrow."

"Good, good." Jean Claude chuckled. He and Boudreaux walked toward the shore.

Confused, Anna waved as the men got into the boats. "Why are they leaving so soon?"

Ralph's arm was still around her. "Your mind was miles away. Are you sure you didn't drink the wine?"

"I wasn't paying attention. What did I miss?"

"Jean Claude thought Boudreaux brought three cameras, but he brought only one. The little box camera around Jean Claude's neck wasn't enough. So, they'll come back tomorrow, and we will show them the island for a couple of days." He turned toward her and cupped her face in his hands. "You look concerned."

"I was fine, having a wonderful visit. Then..." She told him about Luis, the reminder of Ginusz, and then of Frah.

"Forewarned is a good thing," he said.

⁖ ⁖ ⁖

The next morning at dawn, Anna and Ralph greeted the returning five men.

Jean Claude removed his hat and wiped his moist head. "Let's see the tortoises. I can hardly contain my impatience."

Ralph nodded. "We are both ready to travel. Today, I want to head north and show you the natural beauty of this island. I hope we will see iguanas and tortoises. Tomorrow, we can go south and see the seals." He plopped Anna's pith helmet on her head, strapped a pack containing water jars and cooked rice onto his back, and set off into the jungle.

Much of the trek was uphill. It was slow-going for the two older gentlemen, made slower still by Jean Claude's stopping to photograph birds.

Diego found the first group of tortoises. "Señor," he called.

Jean Claude took photographs as his helpers fed bananas to the three lumbering giants. "Who would believe this?" he cried. "Boudreaux, you stay in the picture so everyone can see the size of these creatures. I want these tortoises to show in the photographs so, so clearly. The word to use is testudinal, which means resembling their own shells."

Jean Claude posed for pictures, then Boudreaux again. Then the slow-moving creatures moved on.

Jean Claude gestured to Anna and Ralph. "Doctor and Mrs. Anna. Please, please." He posed them with flowers. "These smell as sweet as the perfume my French mother put on when Papa took her to dinner."

The midday sun shone down.

"Lunchtime," Ralph declared.

They sat on a bluff and ate cold rice and fruit. Jean Claude added jerky to their repast. The meat he provided was salty and puckered all their lips. Jean Claude took more pictures of Anna and Ralph as they shared their meal.

Another trio of tortoises happened by. Sadly, all the bananas in the area were gone, so the group did not stay as long. After they left, Ralph led the way back to camp.

"Allow us to repay your hospitality by catching some fish for dinner," Jean Claude said.

"All right," Ralph told him, "but the reefs can be tricky. We should go with you."

"A fine idea. We'll make it a party."

So, they got into their rowboats, Anna and Ralph got into his canoe, and they all paddled out past the reef. Anna waited in the boat while all six men slipped into the water and fished with their nets. They caught enough for a banquet.

Yet, Luis and Diego continued to dive, looking for more.

Luis said, "I want something *muy grande*."

Boudreaux and Jean Claude sat in their boat. Boudreaux idly dangled his fingers in the water. Suddenly he jumped up, waving both arms and pointing. "A shark. It is a scalloped hammerhead."

The two swimmers hastily slid into the boat where Carlos waited.

Ralph laughed. "They must have decided they had plenty of food for dinner."

The five guests talked of nothing but the shark on the way to shore.

Back at camp, Carlos prepared their dinner. He seasoned the fish with the usual spices but added his own supply of chopped red onion.

"What are these?" Anna lifted a small orange ball.

"Tree tomatoes," Boudreaux said. "And these are hot peppers. All grow wild on the islands. Our Carlos has a way with the cooking." He licked his lips and smiled.

I'll have to look for such plants. I'm getting tired of plain fish.

They ate eleven fish and wiped the sides of their plates with rice to capture each remaining spiced morsel.

"You have filled up my fish supply for tomorrow," Ralph said.

Jean Claude nodded. "Good, good. We will spend the night here, if we may. Tomorrow, we'll take pictures of your seals. I want to look for the iguanas, too. Then, we must leave. We have a timetable to follow."

Ralph nodded.

Anna said, "Tell me what else you've photographed on these islands, Jean Claude."

"Ah, we have seen, and I hope have taken good photographs of marine iguanas and waved albatrosses. We have seen some scalloped hammerhead sharks. Big, big. Even bigger than today. That was a medium size one, right, my friend, Boudreaux?"

"Indeed," he said.

"We could not use the camera for the sea turtles nor the rays. But, we got pictures of land iguanas. We would like more of those and a few more of swallow-tailed gulls. And of course, your seals."

Ralph smiled. "Tomorrow, you will see more seals than you thought existed in this world."

Jean Claude nodded. "Good, good."

"Incidentally, there are flamingos and penguins here in the Galapagos. Did you catch any of them with your camera?"

"No, that is why we continue to explore these islands. You see why we cannot stop for long?"

"Oh, yes." Ralph stood. "Excuse me, I need to check on something." He walked away.

Anna took up the conversation when Ralph left so abruptly. "I have never seen a penguin. How big do you suppose they would be?"

"The Galapagos penguin is small. Perhaps eighteen-inches high. And they weigh only five pounds. I understand that the female lays her eggs in the crevices of lava flows."

Anna looked at Jean Claude's face but was listening for Ralph's return. Luis entered the common area from off the thicket to their right. Behind her, Ralph cleared his throat.

"Yes, we have enough firewood for a day or two," Ralph said.

"Good, good."

They basked in the heat of the firepit. Sparks rose on the updraft as if trying to catch the stars.

Ralph poked the coals with a stick. "Incidentally, let me show you what we call The East Ones' gift."

"Let us see." Boudreaux got to his feet.

Holding tight to Anna's hand, Ralph led the men to the above-ground shelter. "You would all be comfortable in here."

Jean Claude scowled. "We could not take your dwelling from you."

Ralph shrugged. "Anna and I prefer to sleep under the stars."

"Very well, then. Good night."

"Good night," Anna called as she and Ralph walked away.

They climbed into the hammocks, and Anna fell asleep immediately.

ಬ   ಬ   ಬ

"Anna, turn your head," Ralph said.

She sighed. "I know we need to change clothes in the shed today to prevent the men from speculating about us. But this is a challenge. And now, you turn around while I slip into my dress."

"Oh, I need my shirt. I'm usually dressed before you wake up. Can you handle seeing me without a shirt until I get my clothes outside?"

She slid her frock over her head. "Yes, it will be fine. Remember, I have seen all the East Ones with no clothes above the waist. Why should it be different for you?"

"In our culture, as a sign of respect for women, men cover their chests."

"I never thought of it that way. Yet, I was shocked the first time I saw the men bare-chested. Well, not as shocked as when I saw the women covered above the waist only by chains of flowers, their hair, or nothing."

"Madam, you are very young and naïve. The best I can do for you today is to ask you to trust me. If I feel like you are in trouble, I'll say… Well, I can't say your Jesus, Mary, and Joseph chant, but—"

"Why don't you say Holy Virginia?"

"No, I'll say Holy Petersburg."

"That will be fine." She sat on a wooden crate. "I am pleased Flor brought me these walking shoes." She lifted a foot and rolled her ankle, admiring the sparkling cluster of beads on the leather.

"Can I turn?" he said.

"Do turn."

He laughed then motioned toward her hair. "You look bewitching with your hair a-kilter, dear."

She touched her head, feeling lots of loose curls. "I need my comb and my prayer book. I am behind on my daily devotionals." She picked up her rosary and moved items around in her suitcase until she found her missal.

"Let's go." He ushered her outside and picked up his shirt.

Together, they walked to the cooking area where Luis and Carlos had started the fire.

Anna sniffed the bitter, nutty scent of coffee in the morning breeze. "Smells delicious."

"Yes." Holding her elbow, he guided her to a stump seat.

As they sipped coffee, Carlos tossed several fish, still glistening with ocean water, onto a hot pan, making them sizzle. New spice scents perfumed the air as they cooked.

After a tasty breakfast, the party of seven picked up their hats, cameras, binoculars, and lunch food and started south.

Anna recognized the route they took. She touched some white flowers on a bush. "I have to admit these blossoms are gorgeous."

Jean Claude raised a camera to his eye. "Yes, and I need a photograph of you and the doctor here, Mrs. Anna, please. Remember, I will send a few of the best ones to your family. Sadly, it may be a few years until I finish this project and get them printed. By then, who knows? You two may have a baby or two."

The warmth of her blush crept up her neck. *I am so glad to be wearing this helmet. No one can see anything above my nose.*

They climbed up and down the rough terrain.

"All this beauty leaves me speechless," Boudreaux said.

"Doctor. Wait, wait." Jean Claude exchanged his camera for one that Boudreaux carried. "Another picture, please."

They ascended through sun and shade with ground wet and dry. Mockingbirds sang overhead. Then they began to hear the barking of the seals.

Jean Claude hurried forward. "Oh, I can hardly wait."

On top of the next ridge, they looked down at perhaps a hundred brown seals sunning on the rocks.

Jean Claude's face became radiant. "Only here. Only here would I see this. The thumb of God has marked this place."

His smile was contagious. The other crew members looked pleased as they followed him down the cliff to the ocean's edge. Anna and Ralph stayed atop the cliff. Anna had mixed feelings.

Part of her wanted to see the seals up-close. The babies were so cute. But a larger part was reluctant to be immersed in the seal and fish odor. Jean Claude took pictures. He knelt, stood, and sat on the rocks with the inquisitive creatures. At one point, Anna thought he might swim with the seals.

The sun tipped past noon. At last, the group left the herd. Jean Claude looked exhausted as he climbed back up the cliff. Without a word, they headed back to camp. Anna crinkled her nose as they walked. Jean Claude and his party reeked.

It was late afternoon when they arrived home. Jean Claude pulled Ralph to the side. They had a whispered conversation.

Ralph nodded then went to Anna. "Jean Claude and his men smell awful from the seal encounter. Can you go into the shed for a while so they can bathe with our rainwater?"

"Of course. I can get some reading done."

Anna walked to the hut. It was a distance from the East Ones' Gift and would allow the men some privacy. *This roof really could use some mending. Rays of sunlight are shining through*. She sat on a crate, pulled out her Bible, and began reading. Then she closed her eyes in prayer. When she looked up, Luis clad in only a towel around his waist stood in front of her. He held the towel closed with one hand. With the other, he grabbed her arm.

Her jaw dropped. She felt a heavy knot in her chest. She had a fast intake of breath and said, "Oh."

Ralph's shadow filled the doorway. "Holy Petersburg. Luis."

A Cheshire Cat grin crossed Luis' face. "So sorry, *Señor*. Wrong *casa*."

"Yes, very wrong *casa* for you," Ralph said.

Luis made a hasty retreat, followed by Ralph.

Anna felt disconcerted. *What just happened?* With trembling hands, she placed the Bible into her suitcase and latched the lid. After a few minutes, she went out to the eating area. A rowboat paddled away. She walked to the shore and stood beside Ralph.

Jean Claude said, "Boudreaux had photography chores to do, so he and Luis left. Mrs. Anna, they could not wait long enough to say goodbye."

She nodded.

"We must go as well. I am sorry that we did not see iguanas." He smiled at Anna and shook hands with Ralph. Then he climbed into the rowboat with Diego and Carlos.

Anna watched them go.

Ralph stood stiffly with his arm around her. "Never forget to listen to your inner feelings."

They stood together as the ocean carried their guests away. The sun dipped into the horizon. Ralph led her back to the eating area. He acted angry. She sat meekly before the cold firepit.

He paced before her. "What were we thinking? Letting five men on the island." He stomped so hard it seemed to cement the sand.

"I do not know what you mean." She folded the pleats in her skirt.

"Why do you think Luis was in that hut with you?"

"Maybe to steal money?"

"You don't get it. You really don't get it. Do you?"

"What?" She raised her voice and eyebrows.

"He wanted *you*. And you will be on the next safe boat. Out. Of. Here."

"What would he want of me?"

"Don't you know the facts of life?"

She stood and crossed her hands over her chest. "Of course, I do. When a man and a woman love each other enough, they lie together and have intercourse and sometimes make a baby."

Ralph's eyes sparked. "Whoa, whoa. That's a nice womanly explanation. Now, let me tell you the men's ways of the world. Men see. Men want. There are men who take what they want. It's an entirely different set of rules. Do you understand?"

"So, I was in danger, not our belongings?"

"He wanted to take from you something more precious than belongings." He blew out his breath. "How many ways can I say this? It's called rape."

She lowered her eyes.

"No, look at me. Until you get aboard a safe ship, forget the swimming. We are practicing survival skills."

"Oh?"

"Yes. And I will be remiss if I don't give you at least one tactic tonight. Anna, if some male gets too near you and it doesn't feel right, you first kick them between their legs. And I mean the groin. And second, you scream and run."

She looked away to hide her tears.

He moved closer to her. "This day has been one of the longest I can remember. Time for sleep."

They walked to the hammocks.

THIRTY-NINE

Anna awoke to a howling wind.

Ralph put a hand on her shoulder. "The calendar says it's the dry season, but my intuition feels a big storm a-brewing. Look at the sky."

Dark clouds swooped in from the ocean.

"We need to move to the cave," he said. "I have a kind of sled in the cavern. We can come back for the food if there is time. Safety is most important."

How many trips can we make? Is the food heavy? How soon will the rain come? A gust of salty wind blew hair across her eyes and filled her nose and mouth. She found it hard to talk. "I need my books." *I can't risk having them ruined.*

"I'll carry your suitcase. You grab the fruit basket. We'll come back for the rest."

Leaves and debris swirled around the grassy area as she slipped from the hammock. Grains of sand from the beach rasped against her skin. She rushed to the eating area and grasped the basket with the remains of the East Ones' fruit.

"Can we go now?" she asked.

"Yes."

They sped into the jungle. Tree limbs and palm fronds rattled. He guided her around a downed tree trunk and around a gully.

As she raced to the cave, she said the Rosary. *I believe in God, the Father Almighty, creator of Heaven and Earth.*

Ralph checked the intact threads. They entered the cave and dropped their burdens. She breathed deeply, smelling the familiar musty scent of the dwelling.

He rushed into the shadows and returned pulling a sled. "It

works on grass and sometimes on sand if I don't overload it. Come. I think we can manage only one trip. Decide what you want to bring, dear."

"I am thinking."

She pulled some twine from a pile and gathered all her hair back into a knot as she followed Ralph and the sled out of the cave. There was no rain yet, but the wind nearly picked her up and sent her airborne.

He steadied her arm. "Are you sure you want to come?"

She nodded. *I had better grab the outgoing mail, and maybe we should take down the hammocks. And in Jesus Christ, His only son, our Lord...*

She bent into the wind as she staggered forward. It smelled like newly turned soil in a garden. The palm trees whipped about as if trying to flee. Flying leaves struck her face. Ralph pulled two handkerchiefs out of his pocket. He handed one to her, then tied the other around his nose and mouth, knotting it in back. She did the same. It was easier to breathe without sand and bits of debris in her mouth and nose.

When they finally reached the camp, they pantomimed about where to go and what to include because the wind blew their voices away. He left the sled on the grass and ran to the hammocks. Anna ran to the East Ones' gift and rolled up the side shades. She carried the mail and the bag of rice to the sled. Ralph fought the hammocks as they swung out of reach time and again. The wind won. He left them hanging and rushed to the supply lean-to for their tins of tea and spices. He retrieved a crate of canned food from the shed and stacked it on the sled as well. As he tucked a tarp over the load, it started to sprinkle.

They both grabbed the rope to pull the heavy sled. The tree canopy protected them for only a few minutes before the sky opened. Rain fell in torrents. Anna glanced at Ralph, only able to see his eyes above the cloth. He squinted into the deluge. She kept her eyes half-closed as she trudged beside him.

Even if I pray especially hard, this is a long, wet trail. I hope this storm is a short one. Who was conceived by the Holy Spirit, born of the Virgin Mary...

At last, they reached the cave. They rushed inside.

"That was an adventure," she said. "I'm chilled to the bone."

"I'll start a fire. You go put on dry clothes."

"I will."

She hurried behind the screen in the back of the cave and stripped off her sodden clothing. When she returned, dressed and dry, she watched his silhouette in the darkness. He took matches from the tin box on the small table near the firewood and lit the kindling he'd placed in the pit. A curl of smoke rose up to the chimney.

He glanced at her. "Feel better, dear?"

"Yes."

"Now, I'll change. All right with you?"

"Of course." She stepped out of his way.

He disappeared behind the screen.

She sat on a stump before the growing fire and rubbed the chill from her arms. A powerful coffee aroma caught her by surprise. Turning to the dark, she asked, "Are we drinking coffee? I smell Maxwell House."

"I grabbed the can of used grounds before we left camp. You may have noticed before, we're in a hole in the ground. Like it or not, surrounded by dirt. Sometimes wet dirt. A musty smell can be overpowering. At the hospital, when we got into a pocket of stink, old coffee grounds would absorb it. We put the grounds on little plates in about three or four places in a room."

She looked toward the blackness. "I certainly prefer the smell of coffee."

"Incidentally, this may be a stay of several days to a week. We will have time to plan your self-survival strategies. I am sorry I didn't teach you sooner."

"I admit I am too trusting."

He cleared his throat. She heard the scratch of a match across its box and then watched him lower the flame into a can. Ralph's face was illuminated by the candle. He set it on the table. Then he poured water into a pot and placed it over the firepit.

He sat beside her. Outside, the wind roared. A gust blew spray into the cave. Anna shivered. Ralph got up, took the blue blanket from her bed, and draped it over her shoulders. He sat again and put his arm around her.

"You know, I've been on the island for over a year. Regarding the weather, at first, I went by the almanac. Now, I try to read nature. Counting the kinds and number of birds helps. If I see too few, I expect a storm. I also watch the mighty tortoises. Many of the shelled giants equal calm seas and sunshine. The fewer, the more storms."

"But we did see a few the day before yesterday."

"Only a few. Most days, when I get up at dawn, I can count a dozen." He spooned tea leaves into cups and filled them with boiling water. He handed one to her.

"So, here we are." She sipped from her cup, found it too hot, and put it down.

"Yes. Today is the first day of your defense learning. Let us start with a given. Every man who wants to take advantage of you is a bully. Now, think. What do you know about bullies?"

"I have never been bullied."

"Because?"

"I was always with a group."

He sipped and smacked his lips. "But now there is no group. Just you and me."

She nodded.

"Think alone. Like your prayer interloper yesterday. Let's re-play this, even though it is uncomfortable. What did you do?"

"I closed my eyes."

"What courageous thing could you have done?"

"Screamed. How embarrassing would that be?"

"He was a mean man. It doesn't matter what his pals think. What else could you do?"

"Throw something at him."

"Good. What was near that you could throw?"

"I do not recall."

He prodded. "Ponder, Anna. Plan a strategy. Close your eyes.

Remember the area. What could you throw?"

She closed her eyes and thought of the room. "I was sitting on a crate with cans of tuna. I could have thrown them."

"Good. That would be the right weight. The cans would land loud and call attention to your plight. This is an acceptable first plan. Think about the strategy, and this afternoon, let's talk again about this. Because today we are talking defense. As the week goes by, we need to plan offense."

She sighed.

"I think that's enough discomfort for you for the moment."

She picked up the cup again, took a long sip of tea, and felt it soothe her lips and warm her chest.

I am so blessed to have a friend I trust. I am so relaxed with Ralph. He is comforting now and was my champion yesterday when he confronted Luis.

Ralph added a few twigs to the fire. "Every day since you arrived, we have had distractions. We hardly know each other. If we have a week of solitude, you can tell me how your feelings have changed since you left Pennsylvania, and I can tell you what I've been thinking for the last year."

"What *have* you been thinking, Ralph?"

He took a can of tuna from a crate on the sled and pried it open. "You know why I came to these islands. I was beside myself, as they say. I put up a hammock that I brought from the States and figured I'd vegetate. I did. I laid around and watched the sky and the clouds. Fortunately, I came to my senses a bit, before the rains came."

"I think you had a good reason to want to vegetate."

"Perhaps." He scooped out the tuna. "But, back to my story, I had to stop swinging on that hammock. I had to do some exploring. I discovered this cave and found a clean water supply. I knew how to fish. To catch those fish, one has to put a smaller fish on a hook. Back home if I needed a hook, I could use a bobby pin or a safety pin and attach it to a string. But here, I needed to fish in the water. So, I built a raft." He shook his head. "What a mess that was. Sunk. Just like that. Had to build something else for the water. Luckily, I had a hatchet. The second time, I built a better raft. By then, I was starting to wise up. I could die out here, and no one would know or care."

"How did you find enough food?"

He handed her a plate of tuna with some blackberries. She inhaled the fragrance of the fish. As always, it reminded her of her family.

"Lucky for me, my buddies put a package together for my trip. Until I could figure out how to forage on my own, I had their provisions. Between the three of them, I was well supplied. But when I was happy in the hammock, I'd hear my Pappy's voice inside my head. *Boy, all that schoolin'. You got time to waste? Them hands are healin' ones. What ya doin' about that?* And his voice would not go away."

She watched the berries roll around on her plate. "It is hard when you hear family voices in your head."

"What are your voices saying?"

She closed her eyes to hear them more clearly. "They tell me I am human. They remind me that I am very naïve. My readings tell me about Jesus who prayed a lot but also was out around the crowds. A wise woman said that God danced the day her baby was born. Can you even imagine that? God danced. I think He wants me to dance, too. The more I am away from the convent, the more I see that it is not the life for me. I think I need to seek a different life."

"That is a monumental thought. What comes next?"

Home. But where is home? She looked around at their dwelling. An earthy smell seeped from the walls. Candles flickered in the shadows. "You say I should leave. But, how will Flor deliver her baby if I am gone? I feel I have a responsibility to her."

"Maybe you do, and maybe you don't. Remember, she got pregnant before she knew that a woman was coming here." He shrugged. "Incidentally, she might not even come back for a while. Or she might come back to show you her new baby. These East Ones have rules and ways we will never know."

"Is that an excuse for me?"

Outside, the rain and the wind chased around the entrance and moaned through the homemade chimney.

He raised his voice above the sounds. "You know, you are thinking about them as if the tribe is from Ohio. Do you have any idea what they call right and wrong? We cannot judge them. However, so you know, they have no marriage as we think of it. They choose each other, and that is the bond. It's their way. Does that make a difference to you?"

"No. I will accept it the way it is." She picked up her teacup and drank.

"Is this a new part of you?" He poked the burning wood, making a shower of sparks at the edge of the blaze.

"That visit we had with Jean Claude and Boudreaux and their helpers was such a learning experience for me. I thought I was mature. What could have happened had you not been there? I hate that I was so oblivious."

"Fortunately, as you say, it was only a learning experience."

"I am going to find my missal and start my prayers for the day. I will say a long prayer of thankfulness for our warm and dry cave. Today is the feast of Saint Catherine." She picked up a candle, and still wrapped in the blanket, walked to her cot and began reading.

He added a few more branches to the fire and softly whistled *Rhapsody in Blue*.

She hummed along for a few minutes with pleasure and contentment, then stopped herself. *I better keep my mind on my studies and read my daily devotions. If we have seven days here in the cave, I plan to do a lot of praying, so when we come out, I will be ready to take the first safe boat home. I need to find my life where it started. Right in Pennsylvania.*

FORTY

The wind moaned. *My toes and fingers are cold. My feet ache.* She shivered and layered an extra dress over the one she wore. *This feels like a hug.*

"Good morning, Ralph." She pulled her hair back from her face.

"Did you sleep well?"

"Not bad. Chilly, considering the storm."

"I see you're already dressed for the day." Seated by the fire, he tossed a few branches on the flames then stirred them around with a poker.

"Where in all of this land did you find that metal stick?"

"I discovered it while walking on the beach about two months after I arrived. My foot went deep into the wet sand, and my big toe caught on it. How it got here, I'll never know."

"Could it have floated here?"

"Too heavy. Must have arrived long ago with pirates or explorers."

"That is a real puzzle." She moved closer to the fire.

His shadow danced with the flickers from the flames. "When I finally leave this place, the poker will remain in the cave so it can be a riddle for the next resident."

She put a pot of water on the hook above the fire then pulled out a can of tuna and the rice. *I have been here for a month. He starts the fire, I cook the rice. The two of us move like partners in a waltz.* Scattered drops of rain fell from the less-than-perfect chimney and sizzled in their blaze.

"Listen to the wind. Incidentally, the rain seems to find its way in now and again."

"Yes, it does."

"Tell me when you need a pause from your praying, and we'll continue reviewing the self-defense skills. Always remember, a good swift kick between his legs is the best tactic."

"You made that instruction very clear. I will not forget." She moved plates to the tiny table.

"Next, you promptly leave the area in any way possible."

"All right." She nodded.

He sighed and continued in a softer voice. "When I saw Luis with you, I swear, I could have killed him."

She blinked and raised her head. "You are *serious*?"

"I am serious about you. We two could make an amazing partnership and an extraordinary couple. I should have let you know my feelings long before now."

"I had no idea." She shifted her weight from one foot to the other. "This is one of those moments I hear about when I need to speak the right thing and do not know what it is."

He prodded the blaze with the poker. Flames shot up with glimmers of green and blue in the red tongues of fire.

She edged toward him then lowered herself to the adjoining log seat. She slipped her fingers under his open hand. "Dear Ralph, I am honored to hear you talk about us being a couple. I do not have a response. You certainly make me think."

He curled his fingers around hers. "That's all I can ask, my dear. Shall we talk about this tomorrow?"

"Yes. And I will pray for guidance."

He patted her hand.

She continued preparing their breakfast. But inside, her thoughts whirled. *I am confused. Have I changed my mind and want to be a wife and mother? I have so many new ideas turning around in my head.*

Throughout the day, the storm raged. Anna kept her nose buried in her Bible, only glancing up when she thought he wouldn't see. Ralph paced the cave and kept the fire burning.

At the evening meal, he said, "Madam, what would happen to you here on the island if we were separated?"

"I never considered that. It could not occur."

"Wrong, my Anna. Things happen. What would you do?"

"I would look for you."

"And if I couldn't be found? Would you live in the cave for the rest of your life?"

"Nooo." *What would I do?* She stood, wringing her hands.

"Think. What would your next move be? Could you exist alone on the island?"

"Yes, I could live alone here. But do you plan on leaving?"

"No, dear. We are just talking. Would you move in with the East Ones?"

"With the East Ones?" she yelped. "How bizarre. I do not think I could do that. This is a most uncomfortable discussion."

"May this discomfort be only in your head. Both of us should get some sleep. Tomorrow, we talk strategy. Now, good night."

At sunrise the next morning, Anna dressed, went to the firepit, and struck a match to the tinder.

Ralph sat in a dark part of the cave.

She jumped. "Oh."

He didn't speak. Anna sensed his eyes upon her.

She moved breakfast utensils into place. "About your questions yesterday, I have done hours of thinking. I can fish and swim. I know the animals. I can return to the cave in inclement weather."

"And what of the East Ones?"

"I am good at hide-and-seek. I can cover my tracks."

"Pennsylvania hide-and-seek. You are a foreigner in this environment. You need better plans. You need offensive plans, not defensive ones."

"Tell me what I need to know."

"If you had to defend yourself, could you punch someone?"

She shook her head. "I have never punched anyone."

"I want you to know more about protection. I have stuffed a shirt and pants. Let me show you." He walked to the back of the cave and returned carrying a dummy. He tilted the empty cot on end and tied her target upright. "Punch it as hard as you can again and again."

"You want me to?"

"Make a fist and aim for the belly."

She closed her fist and pushed it into the pretend chest. "Like this?"

"Not a bad start, but aim lower if you want to hit the belly. Can you punch harder?"

She tried again.

"Better," he said. "While you practice, I'd like to hear your thoughts on us."

"I feel safe when I am with you. I am beginning to realize that I must become a completely new, non-nun woman. Yet being a nun has been my whole mindset for years. I need time. A great deal of time."

"I am a patient man."

She smiled.

"That's enough exercise for now," he said. "We need to make more candles. While I find my chunks of wax and string, you get a few empty cans."

She gathered the containers and set them down in a line at the fireside.

"Now I need the little stones."

"Stones?" She raised an eyebrow.

"Come on, kid, figure it out. The stone is the most important element of candle making."

She laughed. "I am stumped."

"You think about it while we pause to eat. We need sustenance and adequate fluids. Can you put on the tea? Oh, let's break the rules and have coffee. There is no one else on our island in this inclement weather."

She pulled out the pot with the glass dome on top and added coffee grounds. Soon the aroma of Maxwell House filled the cave. They ate and sipped coffee. The sound of the rain diminished.

Ralph pulled a bag of small stones from a low shelf. "Right where I left them with the other supplies. These stones are the kind I can tie a coated string to and then place on the bottom of a can. Next, I pour in hot wax, enough to cover the stone with the waxed string." He carefully poured the melted wax. "The next day, we put more wax into the can and have a candle."

"Of course. I should have guessed."

"Incidentally, dear, how far can you swim?"

"I can swim a fairly good distance."

"What thing would help you float on the ocean?"

"Again, you make me think outside my comfort level. I think I could stay afloat. When we fished aboard our boat, I saw pieces of wood float by. I could hang on one if need be."

"How fast can you run?"

"I competed in a few races at school. I can run a long distance. Ralph, I feel like I am filling out an athletic report."

"Then let's get back to your exercises."

Anna spent the rest of the day alternately punching the dummy and laughing about punching the dummy. After dinner, they talked about the East Ones and laughed about Anna's shock at her first sight of the half-naked women.

She smiled at him across the flickering firelight. "I like these quiet times with you."

They blew out the candles and went to sleep.

ॐ ॐ ॐ

At dawn, the cave was silent except for the whistling tune of *Amazing Grace.*

Anna smiled and hummed the same melody.

"Good morning." Ralph started the fire. "How did you sleep?"

"Very soundly. I was tired from all that punching. What's on the agenda for today?"

"We need to finish those candles."

They heated and poured another layer of hot wax into the half-dozen cans.

As they worked, he said, "Do you know how to flag a ship?"

"No."

"To broadcast an emergency, we fly a white flag. One hangs it over any high tree or roof to call a ship into port."

"Like a bedsheet?"

"That would work." Ralph stood. "What silly bird is singing in the rain? I need to see this." He walked to the entrance, then turned to Anna and motioned her to look.

She joined him. "It is only sprinkling. Hard to believe it was storming yesterday. This will be a beautiful day for us."

"I reckon."

They bundled dry branches for a shoreside fire, some dinner rice, put up the threads, and headed toward their camp by the ocean.

He walked quietly beside her. "Have you given any thought to my wanting to be more than a friend?"

"Oh, Ralph. I have had many thoughts about that. I think back to when we met. I was apprehensive and had so much fear. Sister Calista's death showed me your kindness. You were so thoughtful when we paid our last respects."

He nodded. "I have no doubt she's up there laughing at us since she created this dilemma."

"Yes, I will say she had her hand in all of this. Next, I thought of you as strong. Then you helped me learn to light a fire and swim. So, I saw that you were also helpful and caring."

"I feel so much more than that. I like the way you first tilt your chin up when you gaze toward the heavens. I watch you lift your eyebrows when you notice those puffy clouds. It makes me think you are counting them." He held her elbow with his free hand as they walked. "Incidentally, if there were a lake on our island, I would call it Lake Anna."

"What a tender thing to say. And I *do* count the clouds."

"I like having you near. Let's talk about the future."

"But is it wise to talk about a future together? We have only known each other for a matter of weeks. I have spent all of my life planning to be a nun. What would you have said if while you were completing your studies to become a doctor, someone told you to be a lawyer instead?"

Ralph nodded. "I'll have to ponder that."

"I do care about you. You say incidentally so frequently that it has become my favorite word."

"What else do you like about me?

She tilted her head and smiled. "I like the clean soapy smell on your shaved face in the morning. I like your whistling as you do chores. I like you being a gentleman."

"We are living here alone together. I respect your wishes."

"There is all the time in the world. A month more would help me."

"That is a hard request from you."

"I know."

"Both of us acted like a couple for the benefit of the East Ones and the photographers."

"And we did fool them." She lifted her eyebrows.

He paused in the path and looked into her eyes. "Yes, we did. It felt good to have my arm around you. Incidentally, you always took that little half step to get closer to me when the East Ones or the photographers were here. I need that."

"I saw a young married couple from my church act that way. I thought we should look like we were newlyweds."

"You fooled me into believing we were a couple. How did you feel pretending we were just married?"

"I felt like I was learning to be an actress."

A tortoise crossed their path taking plenty of time. They waited and watched.

She said, "I saw your tenderness when you became my dentist. When I had that toothache, you were so considerate."

"You had some silly moments there while you took that pain medicine. Remember?"

She blushed. "I will never forget."

The tortoise pushed through a stand of thicker foliage. Anna and Ralph continued toward the ocean.

"What will my father and family think when they see the pictures of us together?"

"That I am your protector."

"Just like Saint Joseph."

"Oh, no. I am no saint. Never was and never will be. Anna, can't you see how good we are together?"

"Dear Ralph. There are many things to consider. For now, my plan is to not return to the convent."

"That's a back-handed compliment if I ever heard one."

She gazed at egg-white-foam clouds as they crept east across the blue sky. "This tropical forest looks renewed from the storm. That great wind dusted all the dead fronds from the tall palm trees."

Ralph smiled. "Incidentally, one of the relaxing things I did when I was alone was to imagine I was one of a stand of eighty trees. The outside ones were sentinels, the inside smaller trees were secure and protected."

"What a calming thought."

They strolled down the tree-lined path. Ralph walked a few steps ahead. Anna stopped to pick some tiny, white-faced flowers to put on the table. When she looked up, Frah stepped out of the bushes between her and Ralph. He stood with his back to her. His hands were on his hips, and his legs were far apart.

What is that horrible man doing here? He always looks like he is up to no good. I thought we were alone.

A second East One stepped silently out of the forest beside Ralph, and the two men grabbed Ralph's arms.

She gasped. The flowers fell from her hands.

Ralph twisted and fought to break their hold. "What do you want?" Then in a louder voice, he shouted, "Run, Anna."

She turned and rushed into the trees. *Which way do I go?* She swerved to the right then to the left again. Suddenly, a rotund East One blocked her path. She ran into him so hard, her breath was knocked from her chest. With her next breath, she smelled the sour odor of his body as his large hands closed over her arms. He twisted her to face the way she'd come.

What is happening? Why?

The Fat East One gave her a careless shove. She stumbled and fell to her knees. Fat One jammed his hand under her arm and lifted her. She planted her right foot in front of her left and stood in place. *I am not budging. Who is this fat one?* She drove her elbow into his plump belly.

"Ha. Ha." He kept his grip and forced her through the brush.

They caught up with the others. Frah and a tall East One held Ralph. Frah wrestled him forward.

Ralph shouted, "Hey. You're hurting me. What's the big idea?"

Frah gave Ralph a fierce tug. Ralph raised his foot and tried to kick his assailants on either side. Mud covered his shoes and pants. They jostled and kept leading him forward. Anna and Fat One followed.

They burst from the trees and into their camp. Two canoes were pulled onto shore. Sno stood at the firepit. *At last. The voice of reason. I am so glad he is in charge. He will let us loose and explain this whole big mistake. Thank You, God.*

But Sno glared as Ralph was dragged before him.

"Stop this foolishness," Ralph shouted. "What is wrong with you? Is someone sick? I'll remind you, sir, I am a doctor."

Sno struck him across the face. Ralph sagged but was held in place by his two captors.

Anna felt lightheaded. *I will not faint. I will help my friend.* She wriggled free of her captor, but before she could take two steps, she was again encircled by Fat One's arms. "Let. Me. Go." She stomped on his bare feet.

Fat One half-carried her to the firepit. She kicked and squirmed. *What is going on?*

Ralph yelled, "Whatever happens, Anna, remember I love you."

"Ralph," she cried and struggled to loosen Fat One's grip.

Sno strode to his canoe on the beach. His actions were slow and deliberate. He grimaced then took out a small, twine-tied bundle. He returned to Ralph holding his knife in one hand and the package in the other. He slit the cord, unwrapped the cloth, and poked it under Ralph's nose. He screamed, "Muerto."

Ralph moaned. "A dead, newborn baby. It must be Flor's

child. Sometimes these bad storms can cause a woman to deliver prematurely. I am so sorry. We both are so sorry."

"Flor's baby." *How very sad. I wish I could see her and offer my condolences*. She twisted, trying to free herself. Fat One held her tighter.

The tall one and Frah continued to restrain Ralph. Their faces resembled masks. No birds chirped. The surf was a whisper.

Sno raised his arm and plunged the knife into Ralph's chest.

Anna screamed, "No!"

Ralph turned away from the knife as Sno's blade again descended.

"Stop. Stop. Stop."

The East Ones let him go. Ralph dropped.

Sno lifted his head and screamed. The sounds Sno made were ones she had heard only in the zoo.

Ralph did not move. Fat One released Anna. She ran to Ralph, took his face in her hands, and saw death looking back at her.

FORTY-ONE

Anna gazed at Ralph. Blood spread over his chest. She touched his limp arm and felt no pulse. Her eyes opened wide.

Frah grunted and yanked her arm. He forced her to the shore and into a canoe.

They are taking me with them. What do I do now? I feel furious yet frightened. Think Anna. She waited until Frah looked away then jumped out of the boat, splashing water over the men. She picked up her skirts and ran through the damp sand.

A panting Frah ran behind then next to her. He pounced on Anna, hauled her back, and dumped her into the canoe.

The men slipped their oars into the sea. The canoes skimmed through the coral-free channel and turned north. Anna sat with her arms folded across her chest. *There are bloodstains on my skirt. He died. Ralph died. In front of my eyes. I will not let my horror show on my face. Dear Ralph, I remember all the skills you taught me, and I will do what I must to survive. I may be alone, but you are in my thoughts. I am not defeated.*

She watched the home island grow smaller and disappear. The East Ones made a sharp turn east. She repeated the *Zdrowaś Maria*, the Hail Mary, counting the number of prayers for each change of scenery. *We have gone north, then directly east. If anyone looks at me, it will seem like I am frozen in fear and looking straight ahead.*

The two boats slipped smoothly through the now choppy water. The men rowed. *Still traveling east. Is the water rough because of a hidden inlet? The past bad weather? Are we in the path of a permanent current?*

A tract of land appeared on their right. All the men ignored it. *So, we are passing another island south of the route.* She wriggled in her seat and adjusted her blood-stained skirt. Frah's firm hand pressed down on her shoulder. *I know these men are deceitful. How dare they kill my friend because of the death of a baby? Did Flor die too? I have no friends here. Each of these East Ones would just as soon kill me. Why keep me alive?*

Don't be foolish, Anna. You know why they want you.

She again chanted the Hail Mary in her head as she calculated and followed their progress. They cleared the nameless island then turned to the right. *Now, we go south.* She memorized the second number of prayers. The first being the trip north. The second, the trip east. And now she began at the count of one again, going south. *East Ones beware, you have crossed the wrong woman.*

Conversations began between the men in both boats. Frah's name was mentioned in their banter. They paddled with vigor, as if anxious to reach home.

My body posture shows only fear, I hope. I will make an escape plan when I am alone, so help me, God. After she'd said many more Hail Mary's, Anna's boat slowed. It swung onto a beach with about twenty-five structures, duplicates of the hut the East Ones had built for her and Ralph. *Here I am, God. Be in my head and guide me.*

Frah grabbed her arm then pulled her out of the boat and onto the shore. He dragged her toward the huts, smiling as if he won a prize. She counted the huts. They entered the fourth one in the second row. Frah dumped her on a grass mat, tied her to a floor-to-ceiling post, and walked out.

My time of peace and prayer. I will hold in every single tear and let the sorrow remain in my heart. God, take the soul of your beloved servant, Ralph, who came to this part of the world to find himself. He honored and served his fellow man. He loved all creatures. Reward him in Heaven for his good works. I thank You for the privilege of knowing this good man. I will honor him by going back and…

Two girls walked into the hut. The first one untied her, touched her own chest, and said, "Pequena."

The other girl placed a bowl of blackberries, nuts, and a portion of fish in front of her. Anna nodded and pantomimed washing her hands. Neither could comprehend. She found the cleanest part of her damp skirt, wiped her hands, then ate.

"Flor?" she asked.

"No. Verana." The second shook her head.

Anna said again, "Flor."

With a look of comprehension, the second girl rushed out of the hut. She returned with a flower. All Anna could do was smile.

She had just finished eating when Frah walked in. The girls scurried away. Frah tied Anna to the post and checked that the knot was secure. With a sneer, he left her alone again.

Anna thought about what Ralph had said would happen if she were abducted. The East Ones would impregnate her right away. But first, there would be a discussion as to who would get the honor. *I will not honor an East One with my body.*

For the next hour or so, she whispered every prayer she had ever heard or said. She prayed the Christmas ones she knew, the Holy Week devotions, and the Easter incantations, too. She prayed to Mary, The Blessed Mother, who was the child of Saint Anne, for Godspeed because the journey would have to be soon. *I need to leave before I become Frah's mate.*

Footsteps alarmed her.

"Anna," Flor whispered.

"Flor, you are alive. I have prayed for you."

Flor placed a gourd pitcher and a coconut shell cup on the floor. She untied Anna's wrists.

Anna hugged her. She pressed her fingers gently on Flor's belly. "I am so sorry."

Flor was still bleeding from the childbirth. Anna ripped the hem of her petticoat and wiped the blood from Flor's thighs.

Flor poured juice into the cup and waited while Anna drank. Then she re-tied Anna's wrists. After she left, Anna caught the bloody rag with her foot and slid it under her skirt.

Much later, Frah returned. He untied her, handed her a cup of water, and watched her every move. He sat on his haunches and spoke in guttural tones.

You want me to act afraid. Of course, I can do that. I will act intimidated. She leaned away from him and lowered her eyes. Then she reached under her skirt, pulled out the bloody cloth, and showed it to him.

His mouth turned down. He tied her to the post and was gone.

Anna smiled grimly. *I am smart. I know how to swim. I read all about simple knots. I will be working on this one as long as it takes.*

She moved her fingers along every inch of the rope tying her but could get no fix on the type of knot. Through the blinds of reeds, she noticed the sun going down. *Am I running out of time?*

Again, someone climbed the three steps to the hut. It was Flor. She gave a tremulous smile and held out a bowl of food. *Dinner.* While Flor untied her, Anna breathed in a spicy aroma. She accepted the bowl. It contained a scoop of what appeared to be raw fish mixed with chopped red onion, a scoop of a mushy substance that tasted vaguely like potatoes, and a salad of leaves and the orange tree tomatoes she had seen before. Anna ate everything. Even the raw fish, which had a heavy citrus flavor.

When she finished eating, she handed the bowl back. Flor set it on the floor and looked around nervously. Then she placed gentle fingers on Anna's lips. She spread the grass of her skirt to reveal a knife tied to her thigh. Anna swallowed a yelp of surprise. Flor handed the knife to Anna. The blade was short but very sharp. Anna placed it close to the post behind her and sat on it. Flor hugged her.

As Flor re-tied Anna to the post, Frah sauntered in. Flor hastily retreated, leaving her bowl behind.

Anna lowered her eyes as if in prayer.

He took a wide stance, hands on his hips. A lecherous smile parted his lips. "Mañana."

She looked up and feigned fear in her wide-open eyes.

He spent what seemed like forever looking her over as if she were on display at a candy counter. He checked the rope holding her wrists then raised his chin, pivoted, and stomped down the three stairs.

Little weasel. I can smell your stinky fish breath. You think you will have your way with me. You will have your mañana when I am gone tomorrow.

She could hardly wait for the sun to slip into the ocean.

FORTY-TWO

Anna concentrated on the sinking sun. In the hut, it required some contortion to peek outside through the slats of the grass shades. *Sun, you are a sluggish mover.*

She scooted on the mat and moved her fingers with care until she touched the knife.

Jesus, Mary, and Joseph. I know this is a good sign. I can do this.

Gently, she maneuvered the knife until she held it in her palm. Anna bent forward, raised her hands, and shifted the handle. She centered the blade on the rope between her two hands and began to saw, careful of her skin. *Fortunately, this is sharp. God help me.* Valuable minutes passed. Shadows lengthened.

She succeeded. Anna placed the knife on the floor and massaged her freed wrists. She tore a swath from her petticoat and wrapped it around the blade, then tucked it into her waistband. The cut rope went into her pocket.

Laughter and voices drew near. Her heart skipped a beat. With hands behind her, she took her position. But no one entered the hut. The voices faded. A long slow breath escaped her. *This is a nasty group of people, except for Flor. I will pray for her.*

Her ears perked at a rustling noise. *It sounds like a child sweeping with a tiny broom.* There was movement. A diminutive mouse pushed a seed out of a crack in the floor. A slide of her foot made the mouse scurry away.

Night fell. Except for the faraway sound of the waves, all was quiet. In the moonlight streaming into the room, Anna searched for food. Flor's empty wooden bowl was the only reminder of nourishment. Anna picked up the bowl and peeked outside.

Is it late enough? Are they asleep? Whatever the hour, I leave now. There will be plenty of time to wonder about the why of these events while at sea. There have to be boats on shore. God, let there be one canoe for me, or I will be swimming. I remember the boat with the photographers and one exclaiming, "Look at the size of that shark," so a boat is preferable.

Exiting the hut, Anna tiptoed down the few steps. Hardly daring to breathe, she moved from the shadow of one building into the darkness of the next. She halted at a loud exhale. A few seconds later, the exhale repeated as the hut's occupant continued to snore. All was quiet between the next set of buildings. The ocean came into view. Five unguarded canoes lined the shoreline.

I want to be sure that my vessel contains an oar. She stepped into water cool enough to awaken every inch of skin. An oar was in the first canoe. She added the bowl. She took the paddles from the other boats then pushed each boat into the surf. To her delight, they floated from the shore. *What a foolish thing. The plan should have been to first use my knife to punch a small hole in each of the canoes so they would eventually sink. God, thank You for keeping the East Ones asleep.*

She tossed the four paddles into her boat. Then she glided her boat into the surf, rolled into it, pulled out an oar, and paddled. The oar was long and unwieldy with a blade at each end. By maneuvering the wood, the flat part caught the ocean.

I remember last summer when a bunch of us went to Waldamere Park and we were out on the lake. One of the men said that to paddle all you do is keep making a figure eight repeatedly. When Ralph rowed, it looked so easy. It can be done.

Figure eight, Anna. She turned and looked at the village. It was still quiet. The four boats had drifted out of sight. Water sprayed her clothing. Overhead, the moon revealed bundles of stars. *God, give me some time to figure out how to work this oar into the water and get moving. Hail Mary, full of grace.* Still, when the oar was dipped in and pulled out, much of the ocean splashed inside the vessel.

Concentrate. God, help me do the figure eight. Lift to the right, lift to the left. Make a figure eight. Holding the oar as close to the center as possible felt clumsy and gave her no speed, so she widened her grasp. She turned to see any East Ones' activity on the beach and saw none. Sadly, her distance from shore was minimal. She concentrated all her attention on rowing and found a slow and steady pace. A cloud passed under the moon. *Good for hiding, bad for course plotting.*

God, I need to talk to you. I know this is all Your will. Why were there no guards on the shore tonight? Your doing, I know. She gripped the paddle, and the bones in her fingers hurt from the squeeze. *Do what You want with these depraved East Ones. My wish was to burn down their village. At least the wish was to burn their boats and let them watch. But it would be my wrath, not Yours, right Lord? And rowing at this awkward pace, they would be beside me by now. There are probably more canoes hidden somewhere.*

She rowed and prayed. *God, I am in your hands. Figure eight. How could one person be this thirsty? Figure eight. My arms ache. Complaining is not the answer. I am alive and away from my captors. I could be on Ralph's island by morning. As soon as I get on shore, I will have lots to drink.* She looked at the sky and found the one star twinkling alone. *I remember Ralph telling me this was our own southern hemisphere's north compass.* She nodded her head at the lone star.

After a while, several clouds crowded the stars. Rain began to fall. She lifted her head and caught the drops on her tongue. Then she positioned the bowl to catch the shower. She drank gratefully and set back to work. *This is confusing. Where is that star now?* She stopped paddling and heard a splash. *A canoe? Surely not.* The next splash sounded closer. The silver shape of a fish jumped into her boat. It wiggled beside her. *Thank you, Lord, for your gifts of rainwater and fish.*

She concentrated on the water and paddling the figure eight. She was so absorbed, she did not realize her boat was grounding on land. The sun was rising over a beach and palm trees.

"This must be *No Name*, the island between the East Ones' and Ralph's. Thank You, God, for the sunrise. Thank You for guiding me to land in this part of my journey."

The early morning mist shrouded her arrival. Palm trees swayed. Birds chirped. Her bowl was still half-full of rainwater, and she drank it down. Then she peered over the edge of the canoe. *Each time I have climbed out of these island boats, there has been a hand to help me, either Ralph's gentle touch on my elbow or Frah's painful grip on my arm. Now, the only way to exit is a clumsy sort of roll and fall. So be it.* She flopped out onto the sand and got a mouthful of seawater.

Tears clouded her eyes. *I am tired, and I am thirsty. But I need to make this boat disappear. The East Ones will be looking for me.* Inch by inch, she pulled the canoe out of the water. Thinking to make the work go faster, she turned it on its side. All that did was fill it with ocean water, making it heavier. She dumped the water. All five oars and the dead fish spilled out. She managed to rescue the fish and one of the oars, but the others floated away before she could reach them.

With a sigh, she righted the vessel and began anew. She pulled. Nothing happened. She gathered palm fronds, laid them under the path of the boat, and slowly eased the canoe up onto the land. She tugged it over the beach and into the wooded area. She threw all the fronds over the boat. *Still visible from the sea.* She collected more, using them first to erase the path of the craft and her feet then to camouflage the boat. She took the dead fish and rinsed it in the ocean.

Can I eat a raw fish? Not yet, but I suppose I will later. She shook her head. *No, I had better eat it now.* She pulled out her knife, skinned the fish, filleted it, cut it into small pieces, and ate it raw, gagging as she swallowed. *I should have saved some of the water.*

I am so weary. I need sleep. I need water. God help me.

She recalled Ralph's counsel. He found clean water near the thickest trees. She looked at the sun, placed it in the sky for reference, and walked to the thicket of trees to her right. Carrying her empty bowl, she searched for a pool of water. Dark berries peeked out from a few bushes. *Thank God these islands are overrun with blackberries.* She picked a few and ate them. The juicy, sweet fruit erased the raw fish flavor from her mouth. After a short walk, she found a pond of clear water. She dipped her hands into the pond and slurped long gulps of it, then scooped it into her bowl and drank her fill. She sat on the bank among clumps of waist-high bushes.

It is prayer time. God, I feel like the people at the Passover. Probably the only reason the East Ones are not here waiting for me is that I am still very close to their island. They must have figured I either made it to Ralph's island or drowned. You found land for me, and fresh water, a fish, and even berries. I can at least say the Rosary while I thank You for the breeze, the sun, and my sanctuary. Then she prayed the words of the Mass as she could bring them to mind. *I will not fall apart until I am back in Ralph's cave. My plan is to be there tomorrow. All things are possible through You.* She closed her eyes and fell asleep.

Anna thought her brother was awakening her with a soft rub up her shoulder and touch to her neck. She awoke as the fat snake kissed her ear. She swatted it away and rose quickly. The sun was sinking behind the island trees. Anna filled her bowl of water, rinsed out her mouth, then drank. All was quiet except for a few bird calls. *Could those be East Ones' signals? I hope not because I am going.* She tore off another part of her skirt, made a sling, and filled it with berries. Then she carried it and the bowl of fresh water to the shore.

At beachside, she detected a disturbance in the sand. *Was that an animal or were my captors here? Time to go now.* She uncovered the canoe and made a roadway out of the greenery. With her bowl, the berries, and the oar inside the craft, she tugged the boat to the sea. She pushed it into the water then splashed beside it and slid in.

Wet already. No matter. I am on the way back to safety. That setting sun helps me judge true north. The sea at night belongs to only the foolhardy such as I. The East Ones never traveled at night. I wonder why. Could it be a superstition or is there danger? I will ponder that tomorrow in the safety of Ralph's cave. She paddled. The sun slid behind *No Name Island* and dusk moved in. The stars came out. She looked for the *north compass* star. Clearing the island, she felt the current going in her direction.

As she rowed, a school of phosphorescent fish darted around the canoe. But their entertainment was short lived. *My arms are so sore. My hands are so raw. My whole body aches.* She took a break to eat some of the berries and drink a little water. The sea surrounded the boat. Clouds played tag across the moon. It would be an endless night of rowing.

My immediate plan on arrival at the island is to drink a gallon of water and eat multiple cans of tuna fish. I will need to get rid of any evidence of my arrival. All footprints will be swept with branches. The boat, unfortunately, has to go, because it an-nounces my presence. Then I will make a swift escape to the cave.

Hours later, she paused again for berry refreshments. Her eyes searched the water for a splash of another jumping fish. None appeared. The silence brought drooping eyelids. *Figure eight. Figure eight. If I start yawning, I will sit up straight.*

She smiled, remembering Sister Calista who was sure none of the young nuns knew the secret of yawning with their mouths closed and nostrils flared. The girls would snicker when the elders would flare their nostrils and pretend to be wide-awake.

As her arms rowed the figure eight by rote, thoughts of Penn-sylvania filled her mind. So many new things could happen. So many old ideas needed to be evaluated. If the convent was not a choice, what was her future? Did she have one?

The moon emerged from the clouds long enough for her to see land to the south. *It's Ralph's island.* Anna stayed on the west course until the land curved south into the sea, and then did the same.

"God, on this day I will not protect the coral reef but am staying close to shore. If this canoe clears the reefs, wonderful. If it hits the coral and rips, then swimming to shore is possible."

The water path to her destination felt endless. The waves bounced the boat left and right. The frequent spray of salt water kept her alert. *God, get me safely to the correct beach and into the cave.* On her left, she saw Ralph's hut. She turned and touched the canoe to familiar soil.

FORTY-THREE

he front of the boat dug into the beach sand. With the vessel secure, she twisted herself out of the craft. Her gaze moved over the dark and silent beach. *Am I alone here?* A brisk pace brought her to Ralph's body. He lay exactly as she remembered. Her eyes pooled with tears. She touched his face. *My wonderful friend and protector. God bless you. I should not move you because that would show the East Ones my return. Yet you deserve a dignified burial. My dream would be to have your funeral at my church in Pennsylvania. I will sing you all the Polish songs today.*

Footprints covered the entire area. *Are these from the abduction or were the East Ones back? Palm frond sweeps will help cover every new track I make.*

Through the darkness, she made her way to the water barrel. Her hands shook, and her fingers cramped after holding the oar for so long. Her first attempt to grab a cup sent it tumbling into the grass. She retrieved it and dipped it into the water. Her lips felt cracked and tender as she lifted the cup to drink—but the water soothed her throat and her empty stomach. *I now know how one feels in a desert.* She opened two cans of tuna, tipped the cans, and slid the oily chunks into her mouth.

Moving to the supply lean-to, Anna picked up her old life preserver, caressing the familiar cottony feel of the cloth as she carried it down to the shore and placed it in the boat. *I thank You, God, for the foresight of Ralph teaching me to swim and trying to teach me to row.*

The sun began to rise. Pink light glinted on the slow rolling waves. She walked to the pile of logs she saw when she first arrived on the island—the pile of logs where Sister Calista died. They were different lengths. She chose four and dragged them one-by-one to the canoe.

At the East Ones' Gift, she unwound a long rope from one of the posts. She took it to the beach and wove the rope in and out of the four logs. *The raft doesn't have to be pretty. It just needs to get Ralph out to sea*. When she was confident that the logs were securely attached to one another, she took a moment for another drink. She ran her gaze over the horizon, looking for the East Ones' boats.

The next chore was moving a dozen cantaloupe-sized rocks into the boat. By the time she finished, the tropical sun was beating down. She carried Ralph's canvas tarp to his body. With much effort, she rolled him onto the tarp. The body expelled gas as she moved it. She wrapped him tightly and tied the tarp closed. *I'm sorry my good friend, but the holy water is back in the cave. I cannot bless you. But God is much more understanding than we think in times of challenges.*

With the rope wrapped around her hands for a better grip, she tugged the tarp. Ralph's body wouldn't move. A frustrated sob escaped her. In her mind, his body would miraculously be atop the pieces of wood and easily attached to the boat then taken out to sea. *Perhaps I should have built the raft up here. But realistically, how could I roll a platform of logs down to the sea with the body on top?*

She put the rope over her shoulder and pulled with all her weight. Her shoes sank into the sandy ground. *God, You got me this far. Give me the courage to get Ralph's body aboard the raft. Holy Ghost, fill my mind with an idea.*

The rope bit into her oar-weary hands. *I could use Ralph's sled right about now, but it's back in the cave. Imagine if one of the tortoises were tame enough to keep a rope in his mouth and pull the tarp to the water. What a dreamer I am. Where in my mind is an alternate plan? Thank God no visitors are on the horizon. What are the smoothest things I see?*

Anna laid out palm fronds. Again, her eyes scanned the un-inhabited shoreline. Taking hold of the rope, she towed Ralph's remains across the palm leaves to the raft. She climbed aboard on hands and knees and pulled the heavy tarp onto the logs, then centered the bundle in place. The raft was then tied to the rear of the canoe.

What if a big wave comes when I am on the way to the reef, tips the raft, and dislodges the body? That will have to be in Your hands, O Lord.

Anna scrambled back to shore, picked up the palm fronds, and brushed the sand clean. On inspection, it took four sweeps before the beach appeared free of footprints. Then she rushed to the shed, stripped off her layered dress, and hid it and her shoes beneath a crate. She ran to the boat dressed in her underclothes.

At last, the raft and the stolen boat were pushed offshore. She slipped in, paddled, and prayed. *Now I can begin your funeral, dear Ralph. The prayers will all be said in Polish because I am fond of the cadence of the language. I begin with the Sign of the Cross. W Imię Ojca i Syna i Ducha Świętego. Amen. Then the Our Father, Ojche nasz... The Hail Mary, Zdrowaś Maria... A litany to the Blessed Sacrament, Ojchez z nieba, Boże, Zmiłuj się nad nami... And for the last blessing, a Polish dirge, sung at all funerals, Greetings, Queen of Heaven, Witaj, Królovo Nieba... Sorry, but I always cry when singing this melody. That is the final song.*

The boat was well beyond the reef when the prayers were completed. The ocean was free of other canoes. With her paddle, Anna pulled the raft beside the boat and untied the canvas. She placed the rocks at Ralph's head, arms, torso, and feet. Then she closed the tarp and re-tied it.

My heart is so heavy. You deserved so much more. With the knife, she cut the ropes holding the raft together. The body, weighed down by the rocks, sank quietly below the surface and disappeared into the calm ocean. The warm sun offered a sense of peace, but she felt only the urgency of time.

The oar was thrown into the water. It bobbed and moved away. Anna placed the vest around her waist. She slipped out of the canoe, gasping with the chilly water, and pushed the vessel into the current. The sea tried to capture and move her out as well, but she swam briskly. *I have this task, and then I can rest. God, no sharks today. I could use a sailfish to whisk me to shore.*

It was a long way back. She had never swum so far before. Twice, she paused to take a rest, panting and clinging to the life vest around her middle. Tiny fish nibbled on her toes. When at last she reached the shore, dusk was falling. She was so exhausted she couldn't stand. She lay in the surf and allowed the waves to splash around her.

Then she noticed footprints on the beach. The imprint of a canoe marred the sand. She stood slowly. *They were here.*

Alarm rose like a siren in her head. She sprinted to the shed. Her clothes lay undisturbed beneath the crate where she had hidden them. *Thank the Lord. They don't know I'm here. They might suspect, but they don't know for sure. For all they know, Ralph got up and walked away. None of them checked to see if he was truly dead. Or maybe they'll think a pack of wild boars…*

She closed her eyes. *Thank the Lord*.

She dressed and peered out the shed at the gathering shadows. *They can't know I'm here. They can't ever know. They'll never stop looking if they know. Maybe losing the oars at No Name Island was a good thing. Maybe they'll look for me there. Maybe they'll think I drowned.*

Gathering her courage, she ran into the jungle. All the while, Ralph's wisdom rang in her head. *Frah is a sneaky kind of guy. He was always snooping around the woods. But he never found the cave because Ralph always walked a different way so he wouldn't forge a path*.

She veered to and fro as she sped through the jungle. She feared running headlong into Frah or even Fat One as she had before, but no one jumped out at her. At last, she reached the cave. *God, I feel I have arrived at my sanctuary.* She checked the threads. Satisfied that no one had been there, she went inside. Panting and trembling, she sat facing the entrance and stared out at the night.

ꙮ ꙮ ꙮ

She stirred with the thin, gray light of dawn. Birds began their morning songs. Hugging her arms close, she glanced around the cave—then jumped at a silhouette in the shadows. *Is someone there?* But, no, it was only the dummy she'd used for punching practice. Stiff and sore, she climbed to her feet. She untied the dummy and laid it gently on Ralph's cot. Then she lowered the upturned cot into place. *This would have been Sister Calista's bed.*

At the blackened firepit, she piled twigs and branches and prepared to light a fire. *Wait. I can't take the chance. No smoke can rise from this cave. No flicker of light. Tea will brew itself in warm water after a while. My safety is more important than a hot beverage.*

She spooned tea leaves into a cup and covered them with water. As she waited for her drink to change color, she roamed along the shelves. *There is water, tuna fish, cans of peas, and even jars of applesauce. How Ralph saved a few jars, I will never know. We made candles, and if it storms, I will have them.*

Near Ralph's corner of the cave, she found several oilcloth-wrapped bundles. She opened one. The book *Robinson Crusoe* looked up at her.

Pain and sorrow welled up from deep inside. She sat on Ralph's cot and sobbed. *I am alone and afraid. Of course, I would be quite a simpleton if I had no fear in this situation.* Tata's words resounded in her tired mind. *Polish people are strong, Anna. They rarely cry. If something is too hard, turn it around and look at it from another angle. Figure it out.*

With the book cradled in her arms, she sat at the cold firepit and drank her weak, tepid tea. *Will Tata be happy, sad, or accepting if I come home now? I need guidance.*

As if he stood before her, he said*, Córka, chie koham. Daughter, I love you. As for your distance? Your mother, I had to let go. She died. You? Remember, God told Abraham to take his son*

Isaac and offer him as a holocaust. Then, as Abraham raised his knife, God said, Do not do the least thing to him. They returned to their dwelling together. I have been tested. I have given you to God. If you return like Isaac, I will praise God.

Anna roused. *Was I awake, dozing, or asleep?*

As automatic as her morning ritual of washing her face, she began to recite prayers for the day. Next were thank you invocations for her Pennsylvania family and for Ralph. After what seemed hours, she touched her pocket and pulled out the rosary. With closed eyes, she whispered the prayers and touched the beads. As she prayed, she felt a sense of calm and then exhaustion. *I need to rest. This is a good time to lie down for a bit and gather my strength. I am in a place of peace.*

Anna awoke in the black cave to absolute silence. *Ahh. This is the moment I have longed for since leaving the East Ones. Finally, protection surrounds me.* She rolled both arms as if shrugging off an old piece of clothing. *Does my back hurt from the paddling? Or perhaps my thighs and calves from swimming? No. Nothing hurts. No aches. But I am sad. Devastated by Ralph's death. It is all in vain unless I survive unbroken in body and spirit.*

She peered out the cave entrance at the moonlit jungle. A soft breeze played in the trees. *It seems peaceful. But Ralph and I were completely shocked by the sudden appearance of the East Ones on their last arrival. They won't take me unawares again.*

In the darkness, she ate tuna and canned peas. *Today is my transition day. I must plan my island escape. The wait might be a few months long. Can I last? Of course. Tata told me about the trip by boat from Poland. It took many weeks. He and Mama had little personal space in steerage. They kept telling each other of the rewards of a new life in America while crossing the ocean. On the Alexandria, Tommy gave us wonderful accommodations. Here, can I complain? I have plenty of room to walk around. I have fresh air. There are many books.*

"But I can't stay here forever," she whispered.

Still, she did nothing as night edged into the day. After a while, she got up and paced the dim cavern.

"The monumental puzzle is how do I get myself off this island?" *My options are one of two plans. Plan number one is to place rocks on the beach to spell out S O S. Yet with tide changes, I could have ships passing who would never see the sign. Plan number two is to hang a white sheet over the shed. Will the East Ones notice a new flag? They might. However, no strategy is perfect. I need to start somewhere. I must be brave. Polish people have stamina.*

She sat at the table and placed tea in a cup of lukewarm water. "What am I doing? Sitting? No, I need to have the sheet in place today. Today." *Ralph once said that the East Ones might be looking when we are not. For my security, I need to disguise myself as a man, complete with clothes and a new gait. It will confuse an onlooker, I hope, at least at first glance.*

The disguise costume has to be my first task. Pushing the cup away, she went to Ralph's area of the cave. She unbuttoned the dummy's shirt. Inside, she found palm fronds and more clothing used as stuffing. She tried on a familiar shirt, and his soap scent surrounded her like a hug. Tears blurred her vision, and she batted them away. *This was an extraordinary man. He would want me to escape.*

After rolling the sleeves above her elbows, Anna put on his trousers. The pantlegs pooled on the ground. With a sooty stick from the firepit, she marked the fabric at floor level then removed the pants. Her suitcase was still on the sled. She put it on her cot and searched inside for her sewing kit. Then she cut the pants to size. When she tried them on again, the length was fine. She cinched the waist with a rope. *I will pretend to be a man. This is my practice time. A man swings his hands when walking. Some even lean first right then left.* She ambled around the cave trying to move her body side-to-side in a new gait. *I will think of myself as being a man named Paul. My cousin Paul is a lucky kind of person, so it will work for me. Ash on my chin will look like beard stubble. Did Ralph leave a hat here?*

She searched the cave but did not find a hat. The two pith helmets were still in the East Ones' Gift, and both their straw hats were in the supply lean-to. *What should I do? I will not give up.* Picking up the scissors, she cut her hair to her earlobes. A gasp escaped her as she stared at the hank of hair in her hand. *Hair will grow back. Don't think about it.* She stuffed the hair and the excess fabric from the pant legs into a bag and placed it near the cold fireside. From the shelf, she took a small empty tin and filled it with ashes.

Outside, the sun moved too swiftly toward the horizon. *Today, Anna. Complete this project today. A ship could come at any time, even tomorrow. Chances are they will not stop unless they see a white flag on our shed. I need to wear Ralph's shoes when I leave the cave so my footprints will look different. Where are they?*

Another search began. "Surely, the man owned a pair of shoes other than the ones the East Ones gave him." She opened another of his oilcloth bundles and found a pair of black patent leather oxfords. *He trussed these up as if he treasured them. Perhaps he wore them in the hospital where he worked.* "Thank you, Ralph." However, when trying them on, she found each shoe was large enough to hold both of her feet. "A cloth can be wadded into the oversized shoes." When they were stuffed and tried on, the new gait was nothing like the Anna walk.

I will sneak out of the cave at dusk, hang the sheet, and place three letters in the mailbox where someone will see them. One in English explaining where I am and asking for help. Another to Tata in case help never arrives. And one in Polish, in case the Alexandria stops by again. When Tommy brought Sister and me to the island, he talked about continuing south for the next two months and then possibly passing us as they went north.

Anna put more ink in the pen, wrote the letters, then sealed the three envelopes. She pulled a white sheet off the third cot and placed it at the cave entrance.

At the table, she ate a can of tuna and washed it down with weak, tasteless tea. *I wonder what day this is. It is December.*

Maybe the fifth, or the tenth, or as late as the fifteenth. To think I was concerned about the financial crisis at the end of October when I traveled. This is indeed another world.

Dusk fell. Anna dressed in the prepared shirt, pants, and shoes. Ash covered her chin. She carried her three notes, two in English and one in Polish, and a folded white sheet. With the threads in place, she slipped out of the cave. Her breathing was slow and deliberate. *In case of intruders, I need to first walk away from the entrance and into the trees before moving toward the shore. This trip must be made with haste yet with care. Help me, Saint Anne.*

Every few minutes, she paused and listened. Above her head, palm fronds scratched each other. A few tiny insects swiped her face. Birds chased across the path flying to the safety of their nests. Another pause. All was quiet.

This is the same path Ralph and I took. She pushed away memories of the attack. At last, she reached their living area. The sight of it made her heart ache. Their hammocks swayed in the ocean breeze. The lean-to billowed as if breathing. And there was the place where Ralph died. *Concentrate. Put the letter to Tata and the help-me-I-am-in-the-cave notes into the outgoing mail.*

She placed the letters in the mailbox on its appointed stand next to the shed. On tiptoe, she tried to swoop the sheet over the high posts. *Too high.* She looked for something to stand on, then dragged over four tree-stump chairs and made a pyramid. Climbing up, she stretched and struggled to tie the sheet to the high post. It slipped off. *Try again. Did you think this would be easy?*

A soft tumbling of stones at the shore drew her attention. She scanned the horizon. *Something is there. A canoe? Danger.* She hopped down, and with the sheet flapping behind her, ran through the trees to the cave.

Checking the threads, she fled inside and sobbed. *Will I die here? Will I be killed? Will I be captured again?*

With a mind too fearful to remember the prayers she had

uttered daily since her childhood, she pleaded on bended knees. *I am in Your hands. I am in Your hands. I am in Your hands.*

ॐ ॐ ॐ

The next morning, she awoke, prayed, ate tuna, and drank tea-colored tepid water. The white sheet lay crumpled on the cot like a reproach.

Anna, you are acting like a child. Only one person can save you. If you had a mirror and looked into it, you would see what? Panic? So, you did not hang the sheet. Every day is another miracle from the Almighty. He will help you. Flying a white flag is most important. Why did that sheet create a problem? Rethink it. You might need nails and a hammer to get it attached. Where are the tools?

She searched the shelves and finally found a box containing a chisel, a hatchet, a hand drill, and a hammer. The bottom of the box held loose nails. "I know how to use a hammer. It takes two hands to hold the nails and pound them into the hut. I'll go back out, deem it safe, attach that sheet to the shed, and hurry back here. I can make it happen."

At dusk, she donned the same disguise and slid out of the cave. The air was still, as was the sea. The ocean appeared free of any boats or ships. No canoes marred the shore. She repositioned the stump seats next to the shed, climbed up, and nailed the sheet at two corners in only a few minutes. Her eyes scanned the horizon once more. All was clear. Nevertheless, her exit was swift. She ran into the woods and back to the cave. Her hands shook as she inspected the intact threads and went inside.

ॐ ॐ ॐ

The morning sun shone brightly at the cave entrance. *I hope these will be my last few island days. Each of which I will spend in prayer.* She tried to meditate but couldn't focus.

She decided to put together the money for her journey up

the Pacific and east to Pennsylvania. Hers, and if he had any, Ralph's. The train ride from Cincinnati cost $32.70. She would need more than that on the way back. Now that she wasn't traveling as a nun, she would have to pay for her food. She searched the shelves near Ralph's bed. In desperation, she searched under his bed and found a small, metal box. Inside was his marriage certificate, the birth certificate for his little boy, and over four hundred dollars. *Should I take this? Yes. He would certainly want me to have it.* She placed the money into her black purse and into her suitcase.

She made tea with lukewarm water. As she waited for the water to change color, she took out the Polish Bible she had inherited from Sister Hedwiga, the old dead nun at the convent. She opened her Bible. The text that caught her eyes was from Philippians, 4:13. I can do all things through Him who strengthens me. *I believe I came here for a reason. I am in Your hands.*

A noise like the cracking of a baseball bat petrified her. *Is someone there?* She sat perfectly still for the count of one hundred. *Breathe normally. No one can hear.* She heard another snap. *God in Heaven, help me.*

ঝ ঝ ঝ

For the next four days, Anna did little more than listen and pray. Lumbering noises outside the cave made her tremble again and again. She dared not venture outside. But living in a state of constant fear grew tiresome. *Cleaning the entire cave will help me. I always think better when my hands are busy.*

She took a long stick from the box beside the firepit, pulled some palm fronds from the mattress, and made a serviceable broom by wrapping them around and around with a length of twine. She started sweeping at the back of the cave but stopped when she found Sister Calista's suitcase.

Anna opened it. Scents of camphor and wintergreen escaped. Sister's habit lay folded with her rosary and prayer books on top. *Sister, you and I certainly never imagined the magnitude of this journey. Our Kentucky introduction did not prepare us for the Galapagos escapade. What if you had not contracted ptomaine poisoning? How different life would be for the three of us.* She closed the case, cleaned beneath Sister's bed, then stacked all of the nun's belongings on top.

Ralph's side of the cave was neatly arranged. Tin boxes were turned sideways and appeared as a three-tiered shelf. The rack above held his collection of oilcloth-wrapped books. *Robinson Crusoe* lay on his bed where she had left it. She picked up the book and hugged it. *Ralph, you died still professing your love for me. I will try to live a life of gratitude. And I will never forget.*

She carried the book to her suitcase. Inside, there were two sets of women's clothing plus her old lace-up shoes. She nestled Ralph's book beneath her purse.

ಶು ಶು ಶು

She awoke in shadows. Sat up. Listened. The only sound was her own breathing. *Is it night or day?* Only a few steps led her to the entrance. *Dark. Quiet. Safe.* Her eyes had grown accustomed to the lack of light. As she turned, she gazed upon the moonlit cave. Even in darkness, the den was comfortable. *Thank you, Ralph, for creating this haven.*

The following day, she cataloged Ralph's books and placed them on the shelf in the order of her interests. She found an empty tablet among them. *I can use this to keep track of time.* She turned the pages and started with *Day Seven*.

When her tablet said *Day Eleven*, her restlessness peaked. *How long can I wait? Will it take a year?* She tapped her foot "What if the East Ones tore down the white sheet? Am I waiting for a boat that will never come? I need to see the ocean."

At sunset the next day, she dressed in men's clothing, smudged her face, and sneaked out. When she reached their camp, she crept forward with her eyes darting. The sheet was still hanging. But Ralph's boat, the canoe he had so carefully tucked into a safe harbor, was smashed. Footprints covered the beach. With a gasp, she backed away and hurried to the cave.

She sat with fingers intertwined, cradling her head. *I will survive here for as long as it takes to be rescued. What do I know for sure? The East Ones will look for me every chance they have. But they do not travel after sunset, and I do not think they would stay here overnight. Because I need to observe, I will be out at twilight. How dare I act afraid? Ralph tried to teach me self-defense. Now I will live to honor his memory. I am a strong woman and can take care of myself.*

Ralph once told me about a tactic he used for relaxation and calming. He imagined a stand of eighty trees. The outside ones protected the ones in the center. In his mind, he would walk around each tree and admire it then go to the next, counting them down. He was always asleep before he examined all the trees. I need to remember how to climb a tree. I need to observe. Are there any trees near the beach that I could climb and be hidden while I look for a ship?

She searched her memory. The few mangrove trees on the shore were in a poor location. The acacia trees with their umbrella-like tops were too high for her to climb. A few guava trees were promising.

At dusk the next evening, after reflection and prayers, she donned her disguise and slipped out of the cave. Walking with a light tread and keeping off the path, she advanced to the beach. She paused to be certain she was alone then approached the tree. Its many limbs twisted above her. She leaped for the first branch then climbed higher and higher. The task was easier in trousers than in skirts. When she had nearly reached the top, she looked out at the horizon. The ocean was dark with only a smudge of light where the sun would be. No ships. Her only reward was pockets full of guava.

The next evening, she found shoe prints at the beach. A severed tortoise head tossed about with the waves. *So, a ship had been there that day.* Anna hastened to the mailbox. It was empty.

What? But no one had looked for me. In the letters, I asked them to call my name. What went wrong? Disheartened, she returned to her sanctuary.

Once inside, she sank onto a stump chair at the table and buried her face in her hands. *Think of the eighty trees. Calm down. The next ship will be different. But only if I figure out what happened.* She pictured the envelopes in the mailbox. *They took the mail. Hadn't they read the notes? Perhaps not. This time, instead of addressing the envelopes, I will write READ THIS in big, block letters.*

The next morning, while dining on fresh guava, she wrote two more letters, one in English and another in Polish. In them, she asked the reader to walk due east and call her name. As soon as dusk fell, she went back to the campsite and placed the letters in the mailbox. The white flag was still in place. *At least, with all these shoe prints, the East Ones should be convinced that I have been rescued. Maybe they'll forget about me.*

ಚಿ ಚಿ ಚಿ

She spent the next three days sitting at the side of the cave-mouth reading her prayer book in the daylight that streamed into the cave. On the fourth day, she heard the sounds of people pushing through the underbrush. No pretense of quiet. They were coming closer.

Anna leaped to her feet. Her prayer book fell to the floor. She backed away from the entrance, eyes wide in the shadows.

A man's voice called. "Anna. Anna."

Her hands flew to her mouth. *Is this a dream?* "I'm here," she cried, but her voice was barely a whisper.

Then a woman cried out. "*Anna. Anna. Kochana, Anna. Pokaz się.*"

Tears sprang to her eyes. She ran out of the cave. "Yes. I'm here."

Two people stood a short distance away. Pani and Władek.

They turned at her voice. Pani opened her arms, and Anna flew into her embrace, weeping.

Pani held her tight. "*Gdzie doktor?*"

"They killed him," Anna sobbed. "Right in front of me."

Pani nodded. "*Wracemi do domu.*"

Yes. I want to go home. Anna pulled away, smiling through her tears, and wiped her face. Pani smiled and nodded. Władek glanced around the jungle, one hand on the pistol at his hip.

With her head held high, Anna went back inside. She picked up her prayer book. Then she left the cave carrying the small suitcase she'd used at the beginning of her journey. She didn't replace the threads.

CPSIA information can be obtained
at www.ICGtesting.com
Printed in the USA
LVOW10s0012221217
560461LV00026B/972/P